Voyages by
Starlight

by Ian R. MacLeod

Arkham House Publishers, Inc.

Copyright © 1996 by Ian R. MacLeod

LIBRARY OF CONGRESS CATALOGING–IN–PUBLICATION DATA
MacLeod, Ian R., 1956–
    Voyages by starlight / Ian R. MacLeod ; foreword by Michael
Swanwick. — 1st ed.
        p.   cm.
    ISBN 0-87054-171-4 (hardcover : alk. paper)
    1. Fantastic fiction, English.   I. Title.
PR6063.A24996V69   1996
823'.914 — dc20   96-24237

FOR MY PARENTS

Contents

Foreword

There are not many writers whose name on the cover of a magazine will make me buy it without even glancing at the story within. Lucius Shepard comes to mind. Joanna Russ. Gene Wolfe. Maybe a few others.

Definitely Ian R. MacLeod.

I do not place him in such company casually. MacLeod is not merely a good writer, or a promising one. He is, quite simply, one of the best writers at short length today. Nor do I ask you to take my word for this. The proof is here, in this book you hold, waiting to be discovered.

My own voyage of discovery began with "The Giving Mouth." I could hardly have chosen a better introduction. The dark industrial fantasy world therein, inhabited by liveiron draft animals and more-than-Gormenghastian grotesques, is almost shockingly inventive. Its bleak landscape of slagheaps, furnaces, and redbrick towers is magical in the way that dreams are, mingling wonder and horror, beauty and disgust. All unaware, I began reading — and was hooked.

Underpinning this world, with its horses that "hissed and idled their gears," and the hideous Queen Gormal, "as round as a snowberry and twice as bitter," is a prose that is brightly colored, lushly romantic, and — I say this admiringly — not at all subtle. A prose that is perfectly suited for the story.

Compare that to the language of "1/72nd Scale," which is flat and self-effacing and obsessively studded with nervous parenthetical asides, the stylistic equivalent of a stutter. Half the work of characterization is achieved with that (insecure. Fearful. Constantly explanatory) prose. Flip quickly through several other stories here, through "Ellen O'Hara" and "Marnie" and the marvelously strange "Green," and you'll find that with each, MacLeod has reengineered the language, sometimes quietly and sometimes radically, to fit the needs of the work at hand. Yet none of them could be mistaken for the work of any other writer. They are all unmistakably MacLeod.

"1/72nd Scale" was a Nebula Award finalist. Ignore that — a lot of merely good works are nominated for and even win awards. What is worth your close attention is what MacLeod does with an off-the-rack plot. The story — we've all read it before — is a simple one. David's revered older brother Simon is dead, and David knows that his parents wish it had been him instead. His frustrated efforts to regain his family's affection kick into high gear when, in an ambiguous gesture of reconciliation, his father gives him an Airfix 1/72nd-scale Flying Fortress. It is a model kit that his brother had long lusted after, and one that, not coincidentally, David is totally incapable of completing. But one impossible task is as good as another: he sets out to build the model and win back his parents' love.

The familiar story is an unforgiving medium for an artist. It wants to be predictable. It wants to be boring. Yet "1/72nd Scale" is neither. It is constantly surprising, filled with fresh twists and turns of plot, and culminating in a moment that is not only unexpected but inevitable as well.

This ability to surprise, this freshness, helps explain one of MacLeod's chief accomplishments: that he can write science fiction, fantasy, and horror, and all well. I can think of only a handful of writers capable of this feat. Even more remarkably, sometimes a single story will partake of all three genres.

Take "Tirkiluk," for example. It starts out as science fiction, with young Science Officer Seymour being assigned to a lonely Arctic weather station during World War II. With the appearance of the Inuit woman Tirkiluk and her recounting of the legend of the sun and moon coming down to earth to play "dousing the lights," it makes an ostensible shift into fantasy. Then, at the end, as Seymour undergoes his final transformation, it turns into horror.

Or so I was quite sure on first reading. On rereading, however, it was quite clear to me that the final section is not horror at all, but something else, something elevating and hopeful.

This shifting from genre to genre within the course of a story or even between readings is a commonplace in MacLeod's work. (Forgive me if I'm not specific; many of these stories rely on surprise.) What's going on is that MacLeod imagines each story on its own terms, without reference to whatever marketing niche it might fit into. He borrows freely from the genres, but without buying into their expectations. Which sometimes results in a story that can be read as science fiction, fantasy, or horror, depending entirely upon the reader's predisposition.

Thus, "Grownups." Which is set in a world indistinguishable from our own in all ways but one: it has three sexes — men, women, and uncles.

"Grownups" opens in the Arcadia of childhood. With heartbreaking clarity, the innocent pleasures of youth are evoked: bike-riding, skinny-dipping, casual sex. As is the child's perspective on adults. "They drove cars, fought wars, dressed in boring and uncomfortable clothes, built roads, bought newspapers every morning that told them the same thing, drank alcohol without getting merry from it, pulled hard on the toilet door to make sure it was shut before they did their business." Drear indeed! Inevitably, the story moves toward an expulsion from the Garden.

The enabling device in "Grownups" — the uncles — is inexplicable, which would seem to make it fantasy; the biology is closely rationalized, which argues for science fiction; and that we must all one day leave childhood behind — surely that is horrific. So which of the three faces of genre does this story wear?

It hardly matters. The central issue of "Grownups," the horror of growing up, is so basic to our lives that we have most of us forgotten it completely. Using genre tools, MacLeod has made it visible again, in a way not otherwise possible. The result is a story that moves us to emotion and understanding. One that works.

This is, I think, the key to all of MacLeod's work. That he uses the genres, but is not used by them. That his primary loyalty is to the story itself.

Here I must make an end. I regret that I have not said a word about "Papa," in many ways the moral inversion of "Grownups," or "Starship Day," with its sudden shifts of perception, or "The Perfect Stranger," haunted by and fleeing from its own past at whatever cost. A careful examination of these works would cast real light upon MacLeod's oeuvre. And yet I despair of discussing them without ruining them for unwary readers.

Which I refuse to do. Because that's really what I value most about these fictions. It's why I snatch up those magazines. Because when I read one of MacLeod's stories, I never know what to expect. Never know what genre it will turn out to be. Whether its ending will be devastating or exhilarating. Just exactly *what* will happen next.

But I can hardly wait to see.

MICHAEL SWANWICK

Voyages by
Starlight

Ellen O'Hara

The man who came through the back gate into the garden didn't look like a killer.

"Is your dad in?" he asked, dodging the washing, flapping out a handkerchief and mopping the sweat from his face. On this summer evening, Ellen O'Hara didn't think it odd that he wore a thick jacket.

"My dad?"

"It's just a word I want." The man leaned down out of the chimneys and a blue golden sky. He had plump, smiling cheeks that were glazed with stubble. "Will you get him for me, sweet?"

"What do I tell him?"

"Tell him . . ." The man's eyes moved away, narrowing against the lowering sun. "Tell him it's Jim would like a word."

Then Ellen was turning, barefoot over hot paving and slick kitchen linoleum into the front room. The telly on, Ma out cleaning offices, and Dad in his vest after a day at the plant with the tray on his lap that he used to write the letters he sent to the *News*.

"Dad, there's a man called Jim wants to see you."

"Jim?"

"He's at the back."

Dad nodded. His face was a mixture of puzzlement and understanding. Ellen O'Hara had replayed that expression a million times since, had searched for every possible meaning. She knew that evening as she stood by Dad's chair that they were treading a difficult path, staying on here in Hayter Street long after the others of their kind. She knew it from the kicks and the curses that came her way at school, and from the slogans daubed on the walls. She knew it because of evenings she played alone in the back garden when she could hear laughter and the whoosh of bicycles down the alleys. But still, there was nothing unusual about someone wanting to see Dad.

He lifted the tray from his lap. He heaved himself up from the chair. Patting Ellen's head, he ambled out from the front room and through the kitchen, and she followed him into the light of the garden where the man was standing between the washing and the roses, his hand beneath his jacket, the smile still fixed on his face. It was a useful smile. Ellen came to understand that later; one he must have practised, knowing it wasn't possible to keep the facial muscles slack when you were on a job.

Dad was ahead of her, his feet in holed slippers. A vision of his broad fleshy back. The man still smiling as his hand reached into the jacket, and the chimes of an ice-cream van falling softly on the air. The scent of cooking and the tired closed-in heat of the alleys, the scent of the pink-hearted roses. That, and the drone of the bees, the voices. That, and the feel of the killing to come. Ellen could smell it hear it taste it now. It was there in the long moment as the hand slid out from the jacket with the gun with two long black barrels, pointing like a dog's nose. It was there as her mouth filled with a scream.

★ ★ ★

"I've always had good residents in 3A. Some of the stories I could tell you. . . ."

"I'm sure."

Along the corridor, beyond the numbered doors, a kettle was screaming, a couple were arguing, a baby was crying. Someone was coughing and in pain as they lay in bed.

"Here we are."

The old woman turned the key and pushed at the door. There was a bed, a chair, a gas ring. The sound of city traffic broke like a tired sea.

She put her case down on the mattress.

The old woman asked, "I don't suppose you'll be staying long?"

"No," she said, peering at herself in the clouded mirror above the chipped and corroded sink, straightening her hair, checking her face. "It's just a few days. . . ." She was keeping her accent soft. She wanted to sound like the girls who came from the South to the clinics here to get the termination their own laws didn't permit.

"What part of Ireland are you from?"

She turned back to the old woman. Smiling. Taking her in. Kerry. The old woman had memories of Kerry. Of childhood. White cottages. The blue-green hills of long ago.

"Kerry," she said.

"Ahh . . ." The old woman sighed, and momentary brightness filled her eyes.

★　★　★

The Royal Ulster Constabulary came to the house, and the hand-wringing aunts who fluttered with cups of tea, and the people from the telly and the newspapers. Ellen was surprised by all the fuss. After all, it was too late now — wasn't it? But the back garden was taped-off and picked over like a shrine, and people she barely knew kept giving her money and sweets and trying to hug her. She was shown pictures of faces by a police officer. The men were ugly, grainy, in photoflash — they all looked like killers.

Then Ellen saw her dad again. On the telly, on the local news, in a brief clip from an interview he'd given standing out in the street a few months back. She'd missed the broadcast at the time, and her disappointment had been intense. Now she got the chance to see how different the house and Hayter Street looked on the screen, and to hear her dad talking about the Democratic Route in his best jacket and tie, with his shirt collar sticking up. There he was, captured inside the glass of the screen like some rare fish, a Republican Catholic who'd chosen to stay on in the wrong street in the wrong area. They said the killing had been claimed by a new and obscure group.

Then came the funeral, which seemed to Ellen like some mad party with all the cooking and the dusting beforehand, and the panics about what to do with the furniture and whether there would be enough booze. She had to wear her school blazer and itchy woollen tights, and a black car slid down the street like something from another world. Men dressed like crows carried away the long box that had lain in the back room. The priest lied during the service, talking as though he'd admired Dad rather than thought him a dreaming fool, and he and everyone else piled into the house afterwards, and the place reeked of sausage rolls and hair oil and mothballed hats and sweet brown sherry.

Ellen waited for them to leave, to stop looking down at her and going on about the poor wee thing and the shame of it all. Eventually, as evening began to close in and the paper plates were stacked in bin liners outside by the roses, they piled into their hired Cortinas, grumbling about the lack of buses and the taxis that wouldn't cross the Peace Line. And the few neighbours who'd come to pay their respects also slipped away along Hayter Street in the deepening twilight, hoping not to be seen.

★ ★ ★

Ellen and her ma moved out soon after the funeral. When the neighbours heard they were going, they became relaxed, almost friendly. Mrs. Hanrahan from 22 helped with the packing, and the Coys at 16 got a special rate for the van. But within days of their leaving, the windows of their house were smashed and the walls were scrawled and the rooms all stank like a toilet.

They went to stay at Kellaford, Uncle Tod's farm near the Border. At first, the arrangement was declared to be temporary, but Dad's pension from the plant wasn't enough to pay any decent rent, and Uncle Tod didn't mind them being there. Kellaford had the space, as long as you were prepared to put up with the rain that dribbled in through the roof and the worms that wriggled out of the taps.

An old orangery leaned against Kellaford's south wall. Many of the panes were broken, and those that remained were clouded with moss and lichen. The ferns had swarmed out of their shattered pots. The trees and vines were still vigorous, but they were sterile. Nothing had been harvested in the years since most of the land had been sold off to pay taxes, but the orangery still gathered heat from the sun over the hills and held it long after the air outside had turned blue and chill.

In the weeks after their arrival, Ellen sat there for many hours, perched on a rusted pipe, gently rocking to and fro. She kept thinking of the man in the back garden with his fat ordinary face who ducked between the washing and the roses. How was she to know, how was she to tell? She replayed the incident again and again, willing something different to happen, willing some extra bud of knowledge to break open in her head. If only she'd *known* about the man. If only she could have warned Dad.

Darkness flowed, climbing over Kellaford's wild gardens, welling inside the green warmth with the beetles, the scurrying mice, and the gleam of the broken glass that she stooped to lift and turn in her fingers as soft wings of shadow gently batted her bare face and her arms. A man leaning out from the chimneys and a blue golden sky. How was she to tell? And Dad going out there, into the garden, summoned by her. And then the shotgun that came out from beneath the man's jacket. Raised in his hand and her voice screaming with the chimes of the ice-cream van and the pink smell of the roses and the drone of the bees. Yes, she had known then, known even in the moment before the man reached into his jacket. The feeling of it had poured into her, buzzing and rattling in her skull. The killing wave. But too late, too late. A fat hard slap of air that wasn't like a gunshot at all, and Dad's back was blown away.

Ellen turned the glass shard as scented darkness deepened. There was blood on her face and hands as the man pushed the shotgun back inside the jacket. A clumsy moment as the barrels caught on a loose button, and Ellen still screaming as the man turned and stumbled through the washing and was gone. Dad falling against the roses. One hand held up, the back of it caught on the thorns of the roses and seeming to wave. And blood on the roses, blood on the pink-hearted roses. Garlands and sprays. Clots of it on the washing.

Ellen O'Hara turned the shard. Over and over in her fingers, up and down her wrists. Her hands and arms were smooth now, slippery warm. The scream of a fox, out in Kellaford's garden, out in the country night. No, it was her. The bees were quiet, there were no roses and no fox in the darkness, and she was screaming. Uncle Tod's wide shoulders came up against the broken panes of the orangery, blocking the stars; a giant from another world. The stable smell of him as he stooped over her and began to mutter about Your poor ma worried sick and what do you think you're up to out late young lady making all this racket? Reaching to lift her and take her inside for a warming spot of tea, then his breath turning quick as his big hands slid from the glossy wounds along her arms.

★　★　★

Early that evening, feeling clean and scared and new, she tied a blue ribbon in her hair, put on a white blouse and a knee-length blue skirt, checked her face in the mirror, and closed the bed-sit door behind her, pulling hard to engage the feeble lock. She walked down the stairs and out into the warm and gauzy evening, along the suburban streets with their half-wild gardens and cars up on bricks, the buttons of the flat numbers and the people passing by; smiling, distracted, homeward-bound. A strange city, a foreign city. Yet so much the same.

Outside the Underground, she waited for an old woman to finish, then stepped past her into the telephone booth. She looked at her watch, then dialled the number she'd memorised and let it ring four times as she watched the cars go by. Then she put down the phone.

★　★　★

Ellen had a fever. Perhaps it came from the wounds on her arms that had barely bitten into the flesh, were scarcely deep enough for danger. More likely it came from sitting out until all hours in that damp cold godforsaken orangery. I mean, she could hear Ma saying to the priest, to the doctor, to Uncle Tod in the creaking hallway beyond the bedroom door, the kid was too young to intend anything. Too young to know just what in God's name she was doing.

Ellen turned over. Her hair and the pillow smelled of damp flesh, like a towel hung out all week in the bathroom. There was a fly buzzing at the window and the curtains were drawn. They were thin and white, damp-stained at the edges. Where the sun broke through them, and she could see the figure of the Blessed Madonna that hung there, and the mark of the fly's shadow. She opened her mouth and let the buzzing fill her head.

"Weeeelllll . . . young lady." Dr. Kelly was sitting beside her with a nest of veins like tree-roots in his nose.

"Yes . . ." The tight white bandages made her arms feel as though they didn't belong. She saw that the red roots also filled the whites of Dr. Kelly's eyes. She thought of the tree that must surely open its boughs there, inside his head.

He leaned over her. Then, without moving, without losing sight of his weary face, she was in another room. She saw a dead hand on a sheet. She saw flowers in a bedside vase. There was no warmth, no pulse, no heartbeat. Only the smell of shit and carnations. A worried voice saying, *Dr. Kelly, I'm sorry about the mess. And him always so finicky.* . . . But never mind, Mrs. Mayo, never fucking mind. The social worker will be around from the Town Hall.

"Who's Mrs. Mayo?"

"Who's Mrs. . . .?"

Dr. Kelly was leaning close over her now, puzzled and blinking, with the drink on his breath and the carbolic and leather smell of the bag he'd opened beside her. The roots of his eyes, the roots of his nose, and a vision from the tree inside. How could the kid know? But then . . . And maybe . . .

Ellen turned over in the bed, making a fretful noise, pushing away his unease. "I feel . . .," she said as Dr. Kelly's fingers moved to undo her buttons for the chill of the stethoscope. "I feel . . ."

★　★　★

Emerging from the Underground into the traffic of another part of the city, she turned right by the smart shops, then again along the trim hedgerows, swinging her heels and her ribboned hair, smiling up at the hazy pink sky.

The signs said PARKING FOR PERMIT HOLDERS ONLY, and the new red Saab wasn't out of place. The trees lined the road on both sides here. Not overlooked, near-on perfect. A dead end. She puzzled for a moment over the key. Then the locks thunked open, and she lifted the boot, and the big black nylon rucksack that Stevie had made up for her was there inside.

★　★　★

By the onset of winter, Ellen had settled into the routine of life at Kellaford. The school bus clanked down the lane, its interior thick with the fumes of tobacco, wet coats, packed lunches, boiled sweets. And the other children, kids of her own age, would sometimes glance at her from their seats or across the playground in their gossiping groups as though she belonged to another race. To them the big town was far away—almost mythic—and they knew about her dad, who had been shot by the Proddies. It was treated as a kind of perverse bad luck. But Ellen wasn't bullied or picked on. She was just left to herself. In the lessons, in the playground, on the streets of the little town, she'd learned how to be alone.

Climbing down each afternoon from the school bus and filling her lungs with the clean air, looking up at damp green hills and relishing the loneliness, Ellen often felt close to her dad. She remembered those afternoons after school when he'd come to collect her after finishing early at the plant and lift her over the railings. All the stuff he'd told her that the teachers had long forgotten, or never known. About Lugh the Bright One, who wore the Milky Way as a chain around his neck. About Finn MacCool, and his warriors of the Fianna.

She remembered the gleam in Dad's eyes and his rolling walk on the long way back past the big houses on Malone Road and down along the lough. Her dad had had dreams of the future as well as the past. He'd tell her that any fool could look on a map and see that this country was all wrong. He'd put his arm around her and tell her that maybe, Ellen O'Hara, your generation will be the one to see it all come right. After all, history was in their favour, and the only thing that could slow it down was the hotheads who shot and maimed.

★　★　★

One evening when the clouds were clearing after a day of rain, Ellen was walking between the gleaming ruts back down towards Kellaford after the school bus had rumbled off when another sound came out of the air. She looked up at the green Army helicopter as the overhanging trees began to stir, shaking heavy droplets down on her. It was close now, close enough for her to see the soldier leaning from the open door. She'd only seen the machines in the distance before, buzzing tiny as dragonflies as they patrolled the Border.

She walked on more quickly, splashing through the rutted puddles. The helicopter followed. She began to run, glancing back, hardly believing the noise and the wash of air, the smell of metal and fuel and sweetish plastic. She was deeply afraid, yet filled also with a sense of awe.

Uncle Tod was out seeing to the tractor in Kellaford's yard. Ellen climbed the loose stone wall and stumbled into his arms, and the helicopter banked away, combing the wet ungrazed grass of the east fields. Uncle Tod shook his oil-stained fist, and Ellen joined him, shouting, waving her arms at the bloody Brits, shooing them off like geese, suddenly filled with release and exhilaration.

★ ★ ★

In her dreams, she'd visited the heart of this city often enough. She'd known about the big buildings, the jangly accents, the policemen who walked without bullet-proof jackets or guns, the cars parked along the shopping streets. Here, there were no boarded-up shops, no checkpoints, no TOUTS WILL BE SHOT, no FUCK THE POPE. No oil drums filled with rubble.

She wandered along hot pavements amid the neon and the cooking smells. Past shops open late to sell popcorn, shrinkwrap porn, and big beefeater teddys strung up in their bags. No matter what she did with the straps, the black nylon rucksack pressed hard on her shoulders. Again, she checked her watch. She tried to open her mind, but felt only the clash and clamour of traffic, the faint oily smell of the stuff inside the bag that her own body heat was warming, and the acid swirling against the thin casing of the vial and the wires that led from it, and gluts of bilious music from the open doorways of bars. Lights and thoughts and faces roared by. Streaming, disconnected.

She stood by the wide river and watched it flow, drawing more of the night out like strands of ink from beneath the bridges. Her throat caught on the rank garbage air. She vomited it out, and saw the light of the stars, and Uncle Tod leaning out from the orangery darkness of Kellaford to lift her. *Now will you come and let me hold you. . . .*

★ ★ ★

His name was Stevie Rork. He was just two years above her at school. He even took the same bus, although he took it so rarely it was years before Ellen realised the fact. Stevie wasn't that much to look at. He was thin, with longish yellow hair and a fox's pointed face. But everyone—even the teachers—had to admit that Stevie was clever, that he was a charmer, even if he'd probably never come to any good. In many ways, Stevie was like Ellen, an outsider for no reason that anyone could really put their finger on. But he was a fierce fighter who would fly at anyone with a weird catlike anger. And he was a fierce dreamer, too. He'd take dares, stay out all night in abandoned and supposedly haunted hovels, go on wild drives in other people's cars. Once, he'd swum to the bottom of Finnebach Lake and swore blind ever afterwards that he'd seen a green enchanted kingdom below.

Ellen saw him tumbling drunk out of the bars with the big lads on market day, with her ma tutting and pulling her on. She saw him walking alone by the misted silver of Finnebach Lake. She saw him at the turn in the stairs at school, and felt the drop in her belly as he looked back at her.

She walked up to Stevie Rork one evening outside school when the trees hung uprooted in the mist. She looked up at him and said, "I want to be your girl."

"When did you decide this?" he asked, glancing back along the fog-wreathed railings for the hook of some joke.

"A while ago," she said. "One day in school when you looked down at me at the turn in the stairs."

Stevie stopped laughing as the memory of her came back to him. And he pushed back his hair. "And you could tell, could you? You could tell just from my look?"

Ellen smiled. She was feeling Stevie's eyes on her, and how she seemed to him with this red scarf around her throat and the mittens her mother had knitted on her hands and beads of yellow-lit moisture catching fire in her eyes and her hair. He wanted her— and already she knew him better than anyone, and knew that she would find the ways of making him want her more.

★   ★   ★

She walked down concrete steps into the bar by the river, where there was whispered music and pale deep-pile. She sat on a high stool with the black nylon rucksack pushed beneath her, and ordered a drink at the bar. She drew a breath, sniffed, and looked around. Lads from the glass cliff-face Government offices that lay around this place sat with their ties loose and their briefcases tucked under the tables. There were older men, solitary or in smaller groups. A few girls, smartly dressed, looking bored.

"Some place to be alone . . ."

She glanced over at the man who sat two empty stools down from her. Bulging buttons, and a pinstripe suit.

"I said—"

"—yeah." She took a swig of the martini she'd hoped would stiffen her resolve. Jesus, it was cold—and had cost enough. The man had a fat ordinary face. As he leaned over, nearly overbalancing, the booze he'd drunk and the food he'd eaten slid out on his breath, rank as the river.

"You staying, or visiting?"

"I'm having a drink. Alone." She looked at him. She'd seen plenty of his kind in the bars on the day the Broo paid out.

"You're *Irish*, aren't you? I *thought* there was something. Some thick bloody Colleen thinks she can come over here. I'll tell you, right, that I can take the blacks, easy. See, they don't go round killing our lads. Smearing shit over cell walls . . ."

She sat and said nothing. Finishing the drink as quickly as she could without choking, feeling the ice cubes chattering in the glass, and the need to be done with this thing. And she was off the stool, bending quickly down towards the black nylon rucksack that her foot had nudged out of sight in the low space beneath the bar, peeling back the Velcro, slipping her hand inside, finding the plunger, and pushing.

Then, turning, she was gone.

★   ★   ★

"You and me, we're not part of this place," Stevie had said one afternoon in the spring after they'd made love in the damp grass by the standing stones at the corner of East Cornu field and were lying wrapped in the blanket that Ellen had brought up the lane from home, looking at the hawk in the sky, the clouds that chased the sun.

She snuggled under the crook of his arm, smelling him and the grass and the wind that lifted off the green and glittering valley. "Where should we be, then?"

"Somewhere where there's no one like us. Where the Brits aren't in charge."

"Your dad got away."

"My dad's hiding in the South. He's a fool. He's been used by the Cause. I'd happier be a decent criminal than that. . . ."

She closed her eyes and snuggled deeper. She could never really tell when he was serious, when he was joking.

She said, "I don't understand you, Stevie."

She felt the rumble in his thin chest as he laughed. She

shrugged and snuggled deeper and kissed his nipple, feeling the red flame inside him. And the image of a room of yellow billowing curtains, a smiling man with hollow eyes leaning down into a cot, bringing the smell of booze and nicotine. Stevie's dad.

He pushed her over, and began to nuzzle at her breasts. He said, "I love you."

She looked up at the hawk in the sky, and at the jewelled trembling grass around her face, and at the white billows of hawthorn, and she felt the lumpen earth dissolve as the warmth began to spread. Stevie's desire was strong again now, always breaking, always rising, green over blue like the wall of a rolling wave. And yes, as he kissed her and the sun broke through the yellow curtains, he did love her. At that moment, he loved the whole world. He loved it as he loved and took Ellen, and as he loved his new Honda motorbike that he kept up the payments for by delivering messages for the local Brigade.

He lay there afterwards with his head propped in his hand, looking down at her with the rug pulled back, trailing his fingers over her skin.

She closed her eyes, feeling the shining air and his gaze on her and the smile on his lips. She felt the sky still hissing in her ears, and the warmth of his thoughts, opening. Layer within layer within layer. A box within a box. Car headlights beaming into a dark road where something, quite suddenly, leaps out. . . .

Suddenly, Stevie sat up on his elbows. "What's that sound?"

★   ★   ★

That night, the streetlamp flickered at her window like a weeping moon, and the old man in the room above was coughing and turning, his pain reaching down through the ceiling on strands of blood and mucus. When she finally slept, she dreamed that a dark-winged beast was squatting on her chest, scratching at her heart with sharp feathery claws, choking her.

★   ★   ★

The sound was an Army Land-Rover, coming up the lane. They saw the machine's mottled green roof riding over the hedges.

Stevie said, "Let's get out," but the soldiers were already coming at them down the field and from both sides at a run. Pushing through the hawthorn, wading through the rutted mud, kids from the mainland with their fear and their rifles and their heavy boots. They must have watched Ellen and Stevie lying on their blanket in the corner of the field, and moved in ahead of the Land-Rover.

Only the captain made a gallant effort to keep a straight face. He told them they were taking a bloody risk, skulking out in a field this close to the Border. He told them that it was the oldest trick, two paddies pretending to fuck so they could touch the wire that led to some culvert. But he'd let them off because they looked like typical young idiots, a thicko micko and his titless whore. As they wandered back down the field in their mud-heavy boots and jingling packs, one of the soldiers stumbled, lunging at Stevie with the butt of his rifle, slamming him hard.

★   ★   ★

She got up early, woken by the chill of her own sweat. She ran the tap into the sink until it produced lukewarm water, shampooed her hair, and listened to the BBC news on her portable radio. There was a lot about the bombing—there always was when it happened on the mainland.

She twisted open the bottle of hair-colour she'd bought at the chemist's on the corner, and read the instructions. *A small explosion in a riverside bar. One dead, three seriously wounded. Now sport—and a bad day for England. . . .* By eight-thirty, she was packed and out, wearing a short green dress, pale tights, with her damp yellow hair hidden under a white headscarf. Around the corner, she dumped her suitcase into a big communal dustbin.

She walked the streets. She was far too early. She unwound her scarf and combed out her hair in a public lavatory and drank coffee in a café on the local high street, gazing at the newspapers the people were reading, with their headlines and rough drawings of impressions of a thin, dark-haired girl. Glancing at the reflection of a stranger in the café window, she checked her watch.

★   ★   ★

Ellen sat in Kellaford's big kitchen. It was already late, and the generator was down. She actually liked the old farmhouse better this way, with the dark coming in rather than the light going out.

Ma had arranged the evening so that the two of them ended up sitting at opposite sides of the kitchen table beside the paraffin lantern with nothing but this silence between them, and Uncle Tod in his parlour chair with a plastic jug beside him, thinking as he always thought of his dead wife, whom Ellen had never known. She'd died in the birth of a son who was already dead, choked on something called the umbilical cord, which Ellen imagined must be like some kind of noose. Ellen studied the table's deeply rutted wood grain, thinking as she had thought before that it looked like a drunkenly ploughed field.

Ma clicked her tongue. "You're still going with Steven Rork, aren't you?"

"I'm not *going* with anyone."

"Then whatever word you choose to use."

"Why ask, if you're so sure?"

Ma sighed and lit a cigarette. The smoke swirled up and around the lantern between them, drawn to the heat of the flame. Ellen watched as it settled, drifting into half-seen hills.

"I know that you're of that age, Ellen. But why choose Stevie?"

"What's wrong with him? He's had a few scrapes, but who hasn't?"

"You know what his father was?"

"Stevie hasn't seen his dad in years."

Which was true; Stevie's memories of his father were virtually nonexistent, just that figure in the room with billowing yellow curtains, the smell of booze and nicotine. And there was a photograph above the coin-in-the-slot TV in the Rorks' terraced house. It showed a thin man with hollow eyes in a wedding suit, smiling awkwardly, looking out of place. That's my dad, Stevie used to say, pointing.

"You know what'll happen to Stevie, Ellen. You deserve better than getting pregnant by a man who's going to spend half his life in the Kesh."

Ma sucked her cigarette down, and ground the coal out in a saucer, her fingers trembling. "Think about it. Think about you and Stevie. And I know, Ellen, that you're still hurting because of what happened in Hayter Street. But your dad hated the Provos, Ellen. Hated the men preening with their guns. . . ." Ma shrank back in the chair, into the shadows, away from the light, almost as if she was falling. There. She'd had her say.

Ellen nodded, thinking *Hayter Street*—of the way that Ma said Hayter Street, and all the faded images it conjured. Dad a younger man than Ellen ever remembered. But as he leaned over in some park, his bones and the sky showed through. It was all so pale, so thin, almost transparent. Then coming back to Hayter Street that day and seeing the blue cars and the circling lights and the neighbours standing out. Knowing what it meant. And everything afterwards like the cold breaking of an endless wave.

"I don't plan to waste my life, Ma," Ellen said eventually, gazing at the half-figure she now saw. The shivering glint of an eye. "Not on Stevie Rork or anyone else . . ."

She stood up and left the kitchen, running along the corridor, pushing at the damp-rotted door at the far end, bursting out into the orangery where shards of glass hung from the roof on threads of dead ivy, turning and tinkling. She sat down on the old rusted pipe and folded her arms close around her chest, rocking gently to and fro.

She was sick of Kellaford's empty longing, sick of school; of the girls with their need for clothes, make-up, and attention, and the boys who spent half their lives thinking about sex and the other half trying to forget it. Stevie might end up gunned down or in the Maze, but at least he had his plans and his dreams. And he had that sense of risk. It might seem more obvious to her, but she knew that others felt it, too. That was why she'd been drawn to him.

It was something her dad had had too, although he'd taken his chances in different ways. Back in the days before the Provos had taken over, he'd been a proud Republican. He'd walked on the civil rights marches, helped print the pamphlets, argued merrily with his Unionist neighbours, and stood on tables in smoky rooms. But then the burnings and the stonings had begun, and people were forced out of their houses. Whilst Dad had made his stand in Hayter Street and talked of peace and power-sharing and Finn MacCool, the IRA had shaken off the cosy drinking-club chat, rearmed itself, and prepared for war. Like the old guard Republicans, her dad had still talked of peace — and where the hell had it got him?

Ellen stooped down and picked up a green-mottled shard of glass from the orangery floor. She turned it in her hands and looked out through the broken panes at the black hills with the stars above, remembering how she'd once stayed out here. In all the years since then, nothing had really changed.

★   ★   ★

When Ellen finished school, she went back to the city to study. She'd worked hard those last terms at school, and had the grades and a place doing Business Studies at Victoria Road to prove it.

Midafternoons, when lectures were finished, she would leave the windswept campus and her neat room and go across the park, passing through the checkpoints that guarded the big shops. Or she'd walk up the streets beside the lough, past the high-gabled houses where the gulls wheeled in the salt-laden air and her dad had once talked of peace and the dawn of Eire Nua as they walked the long way home from school.

She remembered how the walls in the west of the town told you where you were. FUCK THE POPE, GOD SAVE THE QUEEN. HANG THE FENIAN BASTARDS—that meant you were in the camp of the enemy. DIE, SOLDIER. NO STRIP SEARCHING. EIRE NUA in designs of wild Celtic — that meant you were home. Not that there was much else that was different. She once made a point of entering the alien heartlands of the Crumlin Road, trying to find Hayter Street. It had been razed; there was some new estate that was already

grey and tired and old, the houses FOR SALE and the men all pushing prams, out of work. She wondered about the fat, smiling man,
and where he lived. But the faces she saw, and the beery wash of
anger that broke from the doors of the pubs and the drinking
clubs, were the same that she found beyond the barricades and
the checkpoints amongst her own people a few streets away.

The flats rose high over the grey rooftops, tombstones to civic
architecture. Stevie had told Ellen he'd only got one with the help
of some arm-twisting from Brigade, although she found it hard to
believe you could give these places away. It was damp inside —
noisy, hard to heat, poorly plumbed — but Stevie was happy with
it; enjoying his independence after a lifetime of shared beds and
hand-me-down shoes. With his wage from Brigade, plus the Giro
and the job bonuses, he had more than enough to keep himself
in cigarettes and take-aways. Crouching over Stevie on the mattress on the bare floor, letting him pull off her blouse and bra to
suck at her breasts, Ellen would reach towards him and feel only
the continued certainty of his love for her, his innocent need. The
two other boys she'd been with filled their heads with worries and
fantasies when they made love, but Stevie only ever thought of
the sweetness in her. All she'd see in him was Ellen, Ellen. It was
like making love in a hall of mirrors.

Stevie would often fall asleep afterwards and she would lie beside him, studying his face in the pale light that came through the
curtainless window, wondering if anything about him would ever
really change. But Stevie was a killer now. That was the oddest
thing of all. Her Stevie — the thin lad she'd always known — had
shot a soldier dead, and helped stuff the body of an SAS man left
at the roadside with Semtex. But it was hardly there, that part of
him; Stevie had this bright vision of a land free of the Brits, a Shining Isle where there was birdsong and music in the summer fields.
Sometimes, lying tangled in Stevie's arms and close to the edges
of dream, Ellen could even walk beside him along the clean wet
streets of a new city after some redemptive rain, the soldiers gone,
the barricades down, the slogans washed away, the people smiling
and waving as they drove by in new white cars.

Only sometimes, just as his consciousness arose, would she
catch flashes of the things he fought to suppress; the blood-filled
gap between the dream and reality. She saw a shirtsleeved man,
caught in the crosshairs as he walked towards his car. And in some
corner of her mind the fat-faced gunman was still dodging under
the washing, smiling down at her, asking if he could have a word
with her dad. And she was still running inside to get him, not

knowing what a killer felt like, not knowing even now. Was it someone cold? Someone angry? Was it a stranger, a dark angel—or your closest friend?

When Stevie woke, she'd wet the tea for them both and make a few pointless efforts to tidy. She'd let his old dressing gown hang open as she moved around the flat or leave her clothes off entirely, soaking up the glow of his regard, knowing that he was never happier than when he lay there smoking, sated and disconnected, watching the gentle movements of her body.

"I've been thinking," he said one day as she stood by the window, looking down at the rows of narrow streets where she could see the red berets of an Army patrol moving along the Falls. "You should stay here."

"Stay?" She turned towards him, unthinkingly tightening the sash of the dressing gown.

"I mean," he said, affectedly casual as he lay in bed, tapping his cigarette into the ashtray he'd propped on his thin chest, "this is daft, us living apart in the same city. You don't belong with those stuck-up kids."

She nodded. That, at least, was true. The other students at Victoria Road thought she was thin and pale and strange, this girl who looked at you but never said anything. They knew nothing about the Troubles.

"Well, Ellen . . ." He was trying hard not to push it, trying hard not to hope. "You and me. What do you say?"

She walked over to the bed. Looking down at him, meeting his soft brown eyes, she felt a deep tenderness. "I can't."

Stevie blinked, more from hurt than surprise. "Why not? You know I love you."

"Yes."

The kettle in the tiny kitchen started to whistle. She turned away to see to it, but Stevie sat up and grabbed her hand. Although she knew what he was going to say, she let him keep her there.

"Or we could marry, Ellen. Whatever you want. I'd quit active service. I'd look for a job."

"Some chance of that here."

"But what do you want?"

"I don't know."

"What is it with you, Ellen, eh?"

"What do you mean?"

Steve chewed at his lip, suddenly close to anger or tears. "Why did you choose me?"

She pulled back her hand, rubbing away the sudden pressure of his grip. "I didn't *choose* you. We—"

"—what? You could have been anyone. Anything . . ."

"You know that's not true."

Stevie nodded in resignation. He let go of her hand.

That was it—they never really argued. There would some-times be these bitter exchanges, but after a few moments Stevie always gave up in the frustration of trying to say things that he somehow seemed to guess she knew or felt. Even now as she walked across the bedroom towards the tiny kitchen, she could feel him pushing away a vision of his flat with new wallpaper and floral curtains—a boyish dream of femininity—and her smiling down at him in bed each morning.

★   ★   ★

As winter came on, Ellen sometimes agreed to Stevie's pleas and stayed overnight with him in the flat. Late at night, men from Brigade would come sometimes to talk. They'd look at her and smile as she gave them coffee, their eyes passing right through. They'd wait for her to go into the bedroom and close the door be-fore the real business began.

Other times, she'd turn the key he'd given her and find the flat empty. She'd sit and wait then, puffing at Stevie's cigarettes without bothering to inhale, looking out from the window. As the room filled with smoke and the night came in on a purple wind from the hills, she'd wonder which Stevie Rork it would carry through the door. The Stevie who was heavy with drink. Or the Stevie with the pinpoint eyes, the Stevie with the reek of cordite on his jacket and the crack of an Armalite still ringing in his mind.

One night, she waited and Stevie didn't return. Even before word came of his arrest and the young women from the other flats along the corridor offered their consolation, she knew that this was the sign for which she'd been waiting.

★   ★   ★

She sat in the back of the car as the roads hooked deeper into the hills and the headlights picked out the grey corpse of a sheep at the roadside. Water and the lights of a house gleamed faintly in the shadowed valley below, and the standing stones on the far ridge stood out against the purpling sky. There was a gun under the coat on the front passenger seat. The man who sat beside her glanced down at her thighs, and said nothing.

They came to the large abandoned hotel just as darkness fi-nally settled.

★   ★   ★

Ellen O'Hara's hair was short now, and her pale skin was brown from the tube of paste she'd bought with her new clothes at the airport. She wanted it to look as though she'd been here for some time.

She'd slept-in late on the bed in the little villa and had taken breakfast in the café in the square of white houses, watching the playing children, smiling at their happy absorption, and feeling the sun prickling on her bare neck. She'd looked in at a shop and asked about newspapers. But the English newspapers—the ones she could find—were days old and filled with the Royal Family. She changed some money, bought a swimming costume and a towel, and drove her hired car down through the shimmering hills.

She took the steps to a beach and stripped and lay listening to the waves. The heat pressed down, and she thought of the man in the bar, the smell of his rank breath as he leaned towards her. And the sunlight seared through her eyelids—white, yellow, red, black; the flowering colours of high explosive.

The sand burned her feet as she ran past the sprawled bodies, flabby and brown, gleaming like braised meat. The water was colder than she'd expected. It broke and pulled at her, pushed at her, drawing her out into the bay.

Surfacing, gasping, she looked back at the white shore. Even without moving, just treading water, she was being drawn out by the undertow. For a moment, she let the waves push and slide over her shoulders, across her face, filling her mouth. Then she kicked hard, and thrust with her arms, swimming.

★   ★   ★

The naked man was tied to a chair, which was bolted to a wooden pallet, which in turn was weighed down at the corners with blocks of concrete. His head was hooded and his breathing was loud and irregular. A few minutes before, his left foot had been pulped with a hammer.

In the light of a single paraffin lamp, the interrogators sat facing him from across the floor of the old hotel ballroom. Behind them, and on the ceiling, quivered the dusty remains of tinsel and paper streamers; the remnants of some Christmas bash in the days before the place had closed down due to lack of patronage.

One of the interrogators made a note and looked back at the man.

"Repeat the names."

The man did so. None of it was new now, but they listened anyway and fed a new cassette into the machine. There was a weird sense of horror and sadness in the old ballroom; he was, after all, a soldier like them, someone who'd gone undercover and taken the risks his masters weren't prepared to face.

"Is that it?"

The man nodded, then gasped as someone pulled off his hood. "You know what to do."

The man was sobbing now, but he kept his bruised and puffy eyes on Ellen as she walked out from the shadows. Two paces away, standing at the edge of the pallet to which his chair was fixed, she levelled the gun with both her hands. The others here would have to shoot him afterwards, but tonight her bullet was to be the first. And the man didn't hate, didn't love, was hardly there at all. He was just a searing empty pain that wanted to be over.

★   ★   ★

Dusk was falling when Ellen got back to the villa, and the light she'd left on in the bedroom wasn't showing as she looked up from the road. She climbed the steps and saw that the front door had been forced. She pushed it wide, stepping into the heat of the kitchenette and feeling for life, wondering if this was the moment when it ended.

"That you, Ellen?"

It was Stevie's voice.

She ran into the bedroom and fell on the mattress where he lay, knocking the breath out of him.

"Here, let me see you." Stevie elbowed himself up and yanked the light-pull. He blinked. "Your hair . . ."

She put her hand to her bare neck, the skin slightly hot from the sun. Then to his face.

"You look the same," she said. But his cheeks were plumper and the line of his jaw was blunter, less defined. She assumed it came from all those months in the Maze, then at the house where he'd made bombs on the mainland.

She put her hands on his knees and kissed him, liking the way she looked to him now, a different Ellen O'Hara with short blonde hair. Stevie was opening the buttons of her blouse, pushing it off her shoulders and starting to kiss her breasts. She tasted of salt. It was on his tongue.

After they'd made love, he drifted off to sleep and Ellen lay beside him with his dampness inside her. But for the scent of thyme and the sound of the crickets and the warmth in the air, it was just like old days. But for the flab on Stevie's thighs and chest and belly in the moonlight . . .

He grunted and burrowed his head deeper into the pillow. Some dream of a forest. Then headlights, and running. He stumbled in his dream, and muttered and turned over, sinking deeper.

Ellen stood up, padded into the little bathroom, and turned beneath the spray. She dried herself with a towel, went back into the bedroom, and looked down again at Stevie. It wasn't just the weight he'd put on. He'd changed inside, too. Even his dreams had paled. She remembered the Stevie who saw faces in the clouds, the Stevie who swam down through Finnebach Lake and drank the air up on the hills about Kellaford. She remembered the wild tenderness of his eyes.

★   ★   ★

Stevie dressed to go out when he awoke later in the evening. It wasn't what Ellen wanted, but she understood that he was sick of the months of prison and in hiding. They drove in the hired car down the road into town. They weren't used to holidaying abroad. To them, it was a different world, here under the lights and the stars, in the warmth of the night. Stevie took her hand, and they wandered with the other couples beside the dark rigging and the sea-scents of the old harbour. They looked at the pictures outside the restaurants and ate grilled fish in a square by the shore in candlelight.

"You're still looking sad," he said, pouring a second carafe.

She smiled and shook her head. Nearby, street music was playing and the white spire of a church rose into the Mediterranean night. This place truly was lovely.

"You did well, sweet," he said. "What did you think of the Saab?"

She let Stevie take her hand. The tables beside them had been pushed together to accommodate a larger group of people, a family with gran and granddad and the kids all staying up late and sharing the wine. They were Brits, Ellen realised now. It had been a mistake for them to sit this close.

She said, "We should be getting back."

"Hey, laddie!" Stevie clicked his fingers at the waiter, then looked up at the stars. "Did I tell you," he said, "that I saw my dad?"

"No."

"He's back in the city now. . . ." Stevie drank more sangria and belched. She gazed at his fat, shining face. "Living with some sour old bint and her family in the Falls. And not what I expected. Too much of this stuff." He waved his glass. "Still, it was good to meet the old bastard again."

Ellen glanced over at the next table, willing him to shut his mouth. As he poured more wine, she wondered at how simple he'd become, drinking to rid himself of the worry that he might end up alcoholic like his dad.

Later, she drove Stevie out through the town and into the hairpin hills, winding down the window to let in a breeze that carried the scent of dust and orange groves, fearing he might be sick. He lolled beside her, humming to himself. Checking the rearview mirror, she saw headlights glint into view out of the darkness behind them. A siren began to wail.

"Jesus . . .," Stevie hissed.

She guessed what would be in front of them even as the road dipped and the lights of another car were slewed ahead in the darkness.

"Just keep your foot down," Stevie said. Calm now, cold sober. "We haven't come all this way. . . ."

An officer standing at the side of the road was waving his torch to indicate that they should stop. At the last moment, as she swung the wheel, he tumbled out of the way. Branches scraped over the windshield and the wheels skidded, then bit back onto the loose surface of the pale road on the far side. She felt something tug at the car, and heard a series of dull thumps. But she kept the accelerator floored.

She checked the rearview and saw the lights of the following car dip left also towards the trees, then stop as one of them winked out. Then a fork ahead in the road. Then another, and something bright and hot was burning inside her. She chose east, towards the big northern towns. She felt at ease, pushing the car harder now, taking risks, rolling like a cold breaking wave, driving down this dark tunnel with just the headlights pouring ahead of her.

"We'll have to ditch this car soon," she said, looking over at Stevie and seeing the way that he was slumped. For a moment, she thought it was the drink. Then she felt another giddy surge, and saw the wet gleam on his coat and the bulging rents in the passenger door.

★　★　★

"A fine job you did," said the man who was driving, shaking his head as the car bumped and splashed along the rutted cross-Border track.

Ellen gazed out. The steep enclosed hedges were dark beneath the pale flush of the sky.

She said, "You do what you have to," shivering slightly and keeping her handbag pressed down on her lap as a sliver of dawn broke through the woodland of a far hilltop. She guessed that she'd already be the talk of the Falls bars for getting back here. Not that she wanted that. And not that it had been easy.

As the day brightened, she saw a castle's sheep-picked ruins and a hovering fleck that could have been a hawk or a distant

Army helicopter. She thought of Lugh the Bright One, and of Finn MacCool's warriors who were still sleeping beneath these hills, and how the stories that Dad had once told her of this island's past and its future had grown tangled in her head. Ellen O'Hara, he'd said, as the seagulls mewed and drifted over the rooftops of Malone Road and the light flashed up from the lough, everything has to change. But the whole point was that nothing here ever changed. Later on, when all the truth had been forgotten, she'd be in the tales herself, a small new thread in the endless story.

They rejoined the roads, and the air blowing on her face through a gap in the window changed its scent with the textures of familiar soil. Finnebach Lake gleamed in the distance. They passed the pull-in down the lane where the school bus had once dropped her off. And there was Kellaford, ragged and brown and warm with the morning.

The front door swung open as she climbed out of the car, and Uncle Tod hugged her in speechless tears. She hugged him back, saying, "I can't stay long. . . ."

Ma sat alone in the kitchen.

"How much did you hear?" Ellen asked, sitting down across the deeply grained table. They had a dog now. It growled at her from a cardboard box by the Rayburn.

Ma gave a shrug. "I heard you'd done something. That you were in danger. Then, that you were safe. Your hair—"

"—Stevie's dead."

"Well, there . . ." Ma drew on a cigarette. "There's no saying that it wasn't . . ." She blew out a cloud of smoke.

"Look . . ." Ellen took out the photograph from her handbag, the photograph that she'd found in Stevie's wallet, pushing it across the table.

Ma lifted it with trembling fingers, glanced at it, then pushed it back. "They're even looking like each other now," she said, "aren't they?"

The photograph showed Stevie and his dad standing outside a city bar, arm in arm. Their faces were clear enough, even through the bloodstains. They were both plump, and smiling.

Ellen said, "He's the man, Ma. Stevie's dad. He's the fat man who came to Hayter Street. The man with the gun in the garden."

"Hayter Street . . .?" Ma blinked and shook her head, long rays of sunlight pouring through the window into her sleep-tangled hair. Ellen felt grey emptiness, the slow breaking wave.

"Stevie's dad was a Provo, Ma. He was the one who shot Dad. You understand that?"

"What difference does it make now, Ellen, which side it was that killed him?"

"But *why?*"

"Your dad spoke up, Ellen. He was a Republican who stayed on and talked about peace when the Provos wanted war. It was going to happen anyway, one way or another—that was what I kept trying to tell him. . . ."

"They didn't even have the courage to admit it. . . ."

"I thought you'd know enough, Ellen, to realise that courage doesn't count. You of all people—the way you look at everyone. Seeing and not seeing . . ."

Ellen said nothing, staring at Ma as the dog by the Rayburn, now half-asleep, began to growl once again. She felt empty and she felt cold. It was a cold that had never really left her since that night when Stevie died in her arms on that dark foreign roadside beneath the pines. She'd looked into the killing wave then, and it was cold and it was bright. It was pain beyond feeling that swept you on into a place of white. And it was already there, rolling and breaking inside you, long before you died.

"Then *Stevie*, Ellen," Ma said, shaking her head, genuinely amazed. "Of all the ones you could have had, you had to choose Stevie Rork. . . . I mean . . ." Ma began to laugh, then to cry.

★   ★   ★

The man drove her away from Kellaford, up the hill and through the little town towards the safe house up in the plantations that was waiting. In the square where the shops were opening, she asked to stop and use the loo. Too gallant to argue, the man parked his car in the shadow of the memorial. She was out quickly with her handbag into the old toilets, then through the other entrance and past the school railings where she'd met Stevie, into the cobbled streets beyond.

★   ★   ★

She took her time. It was late afternoon before she reached the city; evening as the tombstone flats rose in sunlight over the terraced streets. EIRE NUA. TOUTS WILL BE SHOT. She knew it well. And the kids were out playing, shooshing by on their bicycles, and the sound of familiar voices and the scent of cooking drifted from front doors open to the heat.

She checked the address that Stevie had so carelessly scrawled on the back of the stained photograph. The street was called Plunkett now, although the old A–Z still showed it as Gawain—named after some British hero, then renamed after an Irish one. No one looked at her here, nothing was strange, and the house was like all the others along Plunkett Street, with a gravelly square of front garden. She closed the iron gate and knocked on the half-open door.

She saw the faded tiling of the hall as she waited, and a lemony square of sunlight thrown across a picture on the wall. She heard the chimes, distant and ethereal, of an ice-cream van, and she wondered if they still came here, where the men in helmets and the Saracens patrolled. As the door swung fully back, she realised that her whole face and body were incredibly tense, and that she was smiling. Sliding her fingers into her handbag, feeling for the cold grip, she looked down at the boy who was standing there. He had his school tie on, and his school shorts.

"Is Mr. Rork in? I'd like to . . . He's a . . ."

She swallowed, licking her lips, preparing to begin some generalised description of Stevie's dad in case he was living here by some other name. But the boy knew him all right. He turned and skipped off down the hall. She could even see the man's face. She heard a door bang, and a shrill voice shouting, "Uncle Marty!" Looking down at the half-dead bush in the patch of front garden, she saw the shrivelled pink-and-brownish roses that hung there, and could smell their scent.

She heard footsteps. The slap and sigh of slippers as a dark figure ambled up the hallway, a newspaper clutched in hand, a crumpled shirt half open to the belly. He brought with him the smell of beer and sweat and cigarettes, but he smelled and felt like Stevie too — she hadn't expected that — and he'd been asleep and was still yawning, flapping a hand over his mouth as he puzzled over this young woman standing in the doorway, part of his mind still trailed with the edges of football on the telly and with half-lost dreams.

"What is it that you're . . ." He stood before her now. In the sunlight, she could see the threads of red on his nose and along his grey-stubbled cheeks. Her hand was still in the handbag, clenched around the gun. Sensing the oddness of her posture, he glanced down. When he looked back up again at her face, he seemed to see everything, and knew what she knew.

She said, "Why?"

He shook his head slowly, spreading his arms. "I should do this thing now," he said, "if I were you. . . ." She looked into the dark of his eyes and saw the shape of her own face caught there, and felt the endless cold breaking over her from the depths of this warm summer evening. She realised that he wasn't daring her to use the gun, and that he was like the soldier who'd looked up at her in the old ballroom of that abandoned hotel and had just wanted it all to end. She realised that he was pleading.

She turned away from him, and heard his voice shout after her as she reopened the gate. She walked down Plunkett Street and out along the Falls, past the barbed wire and the rubble-filled barrels and the big murals of the men in masks and the heros of old, on towards the centre of town, where there were still flowers in the parks and the buses and the taxis stopped and the doors, even in this heat, were closed to the world. Nobody dreamed along Malone Avenue. It was solid and it was real. She sat down on a bench overlooking the lough as the sky darkened and a clear salt-and-heather-tanged breeze blew in off the sea and the hills. After a while, as the streetlights came on and the blue darkness deepened, a shadow that might have been her father seemed to sit down beside her. Turning towards it, unsurprised, she opened her mouth to ask him a question, then shook her head and stood up from the bench. Tossing the weight of her handbag over the railings towards the waters of the lough, Ellen O'Hara walked on down the street.

Green

There are many kinds of pest in a garden. Thrips and greenfly. Flea beetles, fairies, and fungi. Manslugs that nibble leaf-heraldry to mark the territory of their bearded king. Leatherjackets. Mealybugs. An unmarshalled army bickering to bore a ripening fruit or wither a well-formed stem.

Mark knew them all. Their names had been his early words. His first memory was horror at the broken, weeping flesh of a blighted tomato. His second, the garden of his parents' cottage in the row at the south-east corner of my Lord Widder's estate. Sitting in sunshine with the drone of the bees. Roses nodding with the weight of summer. The tawny wall. Everything high above, and the hot sky furthest of all, beyond reach even if he could persuade his legs to stand. Then there was movement. Something quick and brown. And there again: sheen of wings and ivory flicker of eyes and teeth in the wall shadow beneath the roses where plumes of lavender scented the air. He watched the tiny figure, something that moved in a world even wider and brighter than his own. Its movements were wild and sharp, like a bird's, hands darting to tuck the furry globes of lavender and push them into a tiny slung pouch. Its head flickered this way and that, looking for danger, and watching Mark, his presence, weighing up the threat.

Brownie. Mark knew the word. A brownie. And even then his

gardener's instincts told him that this one was benign, that the lavender would thrive regardless of its attention. Mark wasn't sure what he did next. Maybe he laughed, perhaps he reached out a hand, but quick as a blink, the brownie was gone.

The wall shrank in a flurry of years until Mark could sit dangling his feet in the high grass on the far side. In the settling warmth of late afternoons, he would watch that special place amid the tunnel shadows of the orchard where the track from the estate gardens turned into sight. From the open kitchen window in the cottage behind, the clip of the chopping board, steam and the smell of vegetables, seemed to draw his father into view, the hobble of his walk, the hump of his leather apron slung across his left shoulder.

Mark remembered the flash of excitement. Turning to call inside to his mother across the little stretch of their garden. And when he thought of those times, when he grew maudlin and tried to make sense of these things, he would always struggle to prolong that glance back through the open window, to penetrate the cooking shadows of the kitchen and glimpse the woman who breathed and lived and hummed to herself there. But even when he forced his mind into fantasy, she remained hidden by the play of summer light. A vague movement, nothing more than the shape of a cloud seen at night on a river. That was his sole memory of his mother.

In later years when he and his father were alone, he'd try to get him to talk about her. But his father's face would cloud with the same puzzlement that Mark recognised within himself. His lips would shape wordless sounds as though he too had lost his memories. And eventually, one way or another, he'd always tell the same story. How they'd honeymooned at the coast, walked the promenade in fresh new clothes like a couple of swells. A stall with striped awnings had offered daguerreotypes for a pound a throw and they'd stood out in the salt air, debating whether to have their likenesses taken. But it was almost all the money they had, and the need for a meal and perhaps even a drink before they went back to the boarding-house won the day. So, to his father's bitter regret, he had no face in a frame to remind him of the life he'd lost.

Mark and his father were close, sharing their forgetful grief, caring haphazardly for the cottage and each other, and, above all, responding to the growth of all things leafed, all things that came from the earth, all things green. Mark went to the school by the chestnut tree in the vale, but the other children found him vague and aloof. Not friend, nor enemy, nor prey. So Mark stood apart from the dusty rabble at playtime and participated woodenly in the organised games. His real lessons took place at home, with his father.

Their own cottage garden was small but, like the intricate petals of a rose, opened layer upon layer of wonder. In the evenings, free from school and work, they tended and watered, often so deep into the twilight that the soil became a dark mist in their hands. And his father, working in the big estate, clipping and hoeing for my Lord Widder, would sometimes bring home a gaudy broken bloom, a vegetable too huge for the pot yet still rejected as a dwarf in the competition greenhouses, or even—as with the blighted tomato—object lessons in decay and disease.

One day in autumn, his father trudged home through brown gusts of leaves and placed a barred wooden trap down on the kitchen table. Then he struck a lamp and held it close so that Mark could see what it was that whimpered and scurried inside.

"I stopped them from dropping this one in the water-butt," he said, crouching down to level his face with Mark and the edge of the table. "Thought you might want to see it."

The creature put its hands to the bars and peered out, a prisoner in a tiny jail. It had damaged its wings in an initial attempt to escape; greenish-blue, they trailed at its back like torn scraps of paper. But now it seemed resigned to its confinement and tilted its head to watch as Mark and his father talked.

"Now, this is called a ferrish. They gather acorns, which no one minds." His father reached out and prodded a calloused finger, dark with ingrained dirt. The creature backed away from the bars. "But they torment the horses in the stables, though only the Devil knows exactly why—and he isn't telling. My Lord Widder will not have his prize mounts tormented."

"Can I keep it?" Mark asked. "Keep it as a pet?"

His father shook his head. "It's a thing from the wild. Doesn't belong here with us any more than you or I belong up a tree."

"But please . . ."

Mark was uncharacteristically pleading and insistent. Although he didn't realise it, he was a lonely child at heart, withdrawing from the companionship of school-friends and the people on the estate as much from fear as from self-sufficiency. He could just picture the ferrish sitting—after weeks of slow and careful persuasion—on his shoulder like a magical parrot. The fun they would have together! The games!

Reluctantly, his father agreed.

Mark hurried into the deepening evening. He waded carelessly through the dead leaves and wind-flattened nettles that stretched

down from the bottom of the garden to the misting river, and retrieved the rabbit hutch that had lain there since the half-forgot-
ten demise of Bobbity the year before. Brushing wood-lice from
its sides, he carried the big, awkward box back into the kitchen.

As his father stoked up the fire and chopped carrots and onions for dinner, Mark used his precocious skills as a carpenter to
tack back the warped boards and tighten the loose mesh at the
front. He worked on his knees on the worn firelit rug, and the ferrish stared down at him from the table through the bars of the
trap. He screwed dowelling rods in as perches, scattered a few
handfuls of straw, and filled Bobbity's old bowl in the corner with
water. It was dark now outside, and food—acorns, he supposed—
would have to wait until morning.

Mark surveyed his work on the hutch, taking proud stew-
scented breaths of the dim kitchen air. But he was unwilling to lift
the trap, and asked his father to take it down from the table.

"Slowly does it." His father wiped potato peelings from his
hands and slid back the door of the trap, pressing it against the
wider entrance to the hutch.

The ferrish cowered at the back, reluctant to come out. His
father gave the little box a tap, then a gentle shake. Just as Mark
was leaning down to peer inside, the ferrish flew from the trap,
then, before he could close the door, out of the hutch again and
into the kitchen.

Its chest heaving with a breathy whistling sound, it perched on
top of the frame of an old engraving by the closed door. Mark and
his father moved towards it, their arms outstretched like zombies.
Before they could close around the ferrish, it flitted between them
and circled the room twice in quick and silent flight before swerv-
ing towards the window and bumping into the pane like a heavy
moth. It fluttered to the floor and dragged itself towards a chair
leg, briefly out of reach of their clasping hands. Slowly, quietly,
they circled around both sides of the kitchen table, but the ferrish
climbed into the air again, settling awkwardly on the stone rim of
the sink. Back bent, body palpitating, wings bedraggled, it regarded them balefully as they approached once more.

The closer of the two, Mark scraped a chair out of the way and
moved towards it, trying to look trustworthy, gentle. It obviously
had little energy left.

"It's all right," he whispered. "Nothing to be afraid of."

The creature took off, batting by chance against Mark's outstretched hand. He felt the quick warmth clawing against his
palm, but before he could close his fingers it was away.

Mark spun around in time to see the ferrish dart towards the fire. The chimney, he thought. Of course, the chimney! But instead of flying upwards into the smoke-drifting darkness and freedom, the ferrish dived into the heat.

There was a scream—neither of pain nor of joy, but like the wind in the treetops on a wild night—and the flames briefly brightened. Then there was only stillness, and the rattle of the teakettle as it came slowly to the boil.

★   ★   ★

The ferrish's death was a sad lesson for Mark to learn. He carried the guilt with him for all of that winter; a long time for someone so young when the dark months stretch like a stony road lit only by the brightness of Christmas, holly berries, and the occasional appearance of an impertinent mushroom. But it taught him that even in a garden, even in my Lord Widder's planned and regimented estate, there were many things that were wild, things that were free.

The earth awoke again. Summer followed spring, and Mark's reputation as a loner increased. In those precious hours when there was no school and little urgent work to be done in the garden at home, he would wander and explore the endless grounds of the Widder estate. There were, of course, strict rules as to where the young son of an undergardener could go—many of the workers lived out their whole lives on the estate without ever even glimpsing the distant, stately white porticos of the great house. These rules Mark never deliberately disobeyed. If he knew a place was forbidden, a laurel or an ivy wall that represented a boundary which only certain privileged gardeners were permitted to cross, he would turn away along less sacrosanct paths. He wandered, avoiding the gardeners and labourers who, seeing him in any part of the estate without any obvious purpose, invariably asked just what he thought he was doing. And, sometimes, he got lost.

In strange and unexplored parts of the garden, the distinctions between the permitted and the outlawed became deliciously vague. Not knowing whether he was allowed to be there was part of the joy of discovering new places, of getting lost, of crossing a stepping-stone stream into a bluebell wood, of finding a marble chair engraved with seahorses overlooking a waterfall in a ferny dell.

Lord Widder's birthday in July was always a special day. In celebration, the entire estate was permitted a day of rest, something that never happened on Sundays and holy days despite the injunctions of the clergy. Then, there were always urgent tasks to be done in the garden, and of course the estate employees used what time they could to work for themselves on their own plots and houses. But, unlike God, when my Lord Widder decreed a day of rest, he meant it. And woe betide anyone found doing anything more strenuous than lifting a mug of tea.

So Mark set out across the orchard after breakfast with the whole day blissfully ahead of him. It was still early, but the sun was strong through the branches, the grass dry underfoot. Off down the slope to his left in the bowl of the valley where the prize Widder sheep grazed, the spire of Saint Pepper's, one of the estate churches, rose from a cluster of cottages and trees to prick the haze. The Ave bell struck once, rippling the still air. Saint Pepper's and all the other churches throughout the estate would continue to strike the hour and half hour until dusk. When my Lord Widder had been much, much younger, the strike enumerated the years of his life, but now and for many years the stars came out before a full account could be given.

Through the white gate and along the raised track between the asparagus beds. Past the greenhouses. And more greenhouses. And yet more. A crystal garden on all sides, mirroring the flash of the sky. Inside, thick growths of cucumber and tomato billowed and clawed the glass like prisoners. Further on, stepping over hosepipes and wheelbarrows left in uncharacteristic abandon by workers careless in the knowledge that no one would be out to inspect their labours, greenhouse after greenhouse was filled with grapevines. Mark knew as well as any gardener that there were plenty of species of grape that could be grown outside on a south-facing wall, but my Lord Widder was said to prefer the softer, sweeter texture of the more delicate varieties. Following the track between the greenhouses, Mark wondered how anyone, even an aristocrat, could eat so many grapes.

He eventually reached the mountainous privet hedge that marked the outermost boundary of the formal gardens. Here, the silence was still more obvious; on almost any other day of the year the priveteers would be up on their ladders, clipping and trimming. Mark's father always said they were the happiest of all the workers on the estate. Privet suffers from few pests and seldom dies if properly mulched. It simply grows.

Mark followed the long shadow of the hedge to a white gate set in it like a door in a wall. He went through, down the dim tunnel under the hedge, thinking, although he'd only seen them in books, of a train racing under a hill towards a widening speck of light. Savouring the moment, he emerged into the heat.

Off in the distance, Saint Pepper's chimed another year of Lord Widder's life. The differing pitches of two other estate churches echoed from opposite directions moments later.

He was on familiar ground here. The mile-long avenue stretched from the perimeter, decked out with roses, dahlias, and comical red-hot pokers, leading him to a circular lake of grass centred by a great stone birdbath big enough to wash a griffon. This was one of his favourite places. From it, like doors leading from a giant hall, paths opened into the mysteries of the garden.

He took the way downhill through long grass and copses of oak. As the sun climbed, the trees gathered in larger masses, darker and thicker, until gradually, like falling into a dream, Mark found that they were all around him, over his head, shutting out all but splinters of the sun.

His toes stubbed upraised roots. Ropes of ivy tumbled into his face. The path was tentative and meandering, but the dense undergrowth gave him little choice but to follow. There was no birdsong, little noise but the faint sea-murmur overhead. Mark gazed around in puzzled wonder as he walked, his gardener's instincts in turmoil. Never before had he seen a place where things were simply left to grow. Not checked, or weeded or staked or deadheaded or pruned.

The whisper of the topmost branches only added to the stillness. He jumped at the sound of a woodpecker hammering in the green shadows. As the path wound on between massive trunks and nettles, he stepped over a trail of marching ants. A squirrel darted up an oak and regarded him as it cleaned its whiskers, and further on he saw a half-dozen manslugs chomping the succulent stems of a clump of wild rhubarb. Unafraid, they raised their heads towards him as he passed, their wet, fronded mouths gaping open as if they were about to break into song.

Then Mark saw a sea-horse. He stopped and stared. It was a little way off the track, swaying gently to and fro in the dreaming heat of the forest, its tail twined around a branch. He worked his way around towering foxgloves to get a better look. Sensing his presence, the sea-horse rippled its fins and drifted slowly, unconcernedly, into the air. Its scales, caught in a ribbon of sunlight, flashed rainbows. Entranced, Mark waded on through the undergrowth.

The sea-horse drifted ahead, unhurried. Mark stumbled after, his hands outstretched like a baby clutching for a bubble. A sea-horse of the air! Even after the experience with the ferrish, there was still a large part of him that wanted to touch, to understand.

Reaching a particularly thick stretch of bramble, the sea-horse floated high and over. Pushing his way blindly through, Mark suddenly felt the ground shoot from under him. He fell, down and out into brilliant sunlight.

Scratched, stung, and muddied, he climbed out from the ankle-deep water of a ditch and looked around. He was in some unknown part of the landscaped gardens — and the sea-horse had vanished. Then, ahead between a screen of holly, something bright flashed. Mark ran towards it, and found himself teetering at the stone lip of a wide pool. Carp glistened like gold in the shade beneath the lilies. Around the edge a boy was riding a bicycle. He tinkled his bell. Polished chrome sparkled.

"Hey!"

Mark stepped out of the way in surprise, but the boy pulled up and dismounted.

He was about Mark's age, but fairer skinned and slightly taller. Freckles splattered his cheeks and joined in a dark stripe across his nose. The clothes he wore were almost as scruffy as Mark's, but still Mark could see they were conspicuously better made.

"And just who are you?"

Mark stammered his name.

"Adrian Widder."

The boy held out his hand. Mark had never shaken hands before, but he took it anyway.

"Not the left hand, stupid. The right. Like this."

"I see."

"Would you like a go on my bike? I don't mind."

Mark glanced down at the smooth lines, the bright red frame, the cream mudguards. "I can't ride."

"You can't do much, can you?"

Mark shrugged.

"Do you want to learn? I mean, anyone can do it as long as they're not an absolute and complete moron."

"Wouldn't mind."

They fell into step together, the wheels of the bicycle ticking and flashing between them.

The boy said, "It's easiest on the big lawn, softer if you fall. Up here, through the rose garden."

"Did you say your name was Widder?" Mark asked.

"Yes, I just told you. Adrian Widder. Are you this stupid naturally or do you take lessons?"

Mark ignored the taunt. He'd realised already that the boy

didn't mean to hurt. "You can't be . . . Lord Widder . . . can you?"

"That's my father."

"It's his birthday."

"When?"

"Today."

"How do you know that?"

"Everyone on the estate knows," Mark said, glad that he was able to put Adrian right on something. "It's a special day. You must have heard the bells tolling."

Adrian shook his head. "Mother will have given him some present from me, I suppose. He's not here, anyway. Spends most of his time up in the capital with the King. The King needs him a lot."

"What for?"

"To fight, that sort of thing. Father's a great swordsman. I've read it in the papers."

They walked on through the rose garden. The bicycle tyres sighed in the gravel. The bees droned. An easy silence fell between them, the sort that didn't demand to be filled by pointless words. For no reason he could easily explain, Mark liked Adrian Widder. He recognised another loner, and their mutual shyness had been overcome by the sheer accident of their meeting. There was no pressure, no reason why they should get on. Nobody *expected* them to be friends. And somehow, without trying, it became easy.

"Well, here we are." Adrian creaked open a gate in a wall.

Mark followed him through.

And stopped.

Adrian turned. "What is it? Come on!"

Mark stepped slowly across rich turf. Ahead in the midday sun, an immense lawn rolled on and on and on. And in the distant green shimmered the spires and domes of something that was too vast, too ornate, to be called simply a building.

"That's the house," Adrian said offhandedly. "Haven't you ever seen a house before? Now, do you want to learn to ride or not?"

Mark did.

Adrian held the handlebars as Mark climbed on.

Mark fell off.

They tried again and again, Adrian shoving at the saddle to get him going and Mark's feet clawing uselessly at the pedals. And, every time, he fell off, down into the softness and the scent of the grass. It all happened so simply, so predictably, that they began to chuckle, then to laugh. Jaws aching, wiping tears from their eyes and noses, they continued. And the dogged stupidity of their repeated actions—Mark getting on, Mark falling off, Mark getting on again—made their laughter even better, even worse. Eventually, they had to lie down on the lawn, giggling in helpless spasms.

Mark was the first to recover. He sniffed, wiped his nose on the back of his hand, picked up the bicycle. Shoulders still shaking, Adrian propped himself up on his elbows to watch. Mark pushed off.

For once, his feet locked on the pedals. Miraculously, the bicycle started to roll forward under him. He pedalled faster. The ground flashed by. It was wonderful, like flying. It could only be magic that kept the thing from falling over.

"Look!" he yelled. "Look at me!"

He glanced back towards Adrian, then gently tilted the handlebars to turn. Immediately, the bicycle became a wild thing again. It bucked, tossing him high into the air. The grass slammed into his face, a pedal banged his shin. They both started to laugh again.

As the afternoon flowed across the great blue sky, Mark learned—slowly and somewhat painfully—how to turn corners, how to start, and trickiest of all, how to stop. And gradually they moved down the lawn towards the house.

At about three, a dark-suited man emerged from a far door in a distant corner of the house and walked slowly over to them. Stretched on the grass as Adrian shot back and forth to demonstrate how to freewheel, Mark watched him advance. He was carrying a tray, and on it were tumblers and a huge jug of something that looked green and thirst-quenching.

Adrian skidded to a halt. "Well done, Lawrence."

Lawrence placed the tray on the grass and looked at Mark oddly. Beads of sweat twinkled in the sunlight on his bald head. "I thought I should bring a glass for your friend as well."

"He's learning to ride my bicycle."

"I see. . . ." Lawrence straightened up and began to walk slowly back towards the house. His bottom wobbled with each step. Mark and Adrian collapsed again into aching laughter. It was too painful, quite beyond the joke.

A short while later, as Mark was coming to terms with the discovery that the bicycle would continue to move even if you didn't pedal, the great French windows in the domed centre of the house opened in a flash of sunlight.

Mark stopped the bicycle and dropped his feet from the pedals.

"Who's that?" he asked.

"Mother."

She was a lady dressed in white, carrying a white parasol. Even through the ghostly shimmer of the heat, Mark could tell she was beautiful. His thoughts struggled once again with the gaping memory of his own mother, the shadows inside that open kitchen window when he looked back from the wall. Please, he thought, make this the way she was.

"What a lovely day," she said, her clear voice and smile carrying ahead as she approached.

"This is Mark," Adrian said. "We met up at the fish pool. He's my friend."

"How do you do." She stopped in front of Mark and held out her hand. Still astride the bicycle, Mark felt stupid and awkward. But he knew which hand to offer.

"Hello," he said. Her hand felt strong and cool. "Your, um, lady."

She smiled again, her lovely face framed in the shade of the parasol. Her eyes were blue. They widened in gentle amusement. "Just hello is plenty," she said.

She glanced towards Adrian—who was brushing grass from his knees and standing up—then back towards Mark. "Can you cycle well?"

Mark grinned. "I couldn't at all until Adrian taught me."

"Just today?"

"Yes, just today."

"Congratulations, Master Mark. You live on the estate?"

"Number three of the cottages up past the main orchards. My, er, father, he's an undergardener."

"What does he do?"

"Mostly berry fruits, I think. Some vegetables."

"It must be lovely, being a gardener, getting things to grow. Is that what you'd like to be?"

Mark nodded. No other option had ever occurred to him.

"You've got something stuck in your hair." She leaned forward. "Here." Close to, almost sharing the shade of the parasol, Mark could smell her scent. By the time she'd pulled back again and dropped the burr on the grass, he'd decided he was in love.

"Well." She twirled the parasol. "I'm afraid Adrian has to come inside now."

Adrian said, "But—"

"—No," she cut in firmly, without raising her voice. "You promised Master Ignatius that you'd finish that project. And a promise is a promise. Isn't that right, Mark?"

"Yes," Mark said. He realised that this wasn't a subject for negotiation. He climbed off the beautiful red-and-cream bicycle and wheeled it over to Adrian, who took it with the seriousness of a priest handling the sacrament. Without a word — children never understand the need for farewells — he followed his mother back towards the great house.

When Adrian had leaned the bicycle against the wall and the French windows had flashed shut again, Mark turned and ran like the wind.

★   ★   ★

The day after was a school day; it should have been an ordinary day. But Mark's father woke him early, a letter clasped awkwardly in his hand.

"This came," he said. "Just now as I was out doing a bit of weeding out the front. A man in uniform . . ."

Mark sat up and took the letter from him. He knew his father's reading was uncertain at the best of times. The paper was creased and slightly grubby from his father's fingers, but was a rich cream with an embossed red crest and letter heading and smelt of books and leather and luxury.

"It's about me," Mark said as comprehension and surprise trickled over him. "It says I've got to leave here and go as an apprentice gardener in the King's estate at Maldon."

"Now . . ." A half-hopeful smile crinkled his father's stubbled face. "That's foolishness, son. What does it really say?"

Mark glanced down at the letter again, almost doubting his own words. "That's what it says. I've got to leave here and go."

★   ★   ★

The black limousine came out of the rain, rumbling and splashing along the cart tracks to the cottage, pursued by drenched and shouting children and watched by arms-folded clusters of incredulous neighbours sheltering in porches and under dripping trees. The liveried driver took Mark's small case and held open the rear door. Mark descended into deep pile and leather. He hardly had time to glance back through the window and the rain before the cottages and his father had gone from sight.

It took most of the day to reach Maldon. Mark had to ask the driver to stop many times — he discovered that he suffered from travel sickness — but at least being ill gave him an excuse for his tears. He hardly noticed the world through which they passed, a world he had never seen before; cut off in his sickness by the rain-beaded windows, none of it seemed real, least of all the great forest that surrounded Maldon. As evening set in, the limousine lost its purr and strained grumpily up and down hills and roads tunnelled by boughs and huge greenery. Wet fingers of bush and fern trailed and whispered along the panels or pushed themselves against the windows like sudden eerie faces.

Finally, a great gate in a huge wall opened ahead. When they were through, it was as though the forest had never been. After swishing along gravel roads across smooth acres of lake and lawn, the limousine finally stopped.

Mark stumbled out. The driver gave him back his case. The rain had faded and the air was evening dim, scented with green. Across the puddled and mossy paving, a great ivy-clad building hunched its red roofs against forest hills and grey sky. So this was Maldon. Mark was impressed, but also a little disappointed; the house was no larger than the Widder house, and certainly less ornate.

"Where does the King live?" he wondered aloud, glancing along the rows of windows.

The driver snorted. "The castle is miles away, not that the King's ever there. This is just the hostel for the apprentices, for little oiks like you."

★   ★   ★

Mark hated Maldon from the start. After the initiations in the trembling darkness of the dormitory, after the forced fights and the preliminary beatings by the hostel masters, life settled into a bleak routine.

No reigning monarch had visited Maldon for more than fifty years. It continued to function, but, like the rain clouds that gathered so frequently on the surrounding hills, a greyness permeated the estate. The lawns and hedges were trimmed, exotic fruits were tended for the royal table, harvested, then left to rot. The solitary yearly rose that blossomed on the Culpen bush, which traditionally was presented to the King on Saint Errig's day in July, opened its petals and let them fall. The King and his court preferred the diversions of the capital, or if they wanted to risk a little fresh air, there were more southerly retreats where the sun could be relied on.

In his misery—misery so predictable that Mark ceased to be conscious of it as anything other than normality—he still found comfort in all things green, all things that grew.

He soon realised that he knew tricks from his father that the gardeners at Maldon had somehow forgotten, or had never known. How apple suckers, sawfly, and earwigs could be collected from fruit trees simply by hanging an open matchbox at the end of the branch. How a scatter of rose petals would draw the fairies away from the cabbages and a circle of clinker would keep the common slug at bay.

His knowledge brought mixed rewards. To stand out in any way from the other apprentices guaranteed a greater number of fights and beatings, but at the same time the hostel masters and undergardeners weren't foolish enough to turn away from good advice. Of course, they usually snatched the credit for Mark's efforts, for an eelworm-free crop of onions or an ancient rose restored to health, but at heart they were lazy and found undue success almost as trying as failure. Gradually, Mark was allowed to rise.

When he was sixteen, he was made an undergardener and allocated a little room of his own away from the dormitory. The previous occupant had hanged himself with green gardening twine looped around the coat hook on the back of the door, but no ghosts disturbed Mark. In the evenings, he could sit by the open sash window where the ivy whispered and nodded and read books from the hostel's mildewed library, or simply gaze out at the green. The pines across the courtyard. The wild and misty hills in the distance.

He was appointed a full gardener at eighteen and a half. Although he was still the same solitary young man living in the same hostel room, Mark was grateful for the small privileges of rank and, in his own way, proud. Now that he had the freedom—and the money—he was able at last to take the charabanc out through the forest and the farmland far beyond to visit his father. He saw how the shapes of remembered trees on the Widder estate had changed; matured and broadened, or bowed into decrepitude. And past the gate and in the low walled garden in front of the kitchen window, he saw how lavender had choked the roses, how moss had darkened the patch of lawn. The man who greeted him, now stooped under a snowfall of white hair, trembled and avoided the eyes of his son. He was in awe of Mark; a gardener before the age of nineteen.

Mark lay sleepless that night in his childhood bedroom as he wondered at the change that had come between them. Was it fear, unfamiliarity, time? He got up from the narrow mattress and went to the window, pushing back the dusty cotton curtains. The moonlight was kind to the signs of neglect in the little garden below. The lawn looked smooth, the roses luxuriant. And then he saw a movement in the grey clouds of lavender beneath. A brownie gathering the fragrant buds. He smiled and watched until the creature finally flitted away into the orchard, then returned to bed and slept soundly through to morning.

★ ★ ★

Maldon was in turmoil when Mark arrived back, travel-sick and tired. Inexplicably, the King had announced that he was going to revive his traditional visit to Maldon on Saint Errig's day, less than a week away.

One of the senior gardeners called Mark to the offices by the orangery next morning. He deposited his umbrella in the hatstand and rapped on the third brass-plated door along the corridor where panicking clerks scuttled. Mr. Parkin bade Mark sit down facing the wide desk. He looked worried; his face was more deeply marbled with veins than ever, the files in the IN tray leaned precariously and the smell of drink was strong.

Mark had expected the interview—there were bound to be duties to be devolved, preparations to be discussed—but as Mr. Parkin spoke, Mark realised that he was being given a far greater responsibility than he would have bargained for, or wished. Biddle, one of the few genuinely experienced gardeners, had been found lying on the marble bench beside the Culpen bush by an estate doctor collecting lichen that dawn, his leather apron soaked with dew and the slugs already feasting at his mouth and eyes. With just a few days to go, Mark would have to take over.

Afterwards, Mark retrieved his umbrella and took the path between the willows around Blackroot Pool. It had already rained twice that morning, and between bursts of sunshine grey clouds were banking up once more over the hills. Every leaf, every blade of grass, was diamonded with moisture; to brush against a tree or bush guaranteed a soaking. But the estate was busy. Priveteers were clipping hedges, assistant gardeners were tying back peonies, and labourers were mowing—mostly doing, Mark suspected, more harm than good in their panic. Of course, there *was* work to be done. Even in his anxiety about the Culpen bush and as the rain came down again, Mark still paused to snap the dead head off a rose and bent to pluck a shoot of bindweed from a flower bed, but his actions were gentle and instinctive. That was the way with a true gardener, not starting, not stopping, not hurrying, but understanding that the task never ends.

Several times before, Mark had visited the far corner of the estate where the Culpen bush grew. He'd been curious to see a plant that flowered so predictably, but he'd always misjudged the date and had never seen the bloom.

A long, wide avenue led to the garden of the Culpen bush. As

Mark walked past the lines of elms through the thinning, drifting rain, the dark Tudor arch at the far end slowly widened. The square little garden beyond that plain span of masonry was an obvious and possibly intentional anticlimax. Even with the sun breaking through after the rain, it was dim and dull. Dense ivy climbed in the shadow of red brick walls, the highest of which, facing the Tudor arch, marked the final boundary of the estate. The oak forest beyond added to the shade, leaning over across the garden and whispering like an aunt admiring a baby. In the centre, rising from a soggy square of grass, the Culpen bush spread its dark leaves.

Mark frowned as he looked around; it was a poor lightless place, and the overhanging boughs of the forest would bring pests, insects, fungi, diseases, and fairies. The Culpen bush was fighting the odds to grow here at all. He walked around it. The outer leaves formed a ragged globe that almost matched his own height. A nerve of worry started to ache behind his eyes as he walked around it again, looking more carefully. There was no sign of a rose bud. And Mark knew where to look, how to look, what to expect. He wandered around the bush again and again, almost growing dizzy. But there was nothing. No sign. No rose.

He sat down on the wet marble bench facing the bush, then remembered Biddle and quickly stood up again. Had a rose ever blossomed on Saint Errig's day? Had anyone ever seen it? After all, more than fifty years had elapsed since it had been cut, placed on a velvet cushion, and paraded before the King; a long time even — or especially — in a garden.

He knew it was pointless telling anyone. Whatever the facts of the case were, the blame would surely settle on him. He walked forward and touched the wet, dark leaves of the bush. And as he did so, he saw a graceful tiara spider at work, spinning a web that gleamed silver between the thorny stalks even in this shadowed place. He smiled despite himself. Perhaps the bush was truly special, perhaps a little magic flowed in its sap. All he could do was tend it, and pray.

Mark worked on the Culpen bush all day, bowed in its shadows. Using his bare hands, he softened and sifted the soil around the base of the plant, chasing the leatherback beetles away, bringing worms from nearby portions of the estate to burrow in some air. The rain came and went. He tried propping up the umbrella, but soon gave up and let the drops patter his head and back and the mud soak in at his knees. Eventually, it grew too dark to see clearly. He stood up, cloaked in the scent of earth, rubbing at the familiar gardener's ache in his back. The bush was a dim cloud now, the leaves no longer separable by sight. In jokey pretence that it had been a fine, uninterrupted day, the sky was deep and pinkish blue. Peering through the powdery air at the overhanging forest, Mark thought he could just make out the darting movements of the spinner fairies as they wove strands of dusk from bough to bough.

Mark wiped the worst of the mud from his hands on the grass, picked up his umbrella, and set off back towards the hostel. The birds were silent. The stately avenue was eerily balanced between day and night, enfolded in glowing shadow.

He heard the rattle of a bell. The sound was odd in the close softness of the evening, yet instantly familiar. Up ahead amid the fading perspectives of the elms, he saw a figure on a bicycle. Curious, yet too tired to run, he increased his step, but when he reached the place there were only tracks shining on the wet grass like a snail's glitter.

Early next day, after a restless night and a dream of chasing something bright through a forest, Mark was back tending the Culpen bush. He worked fine ash into the soil with his fingers, then began the painstaking task of pinching the greenfly from the leaves and stems one by one. He was soon lost in the task, oblivious to the gusting wind that shivered the elms along the avenue and the leaning oaks. Yet then, half buried in the bush, his face and arms scratched and bleeding from the thorns and his hands sticky with the saplike juice of the greenfly, his concentration was suddenly broken by a sense of being watched.

He twisted out from under the bush. A barefoot child was standing close by, dressed in grubby brown. An equally brown and grubby bicycle was propped up against the ivy at the edge of the garden.

"Hello," she said.

Mark grunted discouragingly. He didn't enjoy being watched when he was working.

"You've been spending a lot of time inside that bush."

"It's the Culpen bush."

"Oh." She nodded. "Then it must be s'posed to flower soon."

Mark picked a thorn from his palm. "Four days from now, in fact. Not that there's any sign." He couldn't think of a reason not to tell her—just some grubby urchin, some labourer's child wandering the estate without permission.

"The flower's for the King?" she asked.

He stood up. "That's right."

The wind lifted wisps of light brown hair across her face. Mark was surprised at how tall she was, almost his own height. She was older than he'd thought, too. But then he was no expert, living a semimonastic life at the hostel.

Mark shrugged and glanced back at the bush, feeling stupidly conscious that her eyes were on him. "I suppose I'll just have to hope . . ."

"That a bud suddenly appears?" She laughed. A little girl's laugh; fierce, absorbed, uncaring. The Culpen bush shivered in a sudden gust. "Well," she sniffed, "that would be magic, or a miracle."

Mark shrugged again as she turned away from him; so much, he thought, for sharing your problems.

She climbed back onto her bicycle, rang the bell, and pedalled out of sight along the sighing avenue.

Dealing with the greenfly and tidying up the bush took him all of the rest of the day and the following morning, by which time the labourers were working their ladders along the avenue, trimming and cutting the elms—badly, Mark couldn't help noticing, and out of season—to make them look neat and soldierly for the King's procession to the Culpen bush. The shadowy little garden itself seemed to attract no attention; the labourers probably didn't know or care why the King was coming, and the more senior staff in the estate would be too wrapped up in their own obsessions to think of anything as obvious as the absence of the Culpen rose. After he'd eaten his sandwiches, sitting on the marble bench, Mark trimmed the ivy and the lawn with the shears he'd brought along. That was fairly easily done; the garden was too damp and shady to encourage quick growth.

Then he sat down again and stared at the Culpen bush. He tried thinking positively, he tried willing a flower to grow. Along the avenue, the rip of saws and falling, splintering timber grew closer, then receded. Once, he felt someone's presence behind him and turned, irritated, expecting to see the girl. There was no one there. He gauged it as an indication of the unhappy mood that the irritation then turned to disappointment.

Back at the hostel that evening, Mr. Parkin came to the refectory as Mark sat alone drinking tea.

"Dress rehearsal the day after tomorrow," he said, leaning over Mark and swaying a little. "Will everything be ready then?"

"Everything?"

"The rose."

"Yes." Mark nodded.

"Good." Mr. Parkin backed away, bumping painfully into the edge of a table.

★   ★   ★

It was foggy next morning. The elms along the avenue loomed. Mark felt sleepy and light-headed; he couldn't see beyond the next few days of his life. The dress rehearsal, the formal procession . . . Giants in the mist, barring his way.

The tiara spider had silvered the entire Culpen bush with its web. Mark sat down on the marble bench. Fog wreathed the boughs of the forest, hung from the ivy like rotting lace, closed off the sky.

A bell. The sound glittering in the thick air like a jewel, then closer, and with it the swish of bicycle tyres on the soft grass. Mark waited expectantly.

"Hello." She dismounted, then came fully from the mist and sat beside him. "Any luck?"

She had changed from the grubby brown dress and looked considerably more presentable in a green blouse and skirt.

Mark shook his head.

"Never mind." She smiled, laid a hand on his shoulder.

Embarrassingly, Mark felt himself shiver. "It's too late to do anything," he said.

"Then forget about it. Why worry?"

Her eyes were green, brown, blue. Colours of autumn and summer, sadness and life. She was hardly a girl at all. A woman, yes. A woman. But even as Mark decided, the play of misty light changed her face and all he saw was a child.

She gave him an odd look, almost as though she'd been caught out.

"My name's Mark," he said.

"Mine's Fianna."

"Fiona?"

"No, Fianna." She spelt it out to him.

Mark nodded. He didn't want to hurt her feelings by commenting on her parents' obvious illiteracy—after all, his own father was hardly better.

She squirmed on the bench. "This is cold, cold and wet. You'll give yourself piles."

Mark said nothing. Even in the hostel, he'd lived a sheltered life; he wasn't sure what piles were.

"Can you ride a bicycle?"

"I think so," he said. "I could once."

"Then why don't you try mine? It'll take your mind off the rose. I'll just sit here and get piles and watch."

The bicycle rested against the ivied wall. As Mark placed his hands on the old handlebars, he was filled with doubt. After all these years, could he still make it balance and fly? He wheeled it out, finding the seat, the pedals, pushing off. The bicycle responded, became alive, drawing him into the mist.

He circled the walled garden, turning sharply around the rosebush, past Fianna on the bench. She clapped and cheered. Mark circled again, the quick mist opening and closing ahead and behind him.

Dizzy, breathing hard, he finally braked and set his feet on the soft, solid grass.

She ran over to him and placed a steadying hand upon his arm as he dismounted. "Well done!"

Mark no longer shivered at her touch, but Fianna's closeness brought an extraordinary feeling of softness, yearning. He blinked and found himself looking into her wide beautiful eyes. The mist was thinning, forming a glowing nimbus around her hair.

She pulled back a little, releasing his arm.

"Thank you," Mark said, ". . . for letting me try the bicycle."

"That's all right. I'd better go soon."

The wonderful feeling slackened as she drew away, like a wave hissing back across the shore, but when he passed the handlebars to her and their skin touched, it came crashing in again.

"What are you going to do today?" she asked, backing off, her eyes lowered as she fiddled with the rusty chrome casing of the bell.

"I don't know," he said. "There's nothing left to do. I haven't touched the bush, or hardly looked at it."

"Then how can you be so sure a flower hasn't budded?" She turned the front wheel and climbed on the bicycle. "You can't be, can you?"

"No . . ."

"Good luck." She cycled off.

Mark walked slowly around the spider-webbed bush. Now the sky overhead was almost blue. Something about the clearing mist made this normally shady place fill with brightness. The dewy sparkling bush looked wonderful, Mark had to concede. It hardly needed a rose to decorate itself with. He watched the architect, the tiara spider with its jewel-like cluster of eyes, still embroidering leaf and branch. It paused, as though conscious of Mark's gaze, then moved gracefully on along a green stem to weave its silk around a fresh new rosebud.

★   ★   ★

Rising from a crag at the centre of the estate, the ornate grey battlements of Maldon Castle hemmed the sky. On the day of the dress rehearsal, a red carpet slid like a tongue from the portcullis mouth, down the rhododendron screes of the crag and across the gardens, all the way to the Culpen bush.

The mock procession, the King's new equerry standing in for the King himself, left Maldon Castle at ten in the morning. The head master-gardener, the master-gardeners, the chief horticulturists, and others ranking high in the garden pyramid assumed, to their chagrin, third place in the procession behind the blue-and-silver ceremonial band that led the way through the pleasant sunshine and the courtiers in their tripping robes and feathered hats. The procession started off slowly and, striving for dignity, grew slower.

Mark stood waiting in the Culpen garden with a scatter of senior gardeners and minor officials. It was well after noon before he heard the first faint echo of the band as they turned into the top of the avenue. The sawn, clipped elms stood rigidly to attention.

The sound grew closer.

"Here they come," Mr. Parkin slurred, gripping a nearby shoulder for support. "Ready now."

Half an hour later, the mock procession arrived. The band stood fanfare along the sides of the avenue. The King's young equerry led the gaudy pack.

"So this is it," he said as they finally passed under the Tudor arch. "This place, this bush. Is *this* really what all the fuss is about?"

Silks and shufflings filled the garden. Beautiful patterns and colours. Tired faces, ugly with worry and responsibility. The head master-gardener made a rapid flanking movement to get beside the equerry.

"Tradition, my lord."

"Of course, tradition. Where would we be, eh?"

Peering around the surrounding heads, Mark saw that the equerry was indeed young. Little more than his own age. And oddly, frustratingly, he recognised him from somewhere.

"Then what happens next?"

"That's all . . . um . . ." The head master-gardener opened and closed his mouth like a fish.

"Please let me have your views, sir," the equerry snapped. "I'm hardly likely to know what goes on here, and neither's the bloody King."

"Well, the rose is placed on the very same cushion that . . . oh, here it is."

"I see. And where is the rose?"

"Ah. Let me . . . here. Yes. This."

"And who cuts it?"

The head master-gardener looked around, pleading for assistance. None was forthcoming. "Well . . . I . . ."

"How about someone from the estate?" the equerry suggested, his face puckered with irritation. "Some chappie who, oh, I don't know . . . How about the fellow who looks after the rose?"

"Of course, my lord."

The head master-gardener looked to the master-gardeners, who looked to the senior gardeners.

"Step forward," Mr. Parkin lisped. "Go on."

Mark pushed his way awkwardly to the front of the crowd. "I tend the rose," he announced as feathers bobbed and heads turned towards him.

The equerry regarded him sullenly. "You're rather young, my friend. You really don't look the part. Still, we waste time and this is becoming boring. You'll have to do. What next?" He clapped his hands. His silk sleeves fluttered. "What next?"

The head master-gardener produced a pair of secateurs from the front of his embossed ceremonial apron. Mark took the cold metal in his hands and walked around the bush to the glorious unfolding bloom. He felt let down, angry. Surely it wouldn't be like this tomorrow? Just some foolish ceremony?

"Then let us assume," the equerry said, "that the rose has been cut. It is placed on the cushion just so, and our friend here brings it to the King. That's right, just *try* to pretend that I'm the King."

Mark took the old and rather threadbare cushion and walked towards the equerry. The bland face was maddeningly familiar. Across his nose and cheeks, Mark saw the faint stain of childhood freckles, and as he did so he remembered the wide lawn, the red-and-cream bicycle.

"You're Adrian Widder . . . my lord."

The equerry scowled. "I don't see what right you have to know or speak my name."

"But you taught me to ride your bicycle. That day, your father's birthday . . ."

Briefly, Mark believed he saw a glimmer of recognition, but then it vanished under irritation and disdain.

"You play a trick like that tomorrow before the King," the equerry hissed, his face growing pale and the old freckle marks showing more strongly, "and I swear you'll never dig a single turd of manure in any garden in the kingdom. Anyway"—he turned his back on Mark —"I think we've done enough. At this point, having accepted the rose — which he will pass back to me and I will toss behind a convenient bush — our beloved King will commence his progress back to the castle."

"Here," the head master-gardener said as they left, giving Mark back the silver secateurs. "You might as well keep these for tomorrow."

The crowd departed down the avenue, slowly fading from sight and hearing, leaving Mark standing alone in the walled garden. He pushed the secateurs into his apron pouch and sat down on the marble bench.

It was midafternoon. The birds were quiet. Hazy sunshine gilded the tops of the forest trees. He gazed at the Culpen bush, at the rose, its petals almost fully open from the bud in just one day. It was a miracle; no rose grew and unfurled that quickly. And all for what? He clenched and unclenched his fists, wondering if he was still capable of tears.

He'd never seen a rose of its like, or equal. Despite its size and the dense, heavy mass of its petals, it lifted proudly from its stem, seeking the sun that never graced the walled garden. Even sitting a good couple of yards away from it, Mark was bathed in the scent. It was unlike any other rose, bringing memories of wide lawns and clear skies, of a beautiful lady with a white parasol leaning close to him in sunlight. And it was partly that, Mark realised, that had triggered his memory of Adrian Widder. He shook his head. That was all in the past. Nothing remained, absolutely nothing.

The petals of the Culpen rose were white, but in the shade of their unfurling and in the deep and unrevealed heart was a blackness that went beyond shade or shadow or night. He breathed the fragrance again. It was too sweet and too bitter to ignore.

He heard the tinkle of a bicycle bell, the tick of approaching wheels. Fianna scooted in on one pedal and alighted smoothly, graceful as a swan, leaning the bicycle beside the Tudor arch.

"I've been watching the procession," she said. "I shouldn't really be on this bike. See, with my best clothes on."

She was barefoot as usual, but in a simple white dress. As she crossed the garden, her image flickered dizzily in Mark's mind. Child, girl, woman, child . . .

"Has the rose come?" she asked.

"Yes." Mark's voice quavered. "It's here."

"Then let me see. And why do you look so glum?"

Mark crouched down beside the bloom. She leaned close behind him, but somehow from a vast impossible height. Her scent, the scent of the rose, roared in his senses. The light and the darkness played over her young, old face, in the depths of her eyes.

She looked towards him. "You should be proud."

Mark swallowed, fighting for words through the dryness of his throat. She was Lady Widder, his dreams, his mother. "I am . . . I just can't let those people take it."

Mark stood up. His knees were trembling. She reached forward and pressed his hands into hers. Mark could feel the power passing between them in a delicious aching rush. The shadowed garden waited, hushed in expectancy.

She took a step closer.

She kissed him.

When she drew back, letting go, she smiled at the seriousness of it all.

"It doesn't matter really, does it?" Mark said, dizzy with the sense of her reality. "The King, this bush?"

Gently, she shook her head.

"Look." Mark took the silver secateurs from his apron and gently clasped the Culpen rose between its thorns. The tiara spider scuttled out of his way along the broken web.

"I shouldn't—" she began.

But his mind was made up; he didn't hear the fear and urgency in her voice. He closed the jaws of the secateurs and lifted the incredible weight of the rose towards her.

The petals curled, writhing outwards, black spilling over white like ink through milk. The blackness turned to ash as the Culpen bush shivered in a sudden wind that caught the flaking remains, swirling them up into the arms of the forest.

Mark looked up at Fianna. The darkness was spreading, filling the white of her eyes, blistering and crinkling her dress and her skin. The wind increased, a tunnel billowing into the sky, swirling her hair like smoke. As she began to dissolve, flying upwards in ragged ash, the remains of her mouth opened into a scream, a sound neither of pain nor of joy. Then she was swallowed in the shrieking wind, twirling into shadow, into nothing.

The wind quickly died. Mark stood alone by the flowerless bush. The still, damp shade settled in a cloak of sadness. There are many pests in a garden. Thrips. Manslugs. Greenfly. Fairies. Yes, that he had always known.

The old bicycle still rested beside the Tudor arch. He untangled the handlebars from the ivy and wheeled it over to the far wall, the forest wall. He leaned it there, settling it carefully before climbing onto the saddle and then, clasping the strongest stems, on up through the ivy towards the waiting boughs.

Starship Day

The news was everywhere. It was in our dreams, it was on TV. Tonight, the travellers on the first starship from Earth would awaken.

That morning, Danous yawned with the expectant creak of shutters, the first stretch of shadow across narrow streets. The air shimmered with the scent of warming pine. It brushed through the shutters and touched our thoughts even as our dreams had faded. For this was Starship Day, and from tonight, nothing would ever be the same. Of course, there were parties organised. Yacht races across the bay. Holidays for the kids. The prospect of the starship's first transmission, an instantaneous tachyon burst across the light-years, had sent the wine sellers and the bakers scurrying towards their stocks and chasing their suppliers. And the suppliers had chased *their* suppliers. And the bread, the fruit, the hats, the frocks, the meat, the marquees, the music, had never been in such demand. Not even when . . . Not even when . . . Not even when. But there were no comparisons. There had never been a day such as this.

As if I needed reminding, the morning paper on the mat was full of it. I'd left my wife Hannah still asleep, weary from the celebrations that had already begun the night before, and there were wine glasses scattered in the parlour, the smell of booze and stale conversation. After starting with early drinks and chatter at the Point Hotel, Hannah's sister Bernice and her husband Rajii had stayed around with us until late. At least, they'd stayed beyond the time I finally left the three of them and went to bed, feeling righteous, feeling like a sourpuss, wondering just what the hell I did feel. But some of us still had work to do on this starship morning. I opened the curtains and the shutters and let in the sound and the smell of the sea. I stacked a tray with the butts and bottles and glasses. I squeezed out an orange, filled a bowl with oats and yoghurt and honey. I sat down outside with the lizards in the growing warmth of the patio.

Weighted with a stone, my newspaper fluttered in the soft breeze off the sea. Page after page of gleeful speculation. Discovery. Life. Starship. Hope. Message. Already, I'd had enough. Why couldn't people just wait? All it took was for the tide to go in and out, for the sun to rise and fall, for stars and darkness to come, and we'd all know the truth anyway. So easy—but after all this time, humanity is still a hurrying race. And I knew that my patients would be full of it at the surgery, exchanging their usual demons for the brief hope that something from outside might change their lives. And I'd have to sit and listen, I'd have to put on my usual Caring Owen act. The stars might be whispering from out of the black far beyond this blue morning, but some of us had to get on with the process of living.

★   ★   ★

Hannah was still half-asleep when I went in to say good-bye.

"Sorry about last night," she said.

"Why sorry?"

"You were obviously tired. Rajii does go on."

"What time did they leave?"

"I don't know." She yawned. "What time did you go to bed?"

I smiled as I watched her lying there still tangled in sleep. Now that I had to go, I wanted to climb back in.

"Will you be in for lunch?"

"I'm—meeting someone."

Bad, that. The wrong kind of pause. But Hannah just closed her eyes, rolling back into the sheets and her own starship dreams. I left the room, pulled my cream jacket on over my shirt and shorts, and closed the front door.

★   ★   ★

I wheeled my bicycle from the lean-to beside the lavender patch and took the rough road down into town. For some reason, part of me was thinking, maybe we should get another dog; maybe that would be a change, a distraction.

Another perfect morning. Fishing boats in the harbour. Nets drying along the quay. Already the sun was high enough to set a deep sparkle on the water and lift the dew off the bougainvillaea draped over the seafront houses. I propped my bike in the shadowed street outside the surgery and climbed the wooden steps to the door. I fed the goldfish tank in reception. I dumped the mail in the tray in my office. I opened a window, sat down at my desk, and turned on the PC, hitting the keys to call up my morning's appointments. Mrs. Edwards scrolled up, 9:00. Sal Mohammed, 10:00. Then John for lunch. Mrs. Sweetney in the afternoon. On a whim, I typed in

About the starship.
PLEASE WAIT
What do you think will happen?
Again, PLEASE WAIT.

The computer was right, of course. Wait. Just wait. Please wait. A seagull mewed. The PC's fan clicked faintly, ticking away the minutes as they piled into drifts of hours and days. Eventually, I heard the thump of shoes on the steps and I called, "Come right in," before Mrs. Edwards had time to settle with the old magazines in reception.

"Are you sure, Owen? I mean, if you're busy. . . ."

"The door's open."

Ah, Mrs. Edwards. Red-faced, the smell of eau de cologne already fading into nervous sweat. One of my regulars, one of the ones who keep coming long after they'd forgotten why, and who spend their days agonising new angles around some old neurosis so that they can lay it in front of me like a cat dropping a dead bird.

As always, she looked longingly at the soft chair, then sat down on the hard one.

"Big day," she said.

"It certainly is."

"I'm terribly worried," she said.

"About the starship?"

"Of course. I mean, what are they going to *think* of us?"

I gazed at her, my face a friendly mask. Did she mean whatever star-creatures might be out there? Did she mean the travellers in the starship, waking from stasis after so many years? Now *there* was a thought. The travellers, awakening. I suppose they'll wonder about their descendants here on Earth, perhaps even expect those silver-spired cities we all sometimes still dream about, or maybe corpses under a ruined sky, dead rivers running into poisoned seas.

"Mrs. Edwards, there probably won't *be* any aliens. Anyway, they might be benign."

"Benign?" She leaned forward over her handbag and gave me one of her looks. "But even if they are, how can we ever be sure?"

★ ★ ★

After Mrs. Edwards, Sal Mohammed. Sal was an old friend, and thus broke one of the usual rules of my practice. But I'd noticed he was drinking too heavily, and when I'd heard that he had been seen walking the town at night in his pyjamas — not that either of these things was unusual *per se* — I'd rung him and suggested a visit.

He sat down heavily in the comfortable chair and shook his head when I offered coffee. There were thickening grey bags under his eyes.

He asked, "You'll be going to Jay Dax's party tonight?"

"Probably. You?"

"Oh, yes," he said, tired and sad and eager. "I mean, this is the big day, isn't it? And Jay's parties . . ." He shook his head.

"And how do you really feel?"

"Me? I'm fine. Managing, anyway."

"How are you getting on with those tension exercises?"

His eyes flicked over towards the cork notice-board where a solitary child's painting, once so bright, had curled and faded. "I'm finding them hard."

I nodded, wondering for the millionth time what exactly it was that stopped people from helping themselves. Sal still wasn't able even to sit down in a chair for five minutes each day and do a few simple thought exercises. Most annoying of all was the way he still lumbered up to me at do's, his body stuffed into a too-small suit and his face shining with sweat, all thin and affable bonhomie, although I knew that he'd only managed to get out now by tanking up with downers.

"But today's like New Year's Eve, isn't it?" he said. "Starship Day."

I nodded. "That's a way of seeing it."

"Everything could change — but even if it doesn't, knowing it won't change will be something in itself too, won't it? It's a time to make new resolutions. . . ."

But Sal got vague again when I asked him about his own resolutions, and by the end of our session we were grinding through the usual justifications for the gloom that filled his life.

"I feel as though I'm travelling down these grey and empty corridors," he said. "Even when things happen, nothing ever changes. . . ."

He'd gone on for so long by then—and was looking at me with such sincerity—that I snapped softly back, "Then why don't you give up, Sal? If it's really that bad—what *is* it that keeps you going?"

He looked shocked. Of course, shocking them can sometimes work, but part of me was wondering if I didn't simply want to get rid of Sal. And as he rambled on about the pointlessness of it all, I kept thinking of tonight, and all the other nights. The parties and the dances and the evenings in with Hannah and the quietly introspective walks along the cliffs and the picnics in the cool blue hills. I just kept thinking.

★　★　★

The lunches with John that I marked down on my PC were flexible. In fact, they'd got so flexible recently that one or the other of us often didn't turn up. This particular John was called Erica, and we'd been doing this kind of thing since Christmas, in firelight and the chill snowy breath from the mountains. I've learnt that these kinds of relationships often don't transfer easily from one season to another—there's something about the shift in light, the change in the air—but this time it had all gone on for so long that I imagined we'd reached a state of equilibrium. That was probably when it started to go wrong.

It was our usual place. The Arkoda Bar, up the steps beside the ruins. There was a group a few tables off that I vaguely recalled. Two couples, with a little girl. The girl was older now—before, she'd been staggering like a drunk on toddler's splayed legs; now she was running everywhere—but that was still why I remembered them.

I almost jumped when Erica came up behind me.

"You must be early—or I must be late."

I shrugged. "I haven't been here long."

She sat down and poured what was left of the retsina into the second glass. "So you've been here a while. . . ."

"I was just watching the kid. What time is it?"

"Who cares? Don't tell me you've been working this morning, Owen."

"I can't just cancel appointments because there's some message coming through from the stars."

"Why not?"

I blinked, puzzled for a moment, my head swimming in the

flat white heat of the sun. "I do it because it's my job, Erica."

"Sorry. Shall we start again?"

I nodded, watching the golden fall of her hair, the sweat-damp strands clinging to her neck, really and truly wishing that we could start all over again. Wishing, too, that we'd be able to talk about something other than this goddamn starship.

But no, Erica was just like everybody else — plotting the kind of day that she could twitter on about in years to come. She wanted to rent a little boat so that we could go to some secret cove, swim and fish for shrimps, and bask on the rocks and watch the night come in. She even had a little TV in her handbag all ready for the broadcast.

"I'm sorry, Erica," I said. "I've got appointments. And I've got to go out this evening."

"So have I. You're not the only one with commitments."

"I just can't escape them like you can. I'm a married man."

"Yeah."

The people with the little girl paused in their chatter to look over at us. We smiled sweetly back.

"Let's have another bottle of wine," I suggested.

"I suppose," Erica said, "you just want to go back to that room of yours above the surgery so you can screw me and then fall asleep?"

"I was hoping—"

"—isn't that right? Owen?"

I nodded: it was, after all, a reasonably accurate picture of what I'd had in mind. I mean, all this business with the boat, the secret cove, fishing for shrimps. . . .

I held out my hand to pat some friendly portion of her anatomy, but she leaned back out of my reach. The people with the kid had stopped talking and were staring deeply into their drinks.

"I've been thinking," she said. "This isn't working, is it?"

I kept a professional silence. Whatever was going to be said now, it was better that Erica said it. I mean, I could have gone on about her selfish enthusiasm in bed, her habit (look! she's doing it now!) of biting her nails and spitting them out like seed husks, and the puzzled expression that generally crossed her face when you used any word with more than three syllables. Erica was a sweet, pretty kid. Tanned and warm, forgiving and forgetful. At best, holding her was like holding a flame. But she was still just a rich Daddy's girl, good at tennis and tolerably fine at sex and swimming and happy on a pair of skis. And if you didn't say anything damaging to her kind when you split up, they might even come back to you years later. By then they'd be softer, sadder, sweeter—ultimately more compromising, but sometimes worth the risk.

So I sat there as Erica poured out her long essay on How Things Had Gone Wrong, and the sun beat down and the air filled with the smell of hot myrtle and the sea winked far below. And the little girl chased blue-and-red butterflies between the tables, and her parents sat listening to the free show in vaguely awestruck silence. It even got to me after a while. I had to squint and half-cover my face. Selfish, calculating, shallow, moody. Nothing new —Erica was hardly one for in-depth personal analysis—but she warmed to her subject, searching the sky for the next stinging adjective. Some of them were surprisingly on target—and, for her, surprisingly long. I thought of that scarred and ancient starship tumbling over some strange new world, preparing to send us all a message. And I thought of me, sitting in the heat with the empty bottle of retsina, listening to this.

"You're right," I said eventually. "You deserve better than me. Find someone your own age, Erica. Someone with your own interests."

Erica gazed at me. Interests. Did she *have* any interests?

"But—"

"—No." I held up a hand, noticing with irritation that it was quivering like a leaf. "Everything you said is true."

"Just as long as you don't say we can still be friends."

"But I think we will," I said, pushing back the chair and standing up.

Quickly bending down to kiss her cheek before she could lean away, I felt a brief pang of loss. But I pushed it away. Onward, onward . . .

"You'll learn," I said, "that everything takes time. Think how long it's taken us to get to the stars."

I waved to her, and to the silent group with their sweet little kid. Then I jogged down the hot stone steps to my bike.

★　★　★

Back at the office, there was a note stuffed through the letterbox and the phone was ringing. The phone sounded oddly sad and insistent, but by the time I'd read Odette Sweetney's message cancelling her afternoon appointment on account of what she called "This Starship Thing," it had clanged back into silence.

I decided to clear the flat upstairs. The doorway led off from reception with a heavy bolt to make it look unused—to keep up the charade with Hannah. I'd sometimes go on to her about how difficult it was to find a trusty tenant, and she'd just nod. I'd really given up worrying about whether she believed me.

The gable room was intolerably hot. I opened the windows, then set about removing the signs of Erica's habitation. I pulled off the sheets. I shook out the pillows. I picked up the old straw sunhat that lay beneath the wicker chair. For the life of me, I couldn't remember Erica ever wearing such a thing. Perhaps it had belonged to Chloe, who'd been the previous John; straw hats were more her kind of thing. But had it really sat there all these months, something for Erica to stare at as we made love? It was all so thoughtlessly uncharacteristic of me. Under the bed, I found several blonde hairs, and a few chewed-off bits of fingernail.

I rebolted the door and went back into the surgery. I turned on the PC and rescheduled Odette Sweetney's appointment. Then I gazed at the phone, somehow knowing that it was going to ring again. The sound it made was grating, at odds with the dusty placidity of my surgery, the sleepy white town, and the sea beyond the window. I lifted the receiver, then let it drop. Ahh, silence. Today, everything could wait. For all I knew, we'd all be better tomorrow. Miraculously happy and healed.

I locked the door and climbed onto my bicycle. I was determined to make the most of my rare free afternoon—no John, no patients—but time already stretched ahead of me like this steep white road. It's a problem I've always had, what to do when I'm on my own. The one part of my work at the surgery that invariably piques my interest is when my patients talk about solitude. I'm still curious to know what other people do when they're alone, leaning forward in my chair to ask questions like a spectator trying to fathom the rules of some puzzling new game. But, for the second half of my marriage with Hannah, I'd found it much easier to keep busy. In the days, I work, or I chase Johns and screw. In the evenings, we go to dinners and parties. The prospect of solitude—of empty space with nothing to react to except your own thoughts—always leaves me feeling scared. So much better to be Good Old Owen in company, so much easier to walk or talk or drink or sulk or screw with some kind of audience to respond to.

I cycled on. The kids were playing, the cats were lazing on the walls. People were getting drunk in the cafés, and the yachts were gathering to race around the bay. Our house lies east of the town, nesting with the other white villas above the sea. I found Hannah sitting alone in the shadowed lounge, fresh mint and ice chattering in the glass she was holding, her cello propped unplayed beside the music stand in the far corner. When I come home unexpectedly, I like it best of all when she's actually playing. Sometimes, I'll just hang around quietly and unannounced in some other part of the house or sit down under the fig tree in the garden, listening to that dark sound drifting out through the windows, knowing that she doesn't realise she has an audience — that I'm home. She's a fine player, is Hannah, but she plays best unaccompanied when she doesn't realise anyone is listening. Sometimes, on days when there's a rare fog over the island and the hills are lost in grey, the house will start to sing too, the wind-chimes to tinkle, the floorboards to creak in rhythm, the cold radiators to hum. The whole of her heart and the whole of our marriage is in that sound. I sit listening in the damp garden or in another room, wishing I could finally reach through it to the words and the feelings that must surely lie beyond.

"You should be outside," I said, briskly throwing off my jacket, lifting the phone from its hook. "A day like this. The yacht race is about to start."

"Sussh . . ." She was watching TV. Two experts, I saw, were talking. Behind them was an old picture of the fabled starship.

"You haven't been watching this crap all day?"

"It's *interesting*," she said.

The picture changed to a fuzzy video shot of Old Earth. People everywhere, more cars in the streets than you'd have thought possible. Then other shots of starving people with flies crawling around their eyes. Most of them seemed to be black, young, female.

"I guess we've come a long way," I said, getting a long glass from the marble-topped corner cabinet and filling it with the stuff that Hannah had made up in a jug. It tasted suspiciously nonalcoholic, but I decided to stick with it for now, and to sit down on the sofa beside her and try, as the grey-haired expert on the screen might have put it, to make contact.

Hannah looked at me briefly when I laid my hand on her thigh, but then she recrossed her legs and turned away. No chance of getting her into bed then, either. The TV presenter was explaining that many of the people on the starship had left relatives behind. And here, he said, smiling his presenter's smile, is one of them. The camera panned to an old lady. Her dad, it seemed, was one of the travellers up there. Now, she was ancient. She nodded and trembled like a dry leaf. Some bloody father, I thought. I wonder what excuse he'll give tonight, leaving his daughter as a baby, then next saying hello across light-years to a lisping hag.

"Oh, Jesus . . ."

"What's the matter?" Hannah asked.

"Nothing." I shook my head.

"Did you have an okay morning?"

"It was fine. I thought I'd come back early, today being today."

"That's nice. You've eaten?"

"I've had lunch."

I stood up and wandered back over to the cabinet, topping my drink up to the rim with vodka. Outside, in the bay, the gun went off to signify the start of the yacht race. I stood on the patio and watched the white sails turn on a warm soft wind that bowed the heavy red blooms in our garden and set the swing down the steps by the empty sandpit creaking on its rusted hinges.

I went back inside.

Hannah said, "You're not planning on getting drunk, are you?"

I shrugged and sat down again. The fact was, I'd reached a reasonable equilibrium. The clear day outside and this shadowed room felt smooth and easy on my eyes and skin. I'd managed to put that ridiculous scene with Erica behind me, and the retsina, and now the vodka, were seeing to it that nothing much else took its place. Eventually, the TV experts ran out of things to say and the studio faded abruptly and gave way to an old film. I soon lost the plot and fell asleep. And I dreamed, thankfully and gratefully, about nothing. Of deep, endless, starless dark.

★   ★   ★

We dressed later and drove through Danous in the opentop towards Jay Dax's villa up in the hills. All the shops were open after the long siesta. Music and heat and light poured across the herringboned cobbles, and the trinket stalls were full of replicas of the starship. You could take your pick of earrings, key-rings, lucky charms, models on marble stands with rubies for rockets, kiddie toys. I added to the general mayhem by barping the horn and revving the engine to get through the crowds. And I found myself checking the lamplit faces, wondering if Erica was here, or where else she might be. But all I could imagine were giggles and sweaty embraces. Erica was a bitch—always was, always would be. Now, some other girl, some child who, these fifteen years on, would be almost her build, her age. . . .

Then, suddenly—as we finally made it out of town—we saw the stars. They'd all come out tonight, a shimmering veil over the grey-dark mountains.

"I was thinking, this afternoon," Hannah said, so suddenly that I knew she must have been playing the words over in her head.

"That we need to find time for ourselves."

"Yes," I said. "Trouble is, when you do what I do for a living. . . ."

"You get sick of hearing about problems? You don't want to know about your own?"

Her voice was clear and sweet over the sound of the engine and the whispering night air. I glanced across and saw from the glint of her eyes that she meant what she was saying. I accelerated over the brow of a hill into the trapped sweetness of the valley beyond, wishing that I hadn't drunk the retsina and the vodka, wishing I'd answered that phone in the surgery, fighting back a gathering sense of unease.

I said, "We haven't really got much to complain about, have we? One tragedy in our whole lives, and at least that left a few happy memories. Anyone should be able to cope with that. And time—do you really think we're short of time?"

She folded her arms. After all, *she'd* been the one who'd gone to pieces. *I'd* been the source of strength. Good Old Owen who—all things considered—took it so well. And after everything, after all the Johns, and the warm and pretty years in this warm and pretty location, and with business at the surgery still going well, how could I reasonably complain?

Soon there were other cars ahead of us, other guests heading for parties in the big villas. And there was a campfire off to the right, people dancing and flickering like ghosts through the bars of the forest. We passed through the wrought-iron gates, and Jay Dax's white villa floated into view along the pines, surrounded tonight by a lake of polished coachwork. We climbed out. All the doors were open, all the windows were bright. A waltz was playing. People were milling everywhere.

I took Hannah's hand. We climbed the marble steps to the main doorway and wandered in beneath a cavernous pink ceiling. The Gillsons and the Albarets were there. André Prilui was there too, puffed up with champagne after a good showing in the Starship Day yacht race. Why, if only *Spindrift* hadn't tacked across his bows on the way around the eastern buoy. . . . And look, here comes Owen, Good Old Owen with his pretty cello-playing wife, Hannah.

"Hey!"

It was Rajii, husband of Hannah's sister Bernice. He took us both by the arm, steering us along a gilded corridor.

"Come on, the garden's where everything's happening."

I asked, "Have you seen Sal?"

"Sal?" Rajii said, pushing back a lock of his black hair. "Sal Mohammed?" Already vague with drink and excitement. "No, now you mention it. Not a sign . . ."

This was a big party even by Jay Dax's standards. The lanterns strung along the huge redwoods that bordered the lawns enclosed marquees, an orchestra, swingboats, mountainous buffets. No matter what news came through on the tachyon burst from the starship, it already had the look of a great success.

Bernice came up to us. She kissed Hannah and then me, her breath smelling of wine as she put an arm round my waist, her lips seeking mine. We were standing on the second of the big terraces leading down from the house. "Well," Rajii said, "what's your guess, then? About this thing from the stars."

Ah yes, this thing from the stars. But predictions this close to the signal were dangerous; I mean, who wanted to be remembered as the clown who got it outrageously wrong?

"I think," Hannah said, "that the planet they find will be green. I mean, the Earth's blue, Mars is red, Venus is white. It's about time we had a green planet."

"What about you, Owen?"

"What's the point in guessing?" I said.

I pushed my way off down the steps, touching shoulders at random, asking people if they'd seen Sal. At the far end of the main lawn, surrounded by scaffolding, a massive screen reached over the treetops, ready to receive the starship's transmission. Presently, it was black; the deepest colour of a night sky without stars, like the open mouth of God preparing to speak. But my face already felt numb from the drink and the smiling. I could feel a headache coming on.

I passed through an archway into a walled garden and sat down on a bench. Overhead now, fireworks were crackling and banging like some battlefield of old. I reached beside me for the drink I'd forgotten to bring, and slumped back, breathing in the vibrant night scents of the flowers. These days, people were getting used to me disappearing; Owen walking out of rooms just when everyone was laughing, Owen vanishing at dances just as the music was starting up. Owen going off in a vague huff and sitting somewhere, never quite out of earshot, never quite feeling alone. People don't mind—oh, that's Owen—they assume I'm playing some amusing private game. But really, I hate silence, space, solitude, any sense of waiting. Hate and fear it as other people might fear thunder or some insect. Hate it, and therefore have to keep peeking. Even in those brief years when Hannah and I weren't alone and our lives seemed filled, I could still feel the empty dark waiting. The black beyond the blue of these warm summer skies.

Somewhere over the wall, a man and a woman were laughing. I imagined Bernice coming to find me, following when I walked off, as I was sure she was bound to do soon. The way she'd kissed me tonight had been a confirmation, and Rajii was a fool—so who could blame her? Not that Bernice would be like Erica, but right now that was an advantage. A different kind of John was just what I needed. Bernice would be old and wise and knowing, and the fact that she was Hannah's sister—that alone would spice things up for a while.

I thought again of the day I'd been through: scenes and faces clicking by. Hannah half-asleep in bed this morning; Mrs. Edwards in the surgery; hopeless Sal Mohammed; young and hopeful Erica; then Hannah again and the dullness of the drink and all the people here at this party, the pointless endless cascade; and the starship, the starship, the starship, and the phone ringing unanswered in the surgery and me taking it off the hook there and doing so again when I got home. And no sign of Sal this evening, although he'd told me he was going to come.

I walked back out of the rose garden just as the fog of the fireworks was fading and the big screen was coming on. I checked my watch. Not long now, but still I climbed the steps and went back through the nearly empty house and found the car. I started it up and drove off down the drive, suddenly and genuinely worried about Sal, although mostly just thinking how tedious and typical of me this was becoming, buggering off at the most crucial moment on this most crucial of nights.

But it was actually good to be out on the clean night road with the air washing by me. No other cars about now, everybody had gone somewhere and was doing something. Everybody was waiting. And I could feel the stars pressing down, all those constellations with names I could never remember. Sal Mohammed's house was on the cliffs to the west of the town, and so I didn't have to drive through Danous to get there. I cut the engine outside and sat for a moment listening to the beat of the sea, and faintly, off through the hedges and the gorse and the myrtle, the thump of music from some neighbour's party. I climbed out, remembering days in the past. Sal standing in a white suit on the front porch, beckoning us all in for those amazing meals he then used to cook. Sal with that slight sense of camp that he always held in check, Sal with his marvellous, marvellous way with a story. Tonight, all the front windows were dark, and the paint, as it will in this coastal environment if you don't have it seen to regularly, was peeling.

I tried the bell and banged the front door. I walked around the house, peering in at each of the windows. At the back, the porch doors were open and I went inside, turning on lights, finding the usual bachelor wreckage. I could hear the low murmur of a TV coming from Sal's bedroom. Heavy with premonition, I pushed open the door, and saw the coloured light playing merely over glasses and bottles on a rucked and empty bed. I closed the door and leaned back, breathless with relief, then half-ducked as a shadow swept over me. Sal Mohammed was hanging from the ceiling.

I dialled the police from the phone by the bed. It took several beats for them to respond, and I wondered as I waited who would be doing their job tonight. But the voice that answered was smooth, mechanical, unsurprised. Yes, they'd be along. Right away. I put down the phone and gazed at Sal hanging there in the shifting TV light, wondering if I should cut the cord he'd used, or pick up the chair. Wondering whether I'd be interfering with evidence. The way he was hanging and the smell in the room told me it didn't matter. He'd done a good job, had Sal; it even looked, from the broken tilt of his head, that he'd made sure it ended quickly. But Sal—although he was incapable of admitting it to himself—was bright and reliable and competent in almost everything he did. I opened a window, then sat back down on the bed, drawn despite myself towards the scene that the TV in the corner was now playing.

The announcer had finally finished spinning things out, and the ancient photo of the starship in prelaunch orbit above the moon had been pulled up to fill the screen. It fuzzed, and darkened for a moment. Then there was another picture, in motion this time, and at least as clear as the last one, taken from one of the service pods that drifted like flies around the main body of the starship. In the harsh white light of a new sun, the starship looked old. Torn gantries, loose pipes, black flecks of meteorite craters. Still, the systems must be functioning, otherwise we wouldn't be seeing this at all. And of course it looked weary—what else was there to expect?

The screen flickered. Another view around the spaceship, and the white flaring of that alien sun, and then, clumsily edited, another. Then inside. Those interminable grey tunnels, dimly and spasmodically lit, floorless and windowless, that were filled by the long tubes of a thousand living coffins. The sleepers. Then outside again, back amid the circling drones, and those views, soon to become tedious, of the great starship drifting against a flaring sun.

As I watched, my hand rummaged amid the glasses and the bottles that Sal had left on the bed. But they were all empty. And I thought of Erica, how she was spending these moments, and of all the other people at the gatherings and parties. I, at least, would be able to give an original answer if I was asked, in all the following years—Owen, what were you doing when we first heard from the stars?

The TV was now showing a long rock, a lump of clinker really, flipping over and over, catching light, then dark. Then another rock. Then back to the first rock again. Or it could have been a different one—it was hard to tell. And this, the announcer suddenly intoned, breaking in on a silence I hadn't been aware of, is all the material that orbits this supposedly friendly cousin of our sun. No planets, no comets even. Despite all the studies of probability and orbital perturbation, there was just dust and rubble here, and a few mile-long rocks.

There would be no point now in waking the sleepers in their tunnels and tubes. Better instead to unfurl the solar sails and use the energy from this sun to find another one. After all, the next high-probability star lay a mere three light-years away, and the sleepers could dream through the time of waiting. Those, anyway, who still survived. . . .

I stood up and turned off the TV. Outside, I could hear a car coming. I opened the front door and stood watching as it pulled in from the road. Hardly a car at all, really, or a van. Just a grey colourless block. But the doors opened, and the police emerged. I was expecting questions—maybe even a chance to break the news about the starship—but the police were faceless, hooded, dark. They pushed by me and into the house without speaking.

Outside, it was quiet now. The noise of the neighbour's party had ceased, and there was just the sound and the smell of the sea. People would be too surprised to be disappointed. At least, at first. Sal had obviously seen it coming—or had known that there was nothing about this Starship Day that could change things for him. Death, after all, isn't an option that you can ever quite ignore. And it's never as random as people imagine, not even if it happens to a kid just out playing on a swing in their own back garden. Not even then. You always have to look for some kind of purpose and meaning and reason, even inside the dark heart of what seems like nothing other than a sick and pointless accident.

The police came out again, lightly carrying something that might or might not have been Sal's body. Before they climbed back into their grey van, one of them touched my shoulder with fingers as cool as the night air and gave me a scrap of paper. After they'd driven off, I got back into my car and took the road down into the now quiet streets of Danous, and parked by the dark harbour, and went up the steps to my surgery.

It all seemed odd and yet familiar, to be sitting at my desk late on Starship Day with the PC humming. The screen flashed PLEASE WAIT. For what? How many years? Just how much longer will the dreamers have to go on dreaming? I felt in my pocket for the piece of paper and carefully typed in the long string of machine code. Then I hit RETURN.

PLEASE WAIT.

I waited. The words dribbled down off the screen, then the screen itself melted, and me with it, and then the room. The lifting of veils, knowing where and what I truly was, never came as the surprise I expected. Each time it got less so. I wondered about what Sal Mohammed had said to me in the dream of this morning. All that stuff about grey endless corridors—was he seeing where he really was? But I supposed that after this number of journeys and disappointments, after so many dead and lifeless suns, and no matter how well I did my job, it was bound to happen. How many Starship Days had there been now? How many years of silence and emptiness? And just how far were we, now, from Earth? Even here, I really didn't want to think about that.

Instead, and as always, I kept busy, moving along the cold airless tunnels on little drifts of gas, my consciousness focused inside one of the starship's few inner drones that was still truly functioning and reliable, even if it didn't go quite straight now and I had to keep the sensors pointing to one side. Outside, through the occasional porthole, I could see others like me who were helping to prepare the starship for another journey. A spindly thing like a spider with rivet guns on each of its legs went by, and I wondered about Erica, whether that really *was* her. I wondered whether it was actually possible, with your consciousness inside ancient plastic and metal, to laugh.

Details scrolled up of how many sleepers we'd lost this time. A good dozen. It mostly happened like Sal; not from soft- or hard-systems failure, but simply because the dream of Danous had ceased to work. That, anyway, was the only reason I could find. I paused now beside Sal's coffin. Ice had frosted over the faceplate entirely. I reached out a claw to activate the screen beside him and saw that he was actually an even bigger loss than I'd imagined—a specialist in solar power. Just the kind of man we'd need out there on some mythical friendly planet. Then I found my own coffin, and paused my hovering drone to look down through the faceplate at the grey and placid version of the features I saw each day in the mirror. In the coffin just above me—or below—was Hannah. Ah, Hannah, a few strands of brittle hair still nestled against her cheek, and that gold chain around her bare neck that she'd insisted on wearing back on Earth when we set out together on this great adventure. Just looking at her, part of me longed to touch, to escape these lenses and claws and get back into the dream. Next time, I promised myself, tomorrow, I'll change, I'll do things differently. No, I won't screw John—Bernice. I might even admit to being unfaithful. After all, Hannah knows. She must know. It's one of the things that's keeping this sense of separateness between us.

I tilted the gas jets and drifted to the coffin that lay beside mine and Hannah's. Like Sal's, like so many others I'd passed, the faceplate was iced over, the contents desiccated by slow cold years of interstellar space. There was really no sign, now, of the small body inside it that had once lived and laughed and dreamed with us. Our child, gone, and with every year, with every starfall, with the hard cold rain that seeps through this starship, and with every John, the chances of Hannah and I ever having another are lessened. But first, of course, we need that green or blue or red world. We need to awake and stretch our stiff limbs, and breathe the stale ancient air that will flood these passages, and move, pushing and clumsy, to one of the portholes, and peer out, and see the clouds swirling and the oceans and the forests and the deserts, and *believe*. Until then . . .

I snapped back out from the drone, passing down the wires into the main databank where Danous awaited. And yes, of course, the morning would be warm again, and perfect, with just a few white clouds that the sun will soon burn away. Nothing could be done, really, to make it better than it already is. There's nothing I can change. And as I turned off my PC and left the surgery and climbed back into my car for the drive home, I could already feel the sense of expectation and disappointment fading. Tomorrow, after all, will always be tomorrow. And today is just today.

Rajii's car was sitting in the drive, and he was inside in the lounge with Bernice and Hannah. I could hear their laughter as I banged the door, and the clink of their glasses.

"Where were you?" Rajii asked, lounging on the rug. Bernice

pulled on a joint, and looked at me, and giggled. Hannah, too, seemed happy and relaxed—as she generally gets by this time in the evening, although I haven't quite worked out what it is that she's taking.

I shrugged and sat down on the edge of a chair. "I was just out."

"Here . . ." Hannah got up, her voice and movements a little slurred. "Have a drink, Owen."

I ignored the glass she offered me. "Look," I said, "I'm tired. Some of us have to work in the morning. I really must go to bed. . . ."

So I went out of the room on the wake of their smoke and their booze and their laughter, feeling righteous, feeling like a sourpuss, wondering just what the hell I did feel. And I stripped and I showered and I stood in the darkness staring out of the window across our garden where the swing still hung beside the overgrown sandpit, rusting and motionless in the light of a brilliant rising moon. And I could still hear the sound of Hannah and Bernice and Rajii's laughter from down the hall, and even sense, somehow, the brightness of their anticipation. I mean . . . What if . . . Who knows . . . Not even when . . . Not even when . . . Not even when . . . Not even . . .

Shaking my head, I climbed into bed and pulled over the sheets. And I lay there listening to their voices in the spinning darkness as I was slowly overtaken by sleep. In my dreams, I found that I was smiling. For tomorrow would be Starship Day, and anything could happen.

The Giving Mouth

I was a child before I was your King. And even though the red-brick tower where I lived with my parents had many windows that gazed over the Pits, I was raised in what you think of as poverty. Each morning I woke on my pallet of stale straw to the scream of the shift whistle and the clang of the pitwheels. The sound was as familiar to me as birdsong, but the shock of the grey light and mineral stench always came like a physical blow.

Put simply, I was a dreamer. And righteous youth made me certain that my dreams were real. I was convinced that there was a better world than the one I found myself in—and not as some abstraction, but as tangible as the grit in my hair and the dirt in the seams of my clothing. Sometimes I could almost see it shimmering at the corners of my eyes; on saint's days when the wind came from the right direction—from the east, and not too strong—when the church bells rang and the underworkers donned ribbons to roam the fair camped in the dust before Castleiron.

But I could only pretend. Everyone knew that there had always been mines. That since the day that the Great Beast first spewed out this mineral Kingdom, Castleiron had always risen like a fist from the green moat at the floor of the valley. And that live-iron and plain iron and copper and zinc were all that separated us humans from the fleas we plucked from our skin.

I remember that on the afternoon when my story truly begins, I had been wandering in the marshes between the slagheaps and the Pits, where the waters rainbowed oil and exposed minerals made grasses and flowers in the colours of dream. Copper green. Cobalt blue. Oxide red. A lonely place, usually pretty, although often things nested and grew there that sent me stumbling away in disgust. So I was always looking around in the wash of light, half in joy, half in fear. And glancing up that afternoon, I saw a figure sitting atop a drift of ash thrown up by the summer gales and honeycombed by the burrowings of a copperworm. A face angled towards the white sun, eyes quivered shut. Just a girl. But she was bathed in light made pure at every angle of cloth and limb. Everything about her was separate. And although part of my mind still knew that she was some underworker crawled up into the light for a few hours, escaping as I tried to escape, that part was drowned in greater knowledge.

I stared. It seemed quite impossible that my gaze wouldn't break the bubble of her perfection. But there she sat, beautiful and unperturbed, glossy coils of hair at her shoulders stirred like ivy by the wind from the Pits. Eventually, afraid the vision would burst inside me, I turned and ran back towards my tower.

Fool that I was, I tried to explain all this to my father that night.

He was standing with his palm pressed against a window high in the tower, in the big empty room he liked to call his study, looking out, his lips trailing white from the cigarette he was smoking, like an old man's beard. He heard my footsteps by the door as I crept by towards places even the servants had forgotten about. I froze at the sound of his voice, but he was only saying, Well Son and How Are You. Come Right In. Here into this big room. He turned, outlined against the flickering light, the cigarette bright at his mouth, glowing red in his eyes. I didn't flinch as he reached out to pat my shoulder, didn't shiver with relief as he thought better of it.

And how are you, son?

I didn't answer. He asked me again. Bittersweet smoke puffed into my eyes. It was hard to make out his face, but I knew that he would be putting on his smile, the one that bared teeth the colour of soot-browned ice. It hovered with the smoke in the air between us, unresolved. I squeaked, Fine, Pop, Just Fine, in a voice that was notched halfway towards breaking.

Something bumped the window. A white nocturnal creature, falling dead from the glass and tumbling down the drop of the tower like spit. I looked out beyond in the direction my father had been staring. The furnaces glowing down the valley, a thousand dogends dropped amid the mines. Up beyond Castleiron, the headlights of a steamhorse hauling some load up the Great Road briefly ribboned the cliffs gold. People living, sweating, burrowing, sleeping . . .

My father crushed his cigarette beneath his boot. He immediately started up another, the match flame making his face first handsome, then old, then hideous. His lips putted wetly. He puffed in silence. I waited. I was unused to his company. When he wasn't working, cursing the underworkers or snatching half-done tasks from the hands of the servants, he spent his time up here alone. I had little contact with him apart from the hotly unreal occasions when he chose to discipline me. Dreamer that I was, I liked to suppose that, up here where the furnaces bled across the moon, my father might also dwell on better worlds than this. And with the image of the girl in the marshes still pouring through my blood with a power I could only just begin to understand, it seemed like a time for saying things that didn't usually have words.

So I spoke. I could taste the corroded air. Hear the dusty sigh of a furnace engine. And doubtless I sounded like the fanciful, half-satisfied child that I was. But still I believed in the truth of my feelings. And I would like to think that there was some poetry in my expression, that it was that which made my father react as he did. For although children may dream of other worlds, every adult has had childhood stolen from them. Even my father was filled to the brimming with hidden dreams.

He nodded and drew on his cigarette with that hasty and somehow furtive gesture that—like his smile—was all his own, pooling red shadows in his hollowed cheeks. He waited without interruption for me to finish.

"What you're telling me, son," he said, "is that you think what you see out of this window is wrong? That nothing is as it should be. Is that exactly right?"

No, of course, not *exactly*. But still I nodded.

"And where do you think all this is going to get you?"

"I"—the jaggedly precise tone in his voice was enough to make me hesitate—"I don't know. It's just a feeling."

"Just a feeling." He took a long drag on his cigarette. A golden worm trembled at his mouth. "Hold out your hand."

I was no fool. I did as he said. I watched and waited as he ground the cigarette out in my palm. And I stood for as long as

I could while he beat me. Then I crouched. Then I lay. My father wanted to teach me a lesson, and for once he did. He was a man raised from this Kingdom, risen from the gritty soil. When he looked out the window of this room he liked to call his study, he saw the world as it was and admitted no room for love or hope or beauty. Not in himself, nor in anyone else who came close to him.

I realised later as I lay sobbing in my pallet, splattered with droppings of moonlight, that tonight had been a bad time to approach my father about anything. He was a dour man at the best of times, but tomorrow Queen Gormal had decreed that all the nobility should attend Castleiron. No one who had received that command would rest easy tonight.

★   ★   ★

I stood outside the tower with the servants next morning, shivering in the dusty wind as our best steamhorse was led from the stables to carry my parents down the valley to Castleiron. My father's jaw was clenched tight. My mother looked white and ill. A bruise — remnant of a week-old argument — was fading to orange on her cheek. I was more than old enough to have an idea of what they might expect at Castleiron. How the Queen would harangue them from the throne set within the cavernous skeletal mouth of the Great Beast that had spewed out this Kingdom and all the riches beneath. How they would have to watch as the royal sentinels hauled some poor wretch from the crowd. How the noblest houses of this land would all stand stiff-faced as the daggers flashed and agony pattered the stones.

You will understand by now that my father kept himself to himself. He had no more time for the other noble houses than he had for the excesses of Queen Gormal. And my mother was a quiet woman who shared his bed when he demanded and checked the books and placated the servants when his brutality went too far. They were trapped by their high birth in the machinations of Castleiron, but in their different ways they were both well equipped to ride the various bloody tides. In his own sullen way, my father managed to keep balance during the more severe swings of power, even when the rooks that nested in the abandoned mines near our tower were absent for days as they feasted on the bodies hung out as example from the walls of Castleiron.

That morning, after my father had climbed aboard the steamhorse and hauled my mother up after him, he looked around at the grey landscape and sniffed the sulphurous air. His colourless eyes travelled over the flaking brick of the tower, the upturned faces of the servants. For a moment, I imagined that he was taking in what he thought might be his last glimpse of home. But then his gaze settled on me as I stood unconsciously rubbing my freshening bruises, cupping my fingers around the weeping blisters on my palm. In an instant, I realised that my punishment was not yet finished.

He cracked his lips into a smile. Teeth like discoloured ice. A sudden gust of wind batted a scrap of ash into his face. He pushed it away and it tumbled into the sky.

"Come on, son," he said, a grey smear now on his cheek. "About time you grew up. Hop aboard."

I stepped forward. He held out thin fingers. They were tight on my wrist, jerking me up like a rope.

The steamhorse sighed and tensed its copper flanks. The gears spun and the flywheels strained. I gripped my mother's waist as we left the tower behind. Through the slagheaps. Burrow openings to the corrugated realm of the underworkers. Towards Castleiron. Ashlar stone black as coal. My stomach coiled like a slug in acid as we crossed the stinking green moat. In the cold shadow of the courtyard, other steamhorses hissed and idled their gears. We joined the thin drift of nobility under the rusted archway that led to the State Rooms. I looked around, breathing the ferrous reek of power, my curiosity battling with my fear. In those declining times when the daylight plundered all dreams, the soot-encrusted ceilings and rotting drapes still had a kind of beauty, albeit one that was not pleasant to behold.

Queen Gormal had arranged a banquet that filled the tables stretched far back into the mildewed darkness of the Great Hall. Through some quirk, my father and my mother and I were destined to sit close to the throne, our faces illuminated in the glare of the smoking sheep's-head lanterns chained from the weary roof. The food was actually quite good by the sour standards of that time. It had been the custom of her predecessor, Cardinal Reichold, to compel the nobility to eat substances too vile for easy description whilst he rocked with laughter on the throne and sipped lemon tea, but Queen Gormal wished to impress us all with her generosity. She had set before us silver platters steaming with heart of agront, hot pickled turnip, and salt loin of lamb.

The jaws of the Great Beast yawned up towards the dim ceiling. Only something so huge could have dwarfed the Queen as she sat overlapping her throne, set like a white epiglottis inside the skeletal throat. She was as round as a snowberry and twice as bitter. Not one to waste energy, she had an eater machine clamped over her face in much the same manner as a hound might wear a muzzle, although with the opposite intention. Some inventor had cast its prototype in liveiron decades before, the intention being to help those who were too weak or ill to work their jaws and swallow. But the device had been taken up instead by those such as the Queen, who wished to avoid the effort of working their throat and jaws as they ate. Two sentries had put aside their ceremonial halberds to load choice items from the feast into the hopper at the front.

I drank the hot wine from the goblet at my side and worked at the food left-handed. I was old enough to relish the ease that the unaccustomed tartness of the wine brought to my bruises and my anxiety. But the grease-smeared faces, the clangorous music, and the squelching of the eater machine all struck a false note. These were worse than average times. Out in the flatlands to the east, beyond the forest where the Great Road met farms and fields and the sky was reportedly blue in summer, close to where mythical Ocean was said to support the land, there was reported to be a Blight. Not canker or insect or disease, but a half-creature that flapped from tree to tree like sheeting caught in a storm, and that dragged itself moaning through the fields and orchards, drawing away nutrition and flavour. Something that enveloped cattle whole and sucked on them like a baby at the nipple, leaving their meat rancid and off-white. At night it howled against the church bells and was rumoured to slide through the windows of hovels to suck the minds from those who were sleeping, leaving the bodies behind, breathing and empty.

It all sounded like the kind of story that starts with a grain of deceit and grows tumorous in the retelling, yet only two days before, my mother had purchased one of the first of the year's crop of cabbage from the market beneath Castleiron. Almost fresh from its journey west on the trains of steamhorses, it had seemed a bargain, yet the cooking of it had filled our tower with a stink redolent of the smell that came from the straw of my pallet on the hottest of days. And when we tried to eat it, the texture of the plump leaves was like gritty snow. I guessed that in this banquet Queen Gormal was using up the last of the previous year's stores in the kind of binge that the weak use to try to stave off the future. In any event, the signs were bad.

So it seemed to me that this meal might be the last decent one any of us would have for some time. And for all the falsity of the celebration, I was determined to enjoy it. Whilst others shouted and banged their goblets and dropped morsels of their food to the stone flags, where the rats of Castleiron scurried them away, I kept my head down and chewed every last scrap to the peel and the marrow, and wiped up the remaining juices with a slab of bread until I could see my face staring back at me from my plate. Making the most of the rare sense of well-being brought on by the wine and a full belly, I leaned back on the bench and looked around. My mother—normally a delicate eater—had virtually finished too and was dabbing grease from her lips with the corner of her sleeve. The sounds of eating were quietening along the huge tables, and many were already climbing over the backs of the benches to stagger behind the screens and make use of the privy buckets. I reached for a dried apple from the pile in the centre of the table, then drew back in surprise when I saw that the food on my father's plate was virtually untouched.

I looked at him. His face was the colour of a slagheap. I risked asking him if he felt all right.

"I cannot abide the sweet meaty flavour of the agront," he growled. "The juice of the thing has soaked through everything on this dish."

I nodded, even though I knew nothing of the sort. I rarely ate with my father in our tower, and the pinkish flesh of agront, harvested wild from the mountainsides around the valley, was rare and expensive. But admittedly it did not do to think of the plant's nocturnal habits and its questing mouth when you were eating, nor of the strange fluorescence it brought to the stools.

I looked along the flickeringly lit table, sprawling with shadows. My father's full plate was already obvious amid the ruins of the banquet.

"Look," I said to him. My palm was throbbing and I could still feel the bruises from my beating, but I was bold with the wine. "Pass what you can over to my plate and drop the rest on the floor. We can't be seen—"

My voice trailed off in the sudden wave of silence as Queen Gormal smashed her goblet against the iron arm of her throne. She waved the sentries to unclasp the bolts and flywheels of the eater machine from her face.

"Now," she spoke. A pretty almost songlike voice that was at odds with everything else about her. I risked glancing up at the throne. My heart kicked me twice in the chest, then seemed to stop. Her arm was raised, and her index finger was pointing straight at my father. Some odd corner of my mind that was still ticking over noted how the rings she wore sunk deep, so that even the stones barely showed, and how the clamps of the eater machine had mottled her face like ringworm.

"You," she crooned, "you who have not eaten. Stand up."

My father hesitated a fraction, just to make certain that she did indeed mean him. But there was no doubt. He climbed to his feet awkwardly, his knees bent forward by the edge of the bench. All jollity had died. The whole hall was brimming with a silence broken only by the squabbling rats and the puttering lanterns. As with every other audience, the time had come for the screeching of agony and denial. I saw that the sentries who stood beside the jaws of the Great Beast were resting their hands on their knives and smirking like children who couldn't wait to open a present.

"Tell me why," the Queen said, her cheeks trembling, "you have chosen to revile my hospitality."

"Your Majesty," my father spread his nicotined hands; an unconscious gesture of helpless innocence that fitted the man as badly as an undersized coat. "The taste of agront — even agront of this undoubted excellence — is like a poison to me. Just as you yourself — "

"Shut up!" Trickles of oily moisture that could have been tears or sweat or the juices of what she had been eating ran down her cheeks and settled in the folds of her neck.

My father let his hands drop. My mother gave a burping sob and stifled it with her hand.

The Queen leaned forward in her throne, out of the mouth of the Great Beast, squinting at him through the smoky light. "I hardly recognise you. What house are you of?"

Hemmed in by the table, my father just managed a bow. More inappropriate than ever now, a half-smile drew shadows across his face. Glancing up at him, this lonely creature of fear and power, I felt a sick frisson of joy that he had come to this. I hated myself for the feeling, but I couldn't help it: I hated my father still more. "The redbrick tower, Your Majesty."

She slumped back. "Then eat the agronts."

Whispers rippled down the tables into the yellow depths of the hall. Was that all? To eat the agronts? The luck of the man! Why, I would eat —

Slowly, my father shook his head. "No, Your Majesty. I will do your bidding on any other matter. But as I have explained in all humility, the taste is abhorrent to me."

She sat rigid. Even the rats seemed to quieten. Yet his face was set firm.

The Queen gripped the edges of the throne. Her mountainous breasts began to tremble, and the facets and chains of her necklaces flashed red. Then she opened her mouth and let out a barking yelp, a sound oddly similar to that made by the agront when immersed in boiling oil. She yelped again. Her face reddened. There was a long and excruciating pause before anyone realised that she was laughing. But as soon as people began to force grins to their lips, she waved her hand for silence.

"Well, my lord of the redbrick tower. You have the stupidity to honour your stomach above your Queen—"

"—Majesty, I—"

"—and yet, you also seem to have a stubborn bravery about you that these swine around you lack." She put out a pink tongue to draw the saliva back from her chin. "Sir, we have a task for you. You will have heard of the Blight that haunts the edge of our lands. Doubtless some plot of those who would lay all bounty to waste. But so far wizardry has failed. I command you, O lord of the delicate stomach, to don your armour and go on Quest. I command you to slay the Blight."

My father bowed. "Willingly, Your Majesty." He obviously realised that, virtual death sentence that this was, it was as good as he was likely to get. And at least it avoided the indignities that the sentries would inflict with their knives.

She waved him to sit down. And the pudding was carried forth steaming from the kitchens. Orangebark on a bed of sweet lettuce. My father ate his portion with mechanical absorption, his grey jaws tensing and untensing like liveiron.

★　★　★

The family suit of armour had hung for decades from hooks in a high and draughty corner of our tower, greased with rancid goose oil to keep it from rusting. I remember first stumbling across it on some early exploratory jaunt through the rambling stairwells and dusty rooms—and how the sight of it gleaming black as a sloughed snakeskin had robbed me for nights of my sleep. When the wind howled down from the Ferrous Mountains and the tower rattled like a dry poppyhead, the suit would sway and clang in the darkness, filling my dreams with the clamour of cracked bells.

The morning after the banquet, my father commanded my mother and myself to watch as he was clad in the suit. The servants muttered and trembled as they puzzled over how it should be reassembled. Every poitrel and plate was black as the kitchen caldrons. My father struck out at them and clanged and howled his impotent rage. But slowly the task was accomplished. His thin body was swallowed in iron.

He clashed his way out into the bitter air. His heavy sabots sunk deep into the ash. The rooks were cawing, circling. The waiting steamhorse was chuffing restlessly. It had had its fill of the best coal in the stables, and although it was too stupid to understand the importance of the journey, it sensed that something unusual was afoot. Its headlights glowed. Its piston arms were hot with anticipation. My father lumbered over. Pushing away all offers of help, he climbed aboard. He looked loose and heavy as a sack of clinker.

He donned his helmet and creaked up the visor. His white, bitter face peered down at us like some martyr looking out from the devouring mouth of a dragon. He shouted to my mother. She fumbled matches and a cigarette, coughing as she drew on the flame to get it alight. She passed it up towards him. He seized it in his gauntlet and sat there smoking clumsily through clenched lips. I think the thing that angered him more than anything was the realisation of how foolish he appeared inside the armour. It really did look as though it had eaten him. He tried to say something, but his words were lost in the sigh of idling pistons and the hiss of the boiler. He threw the cigarette into the dust. Before he let the visor clang down, I had one last glimpse of his face. It was twisted in disgust.

A clanking automaton, less flesh and blood than the steamhorse itself, he let in the gears. The steamhorse tensed its wheels. The whistle screeched, and it rumbled away between the slagheaps trailing a flag of sparks and steam, off towards the Great Road and the forest and the flatlands, to do battle with the Blight. Dogs and children followed for a while in his tracks, but my mother and I remained standing beside our tower where the rooks cawed and circled the grey air that—amid the scents of coal and toil—carried the fading odours of tobacco and goose grease. We turned and hugged each other in a brief, stiff embrace that at least avoided the necessity for words. Then we went inside to wait for news.

★　★　★

The harvest in the flatlands was a nightmare. My father must have passed the straggling trains of steamhorse-drawn wagons as he headed along the Great Road, each hopper brimming with glossy apples, parsnips as long as your arm, and mountains of blackberries dribbling juice into the mud. As always, most were destined for the salt vats, the presses, the smoke-houses, and the drying racks, but those which did find their way to the markets soon spread panic. The apples had the texture of pustules, the parsnips had the flavour of ancient dung: or so it was said by those who claimed the dubious enlightenment of such comparisons. In any event, they were indisputably foul and gave no nourishment.

The minewheels still turned. The smokestacks poisoned the sky. By some irony a new seam of liveiron was struck that promised the finest pedigree of steamhorse in decades, and these were prosperous times for underworkers, with bonus hours for anyone fit enough to work them. But the fresh money chased fewer and fewer goods. What remained of last year's supplies were bought for figures — and, increasingly, other types of currency — that only the most wealthy or the most desperate could afford to pay.

We were fortunate in our tower. My mother invariably expected the worst, and she always saw to it that the larders were full. Now that my father was absent, she could make the most of her pessimist's satisfaction at being right.

Late autumn fell in filthy torrents from the sky. The bricks in our tower oozed the smell of the ancient river clay from which they had been made. I would stare for hours from the window of a forgotten room I had taken to thinking of as my own, watching the mines claw through the mud, still thinking of that girl I had seen sitting on the drift of ash above the marsh, her face tilted to the sun. Although my room was far distant from the place in the tower that my father had liked to call his study, sometimes I would look around me with a start. But then I would smile. Even in this grim season, there was a fresh sense of ease about the tower with my father gone. I was free to dream of things that never were. Worlds of pretty and of gold. And to watch the puddles along the empty track that led towards the Great Road.

I remember the morning that my father returned. Several weeks before, I had discovered a stock of his old cigarettes. I suppose that curiosity must have driven me to try them, but even now I cannot say what made me persist in breathing the foul smog that was quite different from what I expected and yet so reminiscent of my father. But I did persist. And I was smoking as I stood with my palm pressed against the streaming glass of my own empty room. I had grown used to it, almost to like it, although the bitter grey still stung my eyes. My thoughts were anywhere but on the world outside the window. But I instantly heard, faint but unmistakable over the rain, the chuff of the steamhorse and the squelch of iron wheels pulling through the jellied mud. I crushed out my cigarette and half-fell down the tumbling stairways. Into the sooty rain.

It was a steamhorse. With redgold livery showing through the rust. And there was my father, fully suited and balanced atop the iron saddle, water running off the oiled plates of his armour. I splashed out towards him, still half-hoping that it wasn't true. I grabbed the raised stirrups of the steamhorse. As I looked up, the rain streaming into my eyes, the breastplate dropped from his chest. I had to jump backwards as metal tumbled by. White flesh showed. Then my father fell too, half-naked into the mud. The visor broke up over his face. He was smiling. The steamhorse ambled on through the rain towards the tower, shedding what remained of the suit.

I bellowed for the servants to pick up the body and the jigsaw trail of armour. Cowering at my threats, they did as I commanded. They stripped him in the rain. He was like one of the dead chicks that the rooks tossed out from their nests each spring. But he had no beak. And he was breathing. He was smiling. As my mother sobbed and chewed her knuckles, the servants formed a makeshift stretcher. They carried him through cold halls, along damp corridors, up stairways. His limbs rolled off the stretcher and scuffed the steps. I ordered them to take him to the room he had liked to call his study, to place him atop a table beside the window where he used to stand. And then I drove them all away.

I looked into eyes that were the no-colour of rain. At least that hadn't changed. I touched his bony chest and felt the birdcage flutter of his heart, the stirring of his lungs. The Blight had taken him: pushed him through to another world. That smile came from somewhere deep within, boring a hole right through me, up through this tower, the rain, up to the place where sunlight beamed blue over candyfloss. There was no sign of damage or injury, but he didn't even smell the same. Certainly not the sour and disappointed aroma of sweat and cigarettes that I associated with my father's body . . . that I had come to associate with myself.

How pleasant it would be to tell you that I set out clad in greasy armour and mounted aboard a steamhorse to overcome the Blight. And imagine your pride to know that your King was a hero. But in truth if there had been a knife in my hand, I would have killed my father. Driven the steel in hard, and again. I hated that smile. It was everything that he had denied in himself and in me.

But I told myself that I was head of the household now. And I was afraid that violence would only make me more like him than I already was. Losing your father—even in a way such as this— simply brings you face to face with who and what you are. That was the most hateful thing of all.

I let him live. I screamed for the servants. He was thin now beyond malnourishment. I ordered them to search every room in the tower until they found an eater machine to feed him. And I saw to it that they did so.

★   ★   ★

On Saint Ely's day the moat froze solid around Castleiron. Both despite and because of the privations of the winter and the Blight, it was a signal for jollity. The pitwheels stopped turning. The church bells boomed. Children clambered through barbed wire to tie ribbons to the steamhorses grazing the coal seams at the head of the valley. Feeling sick with myself, I stood at a window in my own empty room, watching the dark streams of underworkers emerge from their chaotic dwellings and spread through the frost like ants in sugar. But to her credit, my mother forced her swollen legs up the stairways in search of me. Freed from the threat of my father, she had become a different, more forceful, person. While I moped and cursed the servants, she ran the tower.

I turned from the window as I heard her dragging footsteps. I drew on my cigarette, blinking through the haze and the shadows. She stood in the doorway, and her expression bore more than frustration at my weary indolence. There was anger and fear. Before I had time to argue, she shouted that no son of hers was going to spend his days like this. No way was she going to let it happen. She was right, of course; saint's days were too rare to waste. She nagged me into boots and woollens. Not that I agreed at the time, but I was still half a child, and going outside seemed like less trouble than arguing.

Outside, the chimneys were topped for once by no more than pinkish sky. With the wagons and the pumps all still, my feet crunched loud on the clinker path. The valley resounded with huge silence, like the last echo of a struck gong. I walked over the shifting slagheap, picking my way down between the tin flaps that covered the passageways to the underworkers' dwellings, on through the maze of the Pits. I was drawn by the sounds of life, of people, not specifically of voices and movement, but the indeterminate rumble that a crowd gives off as readily as the smell of close flesh. People laughing and talking and squabbling, people spending money they didn't have and making happy fools of themselves.

There was a fair close to the ice, on the flat wasteland that spread before Castleiron, which people—in place of any number of more accurate descriptions—called the Meadow. The stallholders had taken their customary pitches. I let the flow of the crowd draw me down the breath-smogged passages, past brass incubi and shawls of woven steel for the wealthy, cast-iron whistles and cheap trinkets for the poor. A liveiron automaton stumbled through the crush, his unoiled legs creaking and the glow almost gone from his headlights, offering the attractions of a tent where

the curious could talk with the still-animated severed head of
Cardinal Reichold. I had no money, but many of the sights were
free. A copperworm from the deepest mines coiled around the
quivering form of a dancer. A down-at-heel magician was offering
LIGHTNING BOLTS WHILE YOU WAIT, although the peeling sign failed
to suggest any useful purpose. Further on, the food stalls were
more thinly spaced than I remembered from previous fairs, and
the miasma of cooking meats and burnt toffee was replaced by the
thinly rancid smell, unpleasantly reminiscent of the private parts
of the human body, that we had all come to associate with the
Blight. But even if there was little on display that would attract
anyone with a full belly, the stalls nevertheless did good business.

But it was the ice that everyone had gathered for. The old to
watch, the young to be truly young for a while. Normally, the
moat was an odorous soup stirred by every imaginable effluent.
But the cold had dispersed all but a ghost of the usual stench and
set the liquid smooth as apple jelly. My grim mood was out of
place: even the frost-cured faces of the malcontents who dangled
from the castle walls seemed to be grinning. I thought of my
father, smiling too through the iron cage of an eater machine. In
his own happy world. Then I tried to forget.

The flat-footed skaters sprawled, stood up, skimmed those
miracle seconds before the next fall. I hardly recognised anyone
beneath the dirty bindings, and those I did were servants and underworkers, not fit company for someone of my birth. But I joined
in anyway, clumsy as a broken spring. Amid the skating figures
there was one that kept returning. We circled. We collided. The
bare palms of my hands skidded through a melting patch, and I
laughed as I hauled myself up from my knees. She was laughing
too. Eyes that were green as the ice between a baggy hat and
bandages of scarf. She had rag-doll limbs, rag-doll clothes, but I
could feel her warmth burning through. And it was just a game
as my arms brushed the softness of her breasts as we skated, just
a game as she bumped her limbs against mine.

The rim of the sun broke evening over the ice. I tried to catch
my breath at the wet edge. The girl skidded over to join me. She
pulled the rags down from her face to her sharp certain chin. I saw
that she was the girl I had seen sitting on the ash heap above the
marsh. And although she was pretty beneath the grime, I felt a
flash of resentment that she should break into my dreams. Still,
I tried to talk to her even though her accent was thick, like the
sound of steamhorse slurry tipped down a chute.

The sky was darkening. The stalls of the fair were stripped to skeletons, fought over by the hungry rooks and the even hungrier rats. The ice was empty. Its glow had almost faded as we picked our way through the slushy earth at the edge of the Meadow. Looking back across the ice, her hand tight as a stone in mine, I thought I glimpsed something blacker than the shadows slide beneath the surface. Maybe some creature. Maybe nothing at all. It wasn't a time for thinking.

That silence in the valley that I had noticed early in the day was now a tight physical presence, something from a box within a box. The girl and I stood awkwardly together: two scarecrows all but ignored by the rooks bickering over the remains of the fair. She loosened the ties of the blanket she was wearing for a coat, and I could see the hollow of her neck, the sweat-glimmered divide of her breasts. The idea of talk was even more useless than before. We had come to that moment that all men and women (children though we still both undoubtedly were) must share without sharing. And I stepped forward in the half-thawed mud. She touched me inside the soft prison of her arms with chilly fingers, and I answered without question.

The wind fluted a discord between the empty stalls. It was no use here. We needed to go somewhere. The tower was out of the question; my mother's instruction to make the most of the day certainly wasn't intended to extend to this. There was of course a well-worn tradition of the nobility taking their pleasure with those who couldn't afford to refuse, but the tradition of hypocrisy was stronger still. And this time was different, just as all times have been different for everyone since the Great Beast first spewed out this mineral land.

She grabbed my hand and we hurried across the misnamed Meadow, on into the Pits. The bleached moon rode the wind above the ash heaps, but the paths led down, through twists and turns I could never have followed. Here the soot settled, the dirt gathered in drifts, the frost and the snow were never white. Tin roofs and pit props broke across tunnel throats. The sky closed over with rubble. She led me down.

Here, she said, and gestured towards some hole that was no different from the rest, probably worse if looked at closely. I glanced back, aware of mutterings and wet eyes twinkling, but the space was darkness without scale. She tugged me through into giving blackness. There were the gathering odours of mortality as we clawed away layers of our clothing, sharp explorations that became urgent and sweet. Her chewed lips hot against mine. But for all the blind clamour of my senses, there was a part of my mind that refused to dissolve, that was playing over the memory of each moment even before it happened.

The vision of the girl above the marsh—dissolved into this. Nothing was quite as it should be. I pulled her limbs the way I wanted them, and she pushed back at me. Inexperienced children though we were, we reached some compromise and took our uncertain pleasure. Everything tunnelled down. It was like the moment of waking when the dream fades. I realised, as I fell back and saw the faint moon-glimmer of her flesh, that even the darkness itself was less than absolute.

I slept. I dreamed the scent of dappled pine needles, some memory of a summer wind from the east that the Pits had yet to taint. When I opened my eyes, I saw the grey slopes of our limbs, entwined but separate. She mewed something half-awake. I smelled tears, and realised that she had been crying.

I asked her why.

We began to talk: talking in the darkness is sometimes easier than making love. She told me about her life, the undoing of certainties, the inexhaustible surprises of loss and age. For the first time, I realised that there are visions at the corner of everyone's eyes. Dreams that we dare not turn and face. Just as I had stumbled away from the sight of this girl above the marsh. Just as my father had tried to dissolve his own dreams in anger and bitterness.

We whispered the same words. Our incantations of humanity. Her face was above me, distant and close as the moon, eyes over my eyes, lips over my lips. And her need was inside my flesh, drawn tight beyond release. I loved her. I could feel the world pouring through me, all power and all innocence. And it was mine and I understood through her. For a moment, I knew everything.

I slept again, sweetly in her arms. I dreamed of the shadow I had seen beneath the ice. It was sliding between us. When I awoke there was enough light to make out the puff-ball rottenness of the cave. She had rolled away from me, still curled asleep, showing nothing but the bony architecture of her back. I touched her skin. I stroked the notches of her spine. I wanted fire and tenderness, but she didn't respond. She lay breathing, lifelessly still. When I pulled her over, her limbs sprawled loose. And she was smiling. Her green eyes wide and staring right through my head and up beyond the clouds.

She was smiling like my father, neither dead nor alive.

I remembered the shadow under the ice. The shadow in my dream. The Blight had been here, taken her from me. Even as

I wept, the Pits were clangorously awakening. My grief was drowned in noise before it left my throat.

On hands and knees, I dragged my clothes together. The face I had seen like a vision atop that heap of ash gazed at me without seeing. I kissed her ragged lips, the softness of her breasts. I breathed her skin. Her beautiful eyes were staring into a place I couldn't touch or feel or smell or see. I spread her hair in a burnished fan, I settled her limbs, her dirty-nailed hands. She looked beautiful beyond words, but even as I stared at her I grew afraid that the vision would shatter. I backed into the tight grip of the tunnel with a different kind of fear in my throat, almost glad to be away.

I entered a cavern, drizzled by daylight from crevices in the roof, bitter with smoke. I stumbled along the paths that seemed to lead upwards. Whole families huddled around spitting fires. In places I had to climb around these shivering mounds of flesh and clothing. But even when I was close enough to reach into the flames, there was hardly any heat.

Walking without thinking or caring, I soon came to broadening ways and the bright open sky. The shift whistles were starting to scream. Underworkers were emerging from the dirt, crossing the sharp landscape on their journeys from the hole where they lived to the one where they toiled. Many more, unseen, made their way underground through the honeycomb soil. The labouring steam-horses, hauling chains, driving pulleys that turned cogs that burrowed darkness, looked well-fed and well-oiled, plump compared to the underworkers who tended them.

The scent of the girl still lingered on my flesh, but already the feeling of loss was distant. All the richness had gone. My whole life seemed like a process of loss, as though the Blight had always been here, emptying the air to grey, draining every dream. Drawing and sucking like a leech until, emboldened, it took a form that this world could see.

I wandered out of a choking drift of steam, still unsure of my directions and in no hurry to find my way. Then I stopped and looked around. Scrap iron clawed the rubble. Grasping hands, trying to reach beyond. An underworker was singing a melody to the rhythm of cogs and chains. Gears within gears; worlds within worlds . . . and then my heart began to pound. Suddenly, I was close to a different dream.

I quickened my pace across the Pits. My way led past a church that pricked the sky amid the chimneys at the edge of the deep-mines. A crowd had gathered on the loose mix of bones and rub-

ble that formed the graveyard. As I approached, I heard screeching and wailing.

I slowed when I reached the spot, stumbling over uptilted
femurs and broken memorials. The people were mostly underworkers, crossing themselves with tattered hands and murmuring
imprecations to the saints. When I looked up at the blackened
spire, I saw why.

A shadow was fluttering from the belfry. It had the texture of
loose grey skin; a living flag. I could hear it muttering over the
cries of the onlookers, words without meaning that were closer to
baby talk than insanity. It was easing its way between the slats like
leaves through a gutter. As it did so it began to sob, as though the
process caused it much pain.

I stared for a few moments. So this was the fabled Blight, the
thing that had made my father smile and robbed me of my love,
flapping here, obvious as a dishcloth thrown against the sky. It
must have been drawn by the resonance of the bells, driven by
whatever hungers possessed it to suck out the potency of cast
bronze. The sight was sickening, without meaning, like the suffering the Blight itself carried. It taught me nothing, not even fear.
I pushed my way through the onlookers without glancing back, on
across the slagheaps beyond. When I reached a fork in the ways
beside the ruins of a mine that led left towards my tower, I turned
right.

It was hard work climbing the coalseamed fields where the
steamhorses grazed each night. The creatures churned the steep
edges of the valley to sand, and twice I had to stop myself tumbling backwards by grabbing barbed wire. It hurt, but did little
damage. And my luck held when I literally fell across a copper-
weave nosebag. I shook out the coaldust and hitched it over my
shoulder like a sack.

Up above the field boundaries, there was nothing but rock and
air. I stopped at last to catch my breath and look down over the
valley. It was grey. White. Black. Every colour that wasn't a colour.
This far off in the chimney haze, even the moat of Castleiron was
no longer green. The stench of sweat and sulphur brimmed over
the mountains to the ravaged sky. This was my home and reality
screamed at me through every pore, but now I was determined to
change it. Maybe the dream had gone, but the Blight wasn't going
to take me: *I* was going to take *it*.

I began to poke among the rocks, exploring the crevices where
agronts sheltered in the day. I found the first one easily, a small
thing still purplish from the seed pod. I ripped out its stamen be-

fore it had time to scream and stuffed it into my makeshift sack. But I needed many more and the search took hours. I climbed. My limbs were agony, and the air raked my cigarette-clotted lungs. But slowly the sack grew heavier. The agronts were sly. They waited for me to commit myself to a lunge across sheer rock before skittering just out of reach. But I was driven. I took risks that the peasants who normally came up here with their sacks and skewers would never have chanced — not if they wished to survive.

And all the while the valley below churned life and sulphur. Faintly, I heard the evening shift whistles. Focusing away from the crevice I was clinging to, I saw that the sun was setting through the teeth of the mountains. My shadow stretched across a nearby peak. I was incredibly high now, and the sack was heavy on my back. I could feel one or two of the larger agronts that I had failed to kill outright still squirming. Maybe I had enough. Those I pursued now were old and wary, survivors of many night forays into the valley to dog the sleeping and the unwary. And doubtless they had been hunted many times before. I chanced looking directly down at the swimming drop. I saw that the granddaddy of all agronts was climbing my leg.

A shock went through me. One moment my fingers were scrabbling at the rock. The next I was in air. Flying. It was easy to fall. But quickly my bones thundered and I realised that I couldn't have dropped far, not if I felt pain at all. I dragged myself up. The sack was nearby, and the wounded agront was trying to haul itself into hiding on knobby arthritic roots. I kicked it to stillness.

There was a way down through the rocks. Half falling, half walking, I followed. Darkness settled. The steamhorses paused in their rootings for coal to track me with their headlights, the beams moted with soot. They were gentle animals; I remember them now with fondness. That night it was almost as though they were trying to help me find the way. Down into the Pits, where there was always black and fire. Across the slagheaps. To the redbrick tower I called my home.

★ ★ ★

My mother was sitting in the main hall. A fire was burning, but it gave off more smoke than light. I was grateful; it meant that she could hardly see me.

She asked me the questions she thought she was expected to ask. Her son missing for a night and a day. Genuinely, I think she loved me. But her voice was without warmth. The Blight was here, too. I could feel it in my own bones, killing even the bruises,

the cracked ribs, the pain. Oh, where have you been, my son.
. . . I stumbled briefly into her arms and let her kiss me, felt her
muted wonder at the state I was in. Her breath smelt of coal.
There were questions she couldn't ask, questions I couldn't answer. In a hurry for it to end, I broke away, banging the copperwire sack up the stairs behind me.

Passages I knew from childhood. Old-friend shadows and grinning cracks in the wall. Places I could shake hands with. The room
that my father liked to call his study. Where he escaped from
everything but life itself. And now even that. He was stretched out
beside the big window where furnacelight and moonlight webbed
the darkness. The smile on his face glowed through the iron bars
of the eater machine. The smile he could never quite manage on
his own.

I was breathing hard, I could smell the tower, bricks and
blocked chimneys and forgotten chamber pots gone cloudy-ripe
under unmade beds. And the hot metal and clinker and oil and
coal dust in the stables. And the smoke and sulphur of the mines,
the reek of clay freshly exposed to air. And the human smells of
the Pits, of dreams forgotten for too long. And the bittersweet
reek of corrupted power from inside the high walls of Castleiron.
And the faint musty odour of the cigarettes my father used to
smoke as he stood looking out.

The eater machine was idling, squatting over his face. The
hopper was empty, and the liveiron muscles gently tensed and
loosened. My father didn't need much food. It was hardly a drain
on his energy, just lying there smiling.

The open mouth of the copperwire sack gave off the mixed
scents of coal dust and agront. I fumbled out the first creature; a
small one. I ripped off the fingery roots and fed the fat leaves one
by one into the hopper. Then another agront from the sack. Bigger, and still living. Its roots curled tight around my wrist. I
plucked out the warm stamen to kill it. The roots shuddered and
went dead. I began to pull off the leaves, then thought better of
it and simply dropped the whole thing into the hopper. The
machine's arms began to move, probing open my father's lips and
reaching between teeth still stained brown to work his tongue and
jaw, pushing chunks of agront inside. I dropped another agront in
whole. And again. And another. The juices began to dribble and
spray as the eater machine picked up speed. My father's jaw
moved jerkily and without volition. Inside his mouth, the gripper
pressed the mush down into his throat, where the constricting
bands around his neck took over. Even to someone like myself,

who would normally have relished the prospect of eating fresh agront, the sight was enough to tangle my stomach.

The machine slithered and pulsed, happy as liveiron only could be when working. It was impossible for my father to smile now, and his eyes gave nothing away as his belly was pumped full. The eager machine had possessed his body, his face. I just kept on feeding the hopper. The remaining agronts began to squirm inside the sack, catching the reek of death, and perhaps sensing in their own small way that something more was about to happen. I had to keep the neck tight to prevent them from escaping.

Then movement made me look up. Something fluttering over and over against the stars. Like ash on a breeze, but bigger. I paused in my labours, the torn roots of an agront twisting in my hands. I smiled. It was coming. The Blight was coming.

Then my eyes were snatched down again as my father gave a liquid belch. His body was trying to vomit, throw out the pulp that the eater machine was forcing inside. But the glistening liveiron tensed and redoubled its efforts, pushing in more and more. His back arched. Iron tensed against flesh, but it seemed as though there was no competition. The eater machine simply quivered and pulsed harder.

The shadow beyond the window widened. Taking out the stars, the moon, the dogend glow of the Pits. The headlights of a steamhorse briefly ribboned the valley cliffs with gold. Then that too was gone. The Blight thumped gibbering against the window, sucking away most of the light. Its grey mass seethed, searching the panes for weakness. It found a gap. Sobbing, it forced a tendril through. The tendril shuddered, feeling blindly. My father coughed and strained again as the eater machine forced the pulp through his smile, down into his dreamworld. A pane shattered, spraying in. A blade of glass sliced past my cheek. More of the Blight flooded in.

Sound was everywhere now. The Blight. Breaking glass. The squealing of the remaining live agronts. The pump of the eater machine. The clamour of the Pits. And then everything was lost in a larger sound as my father opened his mouth wider than the eater machine could hold. Liveiron splintered and flew like axed wood. My father's jaws still widened. I remembered a steelsnake I had seen eating a rat down by the marshes. I thought of the whole world being swallowed. Then for a dizzy moment I was looking down. Flesh, bone, gristle, bursting apart. Impossibly, there was something beyond. My father's mouth yawned wider. It cracked open his head. It spread, floor to ceiling. There was hardly anything left of my father now, just pink rags, but still his mouth continued to grow. As I fell backwards, it began to vomit out a mass that broke louder than any scream.

A billion things happened at once. Many years later, a sentry who was standing guard on the parapets of Castleiron at that moment bowed before this golden throne and told of how he had heard a sound that was deeper than thunder and felt movement that shook him through his boots. He said that he knew it was either the beginning or the end of the world. Then he looked across the swarming darkness of the Pits and saw light.

I saw only chaos. Splashing wounds from the glass, the Blight broke fully into the room. It fought its way against the tide as the whole tower rocked and fountained bricks into the sky. The jaws were still stretching. The Blight stretched, too. Ragged scraps of it circled like leaves in a whirlwind as it poured itself down into the cavernous mouth. Its gibberings ceased forever, and I felt the hot waves of its delight.

As what remained of the Blight and my father joined, there was a moment of silence without scale. Like the quiet of dawn, but impossibly amplified. Then a column of light broke from the giving mouth, upwards out of what remained of the tower. It seared the clouds and arched across the mineral night, spreading faster than any eye could follow. Light. Changing everything. My own senses were blasted as I fell backwards and away.

The Giving Mouth widened. The Age of the Great Beast ended as it began, but now it was sweetness that spewed across the Kingdom. The slagheaps were clothed in meadowgrass. Underworkers were washed from the Pits, beached at the edge of a forest that swayed. The rooks preened their plumage to blue and circled the rising sun. Castleiron crumbled, and silver fish leaped in the crystal moat. The Great Beast closed its jaws forever over the Queen set in her iron throne, then shivered to sparkling dust. Everything was remade.

I stumbled with everyone else amid the wreckage and beauty on that first morning. I opened my eyes to blue sky. Warm sweet air danced against my face. I climbed to my feet in a ruin, green-gold with bricks and ivy. I wandered through an orchard and marvelled at the tall four-legged beasts that whinnied and tossed their manes in the sunlight and blossom. When all had settled and the morning had arrived in full, I found my mother. Her hair was lifting in the breeze, and she looked younger than I could ever remember. She was kneeling in a filigree of flowers. Nearby, a stream was chattering diamonds. White clouds chased shadows across the rolling green. She was looking around in wonder. Tears were streaming down her cheeks.

I embraced her and cried too.

★　　★　　★

I could tell you much more; the end of my particular tale is just a beginning. But you probably know more than I about the wonders of this world. And I pray that the truth of its origins does not sour it for you.

Now as I strain my weary eyes, I can tell from your face that you hear me without comprehension. You still see only this crotchety old King. You frown as you watch me smoking these leaves that grow so sweetly in the herb garden and yet taste so bitter on the tongue. You puzzle over my habits as you puzzle over my sudden angry moods. But eventually you always turn away and smile and shake your head. You put them down to age. You try to understand, but the wonders of adventure always beckon. On banquet days you sit at my right hand beside this throne set inside the yellowed teeth of this Giving Mouth that even now wafts the sweet air of Paradise against your face and stirs the hair around your noble brow. My chosen successor, you are handsome and proud, wise in the ways of goodness. You look out of that window and see the sweetdark river, forests and meadows tumbling like kites in a dream. You sleep soft and long, and morning is always a surprise. Your days are bright with colour. And you smile with your pretty ones at these stories of times when this Kingdom was cursed. Such tales as are only fit for firelight and the brimming comforts of red wine.

My time is not long. For today, you have heard enough. But soon, before the trees turn to fire and my joints become intolerable, I must take your hand and you must help me down the forgotten stairways of this tower. There, in the deepest quietest recesses, where the candles glow and I have decreed that there will be nothing but gold and incense, I will show you a wonder that you will never believe. A beautiful girl who has slept through my life and will sleep beyond yours. Her hands steepled in repose. The green eyes of her smile caught inside dreams beyond anything that even this world will ever show.

And you will let her sleep, for no one would dare to wake her.

The Perfect Stranger

As I watched the flying boat alight in the bay, I thought, this is what heaven must be like. Along the quay, the other island guests were smiling, expectant, nervous, sharing, whispering their secret hopes; laughing, even, at the strangeness of it all. Above the stuccoed buildings of the little town, huge lips on a billboard formed the word *Welcome*, a warm breath that carried on the breeze across blue water, was held shimmering in the arms of tropical hills.

The props of the flying boat slowed, and her prow drifted to face the breeze. A passenger tug fanned across the water. Soon reunited couples were walking back along the quay, hand in hand, arm in arm, but still—and understandably—uncertain of each other. I checked the note again in the pocket of my shorts. Meena. Was that an Indian name? Should I be looking for someone with black hair, dark skin. . . .

Lin the tour guide came over. She was dressed in a gorgeous blue sarong, busy with her clipboard. "Still haven't found your wife, Marius?"

I shrugged. "I wouldn't know if I had."

"Of course." She smiled brightly. She took my arm and led me through the happy press of bodies along the quay.

"Marius, this is Meena," she said.

A tall and elegant woman turned at the sound of her name. Tall, yes, I'd somehow imagined that. But there was no trace of my Indian lady. Meena had pale brown skin, marvellous green eyes . . . or was that just this tropical light? No, I decided. It was her; she was beautiful. I stared at Meena. Meena stared back at me. What else was there to do?

"It's true, isn't it?" Meena said, her face suddenly breaking from seriousness. Laughing. "What they say—I really can't remember you."

I stepped forward. "Anyway, Meena. I'm glad you're here."

She held out her hand. Unable to tell if she was being ironic, I took it in both of mine. Then she leaned forward and let me kiss her cheek. We stepped back and smiled again. On the hillside above the harbour, the lips on the billboard smiled with us. They breathed the word *Welcome.*

"Do you know how long you've been here?" Meena asked as our Jeep took us along the rough coast road to our bungalow. She seemed happy and relaxed, her right foot up on the rusty dashboard, her khaki dress pushed back to her thighs.

"Not long," I said. I lifted my hands from the steering wheel and leaned across the gearstick. Meena let me kiss her, parting her lips, pressing with her tongue. The Jeep slowed, then took control. It rumbled on between the brilliant sea, the white sand, the chattering jungle. Better than us, it knew the way.

When my hand strayed along her thigh, Meena caught it firmly.

"Let's wait," she said. "It's sweeter to wait."

So I sat watching Meena as she drifted across the pine and rugs of our bedroom, lifting dresses from her case. All the doors and windows were thrown wide. She was seemingly casual, absorbed. But sometimes she would lean close to me, let her bare arm brush my cheek. Or she would stand and stretch at the window, where white curtains billowed with the beat of the waves. I wondered if it could ever feel this way with a true stranger, whether this slow, delicious dance was some pattern we instinctively remembered from our life together. Are people ever this happy? I wondered. Could things have ever been this good?

"There's one odd thing," Meena said, closing the doors of the wardrobe, turning to face me. "The tour people don't let you take anything with you, do they? But when the flying boat was over the ocean, I looked in my case and found this."

It was in her hand. She held it out.

"A photograph of me. Now, Marius, isn't that odd . . .?"

★ ★ ★

I found the evidence quite by accident one day when I was going through Meena's drawers. We worked different hours. I generally saw my prospects mornings and evenings at their homes. The people Meena dealt with were mostly retired, available during what would once have been called office hours. But I liked having the middle of the day to myself, I liked the cold solitude of our flat, being able to get stuff done, being able to go through Meena's things.

I was in a good mood that morning as the Volvo took me home through the ruins of the city. I had completed two sales, and another one looked likely. All three were for the Grade A security package, which cost the most, tied the client to an open-ended maintenance agreement, and paid the highest commission. Sensing my mood, the Volvo played Dvořák's *American* Quartet.

Through the automatic gates leading into our estate, the Volvo cruised past sooty Grecian pillars, weeping stucco. But for the perpetual absence of sunlight, it could have been an old Hollywood slum. The flats were higher on the hill, for people like us who couldn't afford houses, closer to the ravaged sky. One of the Big Companies had recently put up an advertising billboard on the roadside. Huge lips parted and smiled down at me. Overriding Dvořák on the Volvo's speakers, they murmured close to my ear, a voice creamy with digitised sexuality. *Escape,* the voice purred, stretching along my spine like a cat. *Treat yourself to the one luxury that money can't buy. Well, maybe only just . . .*

I picked my way across the damp underground car park, unthinkingly ducking the concrete stalactites and shelves of glowing fungi. The lift was in a good mood. Hello, Marius, it said, and took me straight to our flat without demanding an extra credit.

The flat was cool, grey, empty, softly humming to itself, smelling faintly of toast. As she often did, Meena had left our bedroom window running, ticking up the cost of the rental. It showed a scene from a tropical island, nostalgic waves beating the shore with a sound like an old-fashioned record in the run-out groove. I rummaged under the duvet for the remote control, but the flat beat me to it. The window snowed, then cleared to transparency. I stood looking out, feeling the cool, faint breath of reality. We were fairly high here, up on the eighth floor. I could see bruised clouds ploughing over the estate, the lips mouthing silently on the billboard, the grey tangle of the city beyond.

Meena could never understand why I liked daylight. Plain, muggy daylight. There was hardly enough of it to fill the room — but that was the point. It was faint, evanescent, dreamy. And anyway, what *did* she understand nowadays? I wandered over to her drawers. The top one was always a little stiff. You had to lift and then pull. Here, she kept her jumpers and cardigans. Woollens, as — anachronistically — she liked to call them. Here was a Fair Isle, still almost new. I held it up, remembering a rare happy day, the three of us together. Little Robin in his bobble hat, laughing unsteadily as we swung him between us. Then I folded it back carefully, the way Meena had done.

The next drawer down was for her underwear. Everything was loose here, just stuffed in anyhow. In the cobweb shadows, my hands wandered through her things, feeling the poppers, the loose pull of elastic. I liked the specificity of underwear, the sense of secret purpose, that *this* fits *here*. . . . These days, it was the only time I felt close to Meena. When I was alone. Unlike the Meena-of-now, the vision I touched was pliable, loving. The drawer smelled of salt and linen, white memories of freshly crumpled sheets. It reminded me of times when the words came easily, and when they didn't even matter.

I was about to close the drawer when a glimmer of light caught my eye. Down in the tertiary layers of bras she no longer wore, knickers that were starting to wear through. Light. Bright daylight. And a small voice. It came from a corner of the drawer.

My fingers tangled under an old sachet of lavender, then closed on a piece of card. I lifted it out. The light shone on my hands and face. A photograph. It spoke to me.

"—don't—"

Meena, in some park.

"—don't—"

Turning towards the camera.

"—don't—"

A smile of surprise brightening her lips. Her hair a loose bun, strands of it clinging to her cheek. Blue sky. Dappled light from a whispering tree.

"—don't—"

Meena, endlessly turning towards the lens.

"—don't—"

I put the picture down. It went dark and silent for a moment, thinking that I'd gone away. But I had to pick it up, look at it again, hold it in my shaking hands.

"—don't—"

Don't. How could a negative word sound so loving?

★   ★   ★

Lin the tour guide came down to see us in her Jeep that evening, to check that we were settled in. Meena and I were sitting out on

the veranda. The air smelled leafy, salty, earthy, wet. An hour before, there had been rain, flapping the palms, chattering in the
gutters. We had been lying tangled in the damp sheets of our bed,
too happy to move. Just in time, as the first heavy drops fell, the
sensors in the windows had banged them shut. The sound of
the rain pressed down on us through the sweet sudden change in
the air as my fingers traced the streaming shadows across Meena's
skin.

"Hi!" Lin waved. She picked her way between the puddles and
climbed the wooden veranda steps. "You like it here?"

We both smiled at the understatement. Out to sea, the sunset
was under way. The clouds were fairy mountains.

Lin sat down, clipboard on her lap. Her bright blue sarong of
the morning had been replaced with an equally brilliant red one.
Despite the heat, she always managed to look clean and fresh. She
asked us if we'd managed to work the bath and shower, found the
food in the kitchen, explored the entertainment facilities. Of
course, we had done none of these things, but we nodded and said
everything was fine.

"Some people find the amnesia a problem."

Meena said, "I still feel like myself, if that's what you mean."

"That's exactly it." Lin smiled. "Some people don't."

Meena leaned forward in her rattan chair. In this twilight,
against her white dress, her skin was incredibly brown. "We must
have chosen to come here, right?"

Lin tapped her clipboard. It glowed briefly, but she didn't
glance down at it. "Meena, I don't have your particular details.
That's deliberate, of course. Company policy. But I can tell you
that it costs a great deal of money to come to this island. Not that
everyone is a billionaire or anything. People win prizes, the Big
Companies give out these holidays as performance incentives.
. . . You might just have saved." She tapped the clipboard again.
It threw shadows across her face. It was growing darker by the
minute. "Whatever, make the most of it."

"But why would anyone want to forget everything?" Meena
asked. "To leave themselves behind?"

"All sorts of reasons. Just think, you might both have demanding jobs or some other worry. What better way to forget all that?"

Meena nodded, although she didn't look entirely satisfied. Per-
sonally, I couldn't see what the problem was, as long as we were
happy.

Lin stood up, but she obviously hadn't quite finished. "There
are some specific advantages I can tell you about. The books, the

music, the holo library, for example. You won't remember any of that. So you have a whole world to rediscover, if that's what you wish to do. There's a guy comes here every year for two weeks. He rereads the same book. It's new for him every time."

We watched Lin walk back towards her Jeep, her red sarong aflame in the twilight.

★ ★ ★

We made love in our flat that night. Had sex, anyway. I turned over in bed to grab Meena, and Meena didn't push me away. I was self-absorbed, uncaring of her reaction: the photograph gave me a passion that I hadn't felt in years. Have you done this with him? I wondered. Your photographer friend? Or this? Meena was puzzled, although not uncooperative. But she insisted on keeping the bedroom window running. Moonlight. That bloody tropical shore. She used to say she liked the way it shone on our skin. Years before, I had found the habit arousing. Later on, I decided it was narcissistic. Now, I guessed that she simply wanted something interesting to watch while our love-making was going on.

I didn't sleep well. I spent a lot of time gazing at Meena's face on the pillow. The waves in the window frothed irritatingly on moonlit sand. I couldn't find the remote control without turning on the light, and the flat itself got confused when Meena and I had conflicting views about something.

We used to make love anytime, all the time. Now, it had to be in bed, at night, with the window running, a silly ritual that still often ended in a hundred different versions of Not Tonight, Marius, anyway. Before we were married, before we had Robin, before work became more than just work and money didn't matter, Meena always kept some piece of clothing on. One stocking, a necklace, a scarf. I remembered that she had a specially expensive scarf tucked down in one of those drawers, something I'd bought her one Christmas years ago, supposedly to wear in her hair, although we both knew what it was really for. It was night-black, sprinkled with stars. It spread out and out, cool layers of darkness. I remembered kissing Meena through it. I remember feeling the salt sparkle of Aldebaran, Betelgeuse, the way she used to sigh from the back of her throat when she came.

People change, they drift apart. But how could we have lost so much? Don't. That smile. So much. Without even knowing. But I took comfort from that photograph in her drawer. I knew now that it wasn't just *me*, or even simply us.

★ ★ ★

After showering, changing, making love, we lit a fire from the white bones of driftwood we found on the beach. The stars were everywhere. A crablike robot scuttled out from beneath the veranda and across the white sand to see to our needs. It even offered to light the fire, but that would have spoiled the fun. Instead, we sent it running obediently into the phosphorescent waves.

Meena brushed sand from her feet and sat cross-legged, watching me. "Marius and Meena," she said. "Don't you think it's strange, to have such odd names that match?"

"Everything about being here is strange," I said.

"Tell me what you remember."

I recited the names of the Big Companies, dates from history, venues for the Olympics. Meena chipped in, disagreeing over these little facts in the way that people always do. We both found that reassuring, to know that there was a real world out there, and that together we were part of it. It became a game. Capital cities, kings and queens . . . Beyond the firelight, the dark wall of the jungle wailed and chattered.

The crab-robot returned from the sea out of a rising moon. It shook itself like a dog, then ran proudly up to us, a gleaming fish thrashing in each of its five claws. We both had an idea how to gut them, but we left the robot to get on with it, then rigged up a kind of spit from odds and ends in the well-stocked kitchen. We sat in the firelight and ate the meat with our fingers. It was steaming, pink, delicious.

Meena lay back on the sand. I took her hand and licked away the juice and fish scales, worked my way up her arm, parted the buttons of her dress to kiss her breasts. Inch by inch, I eased the cotton from her flesh. The fire crackled, the logs sighed into glowing dust. She had a scarf in her hair. I reached to loosen it and throw it away.

"No," she said. She sat up in the soft white sand to tie it above her knee. "I feel more naked if I keep something on."

"You remember that?" I said.

She lay back. "Yes," she said. She parted her legs. She took hold of me. "That, I remember."

★　★　★

I didn't show Meena the photograph, nor mention it. I simply put it back in her knicker drawer where I had found it. Anyway, I'd stared at it for long enough to see it without looking. Meena turning, smiling. There, in my head. Don't. I didn't recall the scene— and I was sure I hadn't taken it—but I could tell that the photograph was a recent one from the soft lines around her eyes, from the slight hollowing of her cheeks, the things that age was starting to do to her. Just seeing it made me realise Meena hadn't smiled at me in that warm, open way in years. Warm, open. Not that way in years. Probably not since we had had Robin, when we were in love.

Meena came home midway through the evening, after I'd had time to get a little drunk. I grabbed hold of her in the narrow hall before she could push past, kissed her on the cheek, smelling her work clothes, feeling her work manner. My nerves were tingling. I was trying to detect some difference in her indifference, even though I knew that the only thing that had changed since the morning was me.

I watched her in the bedroom as she undressed.

"Good day?" she asked.

"Six sales," I said; I always added a few for luck. "You?"

"Nothing special. You didn't pick up Robin?"

"No," I said, feeling the usual pang of guilt.

"We must spend time with him at the weekend. Um, hold on." She hopped out of her tights. "I've arranged to see this client Saturday morning."

"Isn't that unusual?"

"Look, there's big money in this one, *darling*." She hated it when I queried anything about her work. She thought I didn't take it seriously enough. "He wants to drown in a vat of malmsey."

"Happened to someone in Shakespeare."

"Marius, you can't expect these people to be original. They want some point of reference that they can talk about at the party. I'll have to lunch him, but I'll be back early in the afternoon. And then we get Robin out of stasis, right? Take him to the funfair, give the kid a treat."

She padded into the bathroom and told the flat to turn on the shower, successfully killing any further conversation.

I watched her through the streaming glass. The figure of a woman, no longer Meena. Like a painting by Seurat. A cypher, a stranger. Someone I might once have known.

She came out in a cloud of soapy steam, fumbling for a towel, strands of wet hair clinging to the intricate bones of her neck.

When I reached to touch her, she turned towards me.

"Don't," she said, vaguely annoyed.

★　★　★

A tropical morning. Meena asleep beside me. Sounds of the jungle through the open window beside our bed. I kissed her shoulder. She stirred and smiled, too beautiful to wake.

The white curtains swelled. A light breeze cooled my body. Beyond the window, palm trees swayed. The whole jungle was alive. Movement, colour, light, a thousand different shades of shadow playing across the thick trunks of the palm trees, the dense labyrinth of ferns. A small monkey clung to the bark of the nearest tree. He swung up and along, hand over foot over hand, and hopped soundlessly onto the window ledge. He blinked. A tiny hand worried at his mouth. Everything about him was quick, shy, almost birdlike.

I eased myself up slowly from the bed, expecting the monkey to vanish at any moment. But he froze to watch me. Blink, blink. His irises were silver, the pupils black as a camera lens. He was probably used to visitors—and he wanted food. I padded quickly to the kitchen. I rummaged for biscuits or crisps, but settled on the sultanas I found in a jar, which were probably more suitable anyway.

Meena was awake when I came back, leaning on her elbows and smiling at the monkey on the window ledge. A step at a time, I crept towards him. Meena slid out of bed behind me. The monkey crouched motionless, watching us approach. Meena and I sat down on the sun-warmed pine beneath the window, looking up at him. His tiny pelt was immaculate, lustrous brown, flecked gold where the light caught it. I held out a sultana. The hand took it in a blur. Then another. Meena held out a third. He ate each sultana fastidiously, nibbling around the edges, his eyes flicking from Meena to me, taking everything in. He had a scholarly face, our monkey. While we sat cross-legged beneath the window ledge like naked penitents, it was hard not to feel that Meena and I were in the presence of wisdom.

He didn't run off when the sultanas were finished. And I was sure now that he was gazing at us from curiosity rather than wariness or fear. The palm trees murmured. The warm air burnished the filaments of his fur, stirred Meena's hair. It was a strange moment of equality between one species and another. I felt that he knew us. From the wild serenity amid the treetops, he had come down to consider these strange, sleepy creatures. To see our flesh, our bones, our dreams.

★   ★   ★

I cancelled my first appointment of the morning so that I could leave the flat after Meena. I was tired, a little dazed. I half-expected the photograph not to be there. But it was, and I tucked it into the flap of my briefcase.

The Volvo hummed and harred about what music to play me. It finally settled on Martinů, an ethereal dance. *Escape,* the lips called after me from the billboard as we pulled out from the estate, looming over the rain-rotted villas. *Escape. Treat yourself to the one luxury that money can't buy. Well, maybe only just . . .*

I visited my first prospect. After I'd done my usual spiel, he sat staring at the brochures I'd spread on the coffee table. He was old, with graveyard blotches on his hands, turkey wattles for cheeks. Almost old enough to be one of Meena's clients.

I'd played him this way and that, taken the objections and tossed them easily back. Of course, I agreed, security on your estate is excellent, but that only has to be the first barrier. Why, only yesterday there was that terrible thing on the news. Someone about your age. The kids from outside broke in when the electric fence shorted out, crucified the poor old guy for laughs on his kitchen table. . . .

The prospect risked a glance up at me. The loose flesh of his throat bobbed. Was he about to speak? But no, he looked down again. His trembling fingers brushed the cover of the Grade A booklet. It was printed in red and deep green. They were Christmassy colours, the colours of apples and firelight, childhood and home. I knew, of course, that he ached for me to say something, to break the silence. But I could wait here all day, my friendly-but-serious expression locked into place.

I was good at my job. But then, is there an easier thing to sell than security? Who wants to be without that? I mean, it was *important*, I was doing these people a favour. I'd explained that to Meena often enough. And although she denied it, Meena was in sales too—these days, who isn't? Our two jobs even followed on. After security, death. What could be more natural? And when the time comes and the surgeons can do no more, why not go out with a bang? Attend your own funeral. Jump from the top of the Eiffel Tower. Shoot yourself with an antique Luger that Hitler once owned.

At least, I thought, it's unlikely that Meena met the person who took that photograph through her work. But the idea clicked inside me. I saw trembling age-stained hands clutching a camera. I saw it all. Someone with the greed and the money to get everything they want. And Meena comes to arrange their last needs. A glimpse of her knees as she spreads her quotes and folders. And why not go out with a bang? Why not, indeed.

"Have you ever thought about dying?" I asked my prospect, genuinely curious.

"What?" The withered face looked up at me, then firmed into an expression of refusal.

Dammit.

★   ★   ★

We had breakfast. I wandered around our house. One storey, bare wood and big windows everywhere. Sunlight gleaming, and the smell of the sea. You almost felt as though you were out-of-doors. I paused at the entertainment box, remembering what Lin had said. I skimmed through a few book titles. The famous ones rang a bell, but I had no idea whether I'd ever read any of them. I mean, who ever reads anything now anyway? Billionaires on tropical islands, maybe.

I asked the box to play me some music, just anything it thought I might like. I was curious to know how it would react, whether it had some idea of my taste in these things — which was more than I had.

The sound of a string quartet filled the room. Dvořák, the screen told me. The *American* Quartet, Op. 96. Beautiful stuff, and every note of it was new to me, as fresh as the day it had flowered in the mind of that Czech on a far continent. But at the same time, I felt a warmth towards the piece that I didn't associate with unfamiliar music — as much, that is, as I could associate anything with anything. Yes, I decided, this is a kind of memory, or at least a memory of a memory. It's how I feel when I look into Meena's eyes. Like the stranger you recognise without knowing.

★   ★   ★

At lunchtime I went out from the office to the repo shop opposite. There was a kid at the counter. He had acne, specks of blood on his suit collar. Don't, Meena said to him when he turned her over in his hands. He asked me whether I knew if it was taken on a Canon or a Nikon. I told him, Just get the bloody thing done.

Home early, I put Meena's original photograph back in her knicker drawer with a feeling of relief. At least now that I had my own copy, I wouldn't have the indignity of constantly having to steal hers.

I sat down with the computer in the study, shoved the photograph into the drive.

"— don't —"

Meena turned to me on the screen. I zoomed in on her smiling face as she turned. Then over her shoulder. Some kind of path. Rainbowed at the edge of the shot where the lens was weakest and the digits were thin, I could just make out the wire of a litter bin. The bough over Meena's head was dipping in the breeze, freezing, dipping again. I worked my way through it leaf by leaf, saw flashes of blue sky, a caterpillar in close-up, then snatches of a glittering lake, and an old sign on the far shore. BOATS FOR HIRE, in peeling paint.

Meena said, "—don't—"

I killed the sound of her voice, killed the picture, tumbled down a stairway of menus to maximise the rest of the sound. The murmur of open air. Agitated birdsong. Trees whispering. It was a warm spring day. Somewhere, not too far off, I could hear splashes, shouts. The unmistakable sound of kiddies in a paddling pool. I saw orange water-wings, the fanning blue water frozen forever.

I silenced the birds, the trees, the splashes, the shouts. Then there was the murmur that lies at the back of sound in any open space, like the grinding of a huge machine. I killed all of that, too. Turned up the volume. Listened to what was left.

Someone breathing. Whoever was holding the camera. Huh. Half an intake of breath. Huh.

Huh. The sound was amazingly light, almost feminine. But not quite. My suspicions had moved on from a geriatric to something with pectorals and sweat. Maybe I'd have to rethink again. Huh. It was over so quickly, so hard to tell. Huh. I tried to visualise the hands that held the camera, that touched Meena, that parted the secrets of her flesh.

"What the hell are you doing, Marius?"

Huh.

Meena stood at the door of the tiny study. In her work clothes, her work face, laptop in hand.

I turned, hit the EXIT key. Huh. Do you really want to Quit? Huh. You bet.

I said, "Just pissing around."

"That strange noise . . . like someone crying." She shrugged. "Marius. Have you eaten?"

"No," I said. "I was about to ask you the same thing."

"You didn't pick Robin up?"

"Did you?"

Meena shook her head. "Marius, just how much time do you think I have these days?"

★   ★   ★

Next morning, after the monkey had come again to the window ledge, Meena and I found our yacht at anchor around the headland. In a pirate cove, the water so clear that the yacht seemed to hang suspended above the blue-pink coral.

We swam out towards her. As soon as we had climbed the rope ladder aboard, her ghostly crew set white sails to the fresh breeze.

We dropped anchor out in blue nowhere, alone to the rim of

the horizon. We swam. The water here was impossibly deep, inky blue all the way down to dreams of pirate wrecks, the fallen marble of lost civilisations. Lying beside Meena on the gleaming deck, I wondered at the person I had been. In some grey city. This is the tomorrow that never comes, I thought, trailing my hand down Meena's belly, gently kissing her ear. This is the future.

"How do you think they made the island?" Meena asked later.

I was lying on her. Inside her. Breathing. The water was scudding at her shoulder. Brown flesh, brown wood, white foam. The yacht had filled her sails. The dolphins were leaping ahead of the prow. We were heading home.

"The beaches can't be natural," she said. "There are no beaches left since the ice-caps melted."

I lowered my head to her shoulder, licked down into the hollow. Climate change. Yes, the fact was there in my mind. Climate. Change. But the gleam of brass, the scent of her hair . . .

"It's an island," I said. "Adrift from all the change."

She chuckled. The sound came through my spine. "So you think it's floating?"

I kissed her. Don't all islands float, the proper islands that you dream about?

She raised her arms. Then she pushed me back, rolled over on the warm deck, was astride me, caressing herself against my face, the sky pushing through. I thought of the island, our magical floating island. Anchored, drifting on the shadowed deep-sea chains amid doublooned wrecks, the whispered bones of pirates.

★　★　★

Next afternoon, after five unsuccessful prospect calls and some more sleuthing on the computer, I was taken by the Volvo to pick up Robin from the stasis centre on my way to the park. I couldn't remember asking. Perhaps the car was developing a conscience. Maybe it enjoyed having its back seat thrown-up over, little bits of broken toys wedged down between the upholstery. The Volvo parked in the plastic twilight beneath the stasis centre's massive wigwam roof. Bright arrows beckoned me through the thickening smells of coffee and polythene towards Reception.

Day on day, Robin's stasis bill had mounted up like an old-fashioned library fine. Even the receptionist seemed to think it was a lot. I gave her my card, and stood waiting for the red ACCOUNT OUT OF CREDIT light to flash. But today, whatever software god presided over the link to the bank was on my side. The receptionist dragged out a smile from the back recesses of her teeth. That'll do nicely.

When Meena and I had gone through the financial details

necessary to have Robin, the plan had been that she'd look after him most mornings, I'd have him afternoons. And unless we were going out, we would invariably let the little kid spend evenings in the flat, sleep with Mickey Mouse and Pluto in the little bedroom we'd had specially made. It all seemed fine when you looked at it on a spreadsheet. Stasis wasn't that much cheaper than using a nursery, but the big advantage was that Junior experienced no elapsed time. Mummy or Daddy dropped you into the stasis centre in the morning. Five seconds later, they picked you up again. It could be five hours or—increasingly with us—five days. Still, there were no nannies, no "Well, Sarah Says I Can," nothing to conflict with the parent's role. Robin was all ours—but the way things had worked out, we had to keep him mostly in stasis so that we could earn the money to keep him there.

Robin ran out to greet me. He gave me a hug.

"What day is it now, Daddy?" he asked. That's one thing they don't tell you about in the brochures. Kids aren't stupid.

"Wednesday all day," I said. "And Daddy's going to take you to a park."

Robin was silent in the Volvo. Gazing out of the window at the sunless city, gazing at me.

"You'll be starting school soon," I was saying. "You'll have other kids to play with."

"Yeah," he said.

I drummed my fingers on the steering wheel, pretending to be absorbed in a process I wasn't even performing. We drove in hushed silence. I wished the Volvo would play one of its kiddy tunes. "The Little Red Train." Or the one that went "Scoop, Scoop" at the end of every verse. But the car didn't seem to think that music of any kind was appropriate, and Robin would be sure to notice if I did it manually. Green eyes under a blond fringe watched me, the movement of my hands, the expression on my face. Blink, blink. Click, click. Meena had had Robin seven years before. He was now three and, oh . . . ten months, but I couldn't help wondering whether the wisdom of those extra years hadn't somehow seeped in.

It was billed as autumn in the park. A big red sign flashed over the broken concrete outside the dome, endlessly scattering a neon tumble of falling leaves. It cost a fortune to get in. You got a free Nikon if you paid an extra 10 percent. Throw away the camera, keep the pics.

There was a guy standing at the wicker gate that led into the smoky twilight. I'd seen him and his sort many times before. At the funfair, the sprawling Toys "R" Us that Robin was always wanting to go to, even outside the stasis centre. There was big money in this kind of thing now, selling kids to couples for whom the poisons and the climate had made the simple act of having a child a biological impossibility. Quick as a pick-pocket in reverse, the man tucked a card into my hand. Sweet kid you got there, the card whispered. Got a list of prospective parents as long as your arm. Give a good price, and no fancy paperwork, no questions asked. I tore the card up and threw it into the nearest bin.

Dead leaves clattered on the paths. The low sky trailed through withered trees. The ice-cream stall was boarded and bolted.

"Do you like it here?" I asked Robin, crouching down to help him on with the mittens that hung from elasticated straps.

"It's good," he said, breathing a little grey cloud at me.

"Have you ever been here before?"

"I don't know," he said. "Have you taken me?"

We walked across the damp grass to the swings. I pushed him slowly. The wet chains creaked. Ahead of us, the paddling pool had been drained. A bowl of flaking blue concrete, filled with leaves and the sludge of autumn. I remembered the children's voices, the water-wings, the bright spray.

"I thought Mummy might have come here with you once," I said. "In the spring."

"It would look different then?"

"Yes. All the birds would be singing. The sun shining. I thought Mummy might have taken you, perhaps with a nice uncle."

"A nice uncle?"

"You know, a grownup friend."

Robin tilted his head back from the swing to smile at me. He seemed to think it was some kind of joke.

"Come on," I said.

A gardener was tending a bonfire beside the damp greenhouses, raking the endless fall of leaves into a wheelbarrow, tipping them over the flames to produce more smoke. Robin and I walked up to him.

"Autumn's a popular season," he told us. "You'd think people would want sunshine, but they seem to like this melancholy place."

"What about spring?"

"That doesn't go down so well," he said. There was a dewdrop on his nose. It looked authentic, but as he raised his arm to wipe it on his ragged sleeve, I heard the faint whir of a faulty servo. Not snot, I supposed, but machine oil.

"But you *do* do spring?"

The smoke spiralled into his face. He didn't blink.

"Spring? Oh, yes. A week or so every couple of years."

"And when was the last time?"

He shrugged. "You'll have to speak to the mainframe about that. I don't have a long-term memory. I'm just a gardener, you know." The dewdrop was growing on his nose again: it made you want to sniff.

Robin got bored as we walked along the aimless paths around the boating lake. The boats were locked up for the winter. The sign above the boathouse said BOATS FOR HIRE. Close to, I could see that the peeling paint was actually carefully moulded plastic. I gazed across the black water of the lake. I checked the copy of the picture in my pocket.

"—don't—"

Robin looked up, surprised to hear his mummy's voice. I shrugged, patted his head. This is grownup business, son. Meena turned and smiled. She said, Don't.

I found the spot. Inevitably, it was a disappointment. Here in a different season, with minty smell of decay and the wind rattling the litter baskets. I gazed down at the picture again. Turning, smiling, saying, Don't. There, in sunlight, she looked happy and more real.

Robin was busy clambering up onto the park bench beside me. He was a little unsteady as he stood up. I lifted him in my arms, surprised at his lightness, his weight.

"Will you take me home?" he asked, looking me right in the eye.

I gave Robin a kiss at the stasis centre, ruffled his hair before he scampered off through the sliding doors. I waved. Back at the weekend, I promised. A different woman at Reception smiled. Perhaps I should follow Robin through those sliding doors. And thirty years from now, I could return to Meena, see the sags and wrinkles she couldn't afford to put right. Know her for just what she was, laugh freely in her aged face. But the thought was only a game. Although there was nothing to stop those who could afford it from going into long-term stasis, everyone knew from the bitter experience of the last hundred years that the future was a joke. The only guarantees were that the climate would be worse, and that everything apart from wristwatches, computers, and disposable umbrellas would be more expensive.

When I got back into the estate, I saw that the lips had gone from the billboard. There was a picture there now. A tropical beach. But the voice was still there. *Escape,* it whispered. *Treat yourself to the one luxury that money can't buy.* Invisibly, the lips smiled. *Well, maybe only just . . . Escape.* Beckoning palms, white sand. *Escape.* There, in the car, I couldn't help laughing. The Volvo innocently played me a little Dvořák, thinking I was happy.

★   ★   ★

Meena and I often talked about who we might be. Do *you* feel like a billionaire? Well, no, neither do I. If one of us was rich, it was probably Meena, we decided. She was more decisive, I was more romantic. We were noticing things about ourselves as much as about each other. The whole idea of this process of discovery was charmingly odd. How Meena liked some time alone walking on the beach each afternoon, my interest in the music the entertainment box provided. The foods we liked, the things we hated, the way we made love.

And were we in love? There was a sense of delicious honesty, sitting out on the rattan chairs with the palm trees dripping and the sea still grey after the afternoon rain, talking about ourselves as though we were other people. The things that we surprised each other with came as much a surprise to ourselves.

Yes, we agreed, holding hands as the sun came out and the jungle began to steam. This is a kind of love, a unique childhood innocence, the love you first feel for someone. When you really don't know them. When you ache with the specialness, the closeness, the new sharing. I mean, whoever said that love was about knowledge? And we vowed that we would remember this time, carry it with us like a jewel through whatever lay ahead.

Meena and I ran to the sea before dinner. We made love in the white bridal foam. Then Meena swam towards the sinking sun. She stood up and waved, then cried out as her foot struck something.

I helped her hop back to the bungalow. It was a deep, clean gash in the sole of her right foot. She must have caught the edge of a block of coral that the waves had washed in. She sat patiently as blood and seawater trickled over the veranda. Our little monkey ran out along the wooden rail. We had to smile when he saw Meena and pawed his face, chattering with what sounded like concern.

I called for Lin. You'd assume they would see to this sort of thing, I thought irritably, thumping the digits on the box. With the money we must be paying. But she arrived amazingly quickly.

This time, her sarong was green, shot through with golden yellow. She sprayed Meena's foot with something from the bag she was carrying.

"It'll need stitches," she said. Meena leaned forward to watch with curiosity when Lin got to work with silver and thread, as though it was someone else's foot.

Lin dropped the needle. It fell between a gap in the veranda boards. Lin sighed, then sat back and took a blade from her bag. She used it to cut open both of her wrists, then grasped the dry flaps and peeled the skin away from each hand. Beneath, there was clean steel.

"It'll be a lot quicker this way," she said, snipping her fingers like scissors.

When Lin had sprayed on Meena's bandage, she pulled the skin back onto her hands, smoothing out the wrinkles.

"It's so much easier to hold things, metal to metal," she said, smiling, looking cool and beautiful in her sarong. "I really don't know how you humans manage."

★　★　★

I found out about spring in the park. The last time they'd run it had been two months before. A special promotion, linked in with a new fashion design. SPRING IS FOR LOVERS . . . OF STYLE. Well, how ironic. I asked the park mainframe if it kept a list of visitors. Hauling out some ancient privacy programme from the depths of its memory, it told me to bugger off.

So I started to follow Meena. I hadn't made a sale all week anyway, and was running out of fresh prospects. I'd lost the edge. It's a hard life, being in sales — everyone's at it. It's the only job left, now that the machines see to all the important stuff.

The Volvo enjoyed tailing Meena's Casio. It took to playing Mahler. One minute the music was yearning, the next crashingly ironic; I couldn't decide whether I liked it or not.

Meena went to predeath receptions. She attended performance reviews at the Head Office. She visited clients. I sat in the Volvo under sick skies, watching from a discreet distance amid the rubble and the chattering billboards, the tightly fenced estates. Mahler rumbled on, symphony after symphony. I gazed at my copy of the photograph, propped on the steering wheel. Meena. Turning. Smiling. Don't. The clients Meena saw had big money, big houses. After she'd ducked back into the Casio and driven off through the rain, I had ten or so minutes to check at the door before the Volvo lost contact. Ding, dong, nice place you've got here, sir. And when was the last time you thought about security?

But they were all old, old. I could tell that all they were truly interested in was dying. So, for the hell of it, I started trying to sell that to them instead. And the joke was that they were all interested. Sure, Meena was busy seeing a lot of prospects, but sure as death itself, she wasn't closing her sales.

Meena criss-crossed the city in her Casio. Apart from wildly exaggerating her success rate, she did exactly what she told me she did when I quizzed her each evening. I thought, So this is your life, Meena. Another prospect, another meeting. And just exactly when is it that you smile?

★   ★   ★

I couldn't sleep that night. This island, the false beach, Lin a robot . . .

The moonlight fell brightly through the window nearest our bed. The jungle beyond was black, white. The trunk of the nearest palm was gashed by shadows, like the claw marks of some huge animal. And clinging to it with tiny hands, motionless, precise, was our little monkey. Gazing through our window, watching us with his gleaming eyes.

At dawn, with Meena still sleeping, I took a bucket and walked along the shore until I found a scatter of rock pools. The morning light was still incomplete, misty grey. I fished for little crabs amid the anemones, dropped them into my bucket, where they clambered over each other's backs like the celebrants of an orgy. When I'd collected a dozen or so, I squatted over a wide flat rock, tendrils of the waves running between my toes. I broke the shells open one by one. The first three crabs were pink inside, smelling of flesh and salt. But the fourth tried to scuttle away, trailing a silver necklace of circuits. I hit it again. It gave off a thin wisp of smoke, and was still.

When Meena awoke, and after we had made love, we took the Jeep for a picnic in the jungle. It found us a waterfall, a clear pool to dive in. Shining rocks, drifting clouds, and rainbows. Far above, impassive as a god, the great mountain at the centre of the island was half-veiled in cloud. As we sat like savages in the humid shade, eating with our fingers, drinking chilled wine from the bottle, we wondered if you could really touch the sky from up there. We planned an expedition to find out one day before the holiday ended, knowing that time was already growing shorter, knowing that we never would.

"Look!" Meena pointed as we climbed back into the Jeep. "Up there."

I gazed up into the green canopy.

"Can you see?"

I nodded. And after a few moments, I could.

"Our monkey," she said.

He was looking down at us from a thick vine. Those wise eyes.

"That's not possible," I said, shaking my head.

★ ★ ★

So I arranged a party. I invited all our friends. Meena said, But you hate parties. I insisted. I fixed the catering, bought the booze with money we didn't have. I wanted everyone here, everyone that she knew.

I was drunk before the guests arrived. It was a strange feeling, wandering, smiling, saying Hello, knowing that one of these people was probably The One. That here in my flat at this very moment, drinking my wine and tracing the circles of dust, were The Hands That Touched, The Lips That Kissed. The room swayed; the flat was having a good old time crammed with all these bodies, playing rock and roll. I watched Meena as she squeezed her way from group to group, looking for those secret signs, the smiles, the brush of fingers. Plain avoidance.

But there was nothing. I'd made a fool of myself. I went to throw up. I was swaying against the pull of the room. People were looking my way. I staggered into the cool of Robin's bedroom, slumped down on his tiny bed. Over the music, I yelled at the flat to close the bloody door. Then I lay back in the linen darkness. Mickey Mouse looked down at me, smiling.

Meena came in. She had left the door open and there was silence outside. The party had ended, and the air was stale yellow from all the drink and the talk. I must have slept.

"What the hell is the matter with you, Marius?"

"Too much to drink."

"I don't mean that."

"Do you love me?"

"Look," she said. "I've got a busy day tomorrow. A new customer wants to suffocate in a vat of Venusian atmosphere—something original and expensive for a change."

"You used to wear things when we made love. Said it made you feel more naked."

"You should have some water, take a paintab."

"What's gone wrong with us?"

"This isn't really the time to talk, is it?"

"Are you seeing someone else?"

She gazed down at me. I could hear the dark silence of Robin's little room hissing the word *Yes*.

"Meena, are you?"

"Am I what?"

"Seeing someone else?"

"No," she said. "Yes. Make up your own answer."

"I need to know the truth."

"What difference would that make? You can't imagine what it's like, Marius, living with you."

"We used to be happy."

"Yeah," she said. "We used to be happy."

She turned away.

"No, wait!" I shouted. My voice made the room spin.

She folded her arms. "What exactly is it that you want, Marius?"

"I found . . . there's a photograph of you, in a park. Turning and smiling. You look so happy. I found it in your second drawer."

"My drawer. How fucking typical."

"Meena!"

The flat slammed Robin's door behind her.

★   ★   ★

On another day we went into town. The flying boat had just landed—more new arrivals, with people waiting for them on the quay. The lips on the big billboard breathed *Welcome* across the bay. Feeling vaguely envious, Meena and I stood and watched for a moment, then wandered on through the narrow streets. There were little shops everywhere, wind-chimes and mementos droop-ing outside in the brilliant heat, interiors that reeked of mystery and leather and donkey dung. Of course, there were other tourists here, walking arm in arm, all deeply tanned, deeply in love. It spoilt things somewhat, to see your own feelings mirrored so easily in others. People only visit the town here late in their holidays, an ancient shopkeeper told us after we'd bargained for a soapstone box. When the novelty starts to wear off, he added. I looked at him sharply. Wet eyes, a slack, toothless mouth. Would the tour com-pany ever programme a robot to say something like that? I could even smell his breath. No, I decided. No.

We sat and took coffee in a white colonial square, resting, as-sessing our purchases, knowing that everything else would soon be a memory. We felt we'd bought wisely with our money. Not that the cash we had told us anything about what we could nor-mally afford; every visitor to the island was allocated the same amount.

After a while, a couple sat down with us at the tin table. They were both blond, handsome. I wondered if Meena and I could possibly give off the same scent of easy wealth. And I vaguely resented their intrusion — I was starting to count the remaining hours of our stay together — but they proved to be friendly, amusing. Of course, conversation was limited by our lack of memory, but that proved to be a surprising advantage. There was little scope for back-biting, point scoring. It was an egalitarian society here on the island — everyone could pretend to be a billionaire with reasonable conviction. So we laughed and joked together, fantasised outrageously about our real lives, wandered around more of the shops, watched the natives at work along the harbour until another marvellous tropical sunset began to tear the sky to glowing shreds.

★　★　★

A headache woke me in the morning. I was still dressed, crammed into Robin's cot with Mickey Mouse leering down at me. I hauled myself out and leaned against the window. This one was clear; we hadn't been able to afford the special glass for Robin's room. Not that I was complaining. As far as it was possible to make out from the dismal sky, the sun had been up for some hours. And the flat sounded quiet, empty. Meena had probably left hours ago. No chance of following her today.

I rubbed at my face, probed the weary bags under my eyes. Oh, Meena, Meena. Why can't we just fall back into love? Down on the estate, the lips were back on the poster. They seemed to smile specifically at me through a black flurry of rain. *Escape. Treat yourself to the one luxury that money can't buy. Well, maybe only just* . . . Yeah, I grinned back. If only.

I padded around at Robin's tidy little room. All the toys put away, no fingerprints or crayon marks on the walls, no Play-Doh sticking to the carpet. The poor kid; he was hardly real, hardly here at all. And whose fault was that, I wondered. Whose fault was that? I picked up Teddy from on top of the wardrobe. He grinned at me and said, "Hello, little fella, want to play?" I put him back down. He slumped, looking disappointed.

I opened Robin's top drawer. His tiny clothes. Red dungarees, white socks, blue mittens. Just like Meena, he felt more real to me this way. No sulks, no moaning "Daddy Daddy," no wanting stuff we could never afford, making us feel like inadequate parents. Not that he was a bad kid, but still. A couple of drawers below, I found some of his baby things. I held up a romper suit, still stained around the front from some battle in the high chair. Jesus, had he ever been *that* small? As I moved to put it back, I heard a voice. I glared at the teddy bear to shut up, thinking for a moment that it was him.

"—hey Mu—"

But it was Robin's voice. I looked down into the drawer. Beneath an old bib, I saw daylight, some photographs held together by an elastic band.

"—watch m—"

A park in spring. A tree nodding. Robin by a bench. Then Robin climbing onto it.

"—careful dar—" Meena's happy voice behind the camera.

Robin standing on the bench, giggling. One shot of him from the other side of the path, then another, much closer.

"—let me—" Robin's hand reaching out towards the lens, the fingers huge, unfocused.

Then a shot of the gravel. The dancing spring shadows of the trees. Meena's voice saying:

"—e careful—"

"—now—"

The last shot had drifted somewhere else, got lost in another drawer the way these things always do. But Meena said, Don't. I didn't need the photograph to hear her voice.

★　★　★

The palms were swaying wildly against the moon when the Jeep took us back from town. But there was little wind—we had spent the evening dancing in a lamplit square, and we were both very merry, very drunk.

We stumbled around the bedroom in the bungalow, falling over our clothes as we tried to get out of them.

"Today's the last but one," Meena said with sudden clarity.

I flopped onto the bed to watch the ceiling revolve.

"It'll be your turn to leave first," Meena added, her voice fading off into the bathroom. "Seeing as you arrived here before me."

I heard the shower running. When she came back out, drying her hair, the room was still spinning. I pretended that I was asleep.

She turned off the light, shuffled and grunted, then started to breathe heavily, her bottom sticking out into my side of the bed. I could see the bright darkness of the jungle out of the window. It all looked pretty and safe. No mosquitoes, no snakes, no spiders. And even if there were any such beasts, they would be charming and eccentric. User-friendly.

There on the shadow-slashed trunk of the nearest tree, the wise-faced monkey gazed down at me. Eventually, I had to get up and close the curtains.

★　★　★

Escape. The lips smiled at me. *Treat yourself to the one luxury that money can't buy.* I drove in silence. For once, the Volvo was lost for an appropriate tune. When the automatic gates from the estate failed to open, I had to get out and do it manually, battling my way through a sleet of soot and litter. *Escape.* The voice was loud on the wind. Marius, it called after me. Marius. I climbed back inside and the Volvo slammed the door, getting my mood right for a change. Marius. Marius. Don't. I froze. But no, it was just the wind, just my imagination.

Jealousy, I decided, was like one of the pure states of the soul that the mystics used to strive for. All-encompassing, it lit your every thought. Like moving underwater, or through another world, things had a different life. I realised that, for a while at least, the photograph had given my life meaning. It had helped me remember the Meena I had loved. She had twirled ahead of me on this pointless trail, flowing in bright ribbons of memory, beautiful and strange as a temple dancer. Meena, my smiling Meena. The Meena that existed only in my head. Somehow, she had led the way.

Robin ran out towards me through the sliding doors at the stasis centre. I scooped him up, gave him a hug.

He asked, "What day is it, Daddy?" He smelled like the place itself, of coffee and polythene.

I had to think. Yes, Wednesday. Another Wednesday. Seemed that poor Robin's life was a succession of Wednesdays. Face facts; we weren't good enough for him.

"Let's go to the park," I said, taking his hand. "There's a man there I want you to meet. Or if he's not there, we could go look for him at Toys 'R' Us."

Robin stared at me, mittens swinging on their elastic on the ends of his sleeves. Blink, blink. Click, click. He asked, "Was that the man at the gate, Daddy, the one who gave you the talking card that said I was worth so much money?"

I managed a smile. A sweet, bright kid. Was there anything he didn't notice?

★　★　★

Our last full day together on the island went quickly. The sun was as bright as ever, the beach as white, the sea as warm. But everything was pervaded with the cool melancholy that comes like a wind from nowhere on these occasions. We had planned on going out again on our yacht, but when we walked to the little cove, we found that it had gone, presumably reallocated to one of the new arrivals. With that discovery came the awkward thought that perhaps we hadn't been able to afford to keep a yacht for the whole of our holiday, and also of the days that it had been floating unused in the clear water, muttering sea-shanties to its ghostly crew, clocking up a bill that we would perhaps struggle to pay.

Lin came around in the afternoon. Now that I knew the truth, everything about her seemed artificial. Her smiles, her sarongs. And when she went inside our bungalow, I couldn't help thinking that she was simply checking that we hadn't broken anything. She asked about Meena's foot. She asked if we'd had a good time. I sat on the veranda, listening to the sea, hardly bothering to answer. And that night on the beach, we sent the crab-robot into the sea and lit a fire just as we had done on the first night. But the fish was bony and ill-cooked, and afterwards, even Meena didn't taste the same.

★ ★ ★

Crab-robots were dismantling the billboard when I drove back to the flat, crawling over the silent lips like ants on a corpse. I had the tickets to the island lying on the passenger seat, so I guessed the lips had served their purpose, managed at least one sale. Everyone's at it nowadays, selling things — even the machines. And soon they'll be better than us, and what the hell are we all going to do then?

Through the dripping car park, the lift wanted a bribe to take me up. In an expansive mood, I gave it what it asked for without haggling. The flat smelled of toast and damp daylight, cheap wine still from the party, cheap living, cheap lives. There was a sound coming from the bedroom. Someone was groaning, going uh, uh, uh.

I stood in the narrow hall, my heart racing, the tickets going damp in my hands. Meena's voice. Uh, uh. From the bedroom. I felt vindicated — wronged — but at the same time, my mind was a blank. Step by step, a million miles at a time, I walked towards the half-open door.

Meena was lying on the bed under the light of a tropical moon, tangled in her work clothes, her glowing laptop thrown open beside her. She raised her face and looked up at me through streaming tears.

"I thought," I said. My shoulders slumped. "I don't know. I just thought."

"You know what they've gone and done, don't you?" she said.

I stared at her. She was fumbling under her pillow, searching for a tissue, trying to sniff back the tears, embarrassed to be seen this way, even by me, her husband.

"They've given me the sack." She blew her nose. "Say my performance has dropped below . . . below an acceptable level." The tropical moon settled in the pool in each of her eyes. "Now where the hell does that leave us, you tell me that, Marius? You tell me that."

I sat down beside her. I took her hand. My movements were slow and solid. I felt heavy with control.

"It's all right, my darling," I told her.

She looked at me, wanting me to take over, to take care. Her whole face was shining, washed clean. Like an old-fashioned street after some old-fashioned rain, like something from the past.

She began to sob deeply again when I showed her the tickets, and even more so when I told her what I had done. That I'd sold Robin. But I sat patiently, gazing at her in the light of a tropical moon, listening to the sound of waves. My Meena. I held her hand. My Meena. She trembled to my touch, but she didn't push me away. I kissed her face, and she tasted like the waves of a warm tropical sea laddered by moonlight. Then I told the flat to blank the window, and for once the flat didn't argue, and it was just the two of us and the darkness and the faint humming that lies at the background of everything, like the turning of a huge machine. My Meena. My heart was thick and slow with gratitude, control, love. My Meena. I took her in my arms, knowing at last that she understood.

★   ★   ★

Meena was up early on the final morning, putting all her lovely clothes back into their case. It had been so hot—and we'd been so much in love—that she'd had little chance to wear many of them. Would we be able to keep them? I wondered, watching. When we get back, will we care?

"What are you going to do this afternoon?" I asked Meena after I'd packed my own things. "When you're alone after my flying boat has gone."

"It's only a few hours' wait, isn't it?" she said, pulling out her drawers to check they were empty. "I'll just wander around the town. I mean, Marius, what did you do on the first day?"

I shrugged. Quite honestly, I couldn't remember. Inevitably, and for all the lovely charade at the harbour, you seemed to drift to and away from this island rather than reach it with the solid bump of one moment.

"It's a nice idea, though, isn't it?" Meena said, holding up a final blouse. "Arriving and leaving on different flying boats. Makes everything more happy and sad. . . . Look at this." She fished something from the silk pocket, the photograph she'd found in her case on that very first day. "I'd quite forgotten."

I nodded. So had I—but now I was standing at the bedroom door. I hated hanging around like this, protracted good-byes. Although there was still plenty of time, I wanted us to leave the bungalow now, get into the Jeep and away.

She held the photograph up to her face. The light from it had a different quality. It was softer, bluer. Her voice said, "—don't—"

"I wonder how this got here?" she said. "It's hard to imagine that it was purely an accident. Perhaps it's some kind of message."

"—don't—"

"Yes," I said. "More likely, we'll never know."

"Well, I'll just wander along the beach for a while. Say my good-byes." Meena clicked the catches on her case. "There's plenty of time yet. You don't mind waiting here, darling, do you?"

She had wandered off down the steps of the veranda towards the sea before I had time to compose a reply.

The bedroom seemed to close and darken behind her. Ready now for someone else, it shrugged off our traces so easily.

Hearing a sound on the window ledge, I turned. The monkey, sitting there. Somehow he'd grabbed hold of Meena's photograph, and was studying it. The strange sunlight shone on his wise, nervous face. "—don't—" Meena said. Don't. He just stared. Blink, blink. Click, click. He put the photograph to his mouth, nibbled cautiously at the plastic the way any real monkey would have done. Then he looked at me. A challenging stare, filled with smug knowledge.

Feeling sudden anger, I ran over to him. The monkey was slow, conditioned by our affection and sultanas. I grabbed a thin arm. He was light. He didn't struggle, but went stiff with fear—or more likely, was conserving battery power for a sudden burst of speed.

Right. I spread-eagled him with my hands on the pine floor. I was sick of being watched, analysed. The silver eyes blinked. I stared into them, seeing through and down to a control room somewhere, guys in greasy vests with their feet up, sipping preform cups as they watched the screens, saying, Hey, will you just see that lady. Right. I looked around for something hard, sharp. But the bedroom was clear and empty. I grabbed the monkey roughly by the neck, hauled it into the kitchen. The floor pattered behind me, a watery trail of ordure. Yeah, I thought, how realistic, picturing the guy in the vest at the far end of the link, hitting the appropriate button.

I held the monkey down on the cutting board and reached for the nearest thing on the antique rack. Which turned out to be a meat tenderiser. Through the window, there was blue sea, palm trees, lacy waves. The monkey still wasn't putting up a fight, which I found somehow disappointing. He just stared up at me, his tiny mouth half-bared, showing his tiny teeth, his helpless pink tongue. I released my grip slightly, daring him to try to nip me. The monkey just shivered, stared at me with those old, wise eyes.

I let go, wondering if this was a demonstration of mercy or a simple failure of nerve. The monkey pulled himself up and stared, squatting on the work surface. He gave a shrill chatter and rubbed at his face. Then he looked hopefully up at the jar of sultanas. I had to smile, but when I reached for them, he started, jumped down, and sprinted from the kitchen, through the bedroom door, up out of the window, blurring into the green shadows beyond.

I stood for a while at the window, but there was nothing to see but the tangled beauty of the jungle. Turning back to the bedroom, I saw the photograph of Meena lying on the pine floor. I picked her up. She turned towards me and smiled.

"—don't—"

I smiled back, then tucked the photograph into my back pocket. My Meena. A memory. An odd kind of memento of this odd, happy holiday.

I got the crab-robot to clear up the mess the monkey had left, then carried our cases out to the Jeep. Sitting down on them, I gazed around at heaven for the last time. There was no sign of the monkey, but through the gently nodding palms I could see the white speck of the flying boat as it turned along the island, preparing to touch down. Listening to the faint and somehow reassuring hum of its engines, I sat and waited for my Meena to return along the shore.

Tirkiluk

Radio Transmission from *Queen of Erin* via Lerwick to Meteorological Intelligence, Godalming
Confirm Science Officer Seymour disembarked Logos II Weatherbase Tuiak Bay July 28. Science Officer Cayman boarded in adequate health. No enemy activity sighted. Visibility good. Wind Force 4 east veering north. Clear sea. Returning.

★ ★ ★

Noon, July 29th, 1942
Stood watching on the shingle as the *Queen of Erin* lifted anchor and steamed south. I really don't feel alone. The gulls were screaming and wheeling, the seabirds were crowding the rocks, and just as the *Queen* finally vanished around the headland, the huge grey gleaming back of a whale broke from the water barely two hundred yards from the shore, crashing in billows of spray and steam. I take it as a sign of welcome.

Evening, August 2nd
Have been giving the main and backup generators a thorough overhaul. Warm enough to work outside the hut in shirtsleeves — but you only have to look around to see what winter will bring. The mountains north of this valley look as though they've been here forever, and the glacier nosing between down from the

icefields is just too big to believe. It's twenty miles off, and I can barely span it with my outstretched hand. Feel very small.

Noon, August 3rd

Spent a dreadful night on the bunk as the blackfly and mosquito insect bites began to swell and itch. The itching has gone now, but I'm covered in scabs and weeping sores. Hope that nothing gets infected.

Evening, August 6th

Wish I'd had more of a chance to talk with Frank Cayman before we exchanged, but there were all the technical details to go over, and the supplies to unload. He did tell me he was part of a Cambridge expedition to Patagonia in 1935, which, like my own brief prewar experience with the solar eclipse over South Orkneys, was seen as proof of aptitude for maintaining an Arctic weather station. He's a geologist — but then the prewar specialisations of the Science Officers I met at Godalming made no sense, either. Odd to think that many of us are scattered across the Arctic in solitary huts now, or freezing and rocking through the storms on some tiny converted trawler. Of the two — and after my experience on the *Queen of Erin,* and the all-pervading reek of rancid herring — I think I'm glad I was posted on dry ground.

Frank Cayman looked healthy enough, anyway, apart from that frostbitten nose. But he was so *very* quiet. Not subdued, but just drawn in on himself. Was impressed at the start with how neat he's left everything here, but now I can see that there is no other option. You have to be organised.

Evening, August 9th

My call-sign response from Godalming is Capella, that bright G-type sister of the sun. It means, as I expected, that Kay Alexander is my Monitoring Officer. Funny to think of her, sitting there with her headphones in that draughty hut by the disused tennis courts, noting down these bleeps I send out on the cypher grid. An odd kind of intimacy: without speech transmissions, and with usually just a curt coded reply of Message Received (no point in crowding the airwaves). Find that I'm rereading the two requests I've received for more specific cloud data, as though Kay would do anything more than encode and relay them, chewing her pencil and pushing back strands of red hair.

Too late for regrets now. And at the moment I miss the stars more than the people, to be honest. Even at midnight, the sky is still so pearly bright that I can barely make out the major constellations. But that will change.

Evening, August 12th

A great bull seal came up onto the beach this morning as I was laying out my washing on the rocks to dry. Whiskered, with huge battle-scarred tusks, he really did look like something out of Lewis Carroll. Think we both saw each other at about the same time. He looked at me, and I looked at him. I stumbled back towards the hut, and he turned at speed and lumbered back into the waves. I'm not sure which of us was more frightened.

Evening, August 30th

Really must record what I get up to each day.

I'm usually awake at 7:30, and prime the stove and breakfast at eight. Slop out afterwards, then read from my already dwindling supply of unread books until nine. After that, I have to go out and read the instruments. Twelve-hour wind speed, direction, min and max temperature, air pressure, precipitation, cloud height and formation, visibility, sea conditions, frequency and size of any sighted icebergs—have to do this here at the hut, and then halfway up the valley at the poetically named Point B.

Every other day, if conditions permit, I also have to send up the balloon. On those days—lugging the gas canisters and getting the lines straight, then hauling it all in again—there's time for little else before evening, when I have to read off all the measurements here and then trudge up to Point B again. On the alternate days, there's all the domestic trivia of living. Cooking, cleaning, washing, collecting water from the river, scraping off the grey mould that keeps growing on the walls of this hut. Then I have to encode the information and prime up the generator so that valves are warmed and ready to transmit at nineteen hundred hours local time. Then dinner, and try as I might, the tins and the dry reheated blocks all taste the same.

Then listen to the BBC, if the atmosphere is reflecting the signals my way. Thought the radio would be more of a comfort than it actually is. Those fading voices talking about cafés and trains and air-raids make me feel more alone than gazing out of the window ever does.

September 10th

Saw another human being today. I knew that there are Eskimos in this region, but when you get here everything seems so vast and—*empty* isn't the word, because the sea and the valley are teeming with birds, and I've glimpsed caribou, foxes, what might have been musk oxen, and hare—*unhuman*, I suppose. But there it is. I'm not alone.

Was up at Point B, taking the morning measurements. Point

B is a kind of rocky platform, with a drop on one side down to the valley floor and the river from which I gather my water plunging over the rocks, and ragged cliffs rising in a series of grass-tufted platforms on the other. I heard a kind of grunting sound. I looked up, expecting an animal, fearing, in fact, my first encounter with a polar bear. But instead, a squat human figure was outlined on the clifftop, looking down at me, plaits of hair blowing in the wind, a rifle strapped to his back. In a moment, he stepped out of sight.

Frank Cayman told me that he hadn't seen any Eskimos, but he showed me on the map where there were signs of a campground. The tribes here are nomadic, and my feeling is that they must be returning to this area after some time away, probably stocking up with meat on the high plains below the glacier before moving south as the winter darkness rolls in.

They're likely to be used to seeing white men—the Arctic Ocean was a thriving whaling and fishing-ground before the war—but I was warned at Godalming to be very wary of them. Was told that Eskimos are thieving, diseased, immoral, not averse to selling information to the skipper of any stray German sub, etc., etc.

I suppose I should keep my head down, and padlock my hut and supply shed every time I go out. But now that I know I'm not alone, I think I might try to meet them.

September 14th

A long, long day, and the preternatural darkness that fills the air now that the clouds are moving in and the sun is sliced for so long by the horizon gives the whole exploit a weird sense of dream.

I found the Eskimo encampment. It lies a little west of the place Frank Cayman showed me on the map, and was easily visible once I'd climbed north beyond Point B out of the valley from the rising smoke at the edge of the boggy land before the mountains. It's only about ten miles off, but it took me most of six hours to get there, and my boots and leggings were sodden.

No igloos, of course, but it was still odd to see Eskimos living in what looks remarkably like a red Indian encampment from an American Western movie, and even more so because peat-smoke and the dimming light gave the whole place a sort of cinematic grainy black-and-whiteness.

Was unprepared for the smell, especially inside the tent of caribou skin and hollowed earth that I was taken into. Seem to

regard urine as a precious commodity. They use it for tanning—
which is understandable—but also to wash their hair. But for all
that, I was made welcome enough when I squelched towards the
camp yelling "*Teyma!*" (Peace—one of the few Eskimo words I can
remember), although the children prodded me and the dogs
growled and barked. A man called Unluku, one of the elders,
could speak good English—with a colourful use of language he'd
learned from the whalers. He told me that they knew about my
hut, and that they didn't mind my being there because I wasn't
eating their caribou or their seals. Also asked him what they knew
about the war. Stroking the head of the baby who sat suckling on
his mother's lap beside him, he said they knew that *kaboola*—
white man—was killing himself. They strike me as a decent people; strange and smelly and mercurial, but content with their lives.

September 15th

Rereading my encounter with the Eskimos, I don't think I've
really conveyed their sense of otherness, strangeness.

The liquefying maggoty carcasses of several caribou had been
left at the edge of the camp-ground, seemingly to rot, although I
gathered that this was their store of food. And, although the
people looked generally plump and cheerful, there was one figure
squatting in the middle of the rough ring of tents, roped to a
whalebone stake. The children would occasionally scoop up a pile
of dog excrement and throw it at him, and Unluku took the trouble to walk over and aim a loose kick. He said the figure was Inua,
which I assumed to be some kind of criminal or scapegoat,
although tried to look it up, and the closest I can come is a kind
of shaman. Perhaps it was just his name. I don't know, and the
sense that I got from those Eskimos was that I never could.

September 20th

Supply ship came this morning—the *Tynwald.* Was expecting
her sometime today or tomorrow. I was given a few much-read
and out-of-date copies of the *Daily Mirror,* obviously in the expectation that I would want to know how the world and the war and
Jane are getting on. And more food, and spare lanterns, and a full
winter's supply of oil. And fresh circulars from Godalming, includ-
ing one about the pilfering of blotting paper.

Stood and watched the ship turn around the headland. Say
they'll probably manage to get back one more time before the
route between the islands becomes impassable. Already, I'm losing
the names and the faces.

October 1st

Looking out through the hut window now, Venus is shining through the teeth of white mountains in the halo of the sun where the wind shrieks and growls, and the Milky Way twines like a great river across the deep blue sky, striated by bands of interstellar dust, clearer than I've ever seen before.

I seem to have come a long way, just to make some sense of my life.

October 12th

The Eskimo encampment is gone. Climbed up from Point B to the edge of the valley this morning when the full moon was shining, and my old prewar Zeiss binoculars could make everything out through the clear sharp air.

No moon now. The edge of the sky is a milky shade in the corner that hides the sun, and the wind is up to Force 6. There were snow flurries yesterday, but somehow their absence today makes everything all the more ominous.

October 16th

Three days of dreadful weather—only managed one trip up to Point B, and the balloon was out of the question.

Then this. Been out for hours, slowly freezing, totally entranced by Aurora Borealis, the Northern Lights. Like curtains of silk drawn across the sky. A faintly hissing waterfall of light. Shifting endlessly. Yet vast. There are no words.

I think of charged particles streaming from the sun, swirling around the earth's magnetic field. Even the science sounds half-magical. I must—

An interruption. A clatter outside by the storage shed that sounded too purposeful to be just the wind. And the door was open—forced—flapping to and fro. Must say I felt afraid, standing there with the wind screaming around me in the flickering auroral half-light. I've refixed it now (cut my thumb, but not badly), and I've got the little .22 rifle beside me as I sit at this desk, as though that would be any use. But must say I feel lonely and afraid, as these great hissing curtains of light sway across the sky beyond my window.

But—being practical—it simply means that some of the Eskimos haven't gone south, and that they have light fingers (although I can't find anything missing), just as I was warned by the trainers at Godalming. Suppose this is my first real test.

October 20th

Out today in better weather taking readings in the pallid light before my fingers froze, I saw a ragged human figure about quarter of a mile down the freezing beach. I assume that this must be my Eskimo-thief. Once I'd seen him, somehow didn't feel afraid.

Went down along the beach afterwards. I made out a grey lump in the darkness that the waves were pushing up the shore. It was the body of a *long* dead seal—not something that I would ever like to consider eating, although from the fresh rents and the stinking spillage over the rocks, this was obviously exactly what the figure had been doing.

Was he *that* desperate, or, in view of the rotting caribou I saw at the camp-ground, am I still stuck in the irrelevant values of a distant civilisation? Was always impressed by the story of those Victorian polar explorers like Franklin, who ended up eating each other and dying in a landscape that the Eskimos lived off and regarded as home.

But still, I feel sorry for my Eskimo-thief, and am even tempted to put something outside the hut and see what happens, although I'm probably just going to attract the white wolves or foxes, or the bears. It might seem like an act of foolishness, but more likely it stems from gratitude towards my Eskimo-thief, and for the fact that I don't feel quite as afraid or alone any longer.

October 22

My Eskimo-thief is squatting in the hut with me now. Eating, I have to say, like a dog. There's a gale howling, and alarming drifts of snow. Easily the worst weather so far. He was hauling himself across the beach on hands and knees, crusted in ice, trying to grab a broken-winged tern. He still hasn't spoken. His clothes are filthy, moulting caribou hair all over the hut, and he looks almost a child. Very young.

I think he was probably the figure I saw roped to the whale-bone stake, which I suppose means that he must be some kind of criminal or scapegoat. The tribe has obviously moved south and left him behind. I recall the stories of how the Eskimo are supposed to leave their ill, elderly, and unwanted outside in winter for the cold and the wolves to finish off.

He wants more. If he can devour unheated pemmican like this, he must be very hungry.

But he can't be too ill.

Evening

I've made a stupid assumption. My Eskimo-thief is a woman.

October 24

The storm has died down. The twilight is deepening, but I still get the sun for a few hours around noon and the bay as yet hasn't iced over.

My Eskimo-thief is called Tirkiluk. I discovered her sex when, after she'd finally finished eating, she pulled down the saucepan from over the stove with some effort, unwound her furs, and squatted over it to urinate. She's terribly malnourished. Painfully bare ribs, a swollen belly.

October 27

Hard to tell under all those layers of fur, but Tirkiluk seems to be improving. She still mostly wanders up and down the ashen shore muttering to herself, or sits rocking on her haunches under a sort of awning that she's rigged up in front of the hut out of canvas from the supply shed and driftwood from the shore. Did I really save her life? Was she abandoned by the tribe? Was I just interfering?

October 29

The supply ship came today. The *Silverdale Glen.* Tirkiluk started shrieking *Kaboola!* and I ran out from the hut and saw the red-and-green lights bobbing out in the bay. Thought for one odd moment that the stars were moving.

I got many knowing looks from the sailors when they saw Tirkiluk sitting on a rock down the beach. Many of them fished these waters before the war, and of course there are the stories about Eskimo wives being offered as a gesture of hospitality. So, and despite her appearance, the crew of the *Silverdale Glen* assume that I've taken Tirkiluk to comfort me through the months of Arctic night, and I know that any attempts at denial would have been counterproductive.

They've gone now, and I'm alone for the winter. It's likely as not, I suppose, that word of Tirkiluk will get back to Godalming.

November 1

Went out to collect water this morning. The storm of the past few days has died entirely, and waves are sluggish, black as Chinese lacquer. Down on the shore, discovered that the water around the rocky inlet where the river discharges has formed a crust of ice. You can almost feel the temperature dropping, the ancient weight of the dark palaeocrystic ice-cap bearing down through the mountains, the weather changing, turning, tightening, notch by notch by notch. Soon, I think, the whole bay will freeze over.

Tirkiluk still sits outside.

November 6

Tirkiluk and I are making some progress in our attempts to converse. Her language bears little resemblance to the Inuit I was taught, although she's surprisingly adept at picking up English. Often, as I try to explain what the place I come from is like, and about the war and my monitoring of the weather, or when she describes the myths and rovings and bickerings of her tribe, we meet halfway. Don't think anyone who overheard would understand a word of it, and a great deal of it is still lost between us. She seems to speak with affection for the tribe, and ignores my attempts to discover why she was left here when they moved on.

November 12

The bay is now solid ice, and the weather has cleared. Earlier, I stood outside with Tirkiluk, pointing out the brightest stars, the main constellations, naked-eye binaries. She recognised many stellar objects herself, and gave them names—and myths or stories that were too complex for our pidgin conversation to convey. The Inuit are deeply familiar with the night sky.

Everything is incredibly clear, although somehow the idea of measurement and observation seems out of place. There's an extraordinary sense of depth to the Arctic sky. Really sense the distance between the stars.

One of the oddest things for me is the almost circular movement of the heavens, and the loss in the low horizon of stars like Alkaid, although in this dazzling darkness, many others have been gained. Counted fourteen stars in the Pleiades when my usual record is eleven, and Mu Cephei glows like a tiny coal. There is still *some* degree tilt to the stellar horizon. Aquila (which Tirkiluk calls Aagyuuk and has some significance for her that she tries but can't explain) has now set entirely.

November 20

The gales have returned, and Tirkiluk and I now share the hut. Much to her puzzlement, have rigged up one of the canvas awnings across the roof beam, which makes for two very awkward spaces instead of a single moderately awkward one. She sleeps curled up on a rug on the floor. When I lie awake listening to the wind and the ice in the bay groaning, can hear her softly snoring.

November 22

Must say that, despite reservations about her personal habits, I welcome her company, although I realise that I came here fully expecting—and wanting—to be left on my own. But she doesn't intrude, which I suppose comes from living close to many other people in those stinking little tents. We can go for hours without speaking, one hardly noticing that the other is there, so in a sense I don't feel that I really have lost my solitude. Then at other times, we both become so absorbed in the slow process of communication that yesterday I forgot to go out and knock the ice off the transmitter wires, and nearly missed the evening transmission.

She told me an Inuit story about the sun and the moon, who came down to earth and played "dousing the lights"—a self-explanatory Inuit sex-game of the kind that so shocked the early missionaries. But the sun and the moon are brother and sister, and in the steamy darkness of an Eskimo hut, they unwittingly broke the incest taboo. So when the lamps were relit, the moon in his shame smeared his face with lantern soot, and the sun set herself alight with lantern oil, and the two of them ran out across the sky, where they still chase each other to this day, yet never dare to meet. It all seemed so poetic—and the story was such an effort for Tirkiluk to get out—that I didn't attempt to ask what happens when there's an eclipse.

November 28

This morning, took a shovel from outside to clear a way through the crystal drift that half-covers the supply shed. Hands were bare, and the freezing metal stuck to my skin. In stupid panic, I ripped a big flap of skin off my palm. I staggered back out of the gale into the hut, dripping blood, grabbing the medicine box and trying to open it one-handed. But Tirkiluk made me sit down, and licked the wound—which was oddly soothing—breathing over it, muttering what I imagine is some incantation, making me stretch my fingers. The weirdest thing is that it hardly hurts at all now, and seems to be healing already. But I've dosed it in iodine, just to be safe.

December 1

Hand almost completely healed.

Better weather—the low cirrus sky glows with an odd light that could be the hidden moon or refracted from the sun or even the Northern Lights. Tirkiluk and I went out walking along the flat glistening bay. With her encouragement, I took out the .22 rifle, and had a lucky shot at a seal that was lying on the ice. The bullet was too small to kill, but Tirkiluk ran over to the creature as it lumbered around, apparently too lost or dazed to find its airhole, and slit it wide open with the bone-handled knife she always carries. Blood and hot offal spewed everywhere, dark as ink, and the flanks quivered and those big dark eyes still stared as she proceeded to eat the steaming liver, offering it to me to share.

Somehow, I would never have considered killing any of the local wildlife without Tirkiluk. But with her, and despite the churning in my stomach, it seemed oddly right. Against Tirkiluk's protests, I have lugged the carcass back to the hut and left it outside to freeze. Did have plans to try to cook it, but now I'm just wondering how I'll ever get rid of it in the spring.

December 2

Needn't have worried. I was woken last night by a shuffling and grunting outside the hut, and by Tirkiluk's smelly hand pressed hard across my mouth to make sure I stayed silent. We crept to the window together and cleared a small space in the dirty crust of ice. There was a polar bear, dragging off the carcass of the seal. An incredible beast. Know now why Tirkiluk didn't want me to drag the seal back to the hut. And understand the Inuit word *ilira*, which is the awe which accompanies fear.

December 7

Looking back at this journal, I see that I imagined Tirkiluk's name was Inua when I saw her at the camp-ground. She tells me now that Inua is actually some fingerless hag who lives at the bottom of the sea, although she can't or won't explain why there should be any connection with her.

December 13

Beyond the edge of the bay, hidden in a steep ravine that I must have walked past many times without even noticing, Tirkiluk has shown me a place of bones. Somehow, the ice and snow hardly settle there. Thought at first that it was simply a place where unwary caribou and musk oxen had fallen and died over the years, but to my horror, and in the eerie light of a clear moon, I saw that there were many human skulls amongst the rocks.

Said her tribe has several places like this, where they leave their dead. I suppose there's little chance of burial with the ground frozen for almost half the year, and any bodies left out would be dragged away like my seal. But she's matter-of-fact about it. She kept pointing and saying something about herself, and repeating bits of the story of "dousing the lights," and the sun and the moon. There's some message I don't understand.

December 18

Understand now why Tirkiluk was abandoned. Discovery is of far more than academic curiosity. Hardly know where to begin.

Have seen her seminaked a few times. She doesn't exactly wash herself, but she goes through an elaborate process of scraping her skin clean with her knife. Although I've tried hard not to look at this and other aspects of her toilet, it's difficult to have something like that going on in the hut—usually accompanied by her rambling half-spoken songs—without taking notice. She's put on some weight, but I'd assumed until now that the continued swelling in her belly was a by-product of earlier malnutrition. Now, I realise the significance of the sun and moon incest story that she keeps telling, and the reason why she was thrown out of the tribe.

Tirkiluk is heavily pregnant, by a half-brother named Iquluut. Think he was the hunter I saw looking down at me from Point B all those weeks ago. He's a senior in the tribe, twice her age, and apparently as the male he's regarded as blameless in the liaison, even by Tirkiluk herself. I shouldn't try to judge, but I know that in many ways the Inuit treat their women badly. A "good" wife is regarded as being worth slightly less than a decent team of dogs, and a "bad" one is unceremoniously dumped. And love doesn't come into the Inuit way of life at all, although lust—male, and female—certainly does.

But there's nothing I can do about all this. Winter has closed in, and Tirkiluk and I are stuck together like Siamese twins in this hut. Just hope she can find a better life with some other tribe in the spring—although she says she'll have to travel what she regards as impossibly far to reach any of her people who will take her. Have to see if I can't wrangle her a passage down to one of the southern ports on the supply boat when it finally comes in the spring, although I saw enough of "Westernised" Eskimo life around the docks at Neimaagen not to wish it on anyone. Least of all Tirkiluk.

December 19

Have looked in all the reference books I've been provided with, and wasn't surprised to find that there was no guidance about childbirth. Can't bring myself to radio Godalming for advice. Not sure whether that's pride, or the certainty that they wouldn't respond.

Christmas day—

and I've opened the bottle of rum that I've been saving until now. Tirkiluk spluttered and spat out the first sip, but then a wide grin spread across her broad face, and she held out her cup and asked for more. Eskimos are obviously used to drink. Think, in fact, that she's holding it better than I am.

Did my best this morning to tell the Nativity story—very appropriate in the circumstances. Tirkiluk knows all about Christian heaven and hell. She thinks hell is a warm place where only white man is allowed to go. Can think of worse places than hell. Even now, in the cheery glow that comes from the drink and the light of the stove and the lanterns, the cold penetrates easily through the triple insulated walls of this hut, and a sense of damp chill slides like an embrace around your back and into your bones. You can never escape it. As far as I can tell from talking to Tirkiluk and rereading the books, the Inuit don't believe in an afterlife. The spirits just drift and return, drift and return.

Even today, the war must go on. Both trekked up to Point B to take measurements from the few instruments that haven't frozen solid. The wind was biting, driven with gravel-like ice, but I taught her "Once in Royal David's City" as we felt our way in the wild grey darkness. Somehow managed to sing, even though had to turn our heads away from the wind just to breathe.

Could stand my frozen beaverskin coat up on its own like a suit of armour when we returned to the hut, and somehow it made an odd, dark presence. I think of that line about "the third who walks always beside you" in *The Waste Land,* and Shackleton's account of that terrible final climb over the mountains of South Georgia. Tirkiluk's matted and moulting furs work far better, although that's probably simply because it's her that's wearing them.

Lost the blood from my right foot entirely today, and after nearly roasting the dead white flesh on top of the stove, gave in to Tirkiluk and let her hold it and rub it against her hard round belly, clicking the odd-shaped stones and polar bear teeth that she has strung around her neck. For the first time in my life—and in the oddest imaginable circumstances—I felt a baby kick. But, as usual, she muttered some incantation, and as usual, it seemed to work.

I've just radioed Godalming. Was rather hoping for more than the usual Message Received code I got in return.

★　★　★

Godalming no transmission stopped No ship for months Must live with this pa

Leave my possessions to my beloved Mother in the ho

★　★　★

Strong enough to keep record now. Important if things turn for worst. No excuse for it. My clumsiness. Not Tirkiluk. Stupid accident. I was drunk. The lantern went over. Should have gone out. But lid was loose. My fault. Idiot. Flaming oil. Everywhere.

Tirkiluk and I are sheltering by a wall of rock and of drift-ice, with what remains of one wall of the supply hut for a roof. The fire was terrible. Much worse in this cold place. The wind so strong. It and the flames fuelling each other. Supply hut went up too. Gas canisters. The oil drums. The lanterns. Explosions. Nearly killed. Everything.

Easier to list what we do have. Thought to drag out our clothing before too late. Some of the bedding. Some canvas. Managed to get back in and save some food, not enough to last the winter. Tirkiluk breaks the cans open with her knife. Contents are ice. No way of warming them. Eskimos carry fire with them through the winter. A tribe's greatest treasure.

Beam of roof fell. Hit my legs. Tirkiluk's all right but can hardly walk and there's the baby. Haven't moved for don't know how. Cold incredible to start with there's no pain no cold now. Fever, then this. Can't feel my legs. Graphite breaks and paper is brittle, but if I'm slow writing is easy.

Can watch the stars turn. Everything freezing. Ice drifts through gaps in canvas and roof like smoke. Place stinks of us and the flames. Remember Tirkiluk now. How she healed me. Chanting, salt ice on my lips, teeth chattering. The hard cold holding me in white bony arms. Lights in the sky. Other lights. Could feel the spirits. Whispering, gathering round. Smoke and ice. Cold breath. Their names tumbling on the wind. So many, so old. Wizened faces. The spirits don't mind the cold. This is their home. I don't belong. I leave my bones in a quiet place where the wolves can't get them.

Scratches of light. January meteors. The Quadrantids. I'm freezing. I don't feel cold. Dreamed that Tirkiluk had lost her fingers. Snapped off like icicles. She was Inua, fingerless hag, muttering under dark ice in the depths of the ocean.

★   ★   ★

Tirkiluk is near to her term. Tells me everything in her own language, and now I understand. Our lips are frozen as we speak, but perhaps the truth of it is in our minds. She tells me that she can't move now and that the bleeding is coming and that she and the baby will die.

The tins are useless. Need proper food. Water too. Must make the effort. Foolish *kaboola* white man with my own bare hands. Must try.

Small victory today, but think we now have a chance. Went

out onto the ice with a spear fashioned from hooked and sharpened transmitter strut, aerial cable for a line. No bleeding. Legs gave way once, but otherwise no problem. Knelt down and licked and scraped the new ice with my bared teeth, tasting the salt that is still in it. Thickness impossible to judge by sight alone, but taste is a clue. At the thinnest point lies a clear circle of water, and a tiny ridge of ice around it that seal-breath has made. The ridge tells who and when and how many have used it.

Crouched down. Waited. Time froze over. Just me and the hole in the ice and the cold stiffening my clothes and the mountains like the shoulders of gods behind me and stars turning in the endless glowing darkness. Silence was incredible. Silence is the thing that's struck me most since the burning of the hut. Always associated fear with noise. But fear is silence, and if you face the silence and listen to it and go through it, you eventually come to a dark place of deeper peace, like diving into that black circle of water as I wait for the seal, becoming part of everything. Found I could stop my breathing, and the slow ragged thump of my heart. Felt I was no longer real, yet knew I would snap back into existence when the seal surfaced to breathe.

Over in an instant. Thought of Tirkiluk. Felt no hesitation, no pity. The grunt and gust of salt air, a face like a dog's. Drove the spear down hard, and felt the shock of it strike back into my body. It began to thrash and pull, but the line held, and the sea turned foamy red. Felt the ice cracking and the ocean bubbling up as I heaved it out. Frozen splashes. Somehow found the energy to haul the seal back to Tirkiluk, the heat of it sliding in my hands. She sliced and bit and tore. The way she had before, when I was so disgusted. She offered it to me. I took a little, and the taste of it was good. But all hunger seems to have left me, and even the fresh water she lifted from the grey sack in the seal's belly slaked a thirst I didn't feel.

She made me take the bladder back to the bloodied hole. Dragged it there somehow, partly on hands and knees. It floated, a wounded sack, then was drawn down by a rippling current. Suddenly alive, swam away into the darkness. Tirkiluk tells me the spirit has returned. There will now be seal to hunt again.

Such terrible guilt about the stupidity of the accident. Not just my own life and Tirkiluk's I've endangered. The weather has turned even more against us now, as though it knows, and we've packed the snow around to make walls—a rudimentary kind of igloo, although Tirkiluk didn't even know the word. The wind bites through, threatening to excavate or bury us. Can feel the

great anticyclone the ice-cap inland like a presence, a ghostly con-
jurer drawing gales out of the Arctic waters. And I think of the
lonely men in huts like the one I destroyed, or in the convoys in
the Atlantic, and rounding the terrible North Cape towards
Murmansk.

Cold here is quite incredible, yet Tirkiluk feels it more than
me. Almost a blessing. Looked at my legs today, cut back leggings
that snapped like stiff card. Black skin, a section of dirty white
where bone is showing through. Never thought to see my own
bone. Wounds that should have gone gangrenous long ago. Think
only the cold keeps me alive. A kind of sterility.

Tirkiluk has shown me how to tame the wind. So simple I
should let the boffins at Godalming know. Would have laughed if
the fractured skin on my face would allow. Rattled those teeth
around her neck, and called on Inua. Tied three knots, and the
gale stilled, and a quarter moon brightened over the bay. Says she
needs a time of quiet now that the baby is near. Says she needs
the blood and the liver and the fresh water of the seal.

I resharpened the spear. I went out. Me, the pale hunter.

When I hunt, the cold disappears. Silence engulfs me. I love
the bright darkness, the glassy emptiness. Can hear the glacier
moving, and understand that one day it will eat the mountains.
Ice is stronger than heat or rock or even the ocean. Was there at
the start of the world, and will close over everything at the end,
when the stars blink out. I wait. Then flash of movement, and the
blood-heat that burns like a fire from the open body of the seal.
I leave the cutting of the flesh to Tirkiluk, who eats and drinks
most of it anyway, and buries deep into the warmth. I must keep
back. Not out of squeamishness, but because I fear the heat.

Return the bladder to the ocean and let the current draw it
away, so that the seal will return for me to hunt again.

The baby came. A boy. A living boy. It's like the Aurora — there
are no words. Leaned on her belly as she pushed. The incredible
heat of her flesh, my fingers like cold leather, and fear in eyes
through the pain at what I had become. We made a clean space
for the child, brought in the fresh falling snow. She cleaned him
and lay him on the skin of the seal. Then she gave him his first
name. Naigo. Could feel the spirits crowding in, joining with the
baby which is at its oldest when born. Filled with the memory of
other lives. That's why a baby cries before it can laugh. Said she
wanted to call him Seymour too, when my name floats free.

Tirkiluk fears that the wolves and the polar bear must come

soon, drawn by the blood-stink of life and death that surrounds this dreadful place. I do not believe that she and the baby will survive, yet I know that I fight for their lives.

Keeps Naigo against her flesh. Will hardly let me see. Says the spirits will be offended. I know my grip is cold as the glacier now, and that I must look awful, yet still I wish she would relent. The child feels half-mine. Yet I know from the wild fear in Tirkiluk's eyes that something is wrong. She senses it greatly now that she has Naigo, now that the whispering ancient spirits are gathered around her and the baby. It's me. Something more than the fire and the cold and this terrible place. I know, yet I cannot bring myself to face it.

Inua was once a young girl just like Tirkiluk, yet she committed some crime, and her parents rowed out with her into the ocean in their umiak, and threw her overboard. When she clung to the side, they cut off her fingers, and they tossed a lamp to her as she sank down into the dark water, so that she might find her way.

Think that Inua is still out there, somewhere at the edge of this bay where the ice meets the black water in shattering half-frozen waves. Her long hair streams out in the currents like dark weed, uncombed and verminous because she has no fingers, and her lantern shines up at me as I peer down through the ice waiting for the seal to rise. Or perhaps it's Aquila I see glittering deep down in the water, which Tirkiluk tells me will soon rise back above the horizon. Or some other drowned star.

I sit outside now, leaving Tirkiluk and Naigo with what little warmth and shelter there is. The breath, the damp, the slight radiance that still comes from her half-frozen body, had become intolerable to me, although I think that she is also happier now that she does not have to see me when the ice cracks from her frozen eyelids and she looks up, and when the baby mews and she draws it out from somewhere inside her.

In starlight, I stand up and I pull back the frozen, useless furs. I can see my hands, my arms, my chest. If I drop the furs now, they skitter across the rocks and ice, shattering like filthy glass. Underneath, there are darkened ropes of chilled muscle, pulled tight by shrivelled skin. My fingernails have peeled back like burned and blackened paint. From what little I can feel of my face with these hands, I have no nose, and my lips are stretched back so that my teeth are permanently bared.

The snow has returned. It gathers on these pages, and the

flakes do not melt as I brush them away. It forms drifts, sculpting my body. I settle back into the downy comfort. I lay back as whiteness falls. My jaw creaks and the softness fills my mouth, settles on these eyes that do not blink. Soon, I will be covered, buried.

I think of Godalming. Of that hut by the tennis courts, and the sagging nets that no one has ever bothered to take in after the last set was played before war and the place was requisitioned. I think of Kay Alexander, her face sprayed with freckles, listening to the hissing seashell silence that drifts down from space.

She looks ragged from worry at the loss of the broadcasts from Weatherbase Logos II as she sits each evening at her receiver, although she knows that there's a war on and that this and worse will happen on every day until it's won. She remembers the shy man who was sent there, who sometimes came across the lawns from the main house in the summer, and would sit nearby at the edge of a table and fuss with the cuffs of his uniform or a pencil, barely meeting her eyes, talking about things without somehow ever really saying. Kay's hair is ragged now. Even in Surrey it is winter and the night comes early and the lanterns glow beyond the blackout blinds, and the stars drift down and leaves are tangled like fish in the rotting tennis nets. Kay's red tresses hang in verminous fronds, and as she lays out the code grid and lifts her headphones from the hook where she keeps them, the chill engulfs her and her fingers snap off one by one.

Nearly covered in forgetful snow now. Cannot see. But Tirkiluk is hungry. She and Naigo need blood warmth. Must not give way. Must go and hunt the seal again. I know her face now, the mewling of her pain, the hot scent of her death spilling across the ice, the way the warmth of her blood makes my frozen, blackened flesh liquefy and dissolve.

The sun is starting to pearl the horizon, and Aquila will soon return. Tirkiluk's Aagyuuk. It signals the thaw.

The polar bear came along the frozen beach at midday. He came with the changing wind, just as the sun was rising. I knew that he would have to come, just as the seal always returns, bringing Tirkiluk and Naigo the gift of her life.

A terrible, beautiful scene, the mountains glittering nursery-pink. Then the white pelt, the lumbering flesh. He raised his snout, smelling fire and life and slaughter. He grunted, and howled.

Naigo began to cry in the shelter behind me, and Tirkiluk sang to soothe him, her voice ringing clear over the keening wind, knowing that there was no hiding, knowing that the beast sensed the warm meat that was waiting on their bones. I thought for a moment of the seal, and how death was a kinder thing here than the winter, and that if I could truly finish with dying and return to life, it would be to a warm place with faces and smiles, crying with the grief of ages, hooded in silver drifts of placenta. But the bear had seen me, and smelled the death that my own lungs and mouth no longer have to taste, and smelled that I was an enemy.

I grabbed the harpoon as the bear lumbered towards me, driving it hard. It struck near the massive chest, reddening where the wind riffled the pelt. The beast was slowed, but still he came towards me. I had an odd strength in me — the strength to throw a harpoon harder and faster than the wind — yet I was light, thinly bound by rigored muscle and spongy ropes of blood. The bear reached me and tumbled me over, and his jaw opened and teeth closed over my arm and shoulder. The teeth gave me no pain. It was the carrion-hot breath that terrified me.

Somehow, I pulled away from beneath him, dragged back on the bones of elbows and knees. I think he sensed then that he already had victory. Grey strands of ligament hung from his mouth, and my right collarbone dangled beneath. He shook it away. There was something playful and catlike about the way he struck out at me with the massive pad of his paw. I was blown back as if by the wind as the claws striped my chest. I struck an outcrop of rock, feeling my left hand snap and roll away, and my leg break where the wound had exposed the bone, raising a pointed femur. The bear leapt at me, coming down, blocking the sky.

My broken femur struck into his belly like a stake. He bellowed, and the blood gushed in a salt wave. I knew that I would have to get away before the heat dissolved me entirely.

I didn't kill the bear. He ran back up the beach, trailing blood. The wound, which seemed so terrible as it broke over me from his belly, will probably heal easily enough. Spring is coming soon, and life will regather itself, and the bear will survive. I wish him luck, and the flesh of the seal when we have finally finished with her. I use the harpoon as a kind of crutch now that I can no longer walk easily. I have lashed the remains of my left arm to it, and struggle along the shore like a broken-winged bird.

I have to keep the harpoon lashed that way even when I hunt, but the seal now comes easily. She has died for us so many times that she no longer fears death.

How I envy her. The bear's blood-heat and his teeth and claws have exposed and melted the flesh of my chest and belly. I can look down now as I shelter by a rock from the long ice-glittering shadows of the gathering sunlight. The dark frozen organs inside their cage, furred with ice.

I look up at the rim of the sky. Aagyuuk is rising. Across six-teen light-years, Altair winks at me. While still I have time, I must catch the seal again.

The thaw is coming now, as Tirkiluk said it would once Aagyuuk had risen. There is faint light much of the day, and sud-den flashes of the blazing rim of the sun through the clouds and glaciers that lie piled on the horizon. The wind is veering south. The seabirds are returning.

The ice in the bay booms now, and cracks like thunder. For Tirkiluk and Naigo, even though I know that there will be bitter storms to come, death has receded. She came out to see me today when the sun was sailing clear of the horizon and I was crouching in the ice-shadows where the cold wind drives deepest at the eastern end of the shore. She brought Naigo with her, gathered deep under her furs. She wept when she saw me, yet she held the child out for me to see. He slept despite the chill. Gently, I let the ragged claw of my remaining hand brush against his forehead, where the marks of birth have left his skin entirely. Then she drew him away, and held him to her breast and wept all the more. I would have wept with her, had I any tears left in me.

I went today to the place of bones. I've known for some time that it is where I should seek to avoid the gathering heat. I stood at the rim of the shadowed ravine with rags of my rotting flesh streaming in the wind, gazing down at those clean and serene skulls. But I know that the souls live elsewhere. They live on the wind, in the ice, and beneath the soft lids of Naigo's sleeping eyes.

I write with difficulty now as the skin sloughs off my fingers like old seaweed. These pages are filthy from the mess I leave, and I can only go out when the wind veers north, or in the cold of the night. Why should I strive to continue now, anyway? I can think of no reason other than fear.

A wide crack has appeared in the sheet of ice that covered the bay. It runs like a road from the horizon right up to the shore. Somehow, I believe I can smell the sea on it, the salt breath of the ocean.

Must write before I lose fingers of remaining hand.

Went out onto the beach. As I gazed at the widening gap in the ice, the seal emerged from the wind-ripped water. She lum-bered up across the rocks towards me, and stared without fear with the steam of life rising from her smooth dark pelt. I could only marvel and wonder, and feel a kind of love. She forgives, after all the times that her life has been taken. She turned then, and went back into the water, and dived in a smooth deep ripple.

I thought then I stood alone in the wind, yet when I looked behind me, Tirkiluk was there. A dark figure, standing just as I have stood so many times at the edge of this shore, looking out at the crystal mountains, the glacier, the bay. She let me hold her, and touch the baby again. I knew that we were saying good-bye, although there were no words.

I can hear the seal mewling on the midnight wind. She is out on the shore again. Calling. Waiting. All I must do now is stand, and lift these limbs, and walk down towards the glittering path of water that spreads out across the bay. And the seal will lead me to the place in the ocean where a lantern gleams, dark hair streams, and fingerless hands spread wide in an embrace.

From there, the rest of my journey should be easy.

★   ★   ★

From the log of John Farragar, Ship's Captain, *Queen of Erin*, 12 May 1943

Sailed 1200 hours Tuiak Bay SSE towards Neimaagen. A fire has destroyed Logos II Weatherbase, and a thorough search has revealed no trace of Science Officer Seymour. Have radioed Meteorological Intelligence at Godalming and advised that he should be listed as missing, presumed dead.

Also advised Godalming that an Eskimo woman and infant survived amid the burnt-out wreckage. They are aboard with us now, and I have no reason to doubt that the truth of this sad matter is as the woman has told me:

Seymour befriended her when she was abandoned by her tribe, and the fire was caused by an accident with a lantern at the time broadcasts ceased. He died soon after from injuries caused by his attempts to recover supplies from the burning hut, and the body was subsequently taken by wolves. The later journals I have recovered are undated, and clearly the product of a sadly deranged mind. I would not wish them to reach the hands of his relatives, and I have thus taken the responsibility upon myself to have them destroyed in the ship's furnace.

Tirkiluk, the Eskimo woman, has asked to be landed at Temekscet, where the tribe is very different from her own, and the wooded land is somewhat warmer and kinder. As the deviation from our course is small, I have agreed to her request. Her journey aboard the *Queen* should take little more than two days, but I am sure that by then we shall miss her.

Papa

My grandchildren have brought time back to me. Even when they have gone, my house will never be the same. Of course, I didn't hear them when they arrived—on this as on many other mornings, I hadn't bothered to turn on my eardrums—but a tingling jab from the console beside my bed finally caught my attention. What had I been doing? Lying in the shadowed heat, watching the sea breeze lift the dappled blinds? Not even that. I had been somewhere distant. A traveller in white empty space.

The blinds flicker. My bedhelper emerges from its wallspace, extending mantis arms for me to grab. One heave, and I'm sitting up. Another, and I'm standing. The salt air pushes hot, cool. I pause to blink. Slow, quick, with both eyes. A moment's concentration. Despite everything Doc Fanian's told me, it's never become like riding a bicycle, but then who am I, now, to ride a bike? And my eardrums are *on*, and the sound of everything leaps into me. I hear the waves, the sea, the lizards stirring on the rocks, distant birdsong, the faint whispering trees. I hear the slow drip of the showerhead on the bathroom tiles, and the putter of a rainbow-winged flyer somewhere up in the hot blue sky. I hear the papery breath and heartbeat of an old man aroused from his midmorning slumbers. And I hear voices—young voices—outside my front door.

"He *can't* be in."

"Well, he can't be *out* . . ."

"Let's—"

"—No, you."

"I'll—"

"—listen. I think . . ."

"It's him."

Looking down at myself, I see that, yes, I am clothed, after a fashion: shorts and a tee-shirt—crumpled, but at least not the ones I slept in last night. So I *did* get dressed today, eat breakfast, clean up afterwards, shave. . . .

"Are you in there, Papa?"

My granddaughter Agatha's voice.

"Wait a moment," I croak, sleep-stiff, not really believing. Heading for the hall.

The front door presents an obstacle. There's the voice recognition system my son Bill had fitted for me. Not that anyone mugs or burgles anyone else any longer, but Bill's a worrier—he's past eighty now, and of that age.

"Are you all right in there?"

Saul's voice this time.

"Yes, I'm fine."

The simple routine of the voicecode momentarily befuddles me. The tiny screen says USER NOT RECOGNISED. I try again, and then again, but my voice is as dry as my limbs until the lubricants get working. My grandchildren can hear me outside, and I know they'll think Papa's talking to himself.

At last. My front door swings open.

Saul and Agatha. Both incredibly real in the morning brightness with the cypressed road shimmering behind them. I want them to stand there for a few moments so I can catch my breath—and for the corneas I had fitted last winter to darken—but I'm hugged and I'm kissed and they're past me and into the house before any of my senses can adjust. I turn back into the hall. Their luggage lies in a heap. Salt-rimed, sandy, the colours bleached, bulging with washing and the excitements of far-off places. *Venice. Paris. New York. The Sea of Tranquillity.* Even then, I have to touch to be sure.

"Hey, Papa, where's the *food?*"

Agatha crouches down on the tiles in my old-fashioned kitchen, gazing into the open fridge. And Saul's tipping back a self-cooling carafe he's found above the sink, his brown throat working. They're both in cut-off shorts, ragged tops. Stuff they've obviously had on for days. And here's me worrying about what I'm wearing—but the same rules don't apply. Agatha stands up, fills her mouth with a cube of ammoniac brie from the depths of the fridge. Saul wipes his lips on the back of his hand, smiles. As though he senses that the hug on the doorstep might have passed me by, he comes over to me. He gives me another. Held tight, towered over, I feel the rub of his stubbled jaw against my bald head as he murmurs, *Papa, it's good to be here.* And Agatha joins in, kisses me with cheese crumbs on her lips, bringing the sense of all the miles she's travelled to get here, the salt dust of a million far-off places. I'm tempted to pull away when I feel the soft pressure of her breasts against my arm. But this moment is too sweet, too innocent. I wish it could go on forever.

Finally, we step back and regard each other.

"You should have let me know you were coming," I say, wondering why I have to spoil this moment by complaining. "I'd have stocked up."

"We tried, Papa," Agatha says.

Saul nods. "A few days ago at the shuttleport in Athens, Papa. And then I don't know how many times on the ferry through the islands. But all we got was the engaged flag."

"I've been meaning," I say, "to get the console fixed."

Saul smiles, not believing for one moment. He asks, "Would you like me to take a look?"

I shrug. Then I nod Yes, because the console really does need reprogramming. And Saul and Agatha were probably genuinely worried when they couldn't get through, even though nothing serious could happen without one of my implant alarms going off.

"But you don't mind us coming, do you, Papa? I mean, if we're getting in the way or anything. Just say and we'll go." Agatha's teasing, of course. Just to see the look on Papa's face.

"No, no." I lift my hands in surrender, feeling the joints starting to ease. "It's wonderful to have you here. Stay with us as long as you want. Do whatever you like. That's what we grandparents are for."

They nod sagely, as though Papa's spoken a great truth. But sharp-eyed glances are exchanged across the ancient kitchen table, and I catch the echo of my words before they fade. And I realise what Papa's gone and said. *We. Us.*

Why did I use the plural? Why? When Hannah's been dead for more than seventy years?

★   ★   ★

An hour later, after the hormones and lubricants have stabilised,

I'm heading down to the port in my rattletrap open-top Ford. Off shopping to feed those hungry mouths, even though I want to hold on to every moment of Saul and Agatha's company.

White houses, cool streets framing slabs of sea and sky. I drive down here to the port once or twice a week to get what little stuff I need these days, but today I'm seeing things I've never noticed before. Canaries and flowers on the window ledges. A stall filled with candied fruit and marzipan mice, wafting a sugared breeze. I park the Ford in the square, slap on my autolegs, and head off just as the noonday bells begin to chime.

By the time I reach Antonio's, my usual baker, the display on the fat-wheeled trolley I picked up in the concourse by the fountains is already reading FULL LOAD. I really should have selected the larger model, but you have to put in extra money or something. Antonio grins. He's a big man, fronting slopes of golden crust, cherry-nippled lines of iced bun. Sweaty and floured, he loves his job the way everyone seems to these days.

I'm pointing everywhere. Two, no, three loaves. And up there; never mind, I'll have some anyway. And those long twirly things — are they sweet? — I've always wondered. . . .

"You've got visitors?" He packs the crisp warm loaves into crisp brown bags.

"My grandchildren." I smile, broody as a hen. "They came out of nowhere this morning."

"That's great," he beams. He'd slap my shoulder if he could reach that far across the marble counter. "How old?"

I shrug. What is it now? Bill's eighty-something. So — nearly thirty. But that can't be right. . . .

"Anyway," he hands me the bags, too polite to ask if I can manage. "Now's a good time." My autolegs hiss as I back out towards the door. The loaded trolley follows.

But he's right. Now *is* a good time. The very best.

I drop the bags of bread on my way back to the square. The trolley's too full to help even if I knew how to ask it, and I can't bend down without climbing out of the autolegs, but a grey-haired woman gathers them up from the pavement and helps me back to the car.

"You *drive?*" she asks as I clank across the square towards my Ford and the trolley rumbles behind in attendance. It's a museum piece. She chuckles again. Her face is hidden under the shadow-weave of a straw sunhat.

Then she says, "Grandchildren — how lovely," as nectarines and oranges tumble into the back seat. I can't remember telling her about Saul and Agatha as we walked—in my absorption, I can't even remember speaking—but perhaps it's the only possible explanation for someone of my age doing this amount of shopping. When I look up to thank her, she's already heading off under the date palms. The sway of a floral print dress. Crinkled elbows and heels, sandals flapping, soft wisps of grey hair, the rings on her slightly lumpen fingers catching in sunlight. I'm staring, thinking. Thinking. Thinking, if only.

★ ★ ★

Back at the house, hours after the quick trip I'd intended, the front door is open, unlocked. The thing usually bleeps like mad when I leave it even fractionally ajar, but my grandchildren have obviously managed to disable it. I step out of my autolegs and stand there in my own hall, feeling the tingling in my synthetic hip, waiting for my corneas to adjust to the change in light.

"I'm back!"

There's silence—or as close to silence as these eardrums will allow. Beating waves. Beating heart. And breathing. Soft, slow breathing. I follow the sound.

Inside my bathroom, it looks as if Saul and Agatha have been washing a large and very uncooperative dog. Sodden towels are everywhere, and the floor is a soapy lake, but then they're of a generation that's used to machines clearing up after them. Beyond, in the shadowed double room they've taken for their own, my grandchildren lie curled. Agatha's in my old off-white dressing gown—which, now I've seen her in it, I'll never want to wash or replace. Her hair spills across the pillow, her thumb rests close to her mouth. And Saul's outstretched on the mattress facing the other way, naked, his bum pressed against hers. Long flanks of honey-brown. He's smooth and still, lovely as a statue.

There's a tomb-memorial I saw once—in an old cathedral, in old England—of two sleeping children, carved in white marble. I must have been there with Hannah, for I remember the ease of her presence beside me, or at least the absence of the ache that has hardly ever left me since. And I remember staring at those sweet white faces and thinking how impossible that kind of serenity was, even in the wildest depths of childhood. But it happens all the time. Everything's an everyday miracle.

I back away. Close the door, making a clumsy noise that I hope doesn't wake them. I unload the shopping in the kitchen by hand, watching the contents of my bags diminish as if by magic as I place them on the shelves. So much becoming so little. But never mind; there's enough for a late lunch, maybe dinner. And my grandchildren are sleeping and the house swirls with their dreams. It's time, anyway, to ring Bill.

★　★　★

My son's in his office. Bill always looks different on the console, and as usual I wonder if this is a face he puts on especially for me. In theory, Bill's like Antonio—working simply because he loves his job—but I find that hard to believe. Everything about Bill speaks of duty rather than pleasure. I see the evening towers of a great city through a window beyond his shoulder. The lights of home-ward-bound flyers drifting like sparks in a bonfire-pink sky. But which city? Bill's always moving, chasing business. My console finds him anyway, but it isn't programmed to tell you *where* unless you specifically ask. And I don't know how.

"Hi, Dad."

Two or three beats. Somewhere, nowhere, space dissolves, in-stantaneously relaying this silence between us. Bill's waiting for me to say why I've called. He knows Papa wouldn't call unless he had a reason.

I say, "You look fine, son."

He inclines his head in acknowledgement. His hair's still mostly a natural red-brown—which was Hannah's colour—but I see that he's started to recede, and go grey. And there are deep creases around the hollows of his eyes as he stares at me. If I didn't know any better, I'd almost say that my son was starting to look old. "You too, Dad."

"Your kids are here. Saul and Agatha."

"I see." He blinks, moves swiftly on. "How are they?"

"They're"—I want to say, great, wonderful, incredible; all those big stupid puppy-dog words—"they're fine. Asleep at the moment, of course."

"Where have they been?"

I wish I could just shrug, but I've never been comfortable using nonverbal gestures over the phone. "We haven't really talked yet, Bill. They're tired. I just thought I'd let you know."

Bill purses his long, narrow lips. He's about to say something, but then he holds it back. *Tired. Haven't talked yet. Thought I'd let you know.* Oh, the casualness of it all! As though Saul and Agatha were here with their Papa last month and will probably call in next as well.

"Well, thanks, Dad. You must give them my love."

"Any other messages?"

"Tell them I'd be happy if they could give me a call."

"Sure, I'll do that. How's Meg?"

"She's fine."

"The two of you should come down here."

"You could come *here*, Dad."

"We must arrange something. Anyway, I'm sure you're—"

"—pretty busy, yes. But thanks for ringing, Dad."

"Take care, son."

"You too."

The screen snows. After a few moments' fiddling, I manage to turn it off.

I set about getting a meal for my two sleeping beauties. Salads, cheese, crusty bread, slices of pepper and carrot, garlicky dips. Everything new and fresh and raw. As I do so, the conversation with Bill drones on in my head. These last few years, they can go on for hours inside me after we've spoken. Phrases and sentences tumbling off into new meaning. Things unsaid. Now, I'm not even sure why I bothered to call him. There's obviously no reason why he should be worried about Saul and Agatha. Was it just to brag— Hey, look, I've got your kids!—or was it in the hope that, ringing out of the blue in what were apparently office hours in whatever city he was in, I'd really make contact?

Slicing with my old steel knives on the rainbow-wet cutting board, I remember Bill the young man, Bill the child, Bill the baby. Bill when Hannah and I didn't even have a name for him two weeks out of the hospital. As Hannah had grown big in those ancient days of prebirth uncertainty, we'd planned on Paul for a boy, Esther for a girl. But when he arrived, when we took him home and bathed him, when we looked at this tiny creature like some red Indian totem with his bulbous eyes, enormous balls, and alarmingly erect penis, Paul had seemed entirely wrong. He used to warble when he smelled Hannah close to him—we called it his milk song. And he waved his legs in the air and chuckled and laughed at an age when babies supposedly aren't able to do that kind of thing. So we called him William. An impish, mischievous name. In our daft parental certainty, even all the dick-and-willy connotations had seemed entirely appropriate. But by the time he was two, he was Bill to everyone. A solid, practical name that fit, even though calling him Bill was something we'd never dreamed or wanted or intended.

★   ★   ★

In the heat of midafternoon, beneath the awning on the patio between sky and sea, Papa's with his sibling's siblings, sated with food. I feel a little sick, to be honest, but I'm hoping it doesn't show.

"Your dad rang," I say, finding that the wine has turned the meaning of the sentence around — as though, for once, Bill had actually made the effort and contacted me.

"Rang?" Agatha puzzles over the old unfamiliar phrase. Rang. Called. She nods. "Oh yeah?" She lifts an espadrilled foot to avoid squashing the ants who are carrying off bread-crumbs and scraps of salad. "What did he say?"

"Not much." *I'd be happy if they'd call.* Did he mean he'd be unhappy otherwise? "Bill seemed pretty busy," I say. "Oh, and he wanted to know where you've been these last few months."

Saul laughs. "That sounds like Dad, all right."

"He's just interested," I say, feeling I should put up some kind of defence.

Agatha shakes her head. "You know what Dad gets like, Papa." She wrinkles her nose. "All serious and worried. Not that you shouldn't be serious about things. But not about *everything.*"

"And he's so bloody possessive," Saul agrees, scratching his ribs.

I try not to nod. But they're just saying what children have always said: waving and shouting across a generation gap that gets bigger and bigger. Hannah and me, we put off having Bill until we were late-thirties for the sake of our careers. Bill and his wife Meg, they must have both been gone fifty when they had these two. Not that they were worn out — in another age, they'd have passed for thirty — but old is old is old.

The flyers circle in the great blue dome above the bay, clear silver eggs with the rainbow flicker of improbably tiny wings; the crickets chirp amid the myrtled rocks; the yachts catch the breeze. I'd like to say something serious to Saul and Agatha as we sit out here on the patio, to try to find out what's really going on between them and Bill, and maybe even make an attempt at repair. But instead, we start to talk about holidays. I ask them if they really have been to the Sea of Tranquillity, to the moon.

"Do you want to see?"

"I'd love to."

Saul dives back into the house. Without actually thinking — nearly a century out of date — I'm expecting him to return with a wad of photos in an envelope. But he returns with this box, a little VR thing with tiny rows of user-defined touchpads. He holds it out towards me, but I shake my head.

"You'd better do it, Saul."

So he slips two cool wires over my ears, presses another against the side of my nose, and drops the box onto the rug that covers my lap. He touches a button. As yet, nothing happens.

"Papa, can you hear me?"

"Yes . . ."

"Can you see?"

I nod without thinking, but all I'm getting is the stepped green lawns of my overly neat garden, the sea enfolding the horizon. Plain old actual reality.

Then, Blam!

Saul says, "This is us coming in on the moonshuttle."

I'm flying over black-and-white craters. The stars are sliding overhead. I'm falling through the teeth of airless mountains. I'm tumbling towards a silver city of spires and domes.

"And this is Lunar Park."

Blam! A midnight jungle strung with lights. Looking up without my willing it through incredible foliage and the geodome, I see the distant Earth; a tiny blue globe.

"Remember, Ag? That party."

From somewhere, Agatha chuckles. "And you in that getup."

Faces. Dancing. Gleaming bodies. Parakeet colours. Someone leaps ten, fifteen feet into the air. I shudder as a hand touches me. I smell Agatha's scent, hear her saying something that's drowned in music. I can't tell whether she's in VR or on the patio.

"This goes on for ages. You know, Papa, fun at the time, but . . . I'll run it forward."

I hear myself say, "Thanks."

Then, Blam! I'm lying on my back on the patio. The deckchair is tipped over beside me.

"You're okay? Papa?"

Agatha's leaning down over me out of the sky. Strands of hair almost touching my face, the fall of her breasts against her white cotton blouse.

"You sort of rolled off your chair. . . ."

I nod, pushing up on my old elbows, feeling the flush of stupid embarrassment, the jolt on my back and arse, and the promise of a truly spectacular bruise. Black. Crimson. Purple. Like God smiling down through tropical clouds.

Agatha's helping me as I rise. I'm still a little dizzy, and I'm gulping back the urge to be sick. For a moment, as the endorphins advance and regroup in my bloodstream, I even get a glimpse beyond the veil at the messages my body is really trying to send. I almost feel *pain*, for Chrissake. I blink slowly, willing it to recede. I can see the patio paving in shadow and sunlight. I can see the cracked, fallen box of the little VR machine.

"Hey, don't worry."

Strong arms place me back in my deckchair. I lick my lips and swallow, swallow, swallow. No, I won't be sick.

"Are you okay? You . . ."

"I'm fine. Is that thing repairable? Can I have a look?"

Saul immediately gives the VR box back to me, which makes me certain it's irretrievably busted. I lift the cracked lid. Inside, it's mostly empty space. Just a few silver hairs reaching to a superconductor ring in the middle.

"These machines are incredible, aren't they?" I find myself muttering.

"Papa, they turn out this kind of crap by the million now. They make them fragile 'cos they want them to break so you go out and buy another. It's no big deal. Do you want to go inside? Maybe it's a bit hot for you out here."

Before I can think of an answer, I'm being helped back inside the house. I'm laid on the sofa in the cool and the dark, with the doors closed and the shutters down, propped up on cushions like a doll. Part of me hates this, but the sensation of being cared for by humans instead of machines is too nice for me to protest.

I close my eyes. After a few seconds of red darkness, my corneas automatically blank themselves out. The first time they did this, I'd expected a sensation of deep ultimate black. But for me at least—and Doc Fanian tells me it's different for all of his patients—white is the colour of absence. Like a snowfield on a dead planet. Aching white. Like hospital sheets in the moment before you go under.

★　★　★

"Papa?"

"What time is it?"

I open my eyes. An instant later, my vision returns.

"You've been asleep."

I try to sit up. With ease, Agatha holds me down. A tissue appears. She wipes some drool from off my chin. The clock in the room says seven. Nearly twilight. No need to blink; my eardrums are still on. Through the open patio doors comes the sound of the tide breaking on the rocks, but I'm also picking up a strange buzzing. I tilt my head like a dog. I look around for a fly. Could it be that I've blinked without realising and reconfigured my eardrums in some odd way? Then movement catches my eye. A black-and-silver thing hardly bigger than a pinhead whirs past my nose, and I see that Saul's busy controlling it with a palette he's got on his lap at the far end of the sofa. Some new game.

I slide my legs down off the sofa. I'm sitting up, and suddenly feeling almost normal. Sleeping in the afternoon usually leaves me feeling ten years older—like a corpse—but this particular sleep has actually done me some good. The nausea's gone. Agatha's kneeling beside me, and Saul's playing with his toy. I'm bright-eyed, bushy tailed. I feel like a ninety-year-old.

I say, "I was speaking this morning to Antonio."

"Antonio, Papa?" Agatha's forehead crinkles with puzzlement.

"He's a man in a shop," I say. "I mean, you don't know him. He runs a bakery in the port."

"Anyway, Papa," Agatha prompts sweetly, "what were you saying to him?"

"I told him that you were staying—my grandchildren—and he asked how old you were. The thing is, I wasn't quite sure."

"Can't you guess?"

I gaze at her. Why do she and Saul always want to turn everything into a game?

"I'm sorry, Papa," she relents. "I shouldn't tease. I'm twenty-eight and a half now, and Saul's thirty-two and three-quarters."

"Seven-eights," Saul says, without taking his eyes off the buzzing pinhead as it circles close to the open windows. "And you'd better not forget my birthday." The pinhead zooms back across the room. "I mean you, Ag. Not Papa. Papa never forgets. . . ."

The pinhead buzzes close to Agatha, brushing strands of her hair, almost touching her nose. "Look, Saul," she snaps, standing up, stamping her foot. "Can't you turn that bloody thing off?"

Saul smiles and shakes his head. Agatha reaches up to grab it, but Saul's too quick. He whisks it away. It loops the loop. She's giggling now, and Saul's shoulders are shaking with mirth as she dashes after it across the room.

Nodding, smiling palely, I watch my grandchildren at play.

"What is that thing, anyway?" I ask as they finally start to tire.

"It's a metacam, Papa." Saul touches a control. The pinhead stops dead in the middle of the room. Slowly turning, catching the pale evening light on facets of silver, it hovers, waiting for a new command. "We're just pissing around."

Agatha flops down in a chair. She says, "Papa, it's the latest thing. Don't say you haven't seen them on the news?"

I shake my head. Even on the old flatscreen TV I keep in the corner, everything nowadays comes across like a rock music video. And the endless good news just doesn't feel right to me, raised as I was on a diet of war and starving Africans.

"What does it do?" I ask.

"Well," Saul says, "this metacam shows the effects of multiple waveform collapse. Look . . ." Saul shuffles towards me down the length of the sofa, the palette still on his lap. "That buzzing thing up there is a multilens, and I simply control it from down here—"

"—that's amazing," I say. "When I was young, they used to have pocket camcorders you couldn't even get in your pocket. Not unless you had one made specially. The pockets, I mean. Not the cameras . . ."

Saul keeps smiling through my digression. "But it's not *just* a camera, Papa, and anyway you could get ones this size fifteen years ago." He touches the palette on his lap, and suddenly a well of brightness tunnels down from it, seemingly right through and into the floor. Then the brightness resolves into an image. "You see? There's Agatha."

I nod. And there, indeed, she is: in three dimensions on the palette screen on Saul's lap. Agatha. Prettier than a picture.

I watch Agatha on the palette as she gets up from the chair. She strolls over to the windows. The pinhead lens drifts after her, panning. I'm fascinated. Perhaps it's my new corneas, but she seems clearer in the image than she does in reality.

Humming to herself, Agatha starts plucking the pink rose petals from a display on the window ledge, letting them fall to the floor. As I watch her on Saul's palette screen, I notice the odd way that the petals seem to drift from her fingers, how they multiply and divide. Some even rise and dance, seemingly caught on a breeze, although the air in the room is still, leaving fading trails behind them. Then Agatha's face blurs as she turns and smiles. But she's also still in profile, looking out of the window. Eyes and a mouth at both angles at once. Then she takes a step forward, whilst at the same time remaining still. At first, the effect of these overlays is attractive, like a portrait by Picasso, but as they build up, the palette becomes confused. Saul touches the palette edge. Agatha collapses back into one image again. She's looking out through the window into the twilight at the big yacht with white sails at anchor out in the bay. The same Agatha I see as I look up towards her.

"Isn't that something?" Saul says.

I can only nod.

"Yes, incredible, isn't it?" Agatha says, brushing pollen from her fingers. "The metacam's showing possible universes that lie close to our own. You do understand that, Papa?"

"Yes. But . . ."

Agatha comes over and kisses the age-mottled top of my head.

Outside, beyond the patio and the velvety neat garden, the sea horizon has dissolved. The big white-sailed yacht now seems to be floating with the early stars. I can't even tell whether it's an illusion.

"We thought we'd go out on our own this evening, Papa," she murmurs, her lips ticklingly close to my ear. "See what's going on down in the port. That is, if you're feeling okay. You don't mind us leaving for a few hours, do you?"

★ ★ ★

A flyer from the port comes to collect Saul and Agatha. I stand waving on the patio as they rise into the starry darkness like silver twins of the moon.

Back inside the house, even with all the lights on, everything feels empty. I find myself wondering what it will be like after my grandchildren have gone entirely, which can only be a matter of days. I fix some food in the kitchen. Usually, I like the sense of control that my old culinary tools give me, but the buzzing of the molecular knife seems to fill my bones as I cut, slice, arrange. Saul and Agatha. Everything about them means happiness, but still I have this stupid idea that there's a price to pay.

I sit down at the kitchen table, gazing at green-bellied mussels, bits of squid swimming in oil, bread that's already going stale. What came over me this morning, buying all this crap? I stand up, pushing my way through the furniture to get outside. There. The stars, the moon, the faint lights of the port set down in the scoop of the darkly gleaming coast. If I really knew how to configure these eardrums, I could probably filter out everything but distant laughter in those lantern-strung streets, music, the clink of glasses. I could eavesdrop on what Saul and Agatha are saying about Papa as they sit at some café table, whether they think I've gone downhill since the last time, or whether, all things considered, I'm holding up pretty well.

They'll be taking clues from things around this house that I don't even notice. I remember visiting a great-aunt back in the last century when I was only a kid. She was always punctilious about her appearance, but as she got older she used to cake her face with white powder, and there was some terrible discovery my mother made when she looked through the old newspapers in the front room. Soon after that, auntie was taken into what was euphemistically called a Home. These days, you can keep your own company for much longer. There are machines that will do most things for you: I've already got one in my bedside drawer that crawls down my leg and cuts my toenails for me. But when do you

finally cross that line of not coping? And who will warn you when
you get close?

Unaided, I climb down from the patio and hobble along the
pathways of my stepped garden. Since Bill decided that I wasn't
up to maintaining it any longer and bought me a mec-cultivator,
I really only wander out here at night. I've always been a raggedy
kind of gardener, and this place is now far too neat for me. You
could putt on the neat little lawns, and the borders are a lesson
in geometry. So I generally make do with darkness, the secret
touch of the leaves, the scents of hidden blooms. I haven't seen
the mec-cultivator for several days now anyway, although it's obviously still keeping busy, trundling along with its silver arms and
prettily painted panels, searching endlessly for weeds, collecting
seedheads, snipping at stray fingers of ivy. We avoid each other,
it and I. In its prim determination — even in the flower displays
that it delivers to the house when I'm not looking — it reminds me
of Bill. He tries so hard, does Bill. He's a worrier in an age when
people have given up worrying. And he's a carer, too. I know that.
And I love my son. I truly love him. I just wish that Hannah was
alive to love him with me. I wish that she was walking the streets
of the port, buying dresses from the stalls down by the harbour.
I just wish that things were a little different.

I sit down on the wall. It's hard to remember for sure now
whether things were ever that happy for me. I must go back to
times late in the last century when I was with Hannah, and everything was so much less easy then. We all thought the world was
ending, for a start. Everything we did had a kind of twilit intensity.
Of course, I was lucky; I worked in engineering construction — all
those Newtonian equations that are now routinely demolished —
at a time when rivers were being diverted, flood barriers erected,
seas tamed. I had money and I had opportunity. But if you spend
your life thinking Lucky, Lucky, Lucky, you're really simply waiting for a fall. I remember the agonies Hannah and I went through
before we decided to have Bill. We talked on and on about the
wars, the heat, the continents of skeleton bodies. But we finally
decided, as parents always do, that love and hope is enough. And
we made love as though we meant it, and Bill was born, and the
money — at least for us — kept on coming in through the endless
recessions. There were even inklings of the ways that things
would get better. I remember TV programmes where academics
tried to describe the golden horizons that lay ahead — how unravelling the edges of possibility and time promised predictive intelligence, unlimited energy. Hannah and I were better equipped

than most to understand, but we were still puzzled, confused. And we knew enough about history to recognise the parallels between all this quantum magic and the fiasco of nuclear power, which must once have seemed equally promising, and equally incomprehensible.

But this time the physicists had got it largely right. Bill must have been ten by the time the good news began to outweigh the bad, and he was still drawing pictures of burnt-out rainforest, although by then he was using a paintbox PC to do it. I remember that I was a little amazed at his steady aura of gloom. But I thought that perhaps he just needed time to change and adjust to a world that was undeniably getting better, and perhaps he would have done so, become like Saul and Agatha—a child of the bright new age—if Hannah hadn't died.

I totter back through the garden, across the patio, and into the house. Feeling like a voyeur, I peek into Saul and Agatha's bedroom. They've been here—what?—less than a day, and already it looks deeply lived in; and smells like a gym. Odd socks and bedsheets and tissues are strewn across the floor, along with food wrappers (does that mean I'm not feeding them enough?), shoes, the torn pages of the in-flight shuttle magazine, the softly glowing sheet of whatever book Agatha's reading. I gaze at it, but of course it's not a book, but another game; Agatha's probably never read a book in her life. Whatever the thing is, I feel giddy just looking at it. Like falling down a prismatic well.

Putting the thing down again exactly where I found it, I notice that they've broken the top off the vase on the dresser, and then pushed the shards back into place. It's a thing that Hannah bought from one of those shops that used to sell Third World goods at First World prices; when there was a Third and First World. Thick blue glaze, decorated with unlikely looking birds. I used to hate that vase, until Hannah died, and then the things we squabbled over became achingly sweet. Saul and Agatha'll probably tell me about breaking it when they find the right moment. Or perhaps they think Papa'll never notice. But I don't mind. I really don't care. Saul and Agatha can break anything they want, smash up this whole fucking house. I almost wish they would, in fact, or at least leave some lasting impression. This place is filled with the stuff of a lifetime, but now it seems empty. How I envy my grandchildren this dreadfully messy room, the way they manage to fill up so much space from those little bags and with all the life they bring with them. If only I could programme my hoover not to tidy it all up into oblivion as soon as they go, I'd leave it this way forever.

Saul's stuffed the metacam back into the top of his travelling bag on the floor. I can see the white corner of the palette sticking out, and part of me wants to take a good look, maybe even turn it on and try to work out if he really meant that stuff about showing alternate realities. But I go cold at the thought of dropping or breaking it — it's obviously his current favourite toy — and my hands are trembling slightly even as I think of the possibilities, of half-worlds beside our own. I see an image: me bending over the metacam as it lies smashed on the tiled floor. Would the metacam record its own destruction? Does it really matter?

I leave the room, close the door. Then I reopen it to check that I've left things as they were. I close the door again, then I pull it back ajar, as I found it.

I go to my room, wash, and then the bedhelper trundles out and lifts me into bed even though I could have managed it on my own. I blink three times to turn off my eardrums. Then I close my eyes.

Sleep on demand isn't an option that Doc Fanian's been able to offer me yet. When I've mentioned to him how long the nights can seem — and conversely how easily I drop off without willing it in the middle of the afternoon — he gives me a look that suggests that he's heard the same thing from thousands of other elderly patients on this island. I'm sure a solution to these empty hours will be found eventually, but helping the old has never been a primary aim of technology. We're flotsam at the edge of the great ocean of life. We have to make do with spin-offs as the waves push us further and further up the beach.

But no sleep. No sleep. Just silence and whiteness. If I wasn't so tired, I'd pursue the age-old remedy and get up and actually do something. It would be better, at least, to think happy thoughts of this happy day. But Saul and Agatha evade me. Somehow, they're still too close to be real. Memory needs distance, understanding. That's what sleep's for, but as you get older, you *want* sleep, but you don't need it. I turn over in shimmering endless whiteness. I find myself thinking of gadgets, of driftwood spindrift spin-offs. Endless broken gadgets on a white infinite shore. Their cracked lids and flailing wires. If only I could kneel, bend, pick them up, and come to some kind of understanding. If only these bones would allow.

There was a time when I could work the latest Japanese gadget straight out of the box. I was a master. VCR two-year-event timers, graphic equalisers, PCs and photocopiers, the eight-speaker stereo in the car. Even those fancy camcorders were no problem, although somehow the results were always disappointing. I remember Hannah walking down a frosty lane, glancing back towards me with the bare winter trees behind her, smiling through grey clouds of breath. And Hannah in some park with boats on a lake, holding baby Bill up for me as I crouched with my eye pressed to the viewfinder. I used to play those tapes late at night after she died when Bill was asleep up in his room. I'd run them backwards, forwards, freeze-frame. I'd run them even though she wasn't quite the Hannah I remembered, even though she always looked stiff and uneasy when a lens was pointed at her. I had them rerecorded when the formats changed. Then the formats changed again. Things were redigitised. Converted into solid-state. Into superconductor rings. Somewhere along the way, I lost touch with the technology.

★   ★   ★

In the morning, the door to the room where my grandchildren are sleeping is closed. After persuading my front door to open, and for some stubborn reason deciding not to put on my autolegs, I hobble out into the sunlight and start to descend the steps at the side of my house unaided. Hand over rickety hand.

It's another clear and perfect morning. I can see the snow-gleam of the mainland peaks through a cleft in the island hills, and my neighbours the Euthons are heading out on their habitual morning jog. They wave, and I wave back. What's left of their greying hair is tucked into headbands as though it might get in the way.

The Euthons sometimes invite me to their house for drinks, and, although he's shown it to me many times before, Mr. Euthon always demonstrates his holographic hi-fi, playing Mozart at volume levels that the great genius himself can probably hear far across the warm seas and the green rolling continents in his unmarked grave. I suspect that the Euthons' real interest in me lies simply in the fascination that the old have for the truly ancient — like gazing at a signpost: this is the way things will lead. But they're still sprightly enough, barely past one hundred. One morning last summer, I looked out and saw the Euthons chasing each other naked around their swimming pool. Their sagging arms and breasts and bellies flapped like featherless wings. Mrs. Euthon was shrieking like a schoolgirl, and Mr. Euthon had a glistening pink erection. I wish them luck. They're living this happy, golden age.

I reach the bottom of the steps and catch my breath. Parked in the shadow of my house, my old Ford is dented, splattered with dust and dew. I only ever take it on the short drive to and from the port nowadays, but the roads grow worse by the season, and exact an increasingly heavy price. Who'd have thought the road surfaces would be allowed to get this bad, this far into the future? People generally use flyers now, and what land vehicles there are have predictive suspension; they'll give you a magic carpet ride over any kind of terrain. Me and my old car, we're too old to be even an anachronism.

I lift up the hood and gaze inside, breathing the smell of oil and dirt. Ah, good old-fashioned engineering. V–8 cylinders. Sparkplugs leading to distributor caps. Rust holes in the wheel arch. I learnt about cars on chilly northern mornings, bit by bit as things refused to work. I can still remember most of it more easily than what I had for lunch yesterday.

A flock of white doves clatter up and circle east, out over the silken sea towards the lime groves on the headland. Bowed down beneath the hood, my fingers tracing oiled dirt, I find myself wishing that the old girl actually needed fixing. But over the years, as bits and pieces have given out and fallen away, the people at the workshop in the port have connected in new devices. I'm still not sure that I believe them when they tell me that until they are introduced into the car's system, every device is actually the same. To me, that sounds like the kind of baloney you give to someone who's too stupid to understand. But the new bits soon get oiled-over nicely enough anyway, and after a while they even start to look like the old bits they've replaced. It's like my own body, all the new odds and ends that Doc Fanian's put in. Eardrums, corneas, a liver, hips, a heart, joints too numerous to mention. Endless chemical implants to make up for all the things I should be manufacturing naturally. Little nano-creatures that clean and repair the walls of my arteries. Stuff to keep back the pain. After a while, you start to wonder just how much of something you have to replace before it ceases to be what it was.

"Fixing something, Papa?"

I look up with a start, nearly cracking my head on the underside of the hood.

Agatha.

"I mean, your hands look filthy." She stares at them, these gnarled old tree roots that Doc Fanian has yet to replace. A little amazed. She's in the same blouse she wore yesterday. Her hair's done up with a ribbon.

"Just fiddling around."

"You must give me and Saul a ride."

"I'd love to."

"Did you hear us come back last night, Papa? I'm sorry if we were noisy—and it *was* pretty late." Carved out of the gorgeous sunlight, she raises a fist and rubs at sleep-crusted eyes.

"No." I point. "These ears."

"So you probably missed the carnival fireworks as well. But it must be great, being able to turn yourself off and on like that. What *are* they? Re- or interactive?"

I shrug. What can I say . . .? I can't even hear fireworks—or my own grandchildren coming in drunk. "Did you have a good time last night?"

"It was nice." She gazes at me, smiling. Nice. She means it. She means everything she says.

I see that she's got wine stains on her blouse, and bits of tomato seed. As she leans over the engine, I gaze at the crown of her head, the pale skin whorled beneath.

"You still miss Grandma, don't you, Papa?" she asks, looking up at me from the engine with oil on the tip of her nose.

"It's all in the past," I say, fiddling for the catch, pulling the hood back down with a rusty bang.

Agatha gives me a hand as I climb the steps to the front of the house. I lean heavily on her, wondering how I'll ever manage alone.

★ ★ ★

I drive Saul and Agatha down to the beach. They rattle around in the back of my Ford, whooping and laughing. And I'm grinning broadly too, happy as a kitten as I take the hairpins in and out of sunlight, through cool shadows of forest with the glittering race of water far below. At last! A chance to show that Papa's not past it! In control. The gearshift's automatic, but there's still the steering, the brakes, the choke, the accelerator. My hands and feet shift in a complex dance, ancient and arcane as alchemy.

We crash down the road in clouds of dust. I beep the horn, but people can hear us coming a mile off, anyway. They point and wave. Flyers dip low, their bee-wings blurring, for a better look. The sun shines bright and hot. The trees are dancing green. The sea is shimmering silver. I'm a mad old man, wise as the deep and lovely hills, deeply loved by his deeply lovely grandchildren. And I decide right here and now that I should get out more often. Meet new strangers. See the island, make the most of the future. Live a little while I still can.

★ ★ ★

"You're okay, Papa?"

On the beach, Agatha presses a button, and a striped parasol unfolds. "If we leave this here, it should keep track of the sun for you."

"Thanks."

"Do you still swim?" She reaches to her waist and pulls off her tee-shirt. I do not even glance at her breasts.

Saul's already naked. He stretches out on the white sand beside me. His penis flops out over his thigh; a beached baby whale.

"Do you, Papa? I mean, swim?"

"No," I say. "Not for a few years."

"We could try one of the pedalos later." Agatha steps out from her shorts and knickers. "They're powered. You don't have to pedal unless you want to."

"Sure."

Agatha shakes the ribbon from her hair and scampers off down the beach, kicking up sand. It's late morning. Surfers are riding the deep green waves. People are laughing, splashing, swimming, drifting on the tide in huge transparent bubbles. And on the beach there are sun-worshippers and runners, kids making sandcastles, robot vendors selling ice cream.

"Ag and Dad are a real problem," Saul says, lying back, his eyes closed against the sun.

I glance down at him. "You're going to see him . . .?"

He pulls a face. "It's a duty to see Mum and Dad, you know? It's not like coming here to see you, Papa."

"No."

"You know what they're like."

"Yes," I say, wondering why I even bother with the lie.

Of course, when Hannah died, everyone seemed to assume a deepening closeness would develop between father and son. Everyone, that is, apart from anyone who knew anything about grief or bereavement. Bill was eleven then, and when I looked up from the breakfast table one morning, he was twelve, then thirteen. He was finding his own views, starting to seek independence. He kept himself busy, he did well at school. We went on daytrips together and took foreign holidays. We talked amicably, we visited Mum's grave at Christmas and on her birthday, and walked through the damp grass back to the car keeping our separate silences. Sometimes, we'd talk animatedly about things that didn't matter. But we never argued. When he was seventeen, Bill went to college in another town. When he was twenty, he took a job in another country. He wrote and rang dutifully, but the gaps got bigger. Even with tri-dee and the revolutions of instantaneous communication, it got harder and harder to know what to say. And Bill married Meg, and Meg was like him, only more so: a child of that generation. Respectful, hard-working, discreet, always ready to say the right thing. I think they both dealt in currency and commodities for people who couldn't be bothered to handle their own affairs. I was never quite sure. And Meg was always just a face and a name. Of course, their two kids—when they finally got around to having them—were wildly different. I loved them deeply, richly. I loved them without doubt or question. For a while, when Saul and Agatha were still children and I didn't yet need these autolegs to get around, I used to visit Bill and Meg regularly.

Agatha runs back up the beach from her swim. She lies down and lets the sun dry her shining body. Then it's time for the picnic, and to my relief, they both put some clothes back on. I don't recognise most of the food they spread out on the matting. New flavours, new textures. I certainly didn't buy any of it yesterday on my trip to the port. But anyway, it's delicious, as lovely as this day.

"Did you do this in the last century, Papa?" Saul asks. "I mean, have picnics on the beach?"

I shrug Yes and No. "Yes," I say eventually, "but there was a problem if you sat out too long. A problem with the sky."

"The *sky?*"

Saul reaches across the mat to restack his plate with something sweet and crusty that's probably as good for you and unfattening as fresh air. He doesn't say it, but still I can tell that he's wondering how we ever managed to get ourselves into such a mess back then, how anyone could possibly fuck up something as fundamental as the sky.

Afterwards, Saul produces his metacam palette from one of the bags. It unfolds. The little pinhead buzzes up, winking in the light.

"The sand here isn't a problem?" I ask.

"Sand?"

"I mean . . . getting into the mechanism."

"Oh, no."

From the corner of my eye, I see Agatha raising her eyebrows. Then she plumps her cushion and lies down in the sun. She's humming again. Her eyes are closed. I'm wondering if there isn't some music going on inside her head that I can't even hear.

"You were saying yesterday, Saul," I persist, "that it's more than a camera. . . ."

"Well," Saul looks up at me, and blanks the palette, weighing up just how much he can tell Papa that Papa would understand. "You know about quantum technology, Papa, and the unified field?"

I nod encouragingly.

He tells me anyway. "What it means is that for every event, there are a massive number of possibilities."

Again, I nod.

"What happens, you see, Papa, is that you push artificial intelligence along the quantum shift to observe these fractionally different worlds, to make the waveform collapse. That's where we get all the world's energy from nowadays, from the gradient of that minute difference. And that's how this palette works. It displays some of the worlds that lie close beside our own. Then it projects them forward. A kind of animation. Like predictive suspension, only much more advanced . . ."

I nod, already losing touch. And that's only the beginning. His explanation carries on, grows more involved. I keep on nodding. After all, I do know a little about quantum magic. But it's all hypothetical, technical stuff; electrons and positrons. It's got nothing to do with real different worlds, has it?

"So it really is showing things that might have happened?" I ask when he's finally finished. "It really isn't a trick?"

Saul glances down at his palette, then back up at me, looking slightly offended. The pinhead lens hangs motionless in the air between us, totally ignoring the breeze. "No," he says. "It's not a trick, Papa."

Saul shows me the palette: he even lets me rest the thing on my lap. I gaze down, and watch the worlds divide.

The waves tumble, falling and breaking over the sand in big glassy lumps. The wind lifts the flags along the shore in a thousand different ways. The sky shivers. A seagull flies over, mewing, breaking into a starburst of wings. Grey comet-tailed things that might be ghosts, people, or—for all I know—the product of my own addled and enhanced senses, blur by across the shore.

"You've got implant corneas, haven't you, Papa?" Saul says. "I could probably rig things up so you could have the metacam projected directly into your eyes."

"No, thanks," I say.

Probably remembering what happened to the VR—Saul doesn't push it.

I look down in wonder. "This is . . ."

What? Incredible? Impossible? Unreal?

"This is . . ."

Saul touches the palette screen again. He cancels out the breaking, shattering waves. And Agatha calls the vendor for an ice cream, and somehow it's a shock when she pushes the cool cone into my hand. I have to hold it well out of the way, careful not to drip over the palette.

"This is . . ."

And my ice cream falls, splattering Saul's arm.

Agatha leans over. "Here, let me. I'll turn that off, Papa."

"Yes, do."

There's nothing left on the palette now, anyway. Just a drop of ice cream, and the wide empty beach. The screen blanks at Agatha's touch, and the pinhead camera shoots down from a sky that suddenly seems much darker, cooler. Immense purple-grey clouds are billowing over the sea. The yachts and the flyers are turning for home. Agatha and Saul begin to pack our stuff away.

"I'll drive the car home, Papa," Agatha says, helping me up from the deckchair just as I feel the first heavy drops of rain.

"But . . ."

They take an arm each. They half-carry me across the sand and up the slope to the end of the beach road where I've parked — badly, I now see — the Ford.

"But . . ."

They put me down, and unhesitatingly unfold the Ford's complex hood. They help me in.

"But . . ."

They wind up the windows and turn on the headlights just as the first grey veils strike the shore. The wipers flap, the rain drums. Even though she's never driven before in her life, Agatha spins the Ford's wheel and shoots uphill through the thickening mud, crashing through the puddles towards the first hairpin.

Nestled against Saul in the back seat, too tired to complain, I fall asleep.

★   ★   ★

That evening, we go dancing. Saul. Agatha. Papa.

There are faces. Gleaming bodies. Parakeet colours. Looking through the rooftops of the port into the dark sky, I can see the moon. I'm vaguely disappointed to find that she's so full tonight. Since I've had these corneas fitted, and with the air nowadays so clear, I can often make out the lights of the new settlements when she's hooded in shadow.

Agatha leans over the café table. She's humming some indefinable tune. "What are you looking at, Papa?"

"The moon."

She gazes up herself, and the moon settles in the pools of her eyes. She blinks and half-smiles. I can tell that Agatha really does see mystery up there. She's sat in the bars, slept in the hotels, hired dust buggies, and gone crater-climbing. Yet she still feels the mystery.

"You've never been up there, have you, Papa?"

"I've never left the Earth."

"There's always time," she says.

"Time for what?"

She laughs, shaking her head.

Music is playing. Wine is flowing. The port is beautiful in daylight, but even more so under these lanterns, these stars, this moon, on this warm summer night. Someone grabs Saul and pulls him out to join the dance that fills the square. Agatha remains sitting by me. They're sweet, considerate kids. One of them always stays at Papa's side.

"Do you know what kind of work Bill does these days?" I ask Agatha — a clumsy attempt both to satisfy my curiosity, and to raise the subject of Bill and Meg.

"He works the markets, Papa. Like always. He sells commodities."

"But if he deals in things," I say, genuinely if only vaguely puzzled, "that must mean there isn't enough of everything . . .?" But perhaps it's another part of the game. If everything was available in unlimited supply, there would be no fun left, would there? Nothing to save up for. No sense of anticipation or pleasurable denial. But then, how come Bill takes it all so seriously? What's he trying to prove?

Agatha shrugs So What? at my question anyway. She really doesn't understand these things herself, and cares even less. Then someone pulls her up into the dance, and Saul takes her place beside me. The moment is lost.

Saul's tapping his feet. Smiling at Agatha as her bright skirt swirls. No metacam tonight, no Picasso faces. She doesn't dissolve or clap her hands, burst into laughter or tears, or walk back singing to the table. But it's hard not to keep thinking of all those tumbling possibilities. Where does it end? Is there a different Papa for every moment, even one that sprawls dying right now on these slick cobbles as blood pumps out from fragile arteries into his brain? And is there another one, far across the barricades of time, that sits here with Saul as Agatha swirls and dances, with Hannah still at his side?

I reach for my wine glass and swallow, swallow. Hannah's dead — but what if one cell, one strand of double helix, one atom, had been different . . .? Or perhaps if Hannah had been less of an optimist? What if she hadn't ignored those tiny symptoms, those minor niggles, if she'd worried and gone straight to the doctor and had the tests? Or if it had happened later, just five or ten years later, when there was a guaranteed cure . . .?

But still—and despite the metacam—I'm convinced that there's only one real universe. All the rest is hocus-pocus, the flicker of an atom, quantum magic. And, after all, it seems churlish to complain about a world where so many things have finally worked out right. . . .

"Penny for them."

"What?"

"Your thoughts." Saul pours out more wine. "It's a phrase."

"Oh yes." My head is starting to fizz. I drink the wine. "It's an old one. I know it."

The music stops. Agatha claps, her hands raised, her face shining. The crowd pushes by. Time for drinks, conversation. Looking across the cleared space of the square, down the shadowed street leading to the harbour, I see a grey-haired woman walking towards us. I blink twice, slowly, waiting for her to disappear. But my ears pick up the clip of her shoes over the voices and the retuning of the band. She's smiling. She knows us. She waves. As my heart trampolines on my stomach, she crosses the square and pulls a seat over to our table.

"May I?"

Agatha and Saul nod Yes. They're always happy to meet new people. Me, I'm staring. She's not Hannah, of course. Not Hannah.

"Remember?" she asks me, tucking her dress under her legs as she sits down. "I helped carry your bags to that car of yours. I've seen it once or twice in the square. I've always wondered who drove it."

"It's Papa's pride and joy," Agatha says, her chest heaving from the dance.

The woman leans forward across the table, smiling. Her skin is soft, plump, downy as a peach.

I point at Saul. "My grandson here's got this device. He tells me it projects other possible worlds—"

"—Oh, you mean a metacam." She turns to Saul. "What model?"

Saul tells her. The woman who isn't Hannah nods, spreads her hands, sticks out her chin a little. It's not the choice she'd have made, but . . .

"More wine, Papa?"

I nod. Agatha pours.

I watch the woman with grey hair. Eyes that aren't Hannah's colour, a disappointing droop to her nose that she probably keeps that way out of inverted vanity. I try to follow her and Saul's conversation as the music starts up again, waiting for her to turn back towards me, waiting for the point where I can butt in. It doesn't come, and I drink my wine.

Somewhere there seems to be a mirror—or perhaps it's just a possible mirror in some other world, or my own blurred imagination—and I see the woman whose name I didn't catch sitting there, and I can see me, Papa. Propped at an off-centre angle against the arms of a chair. Fat belly and long thin limbs, disturbingly pale eyes and a slack mouth surrounded by drapes of ancient skin. A face you can see right through to the skull beneath.

Not-Hannah laughs at something Saul says. Their lips move, their hands touch, but I can't hear any longer. I've been blinking too much—I may even have been crying—and I've somehow turned my eardrums off. In silence, Not-Hannah catches Saul's strong young arms and pulls him up to dance. They settle easily into the beat and the sway. His hand nestles in the small of her back. She twirls in his arms, easy as thistledown. I blink, and drink more wine, and the sound crashes in again. I blink again. It's there. It's gone. Breaking like the tide. What am I doing here anyway, spoiling the fun of the able, the happy, the young?

This party will go on, all the dancing and the laughing, until a doomsday that'll never come. These people, they'll live forever. They'll warm up the sun, they'll stop the universe from final collapse, or maybe they'll simply relive each glorious moment as the universe turns back on itself and time reverses, party with the dinosaurs, resurrect the dead, dance until everything ends with the biggest of all possible bangs.

"Are you all right, Papa?"

"I'm fine."

I pour out more of the wine.

It slops over the table.

Saul's sitting at the table again with Not-Hannah, and the spillage dribbles over Not-Hannah's dress. I say fuck it, never mind, spilling more as I try to catch the flow, and I've really given the two of them the perfect excuse to go off together so he can help her to clean up. Yes, help to lift off her dress even though she's old enough to be his—

But then, who cares? Fun is fun is fun is fun. Or maybe it's Agatha she was after. Or both, or neither. It doesn't matter, does it? After all, my grandchildren have got each other. Call me old-fashioned, but look at them. My own bloody grandchildren. Look at them. Creatures from another fucking planet—

But Not-Hannah's gone off on her own anyway. Maybe it was something I said, but my eardrums are off—I can't even hear my own words, which is probably a good thing. Saul and Agatha are staring at me. Looking worried. Their lips are saying something about Papa and Bed and Home, and there's a huge red firework flashing over the moon. Or perhaps it's a warning cursor, which was one of those things Doc Fanian told me to look out for if there was ever a problem. My body is fitted with all sorts of systems and alarms, which my flesh and veins happily embrace. It's just this brain that's become a little wild, a little estranged, swimming like a pale fish in its bowl of liquid and bone. So why not fit a few new extra pieces, get rid of the last of the old grey meat. And I'd be new, I'd be perfect —

★ ★ ★

Whiteness. Whiteness. No light. No darkness.

"Are you in there, Papa?"

Doc Fanian's voice.

"Where else would I be?"

I open my eyes. Everything becomes clear. Tiger-stripes of sunlight across the walls of my bedroom. The silver mantis limbs of my bedhelper. The smell of my own skin like sour ancient leather. Memories of the night before.

"What have you done to me?"

"Nothing at all."

I blink and swallow. I stop myself from blinking again. Doc Fanian's in beach shorts and a bright ridiculous shirt; his usual attire for a consultation.

"Did you know," I say, "that they've installed a big red neon sign just above the moon that says Please Stop Drinking Alcohol?"

"So the cursor *did* work!" Doc Fanian looks pleased with himself. His boyish features crinkle. "Then I suppose you passed out?"

"Not long after. I thought it was just the drink."

"It's a safety circuit. Of course, the body has got one too, but it's less reliable at your age."

"I haven't even got a hangover."

"The filters will have seen to that."

Doc Fanian gazes around my bedroom. There's a photo of Hannah on the far wall. She's hugging her knees as she sits on a grassy bank with nothing but sky behind her; a time and a place I can't even remember. He peers at it, but says nothing. He's probably had a good mooch around the whole house by now, looking for signs, seeing how Papa's managing. Which is exactly why I normally make a point of visiting him at the surgery. I never used to be afraid of doctors when I was fitter, younger. But I am now. Now that I need them. . . .

"Your grandchildren called me in. They were worried. It's un-

derstandable, although there was really no cause. None at all."
There's a faint tone of irritation in Doc Fanian's voice. He's annoyed that anyone should doubt his professional handiwork, or
think that Papa's systems might have been so casually set up that
a few glasses of wine would cause any difficulty.

"Well, thanks."

"It's no problem." He smiles. He starts humming again. He forgives easily. "If you'd care to pop into the surgery in the next week
or two, there's some new stuff I'd like to show you. It's a kind of
short-term memory enhancement. You know — it helps if you forget things you've been doing recently."

I say nothing, wondering what Doc Fanian has encountered
around the house to make him come up with this suggestion.

"Where are Saul and Agatha?"

"Just next door. Packing."

"Packing?"

"Anyway." He smiles. "I really must be going. I'd like to stay for
breakfast, but . . ."

"Maybe some other universe, eh?"

He turns and gazes back at me for a moment. He understands
more about me than I do myself, but still he looks puzzled.

"Yes," he nods. Half-smiling. Humouring an old man. "Take
care, you hear?"

He leaves the door open behind him. I can hear Saul and
Agatha. Laughing, squabbling. Packing.

I shift myself up. The bedhelper trundles out and offers arms
for me to grab. I'm standing when Saul comes into the room.

"I'm sorry about getting the doc out, Papa. We just thought,
you know. . . ."

"Why are you packing? You're not off already, are you?"

He smiles. "Remember, Papa? We're off to the Amazon. We
told you on the beach yesterday."

I nod.

"But it's been great, Papa. It really has."

"I'm sorry about last night. I behaved like an idiot."

"Yes." He claps his hands on my bony shoulders and laughs
outright. "That was quite something." He shakes his head in admiration. Papa, a party animal! "You really did cut loose, didn't you?"

★   ★   ★

Agatha fixes breakfast. The fridge is filled with all kinds of stuff
I've never even heard of. They've restocked it from somewhere,
and now it looks like the horn of plenty. I sit watching my lovely
granddaughter as she moves around, humming.

Cooking smells. The sigh of the sea wafts through the open

window. Another perfect day. The way I feel about her and Saul leaving, I could have done with grey torrents of rain. But even in paradise you can't have everything.

"So," I say, "you're off to the Amazon."

"Yeah." She bangs the plates down on the table. "There are freshwater dolphins. Giant anteaters. People living the way their ancestors did, now the rainforest has been restored." She smiles, looking as dreamy as last night when she gazed at the moon. I can see her standing in the magical darkness of a forest floor, naked as a priestess, her skin striped with green-and-mahogany shadows. It requires no imagination at all. "It'll be fun," she says.

"Then you won't be visiting Bill and Meg for a while?"

She bangs out more food. "There's plenty of time. We'll get there eventually. And I wish we'd talked more here, Papa, to be honest. There are so many things I want to ask."

"About Grandma?" I suggest. Making an easy guess.

"You too, Papa. All those years after she died. I mean, between then and now. You'll have to tell me what happened."

I open my mouth, hoping it will fill up with some comment. But nothing comes out. All those years: how could I have lived through so many without even noticing? My life is divided as geologists divide up the rock crust of Earth's time: those huge empty spaces of rock without life, and a narrow band which seems to contain everything. And Saul and Agatha are leaving, and time — that most precious commodity of all — has passed me by. Again.

Agatha sits down on a stool and leans forward, brown arms resting on her brown thighs. For a moment, I think that she's not going to press the point. But she says, "Do tell me about Grandma, Papa. It's one of those things Dad won't talk about."

"What do you want to know?"

"I know this is awkward, but . . . how did she die?"

"Bill's never told you?"

"We figured that perhaps he was too young at the time to know. But he wasn't, was he? We worked that out."

"Bill was eleven when your Gran died," I say. I know why she's asking me this now: she's getting Papa's story before it's too late. But I'm not offended. She has a right to know. "We tried to keep a lot of the stuff about Hannah's illness away from Bill. Perhaps that was a mistake, but that was what we both decided."

"It was a disease called cancer, wasn't it?"

So she does know something, after all. Perhaps Bill's told her more than she's admitting. Perhaps she's checking up, comparing versions. But, seeing her innocent questioning face, I know that the thought is unjust.

"Yes," I say, "it was cancer. They could cure a great many forms of the disease even then. They could probably have cured Hannah, if she'd gone and had the tests a few months earlier."

"I'm sorry, Papa. It must have been awful."

I stare at my lovely granddaughter. Another new century will soon be turning, and I'm deep into the future; further than I'd ever imagined. Has Agatha ever even known anyone who's died? And pain, what does she know about pain? And who am I, like the last bloody guest at the Masque of the Red Death, to reveal it to her now?

What *does* she want to know, anyway—how good or bad would she like me to make it? Does she want me to tell her that, six months after the first diagnosis, Hannah was dead? Or that she spent her last days in hospital even though she'd have liked to have passed away at home—but the sight of her in her final stages distressed little Bill too much? It distressed me, too. It distressed *her*. Her skin was covered in ulcers from the treatment that the doctors had insisted on giving, stretched tight over bone and fluid-distended tissue.

"It was all over with fairly quickly," I say. "And it was long ago."

My ears catch a noise behind me. I turn. Saul's standing, leaning in the kitchen doorway, his arms folded, his head bowed. He's been listening, too. And both my grandchildren look sad, almost as if they've heard all the things I haven't been able to tell them.

Now Saul comes and puts his arm around my shoulder. "Poor Papa." Agatha comes over too. I bury my face into them, trembling a little. But life must go on, and I pull away. I don't want to spoil their visit by crying. But I cry anyway. And they draw me back into their warmth, and the tears come sweet as rain.

Then we sit together, and eat breakfast. I feel shaky and clean. For a few moments, the present seems as real as the past.

"That car of yours," Saul says, waving his fork, swapping subjects with the ease of youth. "I was thinking, Papa, do you know if there's any way of getting another one?"

I'm almost tempted to let him have the Ford. But then, what would that leave me with? "There used to be huge dumps of them everywhere," I say.

"Really? And then I could come back here with it, Papa. We could race, and I'd get those people in that workshop down by the port to do my car up just like they've done yours. I mean," he chuckles, "I don't want to have to stop for petrol."

Petrol. When did I last buy *petrol?* Years ago, for sure. Yet the old Ford still rattles along.

"Anyway," Agatha says, standing up, her plate empty, although

I've hardly even started on mine. "I'll finish packing."

I sit with Saul as he finishes his food, feeling hugely unhungry, yet envying his gusto. He pushes the plate back, glances around for some kitchen machine that isn't there to take it, then pulls a face.

"Papa, I nearly forgot. I said I'd fix that console of yours."

I nod. The engaged flag that prevented him and Agatha getting through to me before they arrived must still be on: the thing that stops people from ringing.

But Saul's as good as his word. As Agatha sings some wordless melody in their room, he goes through some of the simpler options on the console with me. I nod, trying hard to concentrate. And Hannah holds her knees and smiles down at us from the photo on the wall. Saul doesn't seem to notice her gaze. I'm tempted to ask for his help with other things in the house. How to reprogramme the mec-gardener and the hoover, ways to make the place feel more like my own. But I know that I'll never remember his instructions. All I really want is for him to stay talking to me for a few moments longer.

"So you're okay about that, Papa?"

"I'm fine."

He turns away and shouts, "Hey, Ag!"

After that, everything takes only a moment. Suddenly, they're standing together in the hall, their bags packed. *Venice. Paris. New York. The Sea of Tranquillity.* Ready to go.

"We thought we'd walk down to the port, Papa. Just catch whatever ferry is going. It's such a lovely day."

"And thanks, Papa. Thanks for everything."

"Yes."

I'm hugged first by one, then the other. After the tears before breakfast, I now feel astonishingly dry-eyed.

"Well . . ."

"Yes . . ."

I gaze at Saul and Agatha, my beautiful grandchildren. Still trying to take them in. The future stretches before us and between us.

They open the door. They head off hand-in-hand down the cypressed road.

"Bye, Papa. We love you."

I stand there, feeling the sunlight on my face. Watching them go. My front door starts to bleep. I ignore it. In the shadow of my house, beside my old Ford, I see there's a limp-winged flyer; Saul and Agatha must have used it last night to get me home. I don't know how to work those things. I have no idea how I'll get rid of it.

Saul and Agatha turn again and wave before they vanish around the curve in the road. I wave back.

Then I'm inside. The door is closed. The house is silent.

I head for Saul and Agatha's room.

They've stripped the beds and made a reasonable attempt at clearing up, but still I can almost feel my hoover itching to get in and finish the job. Agatha's left the dressing gown she borrowed on the bed. I lift it up to my face. Soap and sea salt — a deeper undertow like forest thyme. Her scent will last a few hours, and after that I suppose I'll still have the memory of her every time I put it on. The vase that Hannah bought all those years ago still sits on top of the dressing table: they never did get around to telling me that they broke the thing. I lift it up, turning the glazed weight in my hands to inspect the damage. But the cracks, the shards, have vanished. The vase is whole and perfect again — as perfect, at least, as it ever was. In a panic, almost dropping the thing, I gaze around the room, wondering what else I've forgotten or imagined. But it's still all there, the fading sense of my grandchildren's presence. A forgotten sock, torn pages of the shuttle magazine. I put the vase gently down again. When so many other things are possible, I suppose there's bound to be a cheaply available gadget that heals china.

Feeling oddly expectant, I look under the beds. There's dust that the hoover will soon clear away. The greased blue inner wrapper of something I don't understand. A few crumpled tissues. And, of course, Saul's taken the metacam with him. He would; it's his favourite toy. The wonderful promise of those controls, and the green menus that floated like pond-lilies on the screen. REVISE. CREATE. EDIT. CHANGE. And Agatha turning. CHANGE. Agatha standing still. REVISE. Ghost-petals drifting up from her hands, and a white yacht floating with the stars on the horizon. If you could change the past, if you could alter, if you could amend. . . .

But I'd always known in my heart that the dream is just a dream, and that a toy is still just a toy. Perhaps one day, it'll be possible to revisit the pharaohs, or return to the hot sweet sheets of first love. But that lies far ahead, much further even than the nearest stars that those great exploratory ships will soon be reaching. Far beyond my own lifetime.

The broken VR machine sticks out from the top of the wastebin by the window. I take it out, wrapping the wires around the case, still wondering if there is any way to fix it. Once upon a time,

VR was seen as a way out from the troubles of the world. But no-body bothers much with it any longer. It was my generation that couldn't do anything without recording it on whatever new medium the Japanese had come up with. Saul and Agatha aren't like that. They're not afraid of losing the past. They're not afraid of living in the present. They're not afraid of finding the future.

I stand for a moment, clawing at the sensation of their fading presence, dragging in breath after breath. Then the console starts to bleep along the corridor in my bedroom, and the front doorbell sounds. I stumble towards it, light-headed with joy. They're back! They've changed their minds! There isn't a ferry until tomorrow! I can't believe . . .

The door flashes USER NOT RECOGNISED at me. Eventually, I manage to get it open.

"You *are* in. I thought . . ."

I stand there, momentarily dumbstruck. The pretty grey-haired woman from yesterday evening at the café gazes at me.

"They're gone," I say.

"Who? Oh, your grandchildren. They're taking a ferry this morning, aren't they? Off to Brazil or someplace." She smiles and shakes her head. The wildnesses of youth. "Anyway," she points, "that's my flyer. Rather than try to call it in, I thought I'd walk over here and collect it." She glances back at the blue sea, the blue sky, this gorgeous island. She breathes it all in deeply. "Such a lovely day."

"Would you like to come in?"

"Well, just for a moment."

"I'm afraid I was a little drunk last night. . . ."

"Don't worry about it. I had a fine time."

I glance over, looking for sarcasm. But of course she means it. People always do.

I burrow into my hugely overstocked fridge. When I emerge with a tray, she's gazing at the blank screen of my old TV.

"You know," she says, "I haven't seen one of those in years. We didn't have one at home, of course. But my grandparents did."

I put down the tray and rummage in my pocket. "This," I say, waving the broken VR machine in my gnarled hand. "Is it possible to get it fixed?"

"Let me see." She takes it from me, lifts the cracked lid. "Oh, I should think so, unless the coil's been broken. Of course, it would be cheaper to go out and buy a new one, but I take it that you've memories in here that you'd like to keep?"

I pocket the VR machine like some dirty secret, and pour out the coffee. I sit down. We look at each other, this woman and I. How old is she, anyway? These days, it's often hard to tell. Somewhere between Bill and the Euthons, I suppose, which makes her thirty or even forty years younger than me. And, even if she were more like Hannah, she isn't the way Hannah would be if she were alive. Hannah would be like me, staggering on ancient limbs, confused, trying to communicate through senses that are no longer her own, dragged ever forward into the unheeding future, scrabbling desperately to get back to the past, clawing at those bright rare days when the grandchildren come to visit, feeling the golden grit of precious moments slipping through her fingers even before they are gone.

And time doesn't matter to this woman; or to anyone under a hundred. That's one of the reasons it's so hard for me to keep track. The seasons on this island change, but people just gaze and admire. They pick the fruit as it falls. They breath the salt wind from off the grey winter ocean and shiver happily, knowing they'll sit eating toast by the fire as soon as they get home.

"I don't live that far from here," the woman says eventually. "I mean, if there's anything that you'd like help with. If there's anything that needs doing."

I gaze back at her, trying not to feel offended. I know, after all, that I probably do need help of some kind or other. I just can't think of what it is.

"Or we could just talk," she adds hopefully.

"Do you remember fast food? McDonald's?"

She shakes her head.

"ET? Pee-wee Herman? Global warming? Ethnic cleansing? Dan Quayle?"

She shakes her head. "I'm sorry. . . ."

She lifts her coffee from the table, drinking it quickly.

The silence falls between us like snow.

★   ★   ★

I stand in my doorway, watching as her flyer rises and turns, its tiny wings flashing in sunlight. A final wave, and I close the door, knowing that Saul and Agatha will probably be on a ferry now. Off this island.

I head towards my bedroom. Assuming it's time for my morning rest, my bedhelper clicks out its arms expectantly. I glare at the thing, but of course it doesn't understand, and I've already forgotten the trick Saul showed me to disable it. The house is already back to its old ways, taking charge, cleaning up Saul and Agatha's room, getting rid of every sign of life.

But I did at least make an effort with the console, and now I do know how to make sure the engaged flag isn't showing. Child's play, really—and I always knew how to call up my son Bill's number. Which is what I do now.

Of all places, Bill's in London. The precise location shows up on the console before he appears; it was just a question of making the right demand, of touching the right key. Then there's a pause.

I have to wait.

It's almost as if the console is testing my resolve, although I know that Bill's probably having to put someone else on hold so he can speak to me. And that he'll imagine there's a minor crisis brewing—otherwise, why would Papa bother to ring?

But I wait anyway, and as I do so, I rehearse the words I'll have to say, although I know that they'll come out differently. But while there's still time, I'll do my best to bridge the years.

At least, I'll start to try.

1/72nd Scale

David moved into Simon's room. Mum and Dad said they were determined not to let it become a shrine: Dad even promised to redecorate it anyhow David wanted. New paint, new curtains, Superman wallpaper, the lot. You have to try to forget the past, Dad said, enveloping him in his arms and the smell of his sweat, things that have been and gone. You're what counts now, Junior, our living son.

On a wet Sunday afternoon (the windows steamed, the air still thick with the fleshy smell of pork, an afternoon for headaches, boredom, and family arguments if ever there was one), David took the small stepladder from the garage and lugged it up the stairs to Simon's room. One by one, he peeled Simon's posters from the walls, careful not to tear the corners as he separated them from yellowed Sellotape and blobs of Blu-Tack. He rolled them into neat tubes, each held in place by an elastic band, humming along to Dire Straits on Simon's Sony portable as he did so. He was half-way through taking the dogfighting aircraft down from the ceiling when Mum came in. The dusty prickly feel of the fragile models set his teeth on edge. They were like big insects.

"And what do you think you're doing?" Mum asked.

David left a Spitfire swinging on its thread and looked down. It was odd seeing her from above, the dark half-moons beneath her eyes.

"I'm . . . just . . ."

Dire Straits were playing "Industrial Disease." Mum fussed angrily with the Sony, trying to turn it off. The volume soared. She jerked the plug out and turned to face him through the silence. "What makes you think this thing is yours, David? We can hear it blaring all through the bloody house. Just what do you think you're doing?"

"I'm sorry," he said. A worm of absurd laughter squirmed in his stomach. Here he was perched up on a stepladder, looking down at Mum as though he was seven feet tall. But he didn't climb down: he thought she probably wouldn't get angry with someone perched up on a ladder.

But Mum raged at him. Shouted and shouted and shouted. Her face went white as bone. Then Dad came up to see what the noise was, his shirt unbuttoned and creased from sleep, the sports pages crumpled in his right hand. He lifted David down from the ladder and said it was all right. This was what they'd agreed, okay?

Mum began to cry. She gave David a salty hug, saying she was sorry. Sorry. My darling. He felt stiff and awkward. His eyes, which had been flooding with tears a moment before, were suddenly as dry as the Sahara. So dry it hurt to blink.

Mum and Dad helped him finish clearing up Simon's models and posters. They smiled a lot and talked in loud, shaky voices. Little sis Victoria came and stood at the door to watch. It was like packing away the decorations after Christmas. Mum wrapped the planes up in tissues and put them carefully in a box. She gave a loud sob that sounded like a burp when she broke one of the propellers.

When they'd finished (just the bare furniture, the bare walls; growing dark, but no one wanting to put the light on), Dad promised that he'd redecorate the room next weekend, or the weekend after, at the latest. He'd have the place better than new. He ruffled David's hair in a big bearlike gesture and slipped his other arm around Mum's waist. Better than new.

★   ★   ★

That was a year ago.

The outlines of Simon's posters still shadowed the ivy wallpaper. The ceiling was pinholed where his models had hung. Hard little patches of Humbrol enamel and polystyrene cement cratered the carpet around the desk in the bay window. There was even a faint greasy patch above the bed where Simon used to sit up reading his big boy's books. They, like the model aircraft, now slumbered in the attic. *The Association Football Yearbook, Aircraft* of the Desert Campaign, Classic Cars 1945–1960, Tanks and Armoured Vehicles of the World, The Modeller's Handbook . . . all gathering dust, darkness, and spiders.

David still thought of it as Simon's room. He'd even called it that once or twice by accident. No one noticed. David's proper room, the room he'd had before Simon died, the room he still looked into on his way past it to the toilet, had been taken over by Victoria. What had once been his territory, landmarked by the laughing-face crack on the ceiling, the dip in the floorboards where the fireplace had once been, the corner where the sun pasted a bright orange triangle on summer evenings, was engulfed in frilly curtains, Snoopy lampshades, and My Little Ponys. Not that Victoria seemed particularly happy with her new, smart bedroom. She would have been more than content to sleep in Simon's old room with his posters curling and yellowing like dry skin and his models gathering dust around her. Little Victoria had idolised Simon; laughed like a mad thing when he dandled her on his knee and tickled her, gazed in wonderment when he told her those clever stories he made up right out of his head.

David started senior school in the autumn. Archbishop Lacy; the one Simon used to go to. It wasn't as bad as he'd feared, and for a while he even told himself that things were getting better at home as well. Then on a Thursday afternoon as he changed after Games (shower steam and sweat; cowering in a corner of the changing rooms; almost ripping his Y-fronts in his hurry to pull them up and hide his winkle), Mr. Lewis the gamesmaster came over and handed him a brown window envelope addressed to his parents. David popped it into his blazer pocket and worried all the way home. No one else had got one, and he couldn't think of anything he'd done sufficiently well to deserve special mention, although he could think of lots of things he'd done badly. He handed it straight to Mum when he came in, anxious to find out the worst. He waited by her as she stood reading it in the kitchen. The *Blue Peter* signature tune drifted in from the lounge. She finished and folded it in half, sharpening the crease with her nails. Then in half again. And again, until it was a fat, neat square. David gazed at it in admiration as Mum told him in a matter-of-fact voice that the school wanted back the 100-metres swimming trophy that Simon had won the year before. For a moment, David felt a warm wave of relief break over him. Then he looked up and saw Mum's face.

There was a bitter argument between Mum and Dad and the school. In the end—after the local paper had run an article in its middle pages headlined HEARTLESS REQUEST—Archbishop Lacy agreed to buy a new trophy and let them keep the old one. It stayed on the fireplace in the lounge, regularly tarnishing and growing bright again as Mum attacked it with Duraglit. The headmaster gave several assembly talks about becoming too attached to possessions, and Mr. Lewis the gamesmaster made Thursday afternoons hell for David in the special ways that only a gamesmaster can.

Senior school also meant Homework. As the nights lengthened and the first bangers echoed down the suburban streets, David sat working at Simon's desk in the bay window. He always did his best, and although he never came much above the middle of the class in any subject, his handwriting was often remarked on for its neatness and readability. He usually left the curtains open and had just the desk light (blue-and-white wicker shade; stand of turned mahogany on a wrought-iron base. Good enough to have come from British Home Stores, and all Simon's work—all of it) on so that he could see out. The streetlamp flashed through the hairy boughs of the monkey-puzzle tree in the front garden. Dot, dot, dash. Dash, dash, dot. He often wondered if it was a message.

Sometimes, way past the time when she should have been asleep, Victoria's door would squeak open, and her slippered feet would patter along the landing and halfway down the stairs. There she would sit, hugging her knees and watching the TV light flicker through the frosted-glass door of the lounge. Cracking open his door quietly and peering down through the top banisters, David had seen her there. If the lounge door opened, she would scamper back up and out of sight into her bedroom faster than a rabbit. Mum and Dad never knew. It was Victoria's secret, and in the little he said to her, David had no desire to prick that bubble. He guessed that she was probably waiting for Simon to return.

Dad came up one evening when David had just finished algebra and was turning to the agricultural revolution. He stood in the doorway, the light from the landing haloing what was left of his hair. A dark figure with one arm hidden, holding something big behind its back. For a wild moment, David felt his scalp prickle with incredible irrational fear.

"How's Junior?" Dad said.

He ambled through the shadows of the room into the pool of yellow light where David sat.

"All right, thank you," David said. He didn't like being called Junior. No one had ever called him Junior when Simon was alive, and he was now the eldest in any case.

"I've got a present for you. Guess what?"

"I don't know." David had discovered long ago that it was dangerous to guess presents. You said the thing you wanted it to be and upset people when you were wrong.

"Close your eyes."

There was a rustle of paper and a thin scratchy rattle that he couldn't place. But it was eerily familiar.

"Now open them."

David composed his face into a suitable expression of happy surprise and opened his eyes.

It was a big, long box wrapped in squeaky folds of shrinkwrap plastic. An Airfix 1/72nd-scale Flying Fortress.

David didn't have to pretend. He was genuinely astonished. Overawed. It was a big model, the biggest in the Airfix 1/72nd series. Simon (who always talked about these things; the steady pattern of triumphs that peppered his life; each new obstacle mastered and overcome) had been planning to buy one when he'd finished the Lancaster he was working on and had saved up enough money from his paper round. Instead, the Lancaster remained an untidy jumble of plastic, and in one of those vicious conjunctions that are never supposed to happen to people like Simon, he and his bike chanced to share the same patch of tarmac on the High Street at the same moment as a Pickfords lorry turning right out of a service road. The bike had twisted into a half circle around the big wheels. Useless scrap.

"I'd never expected . . . I'd . . ." David opened and closed his mouth in the hope that more words would come out.

Dad put a large hand on his shoulder. "I knew you'd be pleased. I've got you all the paints it lists on the side of the box, the glue." Little tins pattered out onto the desk, each with a coloured lid. There were three silver. David could see from the picture on the side of the box that he was going to need a lot of silver. "And look at this." Dad flashed a craft knife close to his face. "Isn't that dinky? You'll have to promise to be careful, though."

"I promise."

"Take your time with it, Junior. I can't wait to see it finished." The big hand squeezed his shoulder, then let go. "Don't allow it to get in the way of your homework."

"Thanks, Dad. I won't."

"Don't I get a kiss?"

David gave him a kiss.

"Well, I'll leave you to it. I'll give you any help you want. Don't you think you should have the big light on? You'll strain your eyes."

"I'm fine."

Dad hovered by him for a moment, his lips moving and a vague look in his eyes as though he was searching for the words of a song. Then he grunted and left the bedroom.

David stared at the box. He didn't know much about models, but he knew that the Flying Fortress was The Big One. Even Simon had been working up to it in stages. The Everest of models in every sense. Size. Cost. Difficulty. The guns swivelled. The bomb-bay doors opened. The vast and complex undercarriage went up and down. From the heights of such an achievement one could gaze serenely down at the whole landscape of childhood. David slid the box back into its large paper bag along with the paints and the glue and the knife. He put it down on the carpet and tried to concentrate on the agricultural revolution. The crumpled paper at the top of the bag made creepy crackling noises. He got up, put it in the bottom of his wardrobe, and closed the door.

"How are you getting on with the model?" Dad asked him at tea two days later.

David nearly choked on a fish finger. He forced it down, the dry bread-crumbs sandpapering his throat. "I, I, er—" He hadn't given the model any thought at all (just dreams and a chill of unease; a dark mountain to climb) since he'd put it away in the wardrobe. "I'm taking it slowly," he said. "I want to make sure I get it right."

Mum and Dad and Victoria returned to munching their food, satisfied for the time being.

After tea, David clicked his bedroom door shut and took the model out from the wardrobe. The paper bag crackled excitedly in his hands. He turned on Simon's light and sat down at the desk. Then he emptied the bag and bunched it into a tight ball, stuffing it firmly down into the wastepaper bin beside the chair. He lined the paints up next to the window. Duck egg green. Matt black. Silver. Silver. Silver . . . a neat row of squat little soldiers.

David took the craft knife and slit open the shining shrinkwrap covering. It rippled and squealed as he skinned it from the box. Then he worked the cardboard lid off. A clean, sweet smell wafted into his face. (Like a new car, the inside of a camera case, or a hospital waiting room.) A clear plastic bag filled the box beneath a heavy wad of instructions. To open it he had to ease out the whole grey chittering weight of the model and cut open the seal, then carefully tease the innards out, terrified that he might lose a piece in doing so. When he'd finished, the unassembled Flying Fortress jutted out from the box like a huge pile of jack-straws. It took him another thirty minutes to get them to lie flat enough to close the lid. Somehow, it was very important that he closed the lid.

So far, so good. David unfolded the instructions. They got bigger and bigger, opening out into a vast sheet covered with dense type and arrows and numbers and line drawings. But he was determined not to be put off. Absolutely determined. He could see himself in just a few weeks' time, walking slowly down the stairs with the great silver bird cradled carefully in his arms. Every detail correct. The paintwork perfect. Mum and Dad and Victoria will look up as he enters the bright warm lounge. And soon there is joy on their faces. The Flying Fortress is marvellous, a miracle (even Simon couldn't have done better), a work of art. There is laughter and wonder like Christmas firelight as David demonstrates how the guns swivel, how the undercarriage goes up and down. And although there is no need to say it, everyone understands that this is the turning point. The sun will shine again, the rain will be warm and sweet, clear white snow will powder the winter, and Simon will be just a sad memory, a glint of tears in their happy smiling eyes.

The preface to the instructions helpfully suggested that it was best to paint the small parts before they were assembled. Never one to ignore sensible advice, David reopened the box and lifted out the grey clusters of plastic. Like coat-hangers, they had an implacable tendency to hook themselves onto each other. Every part was attached to one of the trees of thin plastic around which the model was moulded. The big pieces such as the sides of the aircraft and the wings were easy to recognise, but there were also a vast number of odd shapes that had no obvious purpose. Then, as his eyes searched along rows of thin bits, fat bits, star-shaped bits, and bits that might be parts of bombs, he saw a row of little grey men hanging from the plastic tree by their heads.

The first of the men was crouching in an oddly foetal position. When David broke him off the plastic tree, he snapped at the neck.

David spent the evenings and most of the weekends of the next month at work on the Flying Fortress.

"Junior," Dad said one day as he met him coming up the stairs, "you're getting so absorbed in that model of yours. I saw your light on last night when I went to bed. Just you be careful it doesn't get in the way of your homework."

"I won't let that happen," David answered, putting on his good-boy smile. "I won't get too absorbed."

But David was absorbed in the model, and the model was absorbed into him. It absorbed him to the exclusion of everything else. He could feel it working its way into his system. Lumps of glue and plastic, sticky-sweet-smelling silver enamel worming into his flesh. Crusts of it were under his nails, sticking in his hair and to his teeth, his thoughts. Homework—which had been a worry to him—no longer mattered. He simply didn't do it. At the end-of-lesson bells he packed the exercise books into his satchel, and a week later he would take them out again for the next session, pristine and unchanged. Nobody actually took much notice. There was, he discovered, a group of boys and girls in his class who never did their homework—they just didn't do it. More amazing still, they weren't bothered about it and neither were the teachers. He began to sit at the back of the class with the cluster of paper-pellet flickers, boys who said Fuck, and lunchtime smokers. They made reluctant room for him, wrinkling their noses in suspicion at their new, paint-smelling, hollow-eyed colleague. As far as David was concerned, the arrangement was purely temporary. Once the model was finished, he'd work his way back up the class, no problem.

The model absorbed David. David absorbed the model. He made mistakes. He learned from his mistakes and made other mistakes instead. In his hurry to learn from those mistakes he repeated the original ones. It took him aching hours of frustration and eye strain to paint the detailed small parts of the model. The Humbrol enamel would never quite go where he wanted it to, but unfailingly ended up all over his hands. His fingerprints began to mark the model, the desk, and the surrounding area like the evidence of a crime. And everything was so tiny. As he squinted down into the yellow pool of light cast by Simon's neat lamp, the paintbrush trembling in one hand and a tiny piece of motor sticking to the fingers of the other, he could feel the minute tickly itchiness of it drilling through the breathless silence into his brain. But he persevered. The pieces came and went; turning from grey to blotched and runny combinations of enamel. He arranged them on sheets of the *Daily Mirror* on the right-hand corner of his desk, peeling them off his fingers like half-sucked Murraymints. A week later the paint was still tacky: he hadn't stirred the pots properly.

The nights grew colder and longer. The monkey-puzzle tree whispered in the wind. David found it difficult to keep warm in Simon's bed. After shivering wakefully into the grey small hours, he would often have to scramble out from the clinging cold sheets to go for a pee. Once, weary and fumbling with the cord of his pyjamas, he glanced down from the landing and saw Victoria sitting on the stairs. He tiptoed down to her, careful not to make the stairs creak and wake Mum and Dad.

"What's the matter?" he whispered.

Little Victoria turned to him, her face as expressionless as a doll's. "You're not Simon," she hissed. Then she pushed past him as she scampered back up to bed.

On Bonfire Night, David stood beneath a dripping umbrella as Dad struggled to light a Roman candle in a makeshift shelter of paving stones. Tomorrow, he decided, I will start to glue some bits together. Painting the rest of the details can wait. The firework flared briefly through the wet darkness, spraying silver fire and soot across the paving slab. Victoria squealed with fear and chewed her mitten. The afterimage stayed in David's eyes. Silver, almost aeroplane-shaped.

The first thing David discovered about polystyrene cement was that it came out very quickly when the nozzle was pricked with a pin. The second was that it had a remarkable ability to melt plastic. He was almost in tears by the end of his first evening of attempted construction. There was a mushy crater in the middle of the left tailplane and grey smears of plastic all along the side of the motor housing he'd been trying to join. It was disgusting. Grey runners of plastic were dripping from his hands, and he could feel the reek of the glue bringing a crushing headache down on him.

"Getting on all right?" Dad asked, poking his head around the door.

David nearly jumped out of his skin. He desperately clawed unmade bits of the model over to cover up the mess as Dad crossed the room to peer over his shoulder and mutter approvingly for a few seconds. When he'd gone, David discovered that the new pieces were now also sticky with glue and melting plastic.

David struggled on. He didn't like the Flying Fortress and would have happily thrown it away, but the thought of Mum and Dad's disappointment—even little Victoria screwing her face up in contempt—was now as vivid as his imagined triumph had been before. Simon never gave up on things. Simon always (David would show them) did everything right. But by now the very touch of the model, the tiny bumps of the rivets, the rough little edges where the moulding had seeped out, made his flesh crawl. And for no particular reason (a dream too bad to remember) the thought came to him that maybe even real Flying Fortresses (crammed into the rear gunner's turret like a corpse in a coffin.

Kamikaze Zero Zens streaming out of the sky. Flames everywhere and the thick stink of burning. Boiling grey plastic pouring like treacle over his hands, his arms, his shoulders, his face. His mouth. Choking, screaming. Choking) weren't such wonderful things after all.

Compared with constructing the model, the painting—although a disaster—had been easy. Night after night, he struggled with meaningless bits of tiny plastic. And a grey voice whispered in his ear that Simon would have finished it by now. Yessiree. And it would have been perfect. David was under no illusions now as to how difficult the model was to construct (those glib instructions to fit this part to that part that actually entailed hours of messy struggle; the suspicious fact that Airfix had chosen to use a painting of a real Flying Fortress on the box rather than a photograph of the finished model), but he knew that if anyone could finish it, Simon could. Simon could always do anything. Even dead, he amounted to more than David.

In mid-November, David had a particularly difficult Thursday at Games. Mr. Lewis wasn't like the other teachers. He didn't ignore little boys who kept quiet and didn't do much. As he was always telling them, he *cared*. Because David hadn't paid much attention the week before, he'd brought along his rugger kit instead of his gym kit. He was the only boy dressed in green amid all the whites. Mr. Lewis spotted him easily. While the rest of the class watched, laughing and hooting, David had to climb the ropes. Mr. Lewis gave him a bruising push to get started. His muscles burning, his chest heaving with tears and exertion, David managed to climb a foot. Then he slid back. With an affable, aching clout, Mr. Lewis shoved him up again. More quickly this time, David slid back, scouring his hands, arms, and the inside of his legs red raw. Mr. Lewis spun the rope; the climbing bars, the mat-covered parquet floor, the horse and the tall windows looking out on the wet playground, all swirled dizzily. He spun the rope the other way. Just as David was starting to wonder whether he could keep his dinner of liver, soggy chips, and apple snow down for much longer, Mr. Lewis stopped the rope again, embracing David in a sweaty hug. His face was close enough for David to count the big black pores on his nose—if he'd had a few hours to spare.

"A real softy, you are," Mr. Lewis whispered. "Not like your brother at all. Now he was a proper lad." And then he let go.

David dropped to the floor, badly bruising his knees.

As he limped up the stairs that evening, the smell of glue, paint, and plastic—which had been a permanent fixture in the bedroom for some time—poured down from the landing to greet him. It curled around his face like a caressing hand, fingering down his throat and into his nose. And there was nothing remotely like a Flying Fortress on Simon's old desk. But David had had enough. Tonight, he was determined to sort things out. Okay, he'd made a few mistakes, but they could be covered up, repaired, filled in. No one else would notice, and the Flying Fortress would look (David, we knew you'd do a good job, but we'd never imagined anything this splendid; we must ring Granny, tell the local press) just as a 1/72nd-scale top-of-the-range Airfix model should.

David sat down at the desk. The branches of the monkey-puzzle tree outside slithered and shivered in the rain. He stared at his yellow-lit reflection in the glass. The image of the rest of the room was dim, like something from the past. Simon's room. David had put up one or two things of his own now: a silver seagull mobile, a big Airlines of the World poster that he'd got by sending off ten Ski yoghurt foils; but, like cats in a new home, they'd never settled in.

David drew the curtains shut. He clicked the PLAY button on Simon's Sony portable, and Dire Straits came out. He didn't think much of the music one way or another, but it was nice to have a safe, predictable noise going on in the background. Simon's Sony was a special one that played one side of a cassette and then the other as often as you liked without having to turn it over. David remembered the trouble Simon had gone to, to get the right machine at the right price, the pride with which he'd demonstrated the features to Mum and Dad, as though he'd invented them all himself. David had never felt that way about anything.

David clenched his eyes shut, praying that Simon's clever fingers and calm confidence would briefly touch him, that Simon would peek over his shoulder and offer some help. But the thought went astray. He sensed Simon standing at his shoulder all right, but it was Simon as he would be now after a year under the soil, his body still twisted like the frame of his bike, mossy black flesh sliding from his bones. David shuddered and opened his eyes to the grey plastic mess that was supposed to be a Flying Fortress. The room was smugly quiet.

Although there was still much to do, David had finished with planning and detail. He grabbed the obvious big parts of the plane that the interminable instructions (slot parts A, B, and C of the rear side bulkhead together, ensuring that the *upper* inside brace of the support joint fits into dovetail *iv* as illustrated) never got around to mentioning and began to push them together, squeezing out gouts of glue. Dire Straits droned on, "Love over Gold," "It Never Rains," then back to the start of the tape. The faint hum of the TV came up through the floorboards. Key bits of plastic snapped and melted in his hands. David ignored them. At his back, the shadows of Simon's room fluttered in disapproval.

At last, David had something that bore some similarity to a plane. He turned its sticky weight in his hands, and a great bird-shadow flew across the ceiling behind him. One of the wings drooped down, there was a wide split down the middle of the body, smears of glue and paint were everywhere. It was, he knew, a sorry mess. He covered it over with an old sheet in case Mum and Dad should see it in the morning, then went to bed.

Darkness. Dad snoring faintly next door. The outline of Simon's body still there on the mattress beneath his back. David's heart pounded loudly enough to make the springs creak. The room and the Airfix-laden air pulsed in sympathy. It muttered and whispered (no sleep for you, my boy; nice and restless for you all night when everyone's tucked up warm and you're the only wide-awake person in the whole grey universe) but grew silent whenever he lay especially still and dared it to make a noise. The street-light filtered through the monkey-puzzle tree and the curtains onto Simon's desk. The sheet covering the model looked like a face. Simon's face. As it would be now.

David slept. He dreamed. The dreams were worse than waking.

When he opened his eyes to Friday morning, clawing up out of a nightmare into the plastic-scented room, Simon's decayed face still yawned lopsidedly at him, clear and unashamed in the grey wash of the winter dawn. He couldn't abide touching the sheet, let alone taking it off and looking at the mess underneath. Shivering in his pyjamas, he found a Biro in a drawer and used it to poke the yellowed cotton folds until they formed an innocuous shape.

It didn't feel like a Friday at school. The usual sense of sunny relief, the thought of two whole days of freedom, had drained away. His eyes sore from lack of sleep and the skin on his hands flaky with glue, David drifted through Maths and Art, followed by French in the afternoon. At the start of Social Studies, the final lesson of the week, he sat down on a drawing pin that had been placed on his chair: now that Mr. Lewis had singled him out, the naughty boys he shared the back of the class with were beginning to think of him as fair game. Amid the sniggers and guffaws, David pulled the pin out of his bottom uncomplainingly. He had other things on his mind. He was, in fact, a little less miserable about the Flying Fortress than he had been that morning. It probably wasn't as bad as he remembered (could anything really be that bad?), and if he continued tonight, working slowly, using silver paint freely to cover up the bad bits, there might still be a possibility that it would look reasonable. Maybe he could even hang it from the ceiling before anyone got a chance to take a close look. As he walked home through the wet mist, he kept telling himself that it would (please, please, O please God) be all right.

He peeled back the sheet, tugging it off the sticky bits. It was like taking a bandage from a scabby wound. The model looked dreadful. He whimpered and stepped back. He was sure it hadn't been that bad the night before. The wings and the body had sagged, and the plastic had a bubbly, pimply look in places as though something was trying to erupt from underneath. Hurriedly, he snatched the sheet up again and threw it over, then ran downstairs into the lounge.

Mum glanced up from *The Price Is Right.* "You're a stranger down here," she said absently. "I thought you were still busy with that thing of yours."

"It's almost finished," David said to his own amazement as he flopped down, breathless, on the sofa.

Mum nodded slowly and turned back to the TV. She watched TV a lot these days. David had occasionally wandered in and found her staring at pages from Ceefax.

David sat in a daze, letting programme after programme go (as Simon used to say) in one eye and out of the other. He had no desire to go back upstairs to his (Simon's) bedroom, but when the credits rolled on *News at Ten* and Dad smiled at the screen and suggested it was time that Juniors were in bed, he got up without argument. There was something less than affable about Dad's affable suggestions recently. As though if you didn't hop to it, he might (slam your head against the wall until your bones stuck out through your face) grow angry.

After he'd found the courage to turn off the bedside light, David lay with his arms stiffly at his sides, his eyes wide open. Even in the darkness, he could see the pin marks on the ceiling where Simon had hung his planes. They were like tiny black stars. He heard Mum go up to bed, her nervous breathing as she climbed the stairs. He heard the whine of the TV as the channel closed, Dad clearing his throat before he turned it off, the sound of the toilet, the bedroom door creaking shut. Then silence.

Silence. Like the taut skin of a drum. Dark pinprick stars on

the grainy white ceiling like a negative of the real sky, as though
the whole world had twisted itself inside out around David and he
was now in a place where up was down, black was white, and people slithered in the cracks beneath the pavement. Silence. He
really missed last night's whispering voices. Expectant silence.
Silence that screamed, Something Is Going To Happen.

Something did. Quite matter-of-factly, as though it was as ordinary as the kettle in the kitchen switching itself off when it came
to the boil or the traffic lights changing to red on the High Street,
the sheet began to slide off the Flying Fortress. Simon's face
briefly stretched into the folds, then vanished as the whole sheet
flopped to the floor. The Fortress sat still for a moment, outlined
in the light of the streetlamp through the curtains. Then it began to crawl across the desk, dragging itself on its wings like a
wounded beetle.

David didn't really believe that this could be happening. But
as it moved, it even made the sort of scratchy squeaky noises that
a living model of a Flying Fortress might be expected to make. It
paused at the edge of the desk, facing the window; it seemed to
be wondering what to do next. As though, David thought with
giggly hilarity, it hasn't done quite enough already. But the Fortress was far from finished. With a jerky insectile movement, it
launched itself towards the window. The curtain sagged and the
glass went bump. Fluttering its wings like a huge moth, it clung
on and started to climb up towards the curtain rail. Halfway up,
it paused again. It made a chittering sound, and a ripple of movement passed along its back, a little shiver of pleasure: alive at last.
And David knew it sensed something else alive in the room. Him.
The Fortress launched itself from the curtains, setting the streetlight shivering across the empty desk and, more like a huge moth
than ever, began to flutter around the room, bumping blindly into
the ceiling and walls. Involuntarily, he covered his face with his
hands. Through the cracks between his fingers he saw the grey
flitter of its movement. He heard the shriek of soft, fleshy plastic.
He felt the panicky breath of its wings. Just as he was starting to
think it couldn't get any worse, the Fortress settled on his face. He
felt the wings embracing him, the tail curling into his neck, thin
grey claws scrabbling between his fingers, hungry to get at the liquid of his eyes and the soft flesh inside his cheeks.

David began to scream. The fingers grew more persistent, pulling at his hands with a strength he couldn't resist.

"David! What's the matter with you!"

The big light was on. Dad's face hovered above him. Mum

stood at the bottom of the bed, her thin white hands tying and untying in knots.

". . ." He was lost for words, shaking with embarrassment and relief.

Mum and Dad stayed with him for a few minutes, their faces drawn and puzzled. Simon never pulled this sort of trick. Mum's hands knotted. Dad's made fists. Victoria's white face peered around the door when they weren't looking, then vanished again, quick as a ghost. All David could say was that he'd had a bad dream. He glanced across the desk through the bland yellow light. The Fortress was covered by its sheet again. Simon's rotting face grinned at him from the folds. You can't catch me out that easily, the grin said.

Mum and Dad switched off the big light when they left the room. They shuffled back down the landing. As soon as he heard their bedroom door clunk shut, David shot out of bed and clicked his light on again. He left it blazing all night as he sat on the side of the bed, staring at the cloth-covered model. It didn't move. The thin scratches on the backs of his hands were the only sign that anything had happened at all.

As David stared into his bowl of Rice Krispies at breakfast, their snap and crackle and pop fast fading into the sugary milk, Mum announced that she and Dad and Victoria were going to see Gran that afternoon for tea; did he want to come along? David said No. An idea had been growing in his mind, nurtured through the long hours of the night: with the afternoon free to himself, the idea became a fully fledged plan.

Saying he was off to the library, David went down to the Post Office on the High Street before it closed at lunchtime. The clouds were dark and low, and the streets were damp. After waiting an age behind a shopkeeper with bags of ten-pence bits to change, he presented the fat lady behind the glass screen with his savings book and asked to withdraw everything but the one pound needed to keep the account open.

"That's a whole eleven pounds fifty-two pence," she said to him. "Have we been saving up for something special?"

"Oh, yes," David said, dragging his good-boy smile out from the wardrobe and giving it a dust-down for the occasion.

"A nice new toy? I know what you lads are like, all guns and armour."

"It's, um, a surprise."

The lady humphed, disappointed that he wouldn't tell her what it was. She took out a handful of dry roasted nuts from a drawer beneath the counter and popped them into her mouth, licking the salt off her fingers before counting out his money.

Back at home, David returned the savings book to the desk (his hands shaking in his hurry to get back out of the room, his eyes desperately focused away from the cloth-covered model on the top) but kept the two five-pound notes and the change crinkling against his leg in the front pocket of his jeans. He just hoped that Dad wouldn't have one of his occasional surges of interest in his finances and ask to see the savings book. He'd thought that he might say something about helping out a poor school-friend who needed a loan for a new pair of shoes, but the idea sounded unconvincing even as he rehearsed it in his mind.

Fish fingers again for lunch. David wasn't hungry and slipped a few across the plastic tablecloth to Victoria when Mum and Dad weren't looking. Victoria could eat fish fingers until they came out of her ears. When she was really full up, she sometimes even tried to poke a few in there to demonstrate that no more would fit.

Afterwards, David sat in the lounge and pretended to watch *Grandstand* while Mum and Dad and Victoria banged around upstairs and changed into their best clothes. He was tired and tense, feeling rather like the anguished ladies at the start of the headache-tablet adverts, but underneath there was a kind of exhilaration. After all that had happened, he was still determined to put up a fight. Finally, just as the runners and riders for the two o'clock Holsten Pils Handicap at rainswept Wetherby were getting ready for the off, Mum and Dad called bye-bye and slammed the front door.

The doorbell rang a second later.

"Don't forget," Mum said, standing on the doorstep and fiddling with the strap of the black handbag she'd bought for Simon's funeral, "there's some fish fingers left in the freezer for your tea."

"No, I won't," David said.

He stood and watched as the Cortina reversed out of the concrete drive and turned off down the estate road through a grey fog of exhaust.

It was a dark, moist afternoon, but the rain that was making the going heavy at Wetherby was still holding off. For once, the fates seemed to be conspiring in his favour. He took the old galvanised bucket from the garage and, grabbing the stiff-bristled outside broom for good measure, set off up the stairs towards Simon's bedroom. The reek of plastic was incredibly strong now — he wondered why no one else in the house hadn't noticed or complained.

The door to Simon's room was shut. Slippery with sweat, David's hand slid uselessly around the knob. Slowly, deliberately, forcing his muscles to work, he wiped his palms on his jeans and tried again. The knob turned. The door opened. The cloth face grinned at him through the stinking air. It was almost a skull now, as though the last of the flesh had been worried away, and the off-white of the sheet gave added realism. David tried not to think of such things. He walked briskly towards the desk, holding the broom out in front of him like a lance. He gave the cloth a push with it, trying to get rid of the face. The model beneath stirred lazily, like a sleeper awakening in a warm bed. More haste, less speed, he told himself. That was what Dad always said. The words became a meaningless jumble as he held the bucket beneath the lip of the desk and prodded the cloth-covered model towards it. More haste, less speed. Plastic screeched on the surface of the desk, leaving a wet grey trail. More waste, less greed. Little aircraft-shaped bumps came and went beneath the cloth. Hasting waste, wasting haste. The model plopped into the bucket; mercifully, the cloth still covered it. It squirmed and gave a plaintive squeak. David dropped the broom, took the bucket in both hands, and shot down the stairs.

Out through the back door. Across the damp lawn to the black patch where Dad burnt the garden refuse. David tipped the bucket over quickly, trapping the model like a spider under a glass. He hared back into the house, snatching up a book of matches, a bottle of meths, firelighters and newspapers, then sprinted up the garden again before the model had time to think about getting out.

He lifted up the bucket and tossed it to one side. The cloth slid out over the blackened earth like a watery jelly. The model squirmed from the folds, stretching out its wings. David broke the cap from the meths bottle and tipped out a good pint over cloth and plastic and earth. The model hissed in surprise at the cool touch of the alcohol. He tried to light a match from the book. The thin strips of card crumpled. The fourth match caught, but puffed out before he could touch it to the cloth. The model's struggles were becoming increasingly agitated. He struck another match. The head flew off. Another. The model started to crawl away from the cloth. Towards him, stretching and contracting like a slug. Shuddering and sick with disgust, David shoved it back with the toe of his trainer. He tried another match, almost dropping the crumpled book to the ground in his hurry. It flared. He forced himself to crouch down — moving slowly to preserve the precious

flame—and touch it to the cloth. It went up with a satisfying
whooph.

David stepped back from the cheery brightness. The cloth
soon charred and vanished. The model mewed and twisted. Thick
black smoke curled up from the fire. The grey plastic blistered and
ran. Bubbles popped on the aircraft's writhing skin. It arched its
tail in the heat like a scorpion. The black smoke grew thicker. The
next-door neighbour, Mrs. Bowen, slammed her bedroom window
shut with an angry bang. David's eyes streamed as he threw on
firelighters and balled-up newspapers for good measure.

The aircraft struggled in the flames, its blackened body rippling in heat and agony. But somehow, its shape remained.
Against all the rules of the way things should be, the plastic didn't
run into a sticky pool. And, even as the flames began to dwindle
around it, the model was clearly still alive. Wounded, shivering
with pain. But still alive.

David watched in bitter amazement. As the model had no
right to exist in the first place, he supposed he'd been naive to
imagine that an ordinary thing like a fire in the garden would be
enough to kill it. The last of the flames puttered on the blackened
earth. David breathed the raw, sick smell of burnt plastic. The
model—which had lost what little resemblance it had ever had to
a Flying Fortress and now reminded David more than anything of
the dead seagull he had once seen rotting on the beach at Black-
pool—whimpered faintly and, slowly lifting its blistered and trembling wings, tried to crawl towards him.

He watched for a moment in horror, then jerked into action.
The galvanised bucket lay just behind him. He picked it up and
plonked it down hard on the model. It squealed: David saw that
he'd trapped one of the blackened wings under the rim of the
bucket. He lifted it up an inch, kicked the thing under with his
trainer, then ran to find something to weigh down the bucket.

With two bricks on top, the model grew silent inside, as though
accepting its fate. Maybe it really is dying (why haven't you got the
courage to run and get the big spade from the shed like big brave
Simon would do in a situation like this? Chop the thing up into
tiny bits) he told himself. The very least he hoped for was that it
wouldn't dig its way out.

David looked at his watch. Three-thirty. So far, things hadn't
gone as well as he'd planned, but there was no time to stand
around worrying. He still had a lot to do. He threw the book of
matches into the bin, put the meths and the firelighters back
where he had found them, hung the broom up in the garage,

pulled on his duffle coat, locked up the house, and set off towards the High Street.

The greyness of a dull day was already sliding into the dark of evening. Pacing swiftly along the wet-leafed pavement, David glanced over privet hedges into warmly lit living rooms. Mums and Dads sitting on the sofa together, Big Sis doing her nails in preparation for a night down the pub with her boyfriend, Little Jimmy playing with his He-Man doll in front of the fire. Be careful, David thought, seeing those blandly absorbed faces, things can fall apart so easily. Please, be careful.

He took the shortcut across the park, where a few weary players chased a muddy white ball through the gloom, and came out onto the High Street by the public toilets. Just across the road, the back tyres of the Pickfords lorry had rolled Simon into the next world.

David turned left. Woolworths seemed the best place to start. The High Street was busy. Cars and lorries grumbled between the numerous traffic lights, and streams of people dallied and bumped and pushed in and out of the fluorescent heat of the shops. David was surprised to see that the plate-glass windows were already brimming with cardboard Santas and tinsel, but didn't feel the usual thrill of anticipation. Like the Friday-feeling and the Week-end-feeling, the Christmas-feeling seemed to have deserted him. Still, he told himself, there's plenty of time yet. Yes, plenty.

Everything had been switched around in Woolworths. The shelves where the models used to sit between the stick-on soles and the bicycle repair kits were now filled with displays of wine coolers and silk flowers. He eventually found them on a small shelf beside the compact discs, but he could tell almost at a glance that they didn't have any Flying Fortresses. He lifted out the few dusty boxes—a Dukes of Hazzard car, a skeleton, a Tyrannosaurus rex; kid's stuff, not the sort of thing that Simon would ever have bothered himself with—then set out back along the High Street towards W. H. Smith's. They had a better selection, but still no Flying Fortresses. A sign in black and orange suggested IF YOU CAN'T FIND WHAT YOU WANT ON DISPLAY, PLEASE ASK AN ASSISTANT, but David was old and wise enough not to take it seriously. He tried the big newsagent across the road, and then Debenhams opposite Safeway where Santa Claus already had a pokey grotto of fairy lights and hardboard and the speakers gave a muffled rendition of "Merry Christmas (War is Over)." Still no luck. It was quarter to five now. The car lights, traffic lights, streetlights, and shop windows glimmered along the wet pavement, haloed by the begin-

nings of a winter fog. People were buttoning up their anoraks, tying their scarves, and pulling up their detachable hoods, but
David felt sweaty and tired, dodging between prams and slow old
ladies and arm-in-arm girls with green punk hair. He was running
out of shops. He was running out of time. Everyone was supposed
to know about Airfix Flying Fortresses. He didn't imagine that the
concerns of childhood penetrated very deeply into the adult
world, but there were some things that were universal. You could
go into a fish-and-chip shop and the man in the fat-stained apron
would say yes, he knew exactly what you meant, they just might
have one out the back with the blocks of fat and the potatoes. Or
so David had thought. A whole High Street without one seemed
impossible. Once he'd got the model he would, of course, have to
repeat the long and unpleasant task of assembling the thing, but
he was sure that he'd make a better go of it a second time. In its
latter stages, the first model had shown tendencies which even
Simon with his far greater experience of model-making had probably never experienced. For a moment, he felt panic rising in his
throat like sour vomit. The model, trapped under its bucket,
squirmed in his mind. He forced the thought down. After all, he'd
done his best. Of course, he could always write to Airfix and complain, but he somehow doubted whether they were to blame.

He had two more shops on his mental list and about twenty
minutes to reach them. The first, an old-fashioned craft shop, had,
he discovered, become the new offices of a building society. The
second, right up at the far end of the High Street beyond the near-
legendary marital aids shop and outside his normal territory, lay
in a small and less than successful precinct built as a speculation
five years before and still half-empty. David ran past the faded TO
LET signs into the square. There was no Christmas rush here.
Most of the lights in the fibreglass pseudo-Victorian lamps were
broken. In the near darkness, a cluster of youths sat drinking
Shandy Bass on the concrete wall around the dying poplar at the
centre of the square. The few shops that were open looked empty
and about to close. The one David was after had a window filled
unpromisingly with giant nylon teddies in various shades of green,
pink, and orange.

An old woman in a grubby housecoat was mopping the tiled
floor, and the air inside the shop was heavy with the scent of the
same cheap disinfectant they used in the school toilets. David
glanced around, pulling the air into his lungs in thirsty gulps. The
shop was bigger than he'd imagined, but all he could see on display were a few dusty Sindy outfits, a swivel stand of practical

jokes, and a newish rack of Slime Balls—"You Squeeze 'Em, and They Ooze"—the fad of the previous summer.

The man standing with his beer belly resting on the counter glanced up from picking the dirt from under his nails. "Looking for something?"

"Um, models, er, please," David gasped. His throat itched, his lungs ached. He wished he could just close his eyes and curl up in a corner somewhere to sleep.

"Upstairs."

David blinked and looked around again. There was indeed a stairway leading up to another floor. He took it, three steps at a time.

A younger man in a leather-tasselled coat sat with his cowboy boots resting upon a glass counter, smoking and reading *Interview with a Vampire*. He looked even less like an assistant than the man downstairs, but David couldn't imagine what else he could be, unless he was one of the nonspeaking baddies who hung around at the back of the gang in spaghetti Westerns. A faulty fluorescent tube flickered on and off like lightning in the smoky air, shooting out bursts of unpredictable shadow. David walked quickly along the few aisles. Past a row of Transformer robots, their bubble plastic wrapping stuck back into the card with strips of yellowing Sellotape, he came to the model section. At first it didn't look promising, but as he crouched down to check along the rows, he saw a long box poking out from beneath a Revell Catalina on the bottom shelf. There was an all-too-familiar picture on the side: a Flying Fortress. He pulled it out slowly, half expecting it to disappear in a puff of smoke. But no, it stayed firm and real. An Airfix Flying Fortress, a little more dusty and faded than the one Dad had given him, but the same grey weight of plastic, the same painting on the box, £7.75, glue and paints not included, but then he still had plenty of both. David could feel his relief fading even as he slowly drew the long box from the shelf. After all, he still had to make the thing.

The cowboy behind the counter coughed and lit up a fresh Rothmans from the stub of his old one. David glanced along the aisle. What he saw sent a warm jolt through him that destroyed all sense of tiredness and fatigue. There was a display inside the glass cabinet beneath the crossed cowboy boots. Little plastic men struck poses on a greenish sheet of Artexed hardboard that was supposed to look like grass. There were neat little huts, a fuel tender, and a few white dashes and red markers to indicate the start of a runway. In the middle of it all, undercarriage down and bomb-bay doors open, was a silver Flying Fortress. His mouth dry, David slid the box back onto the shelf and strolled up to take a closer look, hands casually thrust into the itchy woollen pockets of his duffle coat, placing his feet down carefully to control the sudden trembling in his legs. It was finished, complete; it looked nothing like the deformed monstrosity he had tried to destroy. Even at a distance through the none-too-clean glass of the display case, he could make out the intricate details, the bright transfers (something he'd never been able to think about applying to his Fortress), and he could tell just from the look of the gun turrets that they would swivel up, down, sideways, any way you liked.

The cowboy recrossed his boots and looked up. He raised his eyebrows questioningly.

"I, er . . . just looking."

"We close now," he said, and returned to his book.

David backed away down the stairs, his eyes fixed on the completed Fortress until it vanished from sight behind a stack of Fisher-Price baby toys. He took the rest of the stairs slowly, his head spinning. He could buy as many models as he liked, but he was absolutely sure he would never be able to reach the level of perfection on display in that glass case. Maybe Simon could have done it better, but no one else.

David took another step down. His spine jarred; without noticing, he'd reached the ground floor. The man cleaning his nails at the desk had gone. The woman with the mop was working her way behind a pillar. He saw a door marked PRIVATE behind a jagged pile of unused shelving. He had an idea; the best he'd had all day.

Moving quickly but carefully so that his trainers didn't squeak, he crossed the shining wet floor, praying that his footsteps wouldn't show. The door had no handle. He pushed it gently with the tips of his fingers. It opened.

There was no light inside. As the door slid closed behind him, he glimpsed a stainless steel sink with a few mugs perched on the draining board, a couple of old chairs, and a girlie calendar on the wall. It was a small room; there didn't seem to be space for anything else. Certainly no room to hide if anyone should open the door. David backed his way carefully into one of the chairs. He sat down. A spring boinged gently. He waited.

As he sat in the almost absolute darkness, his tiredness fought with his fear. The woman with the mop shuffled close by outside. She paused for a heart-stopping moment, but then she went on and David heard the clang of the bucket and the whine of the water pipes through the thin walls from a neighbouring room. She came out again, humming a snatch of a familiar but unplaceable tune. *Da-de-da de-de-de dum-dum.* Stevie Wonder? The Beatles? Wham? David felt his eyelids drooping. His head began to nod.

Footsteps down the stairs. Someone coughing. He wondered if he was back at home. And he wondered why he felt so happy to be there.

He imagined that he was Simon. He could feel the mannish strength inside him, the confident hands that could turn chaotic plastic into perfect machines, the warm, admiring approval of the whole wide world surrounding him like the glowing skin of the boy in the Ready Brek advert.

A man's voice calling good-night and the clink of keys drew David back from sleep. He opened his eyes and listened. After what might have been ten minutes but seemed like an hour, there was still silence. He stood up and felt for the door. He opened it a crack. The lights were still on at the windows, but the shop was locked and empty. Quick and easy as a shadow, he made his way up the stairs. The Fortress was waiting for him, clean lines of silvered plastic, intricate and marvellous as a dream. He slid back the glass door of the case (no lock or bolt — he could hardly believe how careless people could be with such treasure) and took it in his hands. It was beautiful. It was perfect, and it lacked any life of its own. He sniffed back tears. That was the best thing of all. It was dead.

It wasn't easy getting the model home. Fumbling his way through the darkness at the back of the shop, he managed to find the fire escape door, but when he leaned on the lever and shoved it open, an alarm bell started to clang above his head. He stood rigid for a moment, drenched in cold shock, then shot out across the loading yard and along the road behind. People stared at him as he pounded the streets on the long aching run home. The silver Fortress was far too big to hide. That — and the fact that the man in the shop would be bound to remember that he'd been hanging around before closing time — made David sure that he had committed a less-than-perfect crime. Like Bonnie and Clyde or Butch Cassidy, David guessed it was only a matter of time before the Law caught up with him. But first he would have his moment of glory; perhaps a moment glorious enough to turn around everything that had happened so far.

Arriving home with a bad cramp in his ribs and Mum and Dad and Victoria still out at Gran's, he found the bucket in the garden sitting undisturbed with two bricks on top. Although he didn't have the courage to lift it up to look, there was nothing to suggest that the old Fortress wasn't sitting quietly (perhaps even dead) underneath. Lying on his bed and blowing at the model's propellers to make them spin, he could already feel the power growing within him. Tomorrow, in the daylight, he knew he'd feel strong enough to get the spade and sort things out properly.

All in all, he decided, the day had gone quite well. Things never happen as you expect, he told himself; they're either far better or far worse. This morning he'd never have believed that he'd have a finished Flying Fortress in his hands by the evening, yet here he was, gazing into the cockpit at the incredible detail of the crew and their tiny controls as a lover would gaze into the eyes of his beloved. And the best was yet to come. Even as he smiled to himself, the lights of Dad's Cortina swept across the bedroom curtains. The front door opened. David heard Mum's voice saying shush, then Dad's. He smiled again. This was, after all, what he'd been striving for. He had in his hands the proof that he was as good as Simon. The Fortress was the healing miracle that would soothe away the scars of his death. The family would become one. The grey curse would be lifted from the house.

Dad's heavy tread came up the stairs. He went into Victoria's bedroom. After a moment, he stuck his head around David's door.

"Everything all right, Junior?"

"Yes, Dad."

"Try to be quiet. Victoria fell asleep in the car and I've put her straight to bed."

Dad's head vanished. He pulled the door shut. Opening and closing the bomb-bay doors, David gazed up at the model. Dad hadn't noticed the Fortress. Odd, that. Still, it probably showed just how special it was.

The TV boomed downstairs. The start of *3-2-1*; David recognised the tune. He got up slowly from his bed. He paused at the door to glance back into the room. No longer Simon's room, he told himself— *His Room*. He crossed the landing and walked down the stairs. Faintly, he heard the sound of Victoria moaning in her sleep. But that was all right. Everything would be all right. The finished model was cradled in his hands. It was like a dream.

He opened the lounge door. The quiz-show colours on the TV filled his eyes. Red and silver and gold, bright and warm as Christmas. Mum was sitting in her usual chair wearing her usual TV expression. Dad was stretched out on the sofa.

He looked up at David. "All right, Junior?"

David held the silver Fortress out towards his father. The fuselage glittered in the TV light. "Look, I've finished the model."

"Let's see." Dad stretched out his hand. David gave it to him.

"Sure . . . that's pretty good, Junior. You'll have to save up and buy something more difficult with that money you've got in the Post Office. . . . Here." He handed it back to David.

David took the Fortress. One of the bomb-bay doors flipped open. He clicked it back into place.

On the TV Steve and Yvette from Rochdale were telling Ted Rogers a story about their honeymoon. Ted finished it off with a punch line that David didn't understand. The audience roared.

Dad scratched his belly, worming his fingers into the gaps between the buttons of his shirt. "I think your mother wanted a word with you," he said, watching as Steve and Yvette agonised over a question. He raised his voice a little. "Isn't that right, pet? Didn't you want a word with him?"

Mum's face turned slowly from the TV screen.

"Look," David said, taking a step towards her, "I've —"

Mum's head continued turning. Away from David, towards Dad. "I thought you were going to speak to him," she said.

Dad shrugged. "You found them, pet, you tell him . . . and move, Junior. I can't see the programme through you."

David moved.

Mum fumbled in the pocket of her dress. She produced a book of matches. "I found these in the bin," she said, looking straight at him. Through him. David had to suppress a shudder. "What have you been up to?"

"Nothing." David grinned weakly. His good-boy smile wouldn't come.

"You haven't been smoking?"

"No, Mum. I promise."

"Well, as long as you don't." Mum turned back to the TV. Steve and Yvette had failed. Instead of a Mini Metro they had won Dusty Bin. The audience was in raptures. Back after the break, said Ted Rogers

David stood watching the bright screen. A grey tombstone loomed towards him. This is what happens, a voice said, if you get AIDS.

Dad gave a theatrical groan that turned into a cough. "Those queers make me sick," he said when he'd hawked his throat clear.

Without realising what he was doing, David left the room and went back upstairs to Simon's bedroom.

He left the lights on and reopened the curtains. The monkey-puzzle tree waved at him through the wet darkness; the rain from Wetherby had finally arrived. Each droplet sliding down the glass held a tiny spark of streetlight.

He sat down and plonked the Fortress on the desk in front of him. A propeller blade snapped; he hadn't bothered to put the undercarriage down. He didn't care. He breathed deeply, the air shuddering in his throat like the sound of running past railings. Through the bitter phlegm he could still smell the reek of plastic. Not the faint, tidy smell of the finished Fortress. No, this was the smell that had been with him for weeks. But now it didn't bring sick expectation in his stomach; he no longer felt afraid. Now, in his own way, he had reached the summit of a finished Flying Fortress, a high place from where he could look back at the remains of his childhood. Everything had been out of scale before, but now he saw, he really saw, 1/72nd scale; David knew what it meant now. The Fortress was huge, as heavy and grey as the rest of the world. It was him that was tiny, 1/72nd scale.

He looked at the Fortress: big, ugly, and silver. The sight of it sickened him more than the old model had ever done. At least that had been his. For all its considerable faults, he had made it.

David stood up. Quietly, he left the room and went down the stairs, past the lounge and the booming TV, into the kitchen. He found the waterproof torch and walked out into the rain.

The bucket still hadn't moved. Holding the torch in the crook of his arm, David removed the two bricks and lifted it up. For a moment, he thought that there was nothing underneath, but then, pointing the torch's rain-streamed light straight down, he saw that the model was still there. As he'd half expected, it had tried to burrow its way out from under the bucket. But it was too weak. All it had succeeded in doing was to cover itself in wet earth.

The model mewed gently and tried to raise itself up towards David.

This time he didn't step back. "Come on," he said. "We're going back inside."

David led the way, levelling the beam of the torch through the rain like a scaled-down searchlight, its yellow oval glistening on the muddy wet grass just ahead. The rain was getting worse; heavy drops rattling on David's skull and plastering his hair down like a wet swimming cap. The model moved slowly, seeming to weaken with every arch of its rotting fuselage. David clenched his jaw and tried to urge it on, pouring his own strength into the wounded creature. Once, he looked up over the roofs of the houses. Above the chimneys and TV aerials, cloud-heavy sky seemed to boil. Briefly, he thought he saw shapes form, ghosts swirling on the moaning wind. And the ghosts were not people, but simple inanimate things. Clocks and cars, china and jewellery, toys and trophies, all tumbling uselessly through the night. But then he blinked and there was nothing to be seen but the rain, washing his face and filling his eyes like tears.

He was wet through by the time they reached the back door. The concrete step proved too much for the model, and David had to stoop and quickly lift it onto the lino inside, trying not to think of the way it felt in his hands.

In the kitchen's fluorescent light, he saw for the first time just how badly injured the creature was. Clumps of earth clung to its sticky blistered wings, and grey plastic oozed from gaping wounds along its fuselage. And the reek of it immediately filled the kitchen, easily overpowering the usual smell of fish fingers. It stank of glue and paint and plastic; but there was more. It also smelt like something dying.

It moved on, dragging its wings, whimpering in agony, growing weaker with every inch. Plainly, the creature was close to the end of its short existence.

"Come on," David whispered, crouching down close beside it. "There's not far to go now. Please try. Please . . . don't die yet."

Seeming to understand, the model made a final effort. David held the kitchen door open as it crawled into the hall, onwards towards the light and sound of the TV through the frosted lounge door.

"You made *that?*" An awed whisper came from halfway up the stairs.

David looked up and saw little Victoria peering down at the limping model, her hands gripping the banister like a prisoner behind bars. He nodded, feeling an odd sense of pride. It was, after all, his. But he knew you could take pride too far. The model belonged to the whole family as well. To Victoria sitting alone at night on the stairs, to Simon turning to mush and bones in his damp coffin—and to Mum and Dad. And that was why it was important to show them. David was old for a child; he knew that grownups were funny like that. If you didn't show them things, they simply didn't believe in them.

"Come on," he said, holding out his hand.

Victoria scampered quickly down the stairs and along the hall, stepping carefully over the model and putting her cold little hand inside his slightly larger one.

The model struggled on, leaving a trail of slimy plastic behind on the carpet. When it reached the lounge door, David turned the handle and the three of them went in together.

Marnie

I'd arranged things so that I woke up on an ordinary morning. It was November, the winter term. My bedroom curtains were veined with frost and sunlight. And for a long time I just lay there, breathing the strange, familiar smells of this house and this bed and my own sleepy body, until the radio alarm lit up with the last pip of the eight o'clock time signal. It was reassuring to find that nothing had really changed. It was just an ordinary morning. I had ordinary things to do.

I got up and went to the bathroom, finding my way unthinkingly. The memories and sensations were crowding in too quickly for me to react, but for now nothing mattered as long as my body knew what to do. Opening doors with just the right pressure, twisting on the shower taps to get the hot water running before stepping in. My skin felt distant as I soaped myself. The contours and textures seemed right, yet didn't belong. I could sense my flesh, yet it was like touching a lover.

But even as I wondered at the strangeness of returning, the feeling was wearing off. The easy movement of my limbs began to seem natural. The full head of hair that I dried with smooth, strong hands that had reached automatically for the towel was no surprise. Age is relative, and one adjusts to its presence. And I reminded myself that I was, in any case, thirty-one—no longer quite young.

I wiped a space in the steamed-up mirror to shave. I recognised my face from the old, cold photographs. Here, moving and alive, I saw that the camera hadn't lied. It was an ungenerous face, the eyes too close, the nose too large. Insincere when it smiled. Pained when it tried to look sincere. I'd never grown used to it, and seeing it again, with the deepened knowledge of what age would do, made me wonder — just as I had done all those years back, just as I had always done — exactly *what* Marnie had seen in me.

The shaving foam was Tesco's own, from the big store by the roundabout. The razor was a Bic. I marvelled at the rightness of the period detail, the bar codes and the price stickers still on the side. It seemed almost a pity to use them, like ransacking a museum. Brut 33 aftershave in a green plastic bottle on the shelf over the sink. Had people still used that stuff in the late 1980s? I unscrewed the silver cap and splashed some on my chest and face, smiling faintly at the thought of the advert they used to run. It was all coming back to me now. All of it. The dark, sweet smell of the aftershave. The toothpaste and brush in a broken-handled Charles and Diana mug. And beside that, sitting just as naturally on the shelf, was a small bottle of Elizabeth Arden cleanser. Everything about the bottle, the casual thought with which Marnie had doubtless left it for next time, the screw top jammed on at a typically careless angle, hit me hard. I reached out to hold the bottle, touching where her fingers had touched. This was real enough. There was nothing to grin at, point at. This wasn't a museum.

Marnie, I thought. Marnie. Look again. She's all around you. Long strands of her blonde hair in the plughole. A half box of Tampax in the cabinet by the sink. The lipstick remains of I *love you* written on the tiles above the bath showing up through the condensation, even though some tidy insanity had made me wipe it off with white spirit. Marnie: the thought that had filled and haunted my whole life. Marnie. Marnie. *Marnie.*

I got dressed, finding my socks and underpants tucked neatly in the right drawer. Hello, old friends. Then cords, a warmish grey cotton shirt, and a loosely knotted woollen tie that was a concession to my position at the University. Looking at myself fully dressed in the long wardrobe mirror, I felt ticklish threads of the ridiculous pulling once again at my mind. That collar, those cords! And that *tie.* I hadn't remembered looking quite as foolish as this. But memories change to suit the present.

I took breakfast listening to the plummy-voiced newscasters on Radio Four. I'd long forgotten the details, but nothing in the news came as a surprise, any more than it had been a surprise to find cartons of orange juice and milk waiting from yesterday in the fridge, or cartons of sugar-free muesli in the fitted cabinets, slit open and resealed neatly and precisely according to the instructions.

I was in two minds about whether to walk or drive to work. The walk was easy enough, but when I toured my house, touching and remembering all those old possessions, I spent longer in the garage than anywhere else, despite the winter chill. There, still looking clean and new, was my car, my pride and joy, the pinnacle of my overdraft. A Porsche: black and glossy as dark water. I'd forgotten just how proud I'd been of it, but that all came back as soon as I saw and touched and smelt it. After brooding at the wheel for some time, gazing at the slumbering dials, I decided it was better to be cautious on this first day. After all, I hadn't driven anything remotely like it for twenty years.

After brushing my teeth, I pulled on a tweed jacket that would, if my life proceeded as it had before, be stolen from under my seat at a cinema in Southport two years later.

The chilly sunlit air beyond my front door was full of the city. It was a short walk to campus. I lived . . . *live* in a close of small and expensive modern semis built as an infill in one of the huge gardens of the big older houses that still characterised this area around the University. Most of my neighbours were young, like me, professional and well-paid, like me, single or married or living together, but always childless. Like me.

Even in this pretty tree-lined area, the smells of parkland and old leaves were half-drowned, to my newly sensitised nose, by the metallic reek of car fumes. I had two main roads to cross. Both were filled with a dangerous sluggish stream of cars. Startled by the bleep of the pelican crossing and urged on by an impatient old lady, I realised it hadn't been a mistake to leave the Porsche in the garage.

The interlinking suburban roads were nicer, more as I remembered them. Landscaped gardens and mock-Tudor gables. There were school-children piling into ugly Volvos in driveways, and joggers and students walking, and students on bikes. This was my usual route, and many of the faces were familiar, people I passed day after day without acknowledgement. Everything was so neat, so orderly, so expected.

I went through the west gate into the campus. Staff and students drifted and talked and walked in the grassy spaces between the red brick and concrete. Faces came out at me from the past. I was a fixture here, part of the crew. Norman Harris from the

Chancellor's office nodded in my direction as he walked away from his Sierra. Then I saw Stephanie Kent hurrying up the wide granite steps of the library, the same old woollen skirt tight as ever over the ample ridges of her knickers. And there was Jack Rattle, my own Head of Department, the latest Penguin in one hand and a sandwich box in the other.

We converged at the swing doors leading to the Graphic Arts Faculty. I held them open for him.

"Morning, Daniel," he said. "Another day, eh? Another few brain cells gone."

"Hardly any left," I said; it didn't sound right, but then I'd never really known how to respond to Jack. I wondered if he'd said the same thing to me on this same day all those years ago, and what my reply had been.

"You must," he tapped my elbow with the corner of his sandwich box, "you must show me what we're getting from that new plotter. Damn thing cost us enough."

"Sure. Just say when."

"I will. I will." Jack wandered off down the admin corridor to his own office, passing in and out of frames of window sunlight. I paused for a moment beneath the frescoes at the foot of the marble stairs, watching him, wondering if it was foreknowledge or if the signs were really there that his heart would kill him in the spring.

A few students pushed past me as I dawdled, huffy and in a rush. In the sixties and seventies, any arts faculty would have been filled with campus peacocks even this deep into winter term, but now, with the odd green-haired exception, the students were heavy with overcoats, anxiety, and books, just like all the trainee lawyers and engineers in the other faculties. Like everyone else, they wanted their grades, they wanted a job, they wanted money.

I checked my watch. It was 9:35. That was just right; my tutorial should have started at half past. Although it was quite impossible that anyone could find me out, I nevertheless felt it was important to give nothing away by changing my habits.

My legs were suddenly a little weak as I took the stairs to the second level: a strong and unexpected return of the feeling that my body didn't belong to me. In a sense, of course, it didn't, but I pushed that thought down as I passed the Burne-Jones stained-glass and the fire hydrants at the stair turns. This was not the time to hesitate, not when I had a tutorial to get through. Just don't think, I told myself. It worked well enough before.

Along the waxed gleam of the east corridor. Notice boards and past students' efforts on the walls. Rooms 212, 213, 213A, 214.

214. I took a deep breath and walked in. The chatter ceased reluctantly. The air smelt a little of someone's BO, and a lot of the plastic of the computer terminals that had only been in place since the start of the term.

"Good morning." I powered up the master screen, proud of the swift and easy way my hands moved across the switches and keys. "This week we'll continue our exploration of the ways we can expand from the basic paintbox options. . . ."

I paused and looked around at the faces, half-familiar now as they had been then. From the bored expressions, it was obvious that they accepted me without question. I knew that I'd passed a test; my nerves were loosening by the moment. I continued talking at a brisk pace, hardly referring to my notes.

Living in the past was easy.

I closed the tutorial at eleven, and the students drifted out, leaving the garish perspective tricks that the inexperienced or untalented generally produce shimmering on their screens. The computer was still logged for our use, and they could have continued, but for all of them the novelty of pressing keys to make things happen on a screen had worn off. Too lazy to walk around the room and look (and how quickly the habits of my lecturing days were coming back!), I called their efforts up, reduced to quarter windows, on my own screen, and saved them for next week's session, unthinkingly hitting the right keys. VIEW, SAVE, NAME, RETURN. It was an oddly absorbing task, and probably the first time this morning that, with the success of the tutorial behind me, I'd felt completely at home.

The students had left the door open, and Marnie entered the room without my noticing. She'd crept up close behind me before I knew, suddenly, that she was there — and that she was real.

It was strange, to come this far and then to be almost taken by surprise. She put her arms around my neck. Her hair brushed my face. I could smell the shampoo and acacia, and the cigarette she'd just smoked, and the wool of her scarf, and the faint, bitter sweetness of her breath.

"When are you going to give this up," she said, her voice serious but trickling down with every word towards laughter. "Why don't you let the machines get on with it?"

"Could I be replaced that easily?"

"That's right," she said. Her hands pressed against my chest, then suddenly released. ". . . old boffin like you . . ." She spun the chair around so that I faced her. ". . . and how is the old boffin, anyway?"

"Same as yesterday," I said. "Let's have coffee."

Marnie's good mood was frail, as I knew it would be. She walked with her head down as we crossed the bright, busy campus, like a child aiming to miss the cracks in the pavement. I'd have liked to have taken her hand, just to be touching her, but I knew it wasn't the sort of thing we'd usually done.

We queued in the cafeteria. Marnie was silent, and I couldn't think of anything to say. The woman at the till shook her head and gave me a funny look when I offered my Visa card to pay for the coffee. I don't think Marnie noticed. We took our cups over to an empty table by the window that two Arab students had just vacated. The plastic seat felt warm. I was noticing these things, the steam rising from the slowly spinning froth of the coffee, and the way someone had spooned the sugar to one side of the bowl that lay between us: with Marnie, everything was more vivid. It always had been.

"Is this a busy day?" she asked, lifting the cup with both hands, blowing with that beautiful mouth, sipping. A little of the froth stayed on the faint down along her top lip.

"We could be together, if you like."

"That could be nice," she said.

"Could?"

"Depends on what sort of let's-be-together-day it is."

"I love you, Marnie." For thirty years, I'd been wanting to say those words to her again.

She put the cup down with a slight bang. Her eyes travelled across my face, onwards to the window, the wandering students amid the winter-bare trees, the big buildings beyond. "I don't feel right in this place," she said. "All this architecture. Look at the people out there. Standing, wandering around, talking. It's all such a pose. You know, like one of those architect's drawings you see. Prospective developments. And little sketches of people in the foreground . . . imaginary people doing imaginary things, just to give the whole neat concept a sense of scale. It's not real, people standing around like that, you only ever get anything actually like it at a University."

"It's just a place," I said. "We're both here. You. Me. That's real enough."

"And this is going to be a you-and-me day?"

"I'd like it to be," I said.

"I've got a couple of lectures and a life study I could skip."

"Then," I said, "there's no problem."

She didn't reply. There was still froth on her lip and I wanted to mention it, but knew I shouldn't. This whole thing was doubly confusing: my searching for the right words to bridge the awkwardness that was already between us was compounded by the continued vague promptings of memory, a feeling of drifting in and out of the flow. I'd imagined that it would be easy to draw things away from the patterns of the past, but Marnie was still the same, and now that I was here, I was surprised at how little I had changed. I decided that the best thing was to take a new tack, and say those things to her that I'd always wanted to say.

I swallowed some coffee. Another distraction. I'd forgotten the way the University coffee used to taste. Something about it always reminded me of floormops. I was like Proust, but instead of drifting away into memory, I was choking and drowning in tea-soaked madeleines.

"I've been thinking," I said, ". . . about the way we've allowed things to . . . drift. I've been a fool to forget that I loved you. Love you . . . no, I never forgot that, but things got in the way. Let's ignore the last couple of weeks. It's just history, a little time in our lives. The arguments don't matter if we have each other."

She glanced back at me from the window as though she was returning from another world. I checked my irritation. No rows, not this time.

"I'm a bit hung-over," she said. "Honesty time. I was pissed last night."

"With your friends."

She shrugged. "With people. They're not you, Dan, don't worry. I'd like to give things a chance, I really would, if we could get it back. When I saw you this morning, sitting in front of that damn screen of yours, it was —"

Her gaze went up. Something slapped my back.

"Dan! Mind if I join you?"

A chair rasped over from the nearest table before I could answer. Ritchie Hanks — one of the specialists who took care of the University mainframe — plonked his heavy boyish self down.

He glanced at Marnie. I wasn't sure whether they'd ever met — my memory failing me again. There was a gratifying moment of hesitation, as the thought that maybe he'd interrupted something passed briefly in ones and zeros through Ritchie's computer-specialist's brain. But he wasn't easily put off when he had a story to tell about some fascinating new glitch he'd found in the system.

We listened politely. I asked a few questions so that he could give the answers he wanted. Marnie was on her best behaviour: none of the sly asides that I'd found so amusing when I'd first known her but had since come to dread. None of that mattered,

I told myself, not here in the past, not when I knew that Ritchie would have a private-sector job on double the pay by the end of next year and I'd never think of him again, or whilst Marnie . . . but it did. Everything mattered.

"Anyway," I said, stopping him quickly before he began a different story. "I'd better be going now. Pressure of work, you know how it is."

"Sure, Dan. Pressure of work. Never stops, does it. I was only — "

" — that's right." I moved to stand. "Marnie, are you coming?"

"Well . . ." She hesitated and looked at me. Just her joke. Of course she'd come instead of staying with a prat like Ritchie. Wouldn't she?

She smiled. "I have some work to do. Us students have work too."

"Students," Ritchie said, as though it was a new concept. "Of course."

Marnie and I walked out into the cold air. Nothing had been decided. Nothing had changed.

Marnie shivered and pushed her hands into the pockets of her jacket. Her hair almost glittered in the sunlight. "It's true," she said. "I do have things to do. Tell you what, I'll come round your place tonight."

I nodded numbly. "What time?"

"Say . . . eight."

I nodded again.

"Ciao."

"Ciao."

She walked away from me. Above her winter boots and red socks were the bare backs of her knees. I wanted to kiss them and taste her skin. In my newly youthful body, the thought brought the odd and unaccustomed stirrings of an erection. It grew and then faded as she diminished in the slow drift of movement, as she became another figure, an artist's brushstroke to give these buildings a sense of scale.

Maybe I should have started earlier back. Perhaps that was part of the problem. Started back at the time when everything was fresh and new and right. But to do that, I would have had to go back to some misty and mythical place where Marnie wasn't Marnie and I wasn't me.

It was simply more complicated than that.

This was Marnie's second year at University. I'd seen her in the first year, of course; she was too pretty and . . . different not to be noticed. I think we might even have been to a couple of the same parties, not the student sort, but the ones around the chintzy academic fringes of the University where people dress up and pretend to stay sober, and start off talking about the Booker Prize and end up bitching about who's screwing whom. But Marnie didn't invite approaches, at least not from me she didn't.

She was twenty-four, a good three years older than the other undergrads. A *mature student:* how she hated that phrase. I suppose she was lonely in the way that older students always are, having to act as a shoulder to cry on, having to ignore or laugh along with the stupidities of her younger friends. She'd spent those extra years drifting in Europe, working as a nanny in Cannes, staying in some kibbutz, doing the sort of things that most people only talk about doing. I was seven years older, but I'd never really left school. She made me feel young, and she made me wonder just where and why and with whom she'd been doing all these things.

I only met her properly, face to face, when she took the computer graphics option in her second year. She didn't belong in the class. She was always sitting a little apart when I came in and the others looked up from their chatter. Marnie stood out in most situations. She just didn't belong. It was everything about her.

By the end of the second week, it was obvious that Marnie and computers weren't going to get on. There wasn't much to learn — the whole purpose of the course was, after all, to allow the students to put computers down on their CVs when they applied for those cherished jobs in design offices and advertising agencies — but even when she hit the right keys, things would go wrong. And after I'd cleared the screen of gibberish, and she'd punched the keys or prodded the light pen or rolled the mouse again, with a simple pessimism that was quite different from the manner of people who are genuinely computer-phobic, something else would go wrong instead. I'd never known anything like it. She nearly brought down the whole mainframe in the third week, something that was theoretically impossible from our access port and doubtless caused Ritchie and his colleagues no end of fascination.

I didn't mind at all. It gave me a legitimate excuse to spend most of the tutorials sitting next to Marnie, to lean close to her as we pondered the latest catastrophe, and to breathe her scent. I kept my eyes on the screen, but that was because I could see her reflection so clearly in the glass.

She gave me no particular signals. Of course, someone as lovely as Marnie gives signals to every man she passes, but that is merely God's unthinking blessing and curse. She dressed differently from the other students, usually in skirts and dresses rather than jeans. She had a striped blue-and-white cotton jacket that she wore when the weather was still mild early in the term that I fell in love with for some reason. She wore her hair long or in a bun. She smelt of acacia and cigarettes and Marnie. There was a slowness about the way she moved, a kind of resignation. She understood how she looked, but unlike most beautiful women, she had a kind of confidence, but absolutely no pride.

I was attracted. I wanted to walk along sunset beaches with her. I wanted to talk through the night. I wanted to go to bed with her, and stay there a long, long time. I wanted my fill of Marnie, and I wasn't sure how much that could possibly be. The whole thing quickly got out of hand. I wanted her too badly to break the silence and risk rejection. And by the fifth week of term, I was being brusque and ignoring her in class and then replaying every word and look endlessly, even in my sleep. I was even beginning to wonder if it really was Marnie, or whether I was simply going a little mad.

Then I saw her one afternoon. I was killing time, wandering in the local botanical gardens, because the Chancellor's department had cocked-up the room allocation for my tutorial. The big tropical house was a common enough place for students to work, and it came as a bigger surprise than it should have to find her there, sitting with an easel beside the goldfish pool, filling in blocks of colour on a squared-off grid.

I said hello and she said hi. She was wearing a loose tee-shirt, and I could see the curves of her shoulders and neck far more clearly than my fantasies had permitted. She seemed quite cheerful and relaxed. Marnie was, as I soon discovered, very partial to warmth, and very averse to the cold. A real hot-house flower. I sat down on the stone rim of the pond amid the bananas and rotting oranges and orchids, and we chatted. When I stood up for us to go down to the tea room by the pagoda, the backs of my trousers were soaking wet. We laughed about that, the first time we'd ever laughed together. When she pulled on her blue-and-white cotton jacket, her bare downy arm brushed against my chest, and the feeling hit me like a huge taut drum.

That was how it began. Now, with an afternoon to get through without her and only those odd unsatisfactory words in the cafeteria to cling to, Marnie seemed almost as distant from me as she had all those years ahead, before I'd returned.

I spent the time wandering. I walked down to the botanical

gardens, feeling more comfortable now with the undirected flood of traffic that growled past. This was, after all, my life. I had lived it. The eighties were as idiosyncratic as any other decade, but at root, nothing was really that different from the true present. It was just a question of emphasis and style. Women pushed prams. Tramps mumbled. All the young people seemed to be plugged into those clumsy music players . . . Walkmans. They stared straight through you. Visitors from another planet. It reminded me of that Bradbury novel, all the people with shells in their ears. A helicopter chittered low and loud over the rooftops. No one glanced up. And some of the new buildings looked as though they belonged on a moonbase. The future was already here. Of course, there were no silver air-cars or monorails, but by now people had realised that there never would be. Things would carry on pretty much as they had always done, and even the tantalising fear of a black and glassy wasteland, the last of those great midcentury fantasies, was fading. These people pushing past and looking through me as they went about their busy, empty lives knew that nothing would ever really change. The holes in the sky would grow larger, and so would their flatter, squarer, sharper, deeper, thinner TV screens. And when the news slipped in between the commercials, the faces that peered out at them from those TV screens would still be ancient and hollow-eyed with starvation. The future was a fact that had arrived and had already been forgotten. It meant as much and as little to them as it would have done to their ancestors, dragging a plough or sheltering in a cave. They knew that what lay ahead was the same as now, only more so.

There were no students in the tropical house today. I drank my coffee in the tea room down by the bandstand alone.

Still not feeling up to risking myself and the Porsche, I took a bus into the centre of town. I still had some change in my pockets, but it was running down. I knew I had a card in my wallet, next to the last five-pound note, that would get me money from one of the many cash machines. But for all my research and revision, I had no idea what my PIN number was.

I made the mistake of sitting on the top deck of the bus, and the ragged movements and the unaccustomed cigarette fumes left me feeling a little sick by the time it finally jerked to a halt outside C&As.

The shops were a revelation. I would have loved to have taken some of this stuff back to the present with me. Condoms (and who could ever forget AIDS? Well, I had, for one). Organic vegetables. Newspapers with real news in them. Compact discs. Posters like wallpaper with the name of the artist printed at the bottom in huge type. Mrs. Thatcher mugs! I guess I just gawked. The store detectives watched me carefully as I picked up this and prodded that. It was just like a museum. They were the museum keepers, and didn't even know it.

The evening rush hour caught me unawares. Everybody was grim, moving all at once. I had to queue in the yellow streetlight to get a place on the bus, and then had to stand most of the way to my stop. It was cold as I walked the last half mile, and I was pondering whether I should give my central heating a call—before I remembered. The house was warm anyway, the timer set thoughtfully to come on in the evening.

I took a bath, feeling a little guilty about how much I'd unthinkingly enjoyed my Marnie-less tour of the local sights. But by seven I was waiting, anxiously clean and freshly clothed, not so much watching the TV as playing with the remote control.

Slices of the Channel Four news. Some quiz programme. An old Doris Day film. *Top of the Pops. Top of the Pops* was the most diverting (did Michael Jackson ever look *that* young?), but none of them held my attention for long. Soon, Marnie would be here. I planned on going out for a meal, maybe that Indian place just along the road, something ordinary and nostalgic, a place where we could sit in peaceful candlelit anonymity and talk longingly. And then we'd walk back, hugging each other close against the cold, our frosty breath entwined in the streetlight, back to my house, to my bed.

Eight o'clock came and went. Marnie was always late, of course. I fixed myself a shot of Famous Grouse at half past, and then another at five to nine. All the usual questions and accusations were starting a headache hammer inside my head. I wandered around the house, looking at the wallpaper I'd chosen, the furniture and the things I hadn't seen in thirty years. Now, if I'd only kept that big plastic Foster's Lager ashtray that Marnie had smuggled out of the local wine bar under her coat and used to roll her joints. Somewhere along the years, it had departed from my life; exactly the sort of bric-a-brac that grew in value because no one thought anything of it at the time. There were a distressingly large number of things like that around the house. I'd been sitting on a gold mine, and I'd never realised it. And where the goddamned hell was she anyway?

Where was Marnie? At any moment since we'd become lovers, and even for some time before, that question was always somewhere in my thoughts. Another half hour, another whisky. I stood at the window and watched the empty pavement. I sat down and tried the TV again. I lay on the bed. I got up. I put the record player on. Old music for these old times. But the question followed me about, tapping at my shoulder, clutching at my elbow, whispering in my ear. What is she doing? She was with someone else, that was what. She'd never been faithful, not truly, not *faithful*, that was what.

I'd seen her walking the campus with another man the morning after the very first night we'd made love. I was still glowing. I sidled behind a tree. I watched them cross the wide and milling spaces. At the steps in front of the library she put her arms around him and laughed and gave him a quick kiss. She said he was just a student when I quizzed her in the corridor as she came out from pottery, clay on her apron and hands and arms like the evidence of a crime, just someone she liked who had said something funny. Just another student. Snob that I was, that hurt more than anything. He was three years younger than her, for Chrissake! And when I followed him into the cafeteria for lunch, I saw that he had greasy hair and a fair sprinkling of pimples.

Ten o'clock. She wasn't coming. No one, *absolutely no one*, let me down like this! And this wasn't the first time, either, oh no, she let me down all the time! No more whisky, I decided, having drunk myself up to some sort of calm plateau. Tonight might be a dead loss, but there would be plenty of other times. Yes, plenty.

I pulled on a coat and went for a walk. I hadn't walked so much in one day for a long time. It was quiet now, the cars passed by in separate flashes of light. The big petrol station by the traffic lights glowed like a Spielberg spaceship. I headed down past the hospital towards Marnie's place. It was pure masochism, I knew I wouldn't find her there.

Architecturally, the big old houses on Westborne Road were similar to those of the sales directors and wine importers who lived around me, but here, a little further out of town, there were dirty net curtains at the windows and bed-sit rows of bell buttons beside the doors.

Hers was the top window, set in a gable, with a wind-chime owl hanging from the casement in perpetual silence. I crunched up the worn tarmac drive, where a Morris Minor was parked beside a wheelless Triumph Herald up on bricks, and tried the buzzer anyway. A typed strip beside it had the name of the previous occupant, one R. Singh. Marnie never got around to changing anything. There was no reply. The shape of the stairs in the low-wattage light of the hall loomed through the coloured door-glass.

I could smell cat's piss. A record player boomed faintly, deep inside. A man was laughing.

I stopped at the Ivy Bush on the way back, just in time for another drink. There was a traditional jazz band playing in the back room, but I stayed out of the noise in the flock wallpaper lounge. The publican recognised me and said hello. I nodded back, but his face was one that I had completely forgotten. Although I didn't feel particularly drunk, I had to fight back a strong urge to tell them that I'd come all the way from the future just for love. But common sense prevailed. Apart from anything else, they were probably quite used to those sorts of conversations in this particular pub.

I got back to the house at about midnight, drank some more whisky—debating for a while the merits of taking it straight from the bottle, but deciding to keep with etiquette and use a tumbler —pulled off a representative assortment of clothes, and flopped on the bed. The room spun a little, but not as much as I'd hoped. This young body could sure hold its drink.

Then the doorbell rang.

"You've got one sock off," Marnie said as she swaggered in.

"You mean I've got one sock on."

She threw her coat over the stair rail. It slid to the floor. She'd been drinking too. She had a blue dress on underneath, one that showed her figure.

"What happened?" I asked, following her into the lounge.

She flopped down on the sofa, kicked off her shoes, put her feet up. "I tried to ring." She gazed at her toes.

"Sure. What time?"

"You don't believe me."

We were sparring, trying to find out who was more pissed. The things one does for love.

"I'd like a drink," she said.

"You've had enough."

"Look, Daniel," she said, switching off the booze in her brain just as she'd switched it on. "I'm sorry."

I poured us each a glass. She ignored it for a moment, then took it and drank it with both hands.

"What time did you ring?"

"Is this a quiz? Do I get a prize?" She smiled. "Men look funny in shirts and underpants . . . and one sock. Put something on, Dan—or take something off."

"I've been waiting for you all night. What happened?"

"I rang you at ten. You weren't in then, were you? I tried

earlier, but the box was vandalised and it stank. I'm truly sorry. It was my fault."

I sat down on the sofa by her feet. "Who were you with?"

So she began to tell me about the Visconti film she'd been to see at the arts centre that turned out to be a two-part epic and how someone had given her a lift to the bus stop but then their car had broken down. I was angry-drunk, sure that reason and right were on my side, but there was an element of bitter comedy to this. I knew the story already. It was like watching an old series on TV and discovering that you're familiar with every twist and turn, that your brain had retained those meaningless facts for so many years. Why, I wondered, gazing at the lovely and abstract curves of Marnie's thighs where the dress had ridden up, hadn't I realised that this would be tonight? Her story stumbled on, an absurd convoluted epic involving a pub and a wine bar and meeting up with a few more friends and the simple fact that she'd forgotten.

"Nothing's ever your fault," I said. "Nothing ever *was*."

Her eyes widened a little. "You almost sound like you mean that."

I wondered if I did. I finished my whisky and put it down. I waited for the room to settle. The dress had gone up, and she'd made no effort to cover herself. Playing the whore, getting at me that way. It made me angry all over again to realise just how easily it worked.

I took hold of her feet and massaged them, greedy for the feel of her flesh under the nylon.

"Do you forgive?" she asked, not wanting to be forgiven.

"Yes," I said, not meaning it, simply watching her body. Nothing had changed. We were back in the same old ways. The same tracks. The same dead-end sidings. The past and the present had
tracks. The same dead-end sidings. The past and the present had
joined and now her skirt rode higher and my hands touched the
joined and now her skirt rode higher and my hands touched the
tension in her calves and thighs and up towards what was prom-
tension in her calves and thighs and up towards what was prom-
ised underneath, widening and sweetening and sharpening to the
ised underneath, widening and sweetening and sharpening to the
place where everything was Marnie.
place where everything was Marnie.

★ ★ ★

We showered separately afterwards to wash away some of the drink, and our guilt at using each other so easily. Nothing had changed. Sex with someone you can hardly talk to afterwards has to be a bad idea. So this was what I'd come all this way for. My Marnie. My love. She pulled back the shower curtains and stepped through the moist heat. There were droplets on her shoulders and face. Nothing had changed. Her hair was dark and smooth and wet, like a swimmer's.

We lay in the same bed through the grey night. Marnie breathed soft and heavy beside me. Sometimes, I remembered, I could talk to her when she was like this, find all the right words. But even that was gone. Nothing had changed, the only difference was that everything I did now reeked of falsity. I was a voyeur, staring out at my own life through keyhole eyes.

And I could press RETURN at any time, clear the screen to end this absurd role-playing game. The thought was a bitter comfort, with Marnie so real and so distant beside me, and yet somehow it drew me into sleep, through the walls and into the sky and deep inside Marnie's eyes, where there was only the sparky darkness of electricity, circuitry, and machine power.

I awoke. The greyness was growing stronger with the winter dawn. My Marnie. The perfect, anonymous curves of wrist and back and cheekbone. The composure of sleep. I touched her skin gently, lovingly, and it rippled and broke. She rolled over and muttered something and stumbled out of bed to go to the loo.

The clock said seven-thirty. I wanted to make love to her again, not really for the sex, but just to convince myself that she was real. But when she came back she began to collect her scattered clothes.

"God, I hate wearing yesterday's knickers."

"You should bring some of your stuff around here," I said, crossing my hands behind my head. "We could even try living together," pleased with myself at how easily I'd managed to slip that one through.

She gave me a be-serious look and pulled her slip on over her head. "Let's have breakfast. I could fix something."

"Something nice . . .?"

"Goes without saying." She picked up her dress and gave it a shake. "I'm the perfect housewife."

Irritatingly fully dressed, she wafted out of the bedroom. I sat up and put my feet on the carpeted floor. I supposed the morning had to begin sometime.

We faced each other across toast and boiled eggs at the breakfast table.

"What about living together?" I asked her again.

She looked wonderfully pretty with no make-up and her hair a mess. I wondered why women had never grasped the fact that men actually preferred them this way, without the paint and plastic.

She thwacked the top off her egg. "What about it?"

"Come on, Marnie." I tackled my own egg, tapping it gently around the sides. "I thought you were always saying you wanted to try anything new."

"Living together isn't new, Dan. We'd row too much. Look at us now. It's great when it's great, but it's like being on a roller coaster. And that wouldn't last for long."

"That's exactly my point," I said, keeping my voice smoothly reasonable and staring back at the watery ruin inside my egg. Marnie was a useless cook. "Things would get better."

"Dan, they would just get the same. You *know* that."

It was hard to stay in love with her for long when she was like this. Mulishly refusing to listen. Her sweet disorder was just an irritant. She was wearing that blue dress of the night before, that smelt of cigarettes and the places she'd been to and the people she'd been with. There was even a red wine stain just above her left breast. It was too easy to imagine some oaf mopping it for her.

"And exactly who were you with last night?"

"We've been through all that." She pushed away her plate and went in search of cigarettes. I followed her as she dug into her handbag and under cushions.

"You shouldn't smoke anyway," I said. "Look at you, you're a bloody addict."

"One more word," she said, "and I'm leaving. I don't need this first thing in the morning. I mean, come on, do you?"

But she didn't find her cigarettes, and I did say several more words. This was an easy row by our standards, kid's stuff. Marnie told me to go to hell and a few more places besides, and she used the F-word, which I never liked, especially from a woman. Then she grabbed up her coat and handbag and stormed out, banging the front door so hard that it bounced open again, letting in the cold of the morning. I had to go down the hall and shut it myself.

I poured out some more coffee in the kitchen, ignoring the yellow-eyed stare of the eggs. Until this moment, my body had somehow disregarded its shortage of sleep and excess of alcohol, but something had jogged its memory and now it was making up for lost time. I took the cup through to the lounge and dropped down into a chair, leaving the curtains closed. Marnie's cigarettes peeked out from underneath the dishevelled sofa. I stared at them. What was it about being in love with her? I was acting like a robot, as though I had no free will.

Something would have to change. The thought kept recurring over the next two days as Marnie and I avoided each other, just as we had done before, just as we always did, playing the game of pride, pretending that an acknowledgement of the fact that we needed each other would be a sign of weakness. Something would have to change. Everything was just the same. A petite Taiwanese student had a nosebleed in one of my classes. I got a letter from my parents telling me that old Uncle Derek was in a bad way from a stroke. I broke one of my heavy Waterford whisky glasses and cut my finger when I was washing up. The passage of these days, it seemed, had been pegged out by accidents and misfortunes.

But life had its compensations. I spent a lovely lecture-free Friday morning taking the Porsche up and down the close and along the local roads, just to get the feel of it again. As with everything else, it was really just a matter of letting my subconscious take over. The Porsche obeyed my commands promptly and politely, its great engine purring like an eager-to-please cat. Inside there was still that beautiful smell you got from cars in those days. The whole feel of it was nice, precise. For the first time since I'd returned, I felt as though I was really in command. Around lunchtime, I went for a longer drive, risking the traffic and finding that, with the Porsche, I had nothing to fear. We all used to take driving for granted, but in the right car it could be a real pleasure: the Porsche was the right car.

My route took me through the fringes of a high-rise slum, the Porsche as strange as a spaceship in this land of the dog turd and the abandoned mattress. I turned gratefully back towards the bright and busy hive of the University, along Westborne Road, under the tree shadows, past the big old houses. And there, quite by chance, was Marnie, walking and talking between two men.

I slowed the Porsche to a smooth walking pace and buttoned the window down.

"Fancy a lift, Marnie?"

"Okay," she said, without an ounce of hesitation. I unclicked the door, and she slipped elegantly into the bucket seat. I exchanged a look with the two scruffy postgrads she'd been walking with. Sorry, lads.

We zoomed off.

"I've just been driving around this morning," I said. "I'd forgotten how good the Porsche was."

She laughed. "How can you forget a thing like this? It takes half your salary."

"You like it?"

"Of course I do. It's just a car, but it's a nice car. Why do you have to keep asking people these things? It's like you don't believe them yourself."

I shook my head, shrugged. I touched the brake. The car rooted itself to the line of a junction.

"Last night, whenever it was," she said. "I don't blame you for being angry when I was late. It's just that everything gets so *big* with you and me. When you're sweet, Dan, everything's fine, but we always seem to be looking for ways to hurt each other."

"I've been trying to think what to say," I said. "Really, Marnie . . . I'm sorry, too." Sincerity was always easier when you were driving.

I flashed my pass at the security guard at the east gate. I parked in my usual place by the Arts Faculty.

She slammed the passenger door.

"Careful," I said.

"Careful's my middle name."

"Come round tonight," I said to her across the Porsche's roof. "It doesn't matter what time. And we'll sleep together and when we wake up on Saturday, whenever, we'll go somewhere in this car. A day out, you and me."

She smiled, her perfect face reflected in the perfect, glossy black. "That sounds nice."

Deeply in love, I watched her walk away. She gave me a backwards wave over her shoulder. My Marnie, my one and only.

Because I hadn't stipulated early, the doorbell rang just after six. Marnie stood framed in the light from the hall against the winter black, wearing a tartan shawl and a waxed cotton jacket, carrying her overnight bag.

"Let me help you with that," I said, ever the kindly host.

I dumped her bag by the telephone in the hall and swung the door shut with my foot. Helping her off with her jacket, my hands strayed from her shoulders, spoilt for choice between the curves of her breasts and her lovely behind. She turned and pushed herself against me. Our mouths locked, greedily exchanging breath and saliva. We were half undressed by the time we managed to get up the stairs. Marnie bounced onto the bed, sitting up to undo the remaining buttons of her blouse.

"No," I said, struggling to take off my watch and socks at the same time. "I'll do that. I'll do everything."

We went for a meal later at the nearby Indian restaurant. It was a regular place of ours. The waiters gave us the best table, away from the toilets and the door to the street. I'd managed to get some cash by writing a cheque at the bank, but my recollection of prices was still vague, and even though Marnie always insisted on paying her share, I wasn't sure whether I'd have enough for the meal and to see us through the weekend. When we sat down, I asked Marnie if they'd accept Visa.

"We always pay that way here," she said, pulling her chair in. "You're very forgetful lately."

"You're too much of a distraction."

"Let's see now." She reached across the pink tablecloth and took my hand. She was achingly beautiful in the candlelight. "You tell me who the Chancellor of the Exchequer is."

I went cold. I didn't have the faintest idea. Antony Barber? Too early. Dennis Healey? No, Labour. Then who?

Her golden-lit eyes saw through me for a moment.

I felt as though I wasn't there.

"Time's up," she said, letting go of my hand.

The waiter came over with the menus. In the brief distraction, I remembered. But it was too late to say.

"I'm sorry," I said, studying the long lists of kormas and tandoori dishes to avoid meeting her eyes. "I've been feeling a bit odd lately. You've obviously noticed. Maybe I should see a doctor." I tried a laugh. "Or a psychiatrist."

It was the only fragile moment in an otherwise perfect evening. We got merry on house red. I asked her about her name, just as I'd done all those years before, and she admitted that, yes, her mother really had got it from that Hitchcock movie. Not even a particularly good Hitchcock movie, she added, her eyes dropping towards the candlewax and popadum crumbs. I took her hand and kissed her palm and held it tenderly against my cheek.

Underneath all the looks and all the laughter and all the friends she had, Marnie was vulnerable. There was no doubt about it. Sitting talking or not talking, simply gazing at her, I could also feel my own barriers slipping down. We were so different, so alike: disappointed with a world that had given us many of the things we didn't want and held out on the few we really desired. Between the two of us there was *something*. Like looking in a mirror, it was both a separation and a sharing, a glassy edge between us on which we tried to balance our love. In later years, of course, I romanticised her, idealised her, but now, being with her again, sharing the thoughts and looks and words and silences, of that best kind that you can never recall afterwards, I lost any remaining doubts about our love being ordinary, or even a passing obsession. I loved her. This was, for once in my life, totally and completely real.

We walked home, hugging each other close against the cold,

our frosty breath entwined in the streetlight.

The perfect evening was followed by a perfect night. Everything we did we did slowly, heavily blurred with love. We kissed each other through the edges of sleep. Once, deep in the night, she began to shiver, although it wasn't from the cold. I held her tight until she was still, as I had done before.

"Help me, Dan," she whispered from inside. "Love me."

The dream flowed into the dreamy morning. Bringing coffee to our bed, I could hardly believe that it was this simple and natural to be in love. With the curtains open so we could see the trees and the sky, we sat close under the duvet and debated over a map where we might go. We settled on wherever the roads took us.

I rolled the Porsche proudly out of the garage through a romantic mist of exhaust. My lovely car; it seemed right that it should share our lovely day. I was grinning stupidly, a kid at Christmas. I felt like laughing at the thought of how hard I'd tried to find the words when I'd first returned to Marnie, when all that mattered really was being like this. Together.

I even trusted her to drive for a while, once we were safely out on the country roads. She grated the gears a couple of times, but I managed to keep quiet: no damage was done, and she understood the need to be delicately careful. We swapped back over. It was a wonderful feeling to be driving in this car, with a beautiful woman beside me and nothing but ourselves to fill the day, and the bare trees reaching over the roads, their clawed reflections sweeping the wide hood. We stopped at a country pub and sat in old leather chairs beneath the beams and in the firelight, sipping salty, hoppy beer. They were already playing Christmas tunes on the jukebox, and we talked about where we would go together then. Somewhere with mountains and snow.

Marnie peeled the print off a beer mat and sketched a picture of me with a Biro. When she handed it over, I saw that it was as good as it had always been, a little too accurate for me to appreciate, maybe; a few quick and easy strokes that said things that those old, cold photographs never had. The only difference now was that the card of the mat was softly white again, instead of the yellowed memento I was more used to. Marnie's work was always at its best when she wasn't concentrating or trying. She wasn't really an artist. She had talent, but she was too busy coping with life to turn it into much. She would never have become any kind of artist or designer.

On our way out through the deserted benches of the pub garden, Marnie sat down on the kiddie's wooden swing, not caring about the lichen and moss. She tilted her legs and I pushed her back and forth. The publican came out to bring a barrel up from the cellar. I expected him to tell us to get the hell off, but he just looked and smiled oddly at us, like a man who realises he's lost something.

As we drove on, Marnie told me about a day when she was a child, when it was summer and her father was still alive. He'd pushed her on a creaky swing into the hot sky. He had a tweed jacket that smelt of pipe tobacco and that itched when he hugged her. There were shimmering trees and a lake and a big house of white stone.

"I wish I could find out where that place was," she said. "Just in the past, I guess."

I parked the Porsche under the trees in a country lane. A quiet place. A pretty, nowhere place. The sky was thickly grey. Everything was shadowed and soft, like a room with the curtains drawn. We walked on between the dark hedgerows.

A sign pointed across the fields towards a landmark hill. We followed the track, keeping to the grassy sides to avoid the worst of the mud. A flock of swans flew silently over. Their whiteness seemed to make them ghostly creatures from another world.

From the grassy top of the hill, the whole of a county was spread around us. The grey of the city to the north. Villages and towns. Trees and fields dark with winter. A toy van travelling down a toy road. A big reservoir: tarnished silver, then suddenly bright in the ripples from a breeze that soon touched our faces with cold.

"We haven't *done* anything today," I said.

"That's what's been so good." Marnie hugged me. I could feel the soft pressure of her breasts. "I'd like to have another day like this, please."

I couldn't bring myself to reply.

She let go. "What is it, Dan?"

I shrugged. "Just . . . talking about the future."

"You should know the future never comes."

What was I supposed to do? Nothing had changed. This day. This hill. These words. Marnie. Me.

"What shall we do tonight?" I asked.

"I'll have to go back to my flat."

I nodded, trying very hard to picture her in that cold and

empty room, with the half-finished paintings, the drooping rubber plant in the corner, the owl wind-chime silent at the window.

"I promised to see some people," she said. "A sort of party. Come along with me. It'll be fun."

"It doesn't matter what I say, does it?"

"Don't be like that. Please."

We walked back to the Porsche in our own puzzled and sepa-rate silences. It was waiting under the trees, looking like some-thing out of a calendar or a magazine. Marnie climbed inside and lit a cigarette, exhaling a cloud against the dashboard and wind-screen.

"Couldn't you have done that when you were outside?" I said thickly.

She took another drag. "It's too cold out there, Dan. It'll go when we get moving. . . ." She gave me a pitying look. Poor Daniel, the look said, to be bothered by such an absurd little thing. In truth, I wasn't bothered, as I had been before. But it was too late to change things.

Marnie shivered. "Can't we just get going? I'm cold. I've been cold all day."

Cold all day.

Cold all day.

I gripped the steering wheel hard. "I thought we'd been happy. I thought today was special . . . so special you won't even bloody well stay with me tonight!"

"It *has* been special," she said. She opened the ashtray on the dash between us and manoeuvred her cigarette towards it. But the ash fell on the black carpet beside the gearbox. She gave it a care-less brush, as though that was enough. "I've just been a bit . . . chilly. You know how I am."

The inside of the car was thick with smoke. I clicked the igni-tion key on a turn and pressed the master button that brought both of the windows down. "Why the hell do you have to smoke in here?" I said over the gentle buzz of the window motors. "Espe-cially when we're trying to talk?"

She laughed, or attempted to. I think she was already starting to cry. "You call this talking? All that bothers you is me smoking in this precious bloody car of yours. Marnie messing up your pretty images of the way everything should be. Marnie smoking. Marnie drinking. Marnie actually sometimes wanting to be with people other than you. When all you want is some woman to sit by you in this bloody, bloody car. It's that simple, isn't it?"

I gripped the steering wheel. I said nothing. There was no point.

"Why don't you just fuck off," she said childishly, childishly stubbing the cigarette out on my carpet, getting out of the Porsche, childishly slamming the door.

I got out on my side. She was standing there beneath the big oak tree, with the placid winter countryside all around us, as though none of this was happening.

"If you could see yourself," I said. "How stupid this is."

"Of course it's stupid! We're having a stupid argument. Or perhaps you hadn't noticed?"

"Why?" I asked reasonably.

"Everything has to be so *personal* with you," she said, breathing in and out in shudders, her face puffed with ugly tears. "That bloody car of yours! This was a lovely day until you ruined it."

"I want you to respect me . . . respect my property."

"Your property!" She was yelling. The sound was unnatural, unwomanly. I'd never seen her this angry before.

unwomanly. I'd never seen her this angry before.

"Just listen. . . ."

I stepped towards her. She pushed me away and stumbled over to the car.

"You deserve this"—she was shouting through the thickness of her tears—"you really do. You bastard! Your property! You do deserve this. I love you, you bastard. I'm not. Your property. Fuck you, I hope you never—"

I watched her fumble open the driver's door. She started the Porsche with the accelerator floored and the gears in reverse. The engine howled, and the car gave a juddering leap backwards into a tree. The bumper crunched, shivering leaves and scraps of bark through swirls of exhaust. Marnie knocked the wiper stalk as she screeched into first. The blades flicked to and fro. Then she pulled away, the fat tyres kicking up a shower of mud and leaf-mould; a rich incongruous scent amid the drifting reek of the petrol.

The engine roar faded into silence. I looked at my watch; almost four o'clock. I began to walk back along the road towards the nearest village. I knew the way: right at the crossroads and straight ahead after that. I was even able to save myself a mile's pointless detour down a badly signed road that petered out to a farm track, but it was still deep twilight, and my shoes were pinching badly by the time I reached the village green and used the phonebox to call for a cab. I waited shivering outside. There were trees and chimneys and a church spire in silhouette against a grainy sky, warmly lit leaded windows in the houses, two ducks circling in the dim pond. The whole scene was heavy with nostalgia for times much earlier than these, the wholesome wood-scented, apple-scented, sunset-coloured days that had never been.

The cab came quickly. Questing headlights swung towards me across the crumbling churchyard wall. It was a Japanese car, I think, not the sort of car that had a real name that anyone remembers. A functional box on wheels. I asked the driver to take me to the nearest town; I didn't bother to explain. I knew that he would perform his role well enough in silence, just as he had done before.

The shops were shut, and the main car park around the big war memorial where he dropped me off was almost empty. No use offering Visa. I paid the fare without a tip. I was left with exactly forty-nine pence in my pockets. A cold wind was starting. A few cans rattled and chimed across the streetlit tarmac.

The police station was on a side road at the back of Woolworths. An old man backing out through the doors with his dog gave me a weary, sharing smile. I told the duty constable at the counter that an acquaintance had driven my car away without permission. I didn't think they were insured. I told him the car was a Porsche. Unimpressed, he nodded towards the empty plastic benches by the doors and told me to wait.

I sat down. Like the few other police stations I've been inside, this one was absurdly quiet, as though it had been waiting for greying, paint-peeling years for something to happen. Something to make up for all the drunks, and all the people like me. I studied the curling posters on the notice board opposite. Oddly, I couldn't remember any of them. I wondered vaguely, irrationally, if that was somehow a sign that things would end up differently.

Two sergeants came out from a room at the back. They flipped up the side of the counter. Before they spoke, I knew from their faces that it had happened. I wondered if this was the time to end it, but part of me wanted to see it again. To be certain.

They drove me to the reservoir. There was a noisy crane there already, and floodlights probing thick yellow shafts into the water. Men in uniforms peered down from the roadside. People were gathering around the fringes of the darkness to watch. One of the sergeants leaned over to the back seat before we stepped out of the car and asked me if I thought it was an accident; just the sort of casual question they try on you before you've had time to put your guard up.

"I used to think so," I said, not caring what they made of it. "But now I don't know. I'm not sure."

The Porsche looked like a big black crab as it broke the surface. It rose into the harsh light, water sluicing out of it in glittering curves. People oohed and aahed. Chains tensed and screamed with the car's weight. The air filled with the smell of green mud, like a bad beach at low tide. The crane paused for a moment, a big insect hesitating with its prey, then swung the car down onto the road. The suspension broke with twiglike snaps. The car was still wet and heavy, dark pools sliding across the verge and down the bank, running eagerly back into the reservoir. Sleepwalking figures broke the door open, and there was a thick rush of mud before they lifted Marnie out. No one hurried. I didn't envy the police their job.

They asked me if it was her. Just confirmation, for the record. I walked through to the front, where an ambulance stood with its lights uselessly circling and its doors uselessly open. A man in a wetsuit pushed past me, wiping something from his hands. They'd just left her on the road. No point in messing the blankets. Her head was turned away, an abstract curve of neck and cheekbone. Her skin was glossy white, and her hair was dark and smooth and wet. Like a swimmer's. I nodded, but this wasn't my Marnie, my one and only, the woman I loved.

I stepped back, away from the flashlights and the floodlights and the spinning blue lights and the people. The time had come, there was no point in going any further. Somewhere from the machine darkness, I would have to summon the will to try again. Try again. Press RETURN. I let the images and sensations fade, the sounds, the sights, the smells.

There will be another time, Marnie. A better time than this, believe me.

I promise.

I promise.

Grownups

Bobby finally got around to asking Mum where babies came from on the evening of his seventh birthday. It had been hot all day, and the grownups and a few of the older children who had come to his party were still outside on the lawn. He could hear their talk and evening birdsong through his open window as Mum closed the curtains. She leaned down to kiss his forehead. She'd been drinking since the first guests arrived before lunch, and her breath smelt like windfall apples. Now seemed as good a time as any. As she turned towards the door, he asked his question. It came out as a whisper, but she heard, and frowned for a moment before she smiled.

"You children always want to know too soon," she said. "I was the same, believe me, Bobby. But you must be patient. You really must."

Bobby knew enough about grownups to realise that it was unwise to push too hard. So he forced himself to yawn and blink slowly so she would think he was truly sleepy. She patted his hand.

After his door had clicked shut, after her footsteps had padded down the stairs, Bobby slid out of bed. Ignoring the presents piled in the corner by the wardrobe—robots with sparking eyes, doll soldiers, and submarines—he peered from the window. They lived at the edge of town, where rooftops dwindled to green hills and the silver curl of the river. He watched Mum emerge from the French windows onto the wide lawn below. She stooped to say something to Dad as he sat lazing in a deckchair with the other men, a beer can propped against his crotch. Then she took a taper from the urn beside the barbecue and touched it to the coals. She proceeded to light the lanterns hanging from the boughs of the cherry trees.

The whole garden filled with stars. After she had lit the last lantern, Mum put the taper to her mouth and extinguished it with her tongue. Then she rejoined the women gossiping on the white wrought-iron chairs. The remaining children were all leaving for home. Cars were starting up, turning out from the shaded drive. Bobby heard his brother Tony call good-night to the grownups and thunder up the stairs. He tensed in case Tony should decide to look in on him before he went to bed, but relaxed after the toilet had flushed and his bedroom door had slammed. It was almost night. Bobby knew that his window would show as no more than a darker square against the wall of the house. He widened the parting in the curtain.

He loved to watch the grownups when they thought they were alone. It was a different world. One day, Mum had told him often enough, one day, sweet little Bobby, you'll understand it all, touching his skin with papery fingers as she spoke. But give it time, my darling one, give it time. Being a grownup is more wonderful than you children could ever imagine. More wonderful. Yes, my darling. Kissing him on the forehead and each eye and then his mouth the way she did when she got especially tender.

Bobby gazed down at the grownups. They had that loose look that came when the wine and the beer had gone down well and there was more to come, when the night was warm and the stars mirrored the lanterns. Dad raised his can from his crotch to his lips. One of the men beside him made a joke and the beer spluttered down Dad's chin, gleaming for a moment before he wiped it away. The men always talked like this, loud between bursts of silence, whilst the women's voices—laughing serious sad— brushed soft against the night. Over by the trellis archway that led by the bins to the front, half a dozen uncles sat in the specially wide deckchairs that Dad kept for them behind the mower in the shed.

Bobby couldn't help staring at the uncles. They were all grossly fat. There was Uncle Stan, Uncle Harold, and of course his own Uncle Lew. Bobby saw with a certain pride that Lew was the biggest. His tie was loose, and his best shirt strained like a full sail across his belly. Like all the uncles, Lew lived alone, but Dad or the father of one of the other families he was uncle to was always ready to take the car down on a Saturday morning, paint the windows of his house, or see to the lawn. In many ways, Bobby thought it was an ideal life. People respected uncles. Even more than their girth required, they stepped aside from them in the street. But at the same time, his parents were often edgy when Lew was around, uncharacteristically eager to please. Sometimes late in the night, Bobby had heard the unmistakable clatter of his van on the gravel out front, Mum and Dad's voices whispering softly excited in the hall. Gazing at Lew seated with the other uncles, Bobby remembered how he had dragged him to the moist folds of his belly, rumbling, Won't You Just Look At This Sweet Kid? His yeasty aroma came back like the aftertaste of bad cooking.

Someone turned the record player on in the lounge. Sibilant music drifted like smoke. Some of the grownups began to dance. Women in white dresses blossomed as they turned, and the men were darkly quick. The music and the sigh of their movement brushed against the humid night, coaxed the glow of the lanterns, silvered the rooftops and the stars.

The dancing quickened, seeking a faster rhythm inside the slow beat. Bobby's eyes fizzed with sleep. He thought he saw grownups floating heartbeat on heartbeat above the lawn. Soon they were leaping over the lanterned cherry trees, flying, pressing close to his window with smiles and waves, beckoning him to join them. Come out and play, Bobby, out here amid the stars. The men darted like eels, the women did high kicks across the rooftop, their dresses billowing coral frills over their heads. The uncles bobbed around the chimney like huge balloons.

When Bobby awoke, the lanterns were out. There was only darkness, summer chill.

As he crawled back to bed, a sudden sound made him freeze. Deep and feral, some kind of agony that was neither pain nor grief, it started loud then came down by notches to a stuttering sob. Bobby unfroze when it ended and hauled the blankets up to his chin. Through the bedroom wall, he could hear the faint mutter of Dad's voice, Mum's half-questioning reply. Then Uncle Lew saying good-night. Slow footsteps down the stairs. The front door slam. Clatter of an engine coming to life.

Sigh of gravel.

Silence.

★   ★   ★

Bobby stood at the far bank of the river. His hands clenched and unclenched. Three years had passed. He was now ten; his brother Tony was sixteen.

Tony was out on the river, atop the oil-drum raft that he and the other kids of his age had been building all summer. The wide sweep that cut between the fields and the gasometers into town had narrowed in the drought heat. Tony was angling a pole through the sucking silt to get to the deeper current. He was absorbed, alone; he hadn't noticed Bobby standing on the fissured mud of the bank. Earlier in the summer, there would have been a crowd of Tony's friends out there, shouting and diving, sitting with their heels clutched in brown hands, chasing Bobby away with shouts or grabbing him with terrible threats that usually ended in a simple ducking or just laughter, some in cutoff shorts, their backs freckled pink from peeling sunburn, some sleekly naked, those odd dark patches of hair showing under their arms and bellies. Maggie Brown, with a barking voice you could hear half a mile off, Pete Thorn, who kept pigeons and always seemed to watch, never said anything, maybe Johnnie Redhead and his sidekicks, even Trev Lee, if his hay fever, asthma, and psoriasis hadn't kept him inside, the twin McDonald sisters, whom no one could tell apart.

Now Tony was alone.

"Hey!" Bobby yelled, not wanting to break into his brother's isolation, knowing he had to. "Hey, Tony!"

Tony poled once more towards the current. The drums shook, tensed against their bindings, then inched towards the main sweep of the river.

"Hey, Tony, Mum says you've got to come home right now."

"All right, *all right.*"

Tony let go of the pole, jumped down into the water. It came just below his naked waist. He waded out clumsily, falling on hands and knees. He crouched to wash himself clean in a cool eddy where the water met the shore, then shook like a dog. He grabbed his shorts from the branch of a dead willow and hauled them on.

"Why didn't you just come?" Bobby asked. "You must have known it was time. The doc's waiting at home to give you your tests."

Tony slicked back his hair. They both stared at the ground. The river still dripped from Tony's chin and made tiny craters in the sand. Bobby noticed that Tony hadn't shaved, which was a bad sign in itself. Out on the river, the raft suddenly bobbed free, floating high on the quick current.

Tony shook his head. "Never did that when I was on it.

Seemed like a great idea, you know? Then you spend the whole summer trying to pole out of the mud."

Around them, the bank was littered with the spoor of summer habitation. The blackened ruin of a bonfire, stones laid out in the shape of a skull, crisp packets, an old flap of canvas propped up like a tent, ringpull cans and cigarette butts, a solitary shoe. Bobby had his own friends—his own special places—and he came to this spot rarely and on sufferance. But still, he loved his brother and was old enough to have some idea of how it must feel to leave childhood behind. But he told himself that most of it had gone already. Tony was the last; Pete and Maggie and the McDonald twins had grown up. Almost all the others too. That left just Trev Lee, who had locked himself in the bathroom and swallowed a bottle of bleach whilst parents hammered at the door.

Tony made a movement that looked as though it might end in a hug. But he slapped Bobby's head instead, almost hard enough to hurt. They always acted with each other as though they were tough; it was too late now to start changing the rules.

They followed the path through the still heat of the woods to the main road. It was midday. The shimmering tarmac cut between yellow fields towards town. Occasionally, a car or truck would appear in the distance, floating silent on heat ghosts before the roar and the smell suddenly broke past them, whipping dust into their faces. Bobby gazed at stalking pylons, ragged fences, the litter-strewn edges of the countryside; it was the map of his own childhood. It was Tony's too—but Tony only stared at the verge. It was plain that he was tired of living on the cliff-edge of growing up.

Tony looked half a grownup already, graceful, clumsy, self-absorbed. He hadn't been his true self through all this later part of the summer, or at least not since Joan Trackett had grown up. Joan had a fierce crop of hair and protruding eyes; she had come to the area with her parents about six years before. Bobby knew that she and Tony had been having sex since at least last winter and maybe before. He'd actually stumbled across them one day in spring, lying on a dumped mattress in the east fields up beyond the waste tip, hidden amid the bracken in a corner that the farmer hadn't bothered to plough. Tony had chased him away, alternately gripping the open waistband of his jeans and waving his fists. But that evening Tony had let Bobby play with his collection of model cars, which was a big concession, even though Bobby knew that Tony had mostly lost interest in them already. They had sat together in Tony's bedroom that smelled of peppermint and socks. I guess you know what Joan and I were doing, he had said. Bobby nodded, circling a black V-8 limo with a missing tyre around the whorls and dustballs of the carpet. It's no big deal, Tony said, picking at a scab on his chin. But his eyes had gone blank with puzzlement, as though he couldn't remember something important.

Bobby looked up at Tony as they walked along the road. He was going to miss his big brother. He even wanted to say it, although he knew he wouldn't find the words. Maybe he'd catch up with him again when he turned grownup himself, but that seemed a long way off. At least five summers.

The fields ended. The road led into Avenues, Drives, and Crofts that meandered a hundred different ways towards home.

The doctor's red estate car was parked under the shade of the poplar in their drive.

"You *don't* make people wait," Mum said, her breath short with impatience, shooing them both quickly down the hallway into the kitchen. "I'm disappointed in you, Tony. You too, Bobby. You're both old enough to know better." She opened the fridge and took out a tumbler of bitter milk. "And Tony, you didn't drink this at breakfast."

"Mum, does it matter? I'll be a grownup soon anyway."

Mum placed it on the scrubbed table. "Just drink it."

Tony drank. He wiped his chin and banged down the glass.

"Well, off you go," Mum said.

He headed up the stairs.

Dr. Halstead was waiting for Tony up in the spare room. He'd been coming around to test him every Thursday since Mum and Dad received the brown envelope from school, arriving punctually at half twelve, taking best-china coffee with Mum in the lounge afterwards. There was no mystery about the tests. Once or twice, Bobby had seen the syringes and the blood-analysis equipment spread out on the candlewick bedspread through the open door. Tony had told him what it was like, how the doc stuck a big needle in your arm to take some blood. It hurt some, but not much. He had shown Bobby the sunset bruises on his arm with that perverse pride that kids display over any wound.

Dr. Halstead came down half an hour later, looking stern and noncommittal. Tony followed in his wake. He shushed Bobby and tried to listen to Mum's conversation with the doc over coffee in the lounge by standing by the door in the hall. But grownups had a way of talking that was difficult to follow, lowering their voices at the crucial moment, clinking their cups. Bobby imagined them stifling their laughter behind the closed door, deliberately uttering meaningless fragments they knew the kids would hear. He found the thought oddly reassuring.

★   ★   ★

Tony grew up on the Thursday of that same week. He and Bobby had spent the afternoon together down at Monument Park. They had climbed the whispering boughs of one of the big elm trees along the avenue and sat with their legs dangling, trying to spit on the heads of the grownups passing below.

"Will you tell me what it's like?" Bobby had asked when his mouth finally went dry.

"What?" Tony looked vague. He picked up a spider that crawled onto his wrist and rolled it between finger and thumb.

"About being a grownup. Talk to me afterwards. I want . . . I want to know."

"Yeah, yeah. We're still brothers, right?"

"You've got it. And—"

"—Hey, shush!"

Three young grownups were heading their way, a man, a woman, and an uncle. Bobby supposed they were courting—they had their arms around each other in that vaguely passionless way that grownups had, their faces absent, staring at the sky and the trees without seeing. He began to salivate.

"Bombs away."

Bobby missed with his lob, but Tony hawked up a green one and scored a gleaming hit on the crown of the woman's head. The grownups walked on, stupidly oblivious.

It was a fine afternoon. They climbed higher still, skinning their palms and knees on the greenish bark, feeling the tree sway beneath them like a dancer. From up here, the park shimmered, you could see everything; the lake, the glittering greenhouses, grownups lazing on the grass, two fat kids from Tony's year lobbing stones at a convoy of ducks. Bobby grinned and threw back his head. Here, you could feel the hot sky around you, taste the clouds like white candy.

"You *will* tell me what it's like to be a grownup?" he asked again.

But Tony suddenly looked pale and afraid, holding on to the trembling boughs. "Let's climb down," he said.

When Bobby thought back, he guessed that that was the beginning.

Mum took one look at Tony when they got home and called Dr. Halstead. He was quick in coming. On Mum's instructions,

Bobby also phoned Dad at the office, feeling terribly grownup and responsible as he asked to be put through in the middle of a meeting.

Tony was sitting on the sofa in the lounge, rocking to and fro, starting to moan. Dad and the doc carried him to the spare bedroom. Mum followed them up the stairs, then pulled the door tightly shut. Bobby waited downstairs in the kitchen and watched the shadows creep across the scrubbed table. Occasionally, there were footsteps upstairs, the rumble of voices, the hiss of a tap.

He had to fix his own tea from leftovers in the fridge. Later, somehow all the house lights got turned on. Everything was hard and bright like a fierce lantern, shapes burned through to the filaments beneath. Bobby's head was swimming. He was someone else, thinking, this is my house, my brother, knowing at the same time that it couldn't be true. Upstairs, he could hear someone's voice screaming, saying, My God No.

Mum came down after ten. She was wearing some kind of plastic apron that was wet where she'd wiped it clean.

"Bobby, you've got to go to bed." She reached to grab his arm and pull him from the settee.

Bobby held back for a moment. "What's happening to Tony, Mum? Is he okay?"

"Of course he's *okay*. It's nothing to get excited about. It happens to us all, it . . ." Anger came into her face. "Will you just get upstairs to bed, Bobby? You shouldn't be up this late anyway. Not tonight, not any night."

Mum followed Bobby up the stairs. She waited to open the door of the spare room until he'd gone into the bathroom. Bobby found there was no hot water, no towels; he had to dry his hand on squares of toilet paper and the flush was slow to clear, as though something was blocking it.

He sprinted across the dangerous space of the landing and into bed. He tried to sleep.

★   ★   ★

In the morning there was the smell of toast. Bobby came down the stairs slowly, testing each step.

"So you're up," Mum said, lifting the kettle from the hob as it began to boil.

It was eight-thirty by the clock over the fridge; a little late, but everything was brisk and sleepy as any other morning. Dad stared at the sports pages, eating his cornflakes. Bobby sat down opposite him at the table, lifted the big cereal packet that promised a scale model if you collected enough coupons. That used to drive Tony wild, how the offer always changed before you had enough. Bobby shook some flakes into a bowl.

"How's Tony?" he asked, tipping out milk.

"Tony's fine," Dad said. Then he swallowed and looked up from the paper—a rare event in itself. "He's just resting, son. Upstairs in his own room, his own bed."

"Yes, darling." Mum's voice came from behind. Bobby felt her hands on his shoulders, kneading softly. "It's such a happy day for your dad and me. Tony's a grownup now. Isn't that wonderful?" The fingers tightened, released.

"That doesn't mean *you* don't go to school," Dad added. He gave his paper a shake, rearranged it across the teapot and the marmalade jar.

"But be sure to tell Miss Gibson what's happened." Mum's voice faded to the back of the kitchen. The fridge door smacked open. "She'll want to know why you're late for register." Bottles jingled. Mum wafted close again. She came around to the side of the table and placed a tumbler filled with white fluid beside him. The bitter milk. "We know you're still young," she said. "But there's no harm, and now seems as good a time as any." Her fingers turned a loose button on her blouse. "Try it, darling, it's not so bad."

What happens if I don't. . . . Bobby glanced quickly at Mum, at Dad. What happens if . . . Through the kitchen window, the sky was summer grey, the clouds casting the soft warm light that he loved more than sunlight, that brought out the green in the trees and made everything seem closer and more real. What happens . . . Bobby picked up the tumbler in both hands, drank it down in breathless gulps the way he'd seen Tony do so often in the past.

"Good lad," Mum sighed after he'd finished. She was behind him again, her fingers trailing his neck. Bobby took a breath, suppressed a shudder. This bitter milk tasted just as Tony always said it did: disgusting.

"Can I see Tony now, before I go to school?"

Mum hesitated. Dad looked up again from his newspaper. Bobby knew what it would be like later, the cards, the flowers, the house lost in strangers. This was his best chance to speak to his brother.

"Okay," Mum said. "But not for long."

Tony was sitting up in bed, the TV Mum and Dad usually kept in their own bedroom propped on the dressing table. Having the TV was a special sign of illness; Bobby had had it twice himself, once with chicken pox, and then with mumps. The feeling of luxury had almost made the discomfort worthwhile.

"I just thought I'd see how you were," Bobby said.

"What?" Tony lifted the remote control from the bedspread, pressed the red button to kill the sound. It was a reluctant gesture that Bobby recognised from Dad.

"How are you feeling?"

"I'm fine, Bobby."

"Did it hurt?"

"Yes . . . Not really." Tony shrugged. "What do you want me to say? You'll find out soon enough, Bobby."

"Don't you remember yesterday? You said you'd tell me everything."

"Of course I remember, but I'm just here in bed . . . watching the TV. You can see what it's like." He spread his arms. "Come here, Bobby."

Bobby stepped forward.

Tony grinned. "Come on, little brother."

Bobby leaned forward over the bed, let Tony clasp him in his arms. It was odd to feel his brother this way, the soft plates of muscle, the ridges of chest and arm. They'd held each other often enough before, but only in the wrestling bouts that Bobby launched into when he had nothing better to do, certain that he'd end up bruised and kicking, pinned down and forced to submit. But now the big hands were patting his back. Tony was talking over his shoulder.

"I'll sort through all the toys in the next day or so. You can keep all the best stuff to play with. Like we said yesterday, we're still brothers, right?" He leaned Bobby back, looked into his eyes. "Right?"

Bobby had had enough of grownup promises to know what they meant. Grownups were always going to get this and fix that, build wendy houses on the lawn, take you to the zoo, staple the broken strap on your satchel, favours that never happened, things they got angry about if you ever mentioned them.

"All the best toys. Right?"

"Right," Bobby said. He turned for the door, then hesitated. "Will you tell me one thing?"

"What?"

"Where babies come from."

Tony hesitated, but not unduly; grownups always thought before they spoke. "They come from the bellies of uncles, Bobby. A big slit opens and they tumble out. It's no secret, it's a natural fact."

Bobby nodded, wondering why he'd been so afraid to ask. "I thought so . . . thanks."

"Any time," Tony said, and turned up the TV.

"Thanks again." Bobby closed the door behind him.

★   ★   ★

Tony finished school officially at the end of that term. But there were no awards, no speeches, no bunting over the school gates. Like the other new grownups, he just stopped attending, went in one evening when it was quiet to clear his locker as though the whole thing embarrassed him. Bobby told himself that that was one thing he'd do differently when his time came. He'd spent most of his life at school, and he wasn't going to pass it by that easily. Grownups just seemed to let things go. It had been the same with Dad when he moved from the factory to the admin offices in town, suddenly ignoring men he'd shared every lunchtime with and talked about for years as though they were friends.

Tony sold his bicycle through the classified pages to a kid from across town who would have perhaps a year's use of it before he too grew up. He found a temporary job at the local supermarket. He and Dad came home at about the same time each evening, the same bitter work smell coming off their bodies. Over dinner, Mum would ask them how everything had gone and the talk would lie flat between them, drowned by the weak distractions of the food.

For Tony, as for everyone, the early years of being a grownup were a busy time socially. He went out almost every night, dressed in his new grownup clothes and smelling of soap and aftershave. Mum said he looked swell. Bobby knew the places in town he went to by reputation. He had passed them regularly and caught the smell of cigarettes and booze, the drift of breathless air and sudden laughter. There were strict rules against children entering. If he was with Mum, she would snatch his hand and hurry him on. But she and Dad were happy for Tony to spend his nights in these places now that he was a grownup, indulging in the ritual dance that led to courtship, marriage, and a fresh uncle in the family. On the few occasions that Tony wasn't out late, Dad took him for driving lessons, performing endless three-point turns on the tree-lined estate roads.

Bobby would sit with his homework spread on the dining-room table as Mum saw to things that didn't need seeing to. There was a distracting stiffness about her actions that was difficult to watch, difficult not to. Bobby guessed that although Tony was still living at home and she was pleased that he'd taken to grownup life, she was also missing him, missing the kid he used to be. It didn't require a great leap of imagination for Bobby to see things that way;

he missed Tony himself. The arguments, the fights, the sharing and the not-sharing, all lost with the unspoken secret of being children together, of finding everything frightening, funny, and new.

In the spring, Tony passed his driving test and got a proper job at the supermarket as trainee manager. There was a girl called Marion who worked at the checkout. She had skin trouble like permanent sunburn and never looked at you when she spoke. Bobby already knew that Tony was seeing her in the bars at night. He sometimes answered the phone by mistake when she rang, her slow voice saying, Is Your Brother About as Tony came down the stairs from his room looking annoyed. The whole thing was supposed to be a secret until suddenly Tony started bringing Marion home in the second-hand coupe he'd purchased from the dealers on the High Street.

Tony and Marion spent the evenings of their courtship sitting in the lounge with Mum and Dad, watching the TV. When Bobby asked why, Tony said that they had to stay in on account of their saving for a little house. He said it with the strange fatality of grownups. They often talked about the future as though it was already there.

Sometimes a strange uncle would come around. Dad always turned the TV off as soon as he heard the bell. The uncles were generally fresh-faced and young, their voices high and uneasy. If they came a second time, they usually brought Bobby an unsuitable present, making a big show of hiding it behind their wide backs.

Then Uncle Lew began to visit more often. Bobby overheard Mum and Dad talking about how good it would be, keeping the same uncle in the family even if Lew was a little old for our Tony.

Looking down at him over his cheeks, Lew would ruffle Bobby's hair with his soft fingers.

"And how are you, young man?"

Bobby said he was fine.

"And what is it you're going to be this week?" This was Lew's standard question, a joke of sorts that stemmed from some occasion when Bobby had reputedly changed his mind about his grownup career three or four times in a day.

Bobby paused. He felt an obligation to be original.

"Maybe an archaeologist," he said.

Lew chuckled. Tony and Marion moved off the settee to make room for him, sitting on the floor with Bobby.

After a year and a half of courtship, the local paper that Tony had used to sell his bicycle finally announced that he, Marion, and

Uncle Lew were marrying. Everyone said it was a happy match. Marion showed Bobby the ring. It looked big and bright from a distance, but close to, he saw that the diamond was tiny, centred in a much larger stub of metal that was cut to make it glitter.

Some evenings, Dad would fetch some beers for himself, Tony, and Uncle Lew, and let Bobby sip the end of a can to try the flat dark taste. Like most other grownup things, it was a disappointment.

★ ★ ★

So Tony married Marion. And he never did get around to telling Bobby how it felt to be a grownup. The priest in the church beside the crematorium spoke of the bringing together of families and of how having Uncle Lew for a new generation was a strengthened commitment. Dad swayed in the front pew from nerves and the three whiskies he'd sunk beforehand. Uncle Lew wore the suit he always wore at weddings, battered victim of too much strain on the buttons, too many spilled buffets. There were photos of the families, photos of the bridesmaids, photos of Lew smiling with his arms around the shoulders of the two newlyweds. Photograph the whole bloody lot, Dad said, I want to see where the money went.

The reception took place at home on the lawn. Having decided to find out what it was like to get drunk, Bobby lost his taste for the warm white wine after one glass. He hovered at the border of the garden. It was an undeniably pretty scene, the awnings, the dresses, the flowers. For once, the boundaries between grownups and children seemed to dissolve. Only Bobby remained outside. People raised their glasses and smiled, drunken uncles swayed awkwardly between the trestle tables. Darkness carried the smell of the car exhaust and the dry fields beyond the houses. Bobby remembered the time when he had watched from his window and the music had beaten smoky wings, when the grownups had flown over the cherry trees that now seemed so small.

The headlights of the hired limousine swept out of the darkness. Everyone ran to the drive to see Tony and Marion duck into the leather interior. Uncle Lew squeezed in behind them, off with the newlyweds to some secret place. Neighbours who hadn't been invited came out onto their drives to watch, arms folded against the nonexistent chill, smiling. Marion threw her bouquet. It tumbled high over the trees and the rooftops, up through the stars. Grownups oohed and aahed. The petals bled into the darkness. It dropped back down as a dead thing of grey and plastic. Bobby caught it without thinking; a better, cleaner catch than anything he'd ever managed in the playing fields at school. Everyone

laughed—that a kid should do that!—and he blushed furiously.
Then the car pulled away, low at the back from the weight of the
three passengers and their luggage. The taillights dwindled, were
cut out by the bend in the road. Dad swayed and shouted something, his breath reeking. People went inside and the party lingered on, drawing to its stale conclusion.

Uncle Lew had Tony and Marion's first child a year later.
Mum took Bobby to see the baby at his house when he came out
of hospital a few days after the birth. Uncle Lew lived in town, up
on the hill on the far side of the river. Mum was nervous about
gradient parking and always used the big pay-and-display down
by the library. From there, you had to cut through the terraced
houses, then up the narrowly winding streets that formed the oldest part of town. The houses were mostly grey pebbledash with
deepset windows, yellowed lace curtains, and steps leading
through tiny gardens. The hill always seemed steeper than it actually was to Bobby; he hated visiting.

Uncle Lew was grinning, sitting in his usual big chair by the
bay window. The baby was a mewing thing. It smelled of soap and
sick. Marion was taking the drugs to make her lactate, and everything was apparently going well. Bobby peered at the baby lying
cradled in her arms. He tried to offer her the red plastic rattle
Mum had made him buy. Everyone smiled at that. Then there
was tea and rock cakes that Bobby managed to avoid. Uncle Lew's
house was always dustlessly neat, but it had a smell of neglect that
seemed to emanate from behind the old-fashioned green cup-
boards in the kitchen. Bobby guessed that the house was simply
too big for him; too many rooms.

"Are you still going to be an archaeologist?" Uncle Lew asked,
leaning forward from his big chair to take both of Bobby's hands.
He was wearing a dressing gown with neatly pressed pyjamas underneath, but for a moment the buttons parted and Bobby
glimpsed wounded flesh.

The room went smilingly silent; he was obviously expected to
say more than simply No or Yes. "I'd like to grow up," he said, "before I decide."

The grownups all laughed. Then the baby started to cry.
Grateful for the distraction, Bobby went out through the kitchen
and into the grey garden, where someone's father had left a fork
and spade on the crazy paving, the job of lifting out the weeds
half-done. Bobby was still young enough to pretend that he
wanted to play.

★ ★ ★

Then adolescence came. It was a perplexing time for Bobby, a grimy anteroom leading to the sudden glories of growing up. He watched the hair grow on his body, felt his face inflame with pimples, heard his voice change to an improbable whine before finally settling an octave, which left him sounding forever like someone else. The grownups themselves always kept their bodies covered, their personal actions impenetrably discreet. Even in the lessons and the chats, the slide-illuminated talks in the nudging darkness of the school assembly hall, Bobby sensed that the teachers were disgusted by what happened to children's bodies, and by the openness with which it did so. The things older children got up to, messy tricks that nature made them perform. Periods. Masturbation. Sex. The teachers mouthed the words like an improbable disease. Mum and Dad both said Yes they remembered, they knew exactly how it was, but they didn't want to touch him any longer, acted awkwardly when he was in the room, did and said things that reminded him of how they were with Tony in his later childhood years.

Bobby's first experience of sex was with May Barton, one afternoon when a crowd of school-friends had cycled out to the meadows beyond town. The other children had headed back down to the road whilst Bobby was fixing a broken spoke on his back wheel. When he turned around, May was there alone. It was, he realised afterwards, a situation she'd deliberately engineered. She said, Let's do it, Bobby. Squinting, her head on one side. You haven't done it before, have you? Not waiting for an answer, she knelt down in the high clover and pulled her dress up over her head. Her red hair tumbled over her freckled shoulders. She asked Bobby to touch her breasts. Go on, you must have seen other boys doing this. Which he had. But still he was curious to touch her body, to find her nipples hardening in his palms. For a moment she seemed different in the wide space of the meadow, stranger almost than a grownup, even though she was just a girl. Here, she said, Bobby, and Here. Down on the curving river, a big barge with faded awnings seemed not to be moving. A tractor was slicing a field from green to brown, the chatter of its engine lost on the warm wind. The town shimmered. Rooftops reached along the road. His hand travelled down her belly, explored the slippery heat of her arousal as her own fingers began to part the buttons of his shirt and jeans, did things that only his own hands had done before. He remembered the slide shows at school, the teacher's bored, disgusted voice, the fat kids sniggering more than anyone at the back, as though the whole thing had nothing to do with them.

May Barton lay down. Bobby had seen the drawings and slides, watched the mice and rabbits in the room at the back of the biology class. He knew what to do. The clover felt cool and green on his elbows and knees. She felt cool too, strangely uncomfortable, like wrestling with someone who didn't want to fight. A beetle was climbing a blade of grass at her shoulder. When she began to shudder, it flicked its wings and vanished.

After that, Bobby tried sex with several of the other girls in the neighbourhood, although he tended to return most often to May. They experimented with the variations you were supposed to be able to do, found that most of them were uncomfortable and improbable, but generally not impossible.

Mum caught Bobby and May having sex one afternoon in the fourth-year summer holidays when a cancelled committee meeting brought her home early. Peeling off her long white cotton gloves as she entered the lounge, she found them naked in the curtained twilight, curled together like two spoons. She just clicked her tongue, turned and walked back out into the hall, her eyes blank, as if she'd just realised she'd left something in the car. She never mentioned the incident afterwards — which was tactful, but to Bobby also seemed unreal, as though the act of sex had made him and May Barton momentarily invisible.

There was a sequel to this incident when Bobby returned home one evening without his key. He went through the gate round the back to find the French windows open. He'd expected lights on in the kitchen, the murmur of the TV in the lounge. But everything was quiet. He climbed the stairs. Up on the landing where the heat of the day still lingered, mewing sounds came from his parents' bedroom. The door was ajar. He pushed it wide — one of those things you do without ever being able to explain why — and walked in. It was difficult to make out the ownership of the knotted limbs. Dad seemed to be astride Uncle Lew, Mum half underneath. The sounds they made were another language. Somehow, they sensed his presence. Legs and arms untwined like dropped coils of rope.

It all happened very quickly. Mum got up and snatched her dressing gown from the bedside table. On the bed, Dad scratched at his groin and Uncle Lew made a wide cross with his forearms to cover his womanly breasts.

"It's okay," Bobby said, taking a step back towards the door, taking another. The room reeked of mushrooms. Mum still hadn't done up her dressing gown, and Bobby could see her breasts swaying as she walked, the dark triangle beneath her belly. She looked little different from all the girls Bobby had seen. Through the hot waves of his embarrassment, he felt a twinge of sadness and familiarity.

"It's okay," he said again, and closed the door.

He never mentioned the incident. But it helped him understand Mum's reasons for not saying anything about finding him in the lounge with May. There were plenty of words for sex, ornate words and soft words and words that came out angry, words for what the kids got up to and special words too for the complex congress that grownups indulged in. But you couldn't use any of them as you used other words; they were surrounded in a space of silence, walled within a dark place that was all their own.

★   ★   ★

Bobby grew. He found to his surprise that he was one of the older kids at school, towering over the chirping first years with their new blazers, having sex with May and the other girls, taking three-hour exams at the ends of term, worrying about growing up. He remembered that this had seemed a strange undersea world when Tony had inhabited it; now that he had reached it himself, this last outpost of childhood, it hardly seemed less so.

The strangeness was shared by all the children of his age. It served to bring them together. Bobby remembered that it had been the same for Tony's generation. Older kids tended to forget who had dumped on whom in the second form, the betrayals and the fights behind the bicycle sheds. Now, every experience had a sell-by date, even if the date itself wasn't clear.

In the winter term when Bobby was fifteen, the children all experienced a kind of growing up in reverse, an intensification of childhood. There was never any hurry to get home after school. A crowd of them would head into the bare dripping woods or sit on the steps of the monument in the park. Sometimes they would gather at Albee's Quick Restaurant and Take Away along from the bridge. It was like another world outside, beyond the steamed windows, grownups drifting past in cars or on foot, greying the air with breath and motor exhaust. Inside, lights gleamed on red seats and cheap wood panelling, the air smelled of wet shoes and coffee, thinned occasionally by a cold draught and the broken tinkle of the bell as a new arrival joined the throng.

"I won't go through with it," May Barton said one afternoon when the pavements outside were thick with slush that was forecasted to freeze to razored puddles overnight.

No one needed to ask what she meant.

"Jesus, it was disgusting."

May stared into her coffee. That afternoon in biology they had seen the last in a series of films entitled *The Miracle of Life*. Halfway through, the pink-and-black cartoons had switched over to scenes that purported to come from real life. They had watched a baby tumble wet onto the green sheet from an uncle's open belly, discreet angles of grownups making love. That had been bad enough—I mean, we didn't *ask* to see these things—but the last five minutes had included shots of a boy and a girl in the process of growing up. The soundtrack had been discreet, but every child in the classroom had felt the screams.

The voice-over told them things they had read a hundred times in the school biology textbooks that automatically fell open at the relevant pages. Chapter thirteen—unlucky for some, as many a schoolroom wit had quipped. How the male's testicles and scrotal sac contracted back inside the body, hauled up on some fleshy block and tackle. How the female's ovaries made their peristaltic voyage along the fallopian tubes to nestle down in the useless womb, close to the equally useless cervix. A messy story that had visited them all in their dreams.

"Where the hell am I supposed to be when all this is going on?" someone asked. "I'm certainly not going to be there."

Silence fell around the corner table in Albee's. Every kid had their own bad memory. An older brother or sister who had had a hard time growing up, bloodied sheets in the laundry bin, a door left open at the wrong moment. The espresso machine puttered. Albee sighed and wiped the counter. His beer belly strained at a grey singlet—he was almost fat enough to be an uncle. Almost, but not quite. Every kid could tell the difference. It was in the way they smelled, the way they moved. Albee was just turning to fat, some ordinary guy with a wife and kids back at home, and an uncle with a lawn that needed mowing and crazy paving with the weeds growing through. He was just getting through life, earning a living of sorts behind his counter, putting up with Bobby and the rest of the kids from school as long as they had enough money to buy coffee.

Harry, who was a fat kid, suggested they all go down to the bowling rink. But no one else was keen. Harry was managing to keep up a jollity that the other children had lost. They all assumed that he and his friend Jonathan were the most likely candidates in the year to grow into uncles. The complicated hormonal triggers threw the dice in their favour. And it was a well-known fact that uncles had it easy, that growing up for them was a slow process, like putting on weight. But for everyone, even for Harry, the facts of life were closing in. After Christmas at the start of the new term, their parents would all receive the brown envelopes telling them that the doctor would be around once a week.

The café door opened and closed, letting in the raw evening air as the kids began to drift away. A bus halted at the newsagent's opposite, grownup faces framed at the windows, top deck and bottom, ordinary and absorbed. When it pulled away, streetlight and shadow filled the space behind. Underneath everything, Bobby thought, lies pain, uncertainty, and blood. He took a pull at the coffee he'd been nursing the last half hour. It had grown a skin and tasted cold, almost as bitter as the milk Mum made him drink every morning.

He and May were the last to leave Albee's. The shop windows were filled with promises of Christmas. Colours and lights streamed over the slushy pavement. The cars were inching headlight to brakelight down the High Street, out of town. Bobby and May leaned on the parapet of the bridge. The lights of the houses on the hill where Uncle Lew lived were mirrored in the sliding water. May was wearing mittens, a scarf, a beret, her red hair tucked out of sight, just her nose and eyes showing.

"When I was eight or nine," she said, "Mum and Dad took me on holiday to the coast. It was windy and sunny. I had a big brother then. His name was Tom. We were both kids and he used to give me piggy-backs, sometimes tickle me till I almost peed. We loved to explore the dunes. Had a whole world there to ourselves. One morning we were sliding down this big slope of sand, laughing and climbing all the way up again. Then Tom doubled up at the bottom, and I thought he must have caught himself on a hidden rock or something. I shouted, Are You Okay, but all he did was groan."

"He was growing up?"

May nodded. "The doc at home had said it was fine to go away, but I realised what was happening. I said, You Stay There, which was stupid really, and I shot off to get someone. The sand kept sliding under my sandals. It was a nightmare, running through treacle. I ran right into Dad's arms. He'd gone looking for us. I don't know why, perhaps it's something grownups can sense. He found someone else to ring the ambulance, and we went back down the beach to see Tom. The tide was coming in, and I was worried it might reach him. . . ."

She paused. Darkness was flowing beneath the river arches. "When we got back, he was twisted and I knew he couldn't be alive, no one could hold themselves that way. The blood was in the sand, sticking to his legs. Those black flies you always get on a beach were swarming."

Bobby began, "That doesn't . . .," but he pulled the rest of the chilly sentence back into his lungs.

May turned to him. She drew the scarf down to her chin. Looking at her lips, the glint of her teeth inside, Bobby remembered the sweet hot things they had done together. He wondered at how close you could get to someone and still feel alone.

"We're always early developers in our family," May said. "Tom was the first in his class. I suppose I'll be the same."

"Maybe it's better . . . get it over with."

"I suppose everyone thinks that it'll happen first to some kid in another form, someone you hardly know. Then a few others. Perhaps a friend, someone you can visit afterwards and find out you've got nothing to say but that it's no big deal after all. Everything will always be fine."

"There's still a long—"

"—How long? What difference is a month more or less?" She was angry, close to tears. But beneath, her face was closed off from him. "You had an elder brother who survived, Bobby. Was he ever the same?"

Bobby shrugged. The answer was obvious, all around them. Grownups were grownups. They drove cars, fought wars, dressed in boring and uncomfortable clothes, built roads, bought newspapers every morning that told them the same thing, drank alcohol without getting merry from it, pulled hard on the toilet door to make sure it was shut before they did their business.

"Tony was all right," he said. "He's still all right. We were never that great together anyway—just brothers. I don't think it's the physical changes that count . . . or even that that's at the heart of it. . . ." He didn't know what the hell else to say.

"I'm happy as I am," May said. "I'm a kid. I feel like a kid. If I change, I'll cease to be me. Who wants that?" She took off her mitten, wiped her nose on the back of her hand. "So I'm not going through with it."

Bobby stared at her. It was like saying you weren't going through with death because you didn't like the sound of it. "It can't be that bad, May. Most kids get through all right. Think of all the grownups . . . Jesus, think of your own parents."

"Look, Bobby, I know growing up hurts. I know it's dangerous. I should know, shouldn't I? That's not what I care about. What I care about is losing *me*, the person I am and want to be. . . . You just don't believe me, do you? I'm not going through with it, I'll stay a kid. I don't care who I say it to, because they'll just think I'm acting funny, but Bobby, I thought you might believe me. There has to be a way out."

"You can't . . .," Bobby said. But already she was walking away.

★   ★   ★

The envelopes were handed out at school. A doctor started to call at Bobby's house, and at the houses of all his friends. Next day there was always a show of bravado as they compared the bruises on their arms. The first child to grow up was a boy named Arthur Mumford, whose sole previous claim to fame was the ability to play popular tunes by squelching his armpits. In that way that the inevitable always has, it happened suddenly and without warning. One Tuesday in February, just five weeks after the doctor had started to call at their houses, Arthur didn't turn up for registration. A girl two years below had spotted the doctor's car outside his house on her paper round the evening before. Word was around the whole school by lunchtime.

There was an unmistakable air of disappointment. When he wasn't performing his party piece, Arthur was a quiet boy: he was tall, and stooped from embarrassment at his height. He seldom spoke. But it wasn't just that it should happen first to someone as ordinary as Arthur—I mean, it has to happen to all of us sooner or later, right? But none of the children felt as excited—or even as afraid—as they had expected. When it had happened to kids in the senior years, it had seemed like something big, seeing a kid they'd known suddenly walking the High Street in grownup clothes with the dazed expression that always came to new grownups, ignoring old school-friends, looking for work, ducking into bars. They had speculated excitedly about who would go next, prayed that it would be one of the school bullies. But now that it was their turn, the whole thing felt like a joke that had been played too many times. Arthur Mumford was just an empty desk, a few belongings that needed picking up.

In the spring, at least half a dozen of the children in Bobby's year had grown up. The hot weather seemed to speed things along. Sitting by the dry fountain outside the Municipal Offices one afternoon, watching the litter and the grownups scurry by, a friend of Bobby's named Michele suddenly dropped her can of drink and coiled up in a screaming ball. The children and the passing grownups all fluttered uselessly as she rolled around on the paving until a doctor who happened to be walking by forced her to sit up on the rim of the fountain and take deep slow breaths. Yes, she's growing up, he snapped, glowering at the onlookers, then down at his watch. I suggest someone ring her parents or get a car. Michele was gasping through tears and obviously in agony, but the doctor's manner suggested that she was making far too much of the whole thing. A car arrived soon enough, and Michele was bundled into the back. Bobby never saw her again.

He had similar, although less dramatic, partings with other friends. One day, you'd be meeting them at the bus stop to go to the skating rink. The next, you would hear that they had grown up. You might see them around town, heading out of a shop as you were going in, but they would simply smile and nod, or make a point of saying Hello, Bobby, just to show that they remembered your name. Everything was changing. That whole summer was autumnal, filled with a sense of loss. In their own grownup way, even the parents of the remaining children were affected. Although there would inevitably be little time left for their children to enjoy such things, they became suddenly generous with presents, finding the cash that had previously been missing for a new bike, a train set, or even a pony.

May and Bobby still spent afternoons together, but more often now they would just sit in the kitchen at May's house, May by turns gloomy and animated, Bobby laughing with her or—increasingly against his feelings—trying to act reassuring and grownup. They usually had the house to themselves. In recognition of the dwindling classes, the teachers were allowing any number of so-called study periods, and both of May's parents worked days and overtime in the evenings to keep up with the mortgage on their clumsy mock-Tudor house.

One afternoon, when they were drinking orange juice mixed with sweet sherry filched from the liquor cabinet and wondering if they dared to get drunk, May got up and went to the fridge. Bobby thought she was getting more orange, but instead she produced the plastic flask that contained her bitter milk. She laughed at his expression as she unscrewed the childproof cap and put the flask to her lips, gulping it down as though it tasted good. Abstractly, Bobby noticed that her parents used a branded product. His own parents always bought the supermarket's own.

"Try it," she said.

"What?"

"Go on."

Bobby took the flask and sipped. He was vaguely curious to find out whether May's bitter milk was any less unpleasant than the cheaper stuff he was used to. It wasn't. Just different, thicker. He forced himself to swallow.

"You don't just *drink* this, do you?" he asked, wondering for the first time whether her attitude wasn't becoming something more than simply odd.

"Of course I don't," she said. "But I could if I liked. You see, it's not bitter milk."

Bobby stared at her.

"Look."

May opened the fridge again, took out a carton of ordinary pasteurised milk. She put it on the worktop, then reached high inside a kitchen cabinet, her blouse briefly raising at the back to show the ridges of her lower spine that Bobby so enjoyed touching. She took down a tin of flour, a plastic lemon dispenser, and a bottle of white wine vinegar.

"The flour stops it from curdling," she said, "and ordinary vinegar doesn't work. It took me days to get it right." She tipped some milk into a tumbler, stirred in the other ingredients. "I used to measure everything out, but now I can do it just anyhow."

She handed him the tumbler. "Go on."

Bobby tasted. It was quite revolting, almost as bad as the branded bitter milk.

"You see?"

Bobby put the glass down, swallowing back a welcome flood of saliva to weaken the aftertaste. Yes, he saw, or at least he was beginning to see.

"I haven't been drinking bitter milk for a month now. Mum buys it, I tip it down the sink when she's not here and do my bit of chemistry. It's that simple. . . ." She was smiling, then suddenly blinking back tears. ". . . that easy . . . Of course, it doesn't taste exactly the same, but when was the last time your parents tried tasting bitter milk?"

"Look, May . . . don't you think this is dangerous?"

"Why?" She tilted her head, wiped a stray trickle from her cheek. "What exactly is going to happen to me? You tell me that."

Bobby was forced to shrug. Bitter milk was for children, like cod-liver oil and rusks. Grownups avoided the stuff, but it was good for you, it *helped.*

"I'm not going to grow up, Bobby," she said. "I told you I wasn't joking."

"Do you really think that's going to make any difference?"

"Who knows?" she said. She gave him a sudden hug, her lips wet and close to his ear. "Now let's go upstairs."

★　★　★

Weeks later, Bobby got a phone call from May one evening at

home. Mum called him down from his bedroom, holding the receiver as though it might bite.

He took it.

"It's me, Bobby."

"Yeah." He waited for the lounge door to close. "What is it?"

"Jesus, I think it's started. Mum and Dad are out at a steak bar, and I'm getting these terrible pains."

The fake bitter milk. The receiver went slick in his hand.

"It can't be. You can't be sure."

"If I was sure I wouldn't be . . . look, Bobby, can you come around?" She gave a gasp. "There it is again. You really must. I can't do this alone."

"You gotta ring the hospital."

"No."

"You—"

"No!"

Bobby gazed at the telephone directories that Mum stacked on a shelf beneath the phone as though they were proper books. He remembered that night with Tony, the lights on everywhere, burning through everything as though it wasn't real. He swallowed. The TV was still loud in the lounge.

"Okay," he said. "God knows what I'm supposed to tell Mum and Dad. Give me half an hour."

His excuse was a poor one, but his parents took it anyway. He didn't care what they believed; he'd never felt as shaky in his life.

He cycled through the estate. The air rushed against his face, drowning him in that special feeling that came from warm nights. May must have been watching for him from a window. She was at the door when he scooted down the drive.

"Jesus, Bobby, I'm bleeding."

"I can't see anything."

She pushed her hand beneath the waistband of her dress, then held it out. "Look. Do you believe me now?"

Bobby swallowed, then nodded.

She was alone in the house. Her parents were out. Bobby helped her up the stairs. He found an old plastic mac to spread across the bed, and helped her to get clean. The blood was clotted and fibrous, then watery thin. It didn't seem like an ordinary wound.

When the first panic was over, he pushed her jumbled clothes off the bedside chair and slumped down. May's cheeks were flushed and rosy. For all her talk about not wanting to grow up, he reckoned that he probably looked worse than she did at that moment. What was all this about? And had she ever had a brother named Tom? One who died? She'd lived in another estate then. Other than asking, there was no way of knowing.

"I think I'd better go and ring—"

"—Don't!" She forced a smile and reached out a hand towards him. "Don't."

Bobby hesitated, then took her hand.

"Look, it's stopped now anyway. Perhaps it was a false alarm."

"Yeah," Bobby said. "False alarm," although he was virtually sure there was no such thing. You either grew up or you didn't.

"I feel okay now," she said. "Really, I do."

"That's good," Bobby said.

May was still smiling. She seemed genuinely relieved. "Kiss me, Bobby," she said.

Her eyes were strange. She smelled strange. Like the river, like the rain. He kissed her, softly on the warmth of her cheek; the way you might kiss a grownup. He leaned back from the bed and kept hold of her hand.

They talked.

Bobby returned home close to midnight. His parents had gone up to bed, but as he crossed the darkened landing he sensed that they were both awake and listening beyond the bedroom door. Next morning, nothing was said, and May was at school with the rest of what remained of their class. The teachers had mostly given up on formal lessons, getting the children instead to clear out stockrooms or tape the spines of elderly textbooks. He watched May as she drifted through the chalk-clouded air, the sunlight from the tall windows blazing her hair. Neither grownup nor yet quite a kid, she moved between the desks with unconscious grace.

That lunchtime, she told Bobby that she was fine. But yes, she was still bleeding a bit. I have to keep going to the little girl's room. I've gone through two pairs of knickers, flushed them away. It's a real nuisance, Bobby, she added above the clatter in the dining hall, as though it was nothing, like hay fever or a cold sore. Her face was clear and bright, glowing through the freckles and the smell of communal cooking. He nodded, finding that it was easier to believe than to question. May smiled. And you will come see me tonight, won't you, Bobby? We'll be on our own. Again, Bobby found himself nodding.

He announced to Mum and Dad after dinner that evening that he was going out again. He told them he was working on a school play that was bound to take up a lot of his time.

Mum and Dad nodded. Bobby tried not to study them too closely, although he was curious to gauge their reaction.

"Okay," Mum said. "But make sure you change the batteries on your lamps if you're going to cycle anywhere after dark." She glanced at Dad, who nodded and returned to his paper.

"You know I'm careful like that." Bobby tried to keep the wariness out of his voice. He suspected that they saw straight through him and knew that he was lying. He'd been in this kind of situation before. That was an odd thing about grownups: you could tell them the truth and they'd fly into a rage. Other times, such as this when you had to lie, they said nothing at all.

★   ★   ★

May was waiting at the door again that evening. As she had promised, her parents were out. He kissed her briefly in the warm light of the hall. Her lips were soft against his, responding with a pressure that he knew would open at the slightest sign from him. She smelled even more rainy than before. There was something else too, something that was both new and familiar. Just as her arms started to encircle his neck, he stepped back, his heart suddenly pounding.

He looked at her. "Christ, May, what are you wearing?"

"This." She gave a twirl. The whole effect was odd, yet hard to place for a moment. A tartanish pleated dress. A white blouse. A dull necklace. Her hair pulled back in a tight bun. And her eyes, her mouth, her whole face . . . looked like it had been sketched on, the outlines emphasised, the details ignored. Then he licked his lips and knew what it was; the same smell and taste that came from Mum on nights when she leaned over his bed and said, you will be good while we're out, won't you, my darling, jewellery glimmering like starlight around her neck and at the lobes of her ears. May was wearing make-up. She was dressed like a grownup.

For a second, the thought that May had somehow managed to get through the whole messy process of growing up since leaving school that afternoon came to him. Then he saw the laughter in her eyes and he knew it couldn't be true.

"What do you think, Bobby?"

"I don't know why grownups wear that stuff. It isn't comfortable, it doesn't even look good. What does it feel like?"

"Strange," May said. "It changes you inside. Come upstairs. I'll show you."

May led him up the stairs and beyond a door he had never been through before. Even though they were out, her parents' bedroom smelled strongly of grownup, especially the wardrobe, where the dark lines of suits swung gently on their hangers. Bobby was reasonably tall for his age, as tall as many grownups, May's father included.

The suit trousers itched his legs and the waist was loose, but not so loose as to fall down. He knotted a tie over a white shirt, pulled on the jacket. May got some oily stuff from the dresser, worked it into his hair and combed it smooth. Then she stood beside him as he studied himself in the mirror. Dark and purposeful, two strange grownups gazed back. He glanced down at himself, hardly believing it was true. He pulled a serious face back at the mirror, the sort you might see behind the counter at a bank. Then he started to chuckle. And May began to laugh. It was so inconceivably easy. They were doubled over, their bellies aching. They held each other tight. They just couldn't stop.

An hour later, May closed the front door and turned the deadlock. Heels clipping the pavement, they walked to the bus stop. Perhaps in deference to their new status as grownups, the next service into town came exactly when it was due. They travelled on the top deck, which was almost empty apart from a gaggle of cleaning ladies at the back. They were busy talking, and the driver hadn't even bothered to look up when he gave them two straight adult fares (don't say please, May had whispered as the tall lights of the 175 had pulled into the stop, grownups don't do that kind of thing). Dressed in this strange way, his back spreading huge inside the jacket shoulder pads, Bobby felt confident anyway. Like May said, the grownup clothes changed you inside.

They got off outside Albee's Quick Restaurant and Take Away. For some reason, May wanted to try visiting a place where they were actually known. Bobby was too far gone with excitement to argue about taking an unnecessary extra risk. Her manner was smooth; he doubted if anyone else would have noticed the wildness in her eyes beneath the make-up. Rather than dodge the cars across the road, they waited for a big gap and walked slowly, sedately. The lights of Albee's glowed out to greet them. They opened the door to grownup laughter, the smell of smoke and grownup sweat. People nodded and smiled, then moved to let them through. Albee grinned at them from the bar, eager to please, the way the teachers were at school when the headmaster came unexpectedly into class. He said, Good evening, Sir, and What'll it be. Bobby heard his own voice say something calm and easy in reply. He raked a stool back for May and she sat down, tucking her dress neatly under her thighs. He glanced around as drinks were served, half-expecting the other grownups to float up from their chairs, to begin to fly. They'd been here after school a hundred times, but this was a different world.

It was the same on a dozen other nights, whenever they hit on an excuse that they had the nerve to use on their unquestioning parents. Albee's, they found, was much further from the true heart of the grownup world than they'd imagined. They found hotel bars where real fountains tinkled and the drinks were served chilled on paper coasters that stuck to the bottom of the glass. There were loud pubs where you could hardly stand for the yellow-lit crush and getting served was an evening's endeavour. There were restaurants where you were offered bowls brimming with crackers and salted nuts just to sit and read the crisply printed menus and say, Well Thanks, But It Doesn't Look As Though Our Friends Are Coming And The Baby Sitter You Know. . . . Places they had seen day in and day out through their whole lives were changed by the darkness, the hot charge of car fumes, buzzing streetlights, glittering smiles, the smell of perfume, transformed into whispering palaces of crystal and velvet.

After changing at May's house back into his sweatshirt and sneakers, Bobby would come home late, creeping down the hall in the bizarre ritual of pretending not to disturb his parents, who he was certain would be listening open-eyed in the darkness from the first unavoidable creak of the front door. In the kitchen, he checked for new bottles of bitter milk. By the light of the open fridge door, he tipped the fluid down the sink, chased it away with a quick turn of the hot tap—which was quieter than the cold—and replaced it with a fresh mixture of wine vinegar, lemon juice, milk, and flour.

★ ★ ★

The summer holidays came. Bobby and May spent all their time together, evenings and days. Lying naked in the woods on the soft prickle of dry leaves, looking up at the green-latticed sky. Bobby reached again towards May. He ran his hand down the curve of her belly. It was soft and sweet and hard, like an apple. Her breath quickened. He rolled onto his side, lowered his head to lick at her breasts. More than ever before, her nipples swelled amazingly to his tongue. But after a moment, her back stiffened.

"Just kiss me here," she said, "my mouth," gently cupping his head in her hands and drawing it up. "Don't suck at me today, Bobby. I feel too tender."

Bobby acquiesced to the wonderful sense of her around him, filling the sky and the woods. She'd been sensitive about some of the things he did before, often complaining about tenderness and pain a few days before she started her bleeding. But the bleeding hadn't happened for weeks, months.

They still went out some nights, visiting the grownup places, living their unbelievable lie. Sometimes as he left the house, or coming back late with his head spinning from the drink and the things they'd done, Bobby would look up and see Mum's face pale at the bedroom window. But he said nothing. And nothing was ever said. It was an elaborate dance, back to back, Mum and Dad displaying no knowledge or denial, each moment at the kitchen table and the rare occasions when they shared the lounge passing without question. A deception without deceit.

The places they went to changed. From the smart rooms lapped with deep carpets and chrome, they glided on a downward flight path through urine-reeking doorways. This was where the young grownups went, people they recognised as kids from assembly at school just a few years before. Bars where the fermented light only deepened the darkness, where the fat uncles sat alone as evening began, looking at the men and the women as the crowds thickened, looking away.

Bobby and May made friends, people who either didn't notice what they were or didn't care. Hands raised and waving through the chaos and empty glasses. Hey, Bobby, May, over here, sit yourselves right down here. Place for the old butt. Jokes to be told, lips licked, lewd eyes rolled, skirt hems pulled firmly down, then allowed to roll far up again. Glimpses of things that shouldn't be seen. They were good at pretending to be grownups by now, almost better than the grownups themselves. For the purposes of the night, Bobby was in town from a university in the city, studying whatever came into his head. May was deadly serious or laughing, saying my God, you wouldn't believe the crap I have to put up with at the office, the factory, the shop. Playing it to a tee. And I'm truly glad to be here and now with you all before it starts again in the morning.

Time broke in beery waves. The account at the bank that Bobby had been nurturing for some unspecified grownup need sunk to an all-time low. But it could have been worse—they were a popular couple, almost as much in demand as the unattached fat uncles when a few drinks had gone down. They hardly ever had to put in for a round.

The best part was when they came close to discovery. A neighbour who probably shouldn't have been there in the first place, a family friend, a teacher. Then once it was Bobby's brother Tony. Late, and he had his arms around a fat uncle, his face sheened with sweat. He was grinning and whispering wet lips close to his ear. There was a woman with them too, her hands straying quick and hard over both of their bodies. It wasn't Marion.

"Let's go," Bobby said. There was a limit to how far you could take a risk. But May would have none of it. She stared straight at Tony through the swaying bodies, challenging him to notice.

For a moment his eyes were on them, his expression drifting back from lust. Bobby covered his hand with his mouth, feeling the grownup clothes and confidence dissolve around him, the school kid inside screaming to get out. Tony made to speak, but there was no chance of hearing. In another moment, he vanished into the mass of the crowd.

Now that the danger had passed, it was the best time of all; catching Tony out in a way that he could never explain. Laughter bursting inside them, they ran out into the sudden cool of the night. May held on to him and her lips were over his face, breathless and trembling from the sudden heightening of the risk. He held tight to her, swaying, not caring about the cars, the grownups stumbling by, pulling her close, feeling the taut rounded swell of her full breasts and belly that excited him so.

"Do you want to be like them?" she whispered. "Want to be a fool and a grownup?"

"Never." He leaned back and shouted it at the stars. "Never!"

Arm in arm, they swayed down the pavement towards the bus stop. Incredibly, Tuesday was coming around again tomorrow; Doc Halstead would be pulling up the drive at home at about eleven, washing his hands one more time and saying, How Are You My Man before taking best-china coffee with Mum in the lounge, whispering things Bobby could never quite hear. May's eyes were eager, gleaming with the town lights, drinking it all in. More than him, she hated this world and loved it. Sometimes, when things were swirling, she reminded him of a true grownup. It all seemed far away from that evening in town after biology, leaning on the bridge alone after leaving Albee's and gazing down at the river, May saying, I won't go through with it, Bobby, I'm not just some kid acting funny. As though something as easy as fooling around with the bitter milk could make that much of a difference.

Dr. Halstead arrived next morning only minutes after Bobby had finished breakfast and dressed. In the spare bedroom, he spread out his rubber and steel. He dried his hands and held the big syringe up to the light before leaning down.

Bobby smeared the fresh bead of blood over the bruises on his forearm, then licked the salt off his fingertips.

Dr. Halstead was watching the readouts. The paper feed gave

a burp and chattered out a thin strip like a supermarket receipt. The doc tore it off, looked at it for a moment, and tutted before screwing it into a ball. He pressed a button that flattened the dials, pressed another to make them drift up again.

"Is everything okay?"

"Everything's fine."

The printer chattered again. He tore it off. "You've still got some way to go."

"How many weeks?"

"If I had a pound for every time I've been asked that question. . . ."

"Don't you know?"

He handed Bobby the printout. Faint figures and percentages. The machine needed a new ribbon.

"Us grownups don't know everything. I know it seems that way."

"Most of my friends have gone." He didn't want to mention May, although he guessed Mum had told him anyway. "How long can it go on for?"

"As long as it takes."

"What if nothing happens?"

"Something always happens."

He gave Bobby a smile.

Bobby and May went out again that night. A place they'd never tried before, a few stops out of town with a spluttering neon sign, a shack motel at the back, and a dusty parking area for the big container rigs. Inside was huge, with bare boards and patches of lino, games machines lining the walls, too big to fill with anything but smoke and tracts of yellowed silence on even the busiest of nights. Being a Wednesday, and the grownups' pay packets being thin until the weekend, it was quiet. They sat alone in the smoggy space for most of the evening. They didn't know anyone, and for once it seemed that no one wanted to know them. Bobby kept thinking of the way Dr. Halstead had checked the readouts, checked them again. And he knew May had her own weekly test the following afternoon. It wasn't going to be one of their better nights. May looked pale. She went out to the Ladies room far more often than their slow consumption of the cheap bottled beer would explain. Once, when she came back and leaned forward to tell him something, he realised that the rain had gone from her breath. He smelled vomit.

At about ten, a fat uncle crossed the room, taking a drunken detour around the chairs.

"Haven't seen you two here before," he said, his belly swaying above the table, close to their faces. "I've got a contract delivering groceries from here to the city and back. Every other day, I'm here."

"We must have missed you."

He squinted down at them, still swaying but now seeming less than drunk. For places like here, Bobby and May wore casual clothes. Bobby dressed the way Dad did for evenings at home, in an open-collared striped shirt and trousers that looked as though they had started out as part of a work suit. May hadn't put on much make-up, which she said she hated anyway. Bobby wondered if they were growing complacent, if this fat uncle hadn't seen what all the other grownups had apparently failed to notice.

"Mind if I . . ." The uncle reached for a chair and turned it around, sat down with his legs wide and his arms and belly propped against the backrest. "Where are you from, anyway?"

Bobby and May exchanged secret smiles. Now they were in their element, back in the territory of the university in the city, the office, the shop, the grownup places that had developed a life of their own through frequent retelling.

It was pleasant to talk to an uncle on equal terms for a change, away from the pawings and twitterings of other grownups which usually surrounded them. Bobby felt he had a lot of questions to ask, but the biggest one was answered immediately by this uncle's cautious but friendly manner, by the way he spoke of his job and the problems he was having trying to find a flat. In all the obvious ways, he was just like any other young grownup. He bought them a drink. It seemed polite to buy him one in return, then—what the hell—a chaser. Soon they were laughing. People were watching, smiling, but keeping their distance across the ranks of empty tables.

Bobby knew what was happening, but he was curious to see how far it would go. He saw a plump hand stray to May's arm—still covered by a long-sleeved shirt to hide the bruises—then up to her shoulder. He saw the way she reacted by not doing anything.

"You don't know how lonely it gets," the uncle said, leaning forward, his arm around Bobby's back too, his hand reaching down. "Always on the road. I stay here, you know. Most Wednesdays. A lot of them sleep out in the cab. But they pay you for it and I like to lie on something soft. Just out the back." He nodded. "Through that door, the way you came in, left past the kitchens."

"Will you show us?" May asked, looking at Bobby. "I think we'd like to see."

The motel room was small. Someone had tried to do it up

years before, but the print had rubbed off the wallpaper by the door and above the green bed. The curtains had shrunk, and Bobby could still see the car park and the lights of the road. A sliding door led to a toilet and the sound of a dripping tap.

The fat uncle sat down. The bed squealed. Bobby and May remained standing, but if the uncle saw their nervousness he didn't comment. He seemed more relaxed now, easy with the drink and the certainty of what they were going to do. He unlaced his boots and peeled off his socks, twiddling his toes with a sigh that reminded Bobby of Dad at the end of a hard day. He was wearing a sweatshirt that had once said something. He pulled it off over his head with his hands on the waistband, the way a girl might do, threw it onto the rug beside his feet. He had a singlet on underneath. The hems were unravelling, but he and it looked clean enough, and he smelt a lot better than Uncle Lew did at close quarters, like unbaked dough. He pulled the singlet off too. His breasts were much bigger than May's. There was hardly any hair under his arms. Bobby stared at the bruised scar that began under his ribcage and vanished beneath the wide band of his jeans, slightly moist where it threatened to part.

"You're going to stay dressed, are you?" he said with a grin. He scratched himself, and the springs squealed some more. "This goddamn bed's a problem."

"We'd like to watch," May said. "For now, if that's okay with you."

"That's great by me. I'm not fussy . . . I mean . . ." He stood up and stepped out of his trousers and underpants in one movement. "Well, you know what I mean."

Under the huge flap of his belly, Bobby couldn't see much of what lay beneath. Just darkness and hair. Every night, he thought, a million times throughout the world, this is going on. Yet he couldn't believe it, couldn't even believe it about his parents with Uncle Lew, although he'd seen them once on that hot afternoon.

"Tell you what," the uncle said. "It's been a long day. I think you'd both appreciate it if yours truly freshened up a bit." He went over to Bobby, brushed the fine hairs at the back of his neck with soft fingers. "I won't be a mo. You two sort yourselves out, eh?"

He waddled off into the toilet, slid the door shut behind him. They heard the toilet seat bang down, a sigh, and the whisper of moving flesh. Then a prolonged fart. A pause. A splash. Then another.

May looked at Bobby. Her face reddened. She covered her mouth to block the laughter. Bobby's chest heaved. He covered his mouth too. He couldn't help it: the joke was incredibly strong. Signalling to Bobby, tears brimming in her eyes, May stooped to pick up the sweatshirt, the shoes, the singlet. Bobby gathered the jeans. There were more clothes heaped in a corner. They took those too, easing the door open as quietly as they could before the laughter rolled them over like a high wind.

They sprinted madly across the car park, down the road, into the night.

★   ★   ★

Next morning, the sky was drab. It seemed to Bobby like the start of the end of summer, the first of the grey veils that would eventually thicken to autumn. Downstairs, Mum was humming. He went first into the kitchen, not that he wanted to see her, but he needed to reestablish the charade of ignoring his nights away from the house. One day, he was sure it would break, she'd have a letter from the police, the doctor, the owner of some bar, a fact that couldn't be ignored.

"It's you," she said. Uncharacteristically, she kissed him. He'd been taller than her for a year or two, she didn't need to bend down, but it still felt that way. "Do you want anything from the supermarket? I'm off in a few minutes."

Bobby glanced at the list she kept on the wipe-clean plastic board above the cooker. Wash powd, loo pap, marg, lemon jce, wne vigr. He looked at her face, but it was clear and innocent.

"Aren't you going to go into the dining room? See what's waiting?"

"Waiting?"

"Your birthday, Bobby." She gave him a laugh and a quick, stiff hug. "I asked you what you wanted weeks ago and you never said. So I hope you like it. I've kept the receipt—you boys are so difficult."

"Yeah." He hadn't exactly forgotten, he'd simply been pushing the thing back in his mind, the way you do with exams and visits from the doctor, hoping that if you make yourself forget, then in time the rest of the world will forget, too.

He was seventeen and still a kid. It was at least one birthday too many. He opened the cards first, shaking each envelope carefully to see if there was any money. Some of them had pictures of archaic countryside and inappropriate verses, the sort that grownups gave to each other. One or two people had made the effort to find a child's card, but there wasn't much of a market for seventeen-year-olds. The most enterprising had combined stick-ons for 1 and 7. Bobby moved to the presents, using his toast knife to slit the tape, trying not to damage any of the wrapping paper, which Mum liked to iron and reuse. Although she hadn't spoken, he was conscious that she was standing at the door and watching. Fighting the sinking feeling of discovering books on subjects that didn't interest him, accessories for hobbies he didn't pursue, model cars for a collection he'd given up years ago, he tried to display excitement and surprise.

Mum and Dad's present was a pair of binoculars, something he'd coveted when he was thirteen for reasons he couldn't now remember. He gazed at the marmalade jar in close-up, through the window at the individual leaves of the nearest cherry tree in the garden.

"We thought you'd find them useful when you grew up too," Mum said, putting her arms around him.

"It's great," he said. In truth, he liked the smell of the case — leather, oil, and glass — more than the binoculars themselves. But he knew that wasn't the point. And then he remembered why he'd so wanted a pair of binoculars, how he'd used to love looking up at the stars.

"Actually, I've lots of stuff to get at the supermarket, Bobby. Dad's taking a half day and we're going to have a party for you. Everyone's coming. Isn't that great?"

Bobby went with Mum to the supermarket. They drove into town past places he and May had visited at night. Even though the sky was clearing to sun, they looked flat and grey. Wandering the supermarket aisles, Mum insisted that Bobby choose whatever he wanted. He settled at random for iced fancies, paté, green-veined cheese. Tony came out from his office behind a window of silvered glass, a name badge on his lapel and his hair starting to recede. He clapped Bobby's shoulder with a Biro-stained hand and said he'd never have believed it, Seventeen, my own little brother. They chatted awkwardly for a while in the chill drift of the frozen meats. Even though there was a longer queue, they chose Marion's checkout. She was back working at the supermarket part-time now that their kid had started nursery school. It wasn't until Bobby saw her blandly cheerless face that he remembered that night with Tony and the other uncle in the bar. He wondered if she knew, if she cared.

There were cars in the drive at home and spilling along the cul-de-sac at three that afternoon, little kids with names he couldn't remember running on the lawn. The weather had turned bright and hot. Dad had fished out all the deckchairs as soon as he got home, the ordinary ones and the specials he reserved for uncles.

People kept coming up to Bobby and then running out of things to say. He couldn't remember whether they'd given him cards or presents, what to thank them for. Uncle Lew was in a good mood, the facets of one of the best wine glasses trembling sparks across his rounded face.

"Well, Bobby," he said, easing himself down in his special deck-chair. He was starting to look old, ugly. Too many years, too many happy events. He was nothing like the fresh fat uncle at the motel. "And what are you going to be when you grow up?"

Bobby shrugged. He had grown sick of thinking up lies to please people. The canvas of Lew's deckchair was wheezing and slightly torn. Bobby hoped that he'd stay a kid long enough to see him fall through.

"Well, get yourself a nice girlfriend," he said. "It means a lot to me that I'm uncle to your Momma and Poppa and to Tony and Marion too." He sucked at his wine. "But that's all up to you."

Looking back up the lawn towards the house, Bobby saw May and her parents emerging into the sunlight from the open French windows. May appeared drab and tired. Her belly was big, her ankles swollen.

She waddled over to them, sweat gleaming on her cheeks.

"Hello, Bobby." She leaned over to let Uncle Lew give her a hug. He put his lips to her ear. She wriggled and smiled before she pulled away.

"Hello, May."

She was wearing a cheap print, something that fell in folds like a tent.

"This whole party is a surprise, isn't it? Your mum insisted that I didn't say anything when she told me last week. Here. Happy birthday."

She gave him a package. He opened it. Five minutes later, he couldn't remember what it contained.

Dad banged the trestle table, and people gathered around on the lawn as he made a speech about how he could hardly believe the way the years had flown, saying the usual things that grown-ups always said about themselves when it was a child's birthday. He raised his glass. A toast. Bobby. Everyone intoned his name. *Bobby.* The sun retreated towards the rooftops and the trees, fill-ing the estate with evening, the weary smell of cooking. Those grownups who hadn't been able to skip work arrived in their work clothes. Neighbours drifted in.

May came over to Bobby again, her face flushed with the drink and the sun.

"Did the doc come over to see you today?" he asked, for want of anything better. The hilarious intimacy of the things they had done in the night suddenly belonged to a world even more distant than that of the grownups.

"Nothing happened," she said, spearing a slice of pickled herring on the paper plate she carried with a plastic fork. "Nothing ever happens." She took a bite of the gleaming vinegared scales, then pulled a face. "Disgusting. God knows how the grownups enjoy this shit."

Bobby grinned, recognising the May he knew. "Let's go somewhere. No one will notice."

She shrugged Yes and propped her plate on the concrete birdbath. They went through the back gate, squeezed between the bumpers on the drive and out along the road.

"Do you still think you'll never grow up?" Bobby asked.

May shook her head. "What about you?"

"I suppose it's got to happen. We're not fooling anyone, are we, going out, not drinking the milk? I'm sure Mum and Dad know. They just don't seem to care. I mean, we can't be the first kids in the history of the world to have stumbled on this secret. Well, it can't be a secret, can it?"

"How about we climb up to the meadows?" May said. "The town looks good from up there."

"Have you ever read *Peter Pan?*" Bobby asked as they walked up the dirt road between the allotments and the saw mill. "He never grew up. Lived in a wonderful land and learnt how to fly." He held open the kissing gate that led into the fields. May had to squeeze through. The grass was high and silvered with seed, whispering under a deepening sky. "When I was young," he said, "on evenings like this, I used to look out of my bedroom window and watch the grownups. I thought that they could fly."

"Who do you think can fly now?"

"No one. We're all the same."

They stopped to catch their breath and look down at the haze below. Hills, trees, and houses, the wind carrying the chime of an ice-cream van, the river stealing silver from the sky. He felt pain spread through him, then dissolve without finding focus.

May took his hand. "Remember when we came up here alone that time, years ago?" She drew it towards her breast, then down. "You touched me here, and here. We had sex. You'd never done it before." She let his hand fall. Bobby felt no interest. May no longer smelled of rain, and he was relieved that he didn't have to turn her down.

The pain came again, more strongly this time. He swayed. The shimmering air cleared, and for one moment there was a barge on the river, a tractor slicing a field from green to brown, a hawk circling high overhead, May smiling, sweet and young as she said, Let's Do It, Bobby, pulling her dress up over her head. He blinked.

"Are you okay?"

"I'm fine," he said, leaning briefly against her, feeling the thickness of her arms.

"I think we'd better go back."

Down the hill, the pain began to localise. First circling in his spine, then gradually shifting orbit towards his belly. It came and went. When it was there, it was so unbelievable that he could almost put it aside in the moments of recession. Like a bad dream. The trees swayed with the rush of twilight, pulling him forward, drawing him back.

Progress was slow. Night came somewhere along the way. Helped by May, he staggered from lamppost to lamppost, dreading the darkness between. People stared, or asked if everything was okay before hurrying on. He tasted rust in his mouth. He spat on the pavement, wiped his hand. It came away black.

"Nearly there," May said, half-holding him around his searing belly.

He looked up and saw houses he recognised, the postbox that was the nearest one to home. His belly was crawling. He remembered how that postbox had been a marker of his suffering one day years before when he'd been desperate to get home and pee, and another time walking back from school when his shoes were new and tight. Then the pain rocked him, blocking his sight. True pain, hard as flint, soft as drowning. He tried to laugh. That made it worse and better. Bobby knew that this was just the start, an early phase of the contractions.

He couldn't remember how they reached home. There were hands and voices, furious diallings of the phone. Bobby couldn't get upstairs and didn't want to mess the settee by lying on it. But the grownups insisted, pushed him down, and then someone found a plastic sheet and tucked it under him in between the worst of the waves. He thrashed around, seeing the TV, the mantelpiece, the fibres of the carpet, the light burning at his eyes. I'm not here, he told himself, this isn't real. Then the biggest, darkest wave yet began to reach him.

Wings of pain settled over him. For a moment without time, Bobby dreamed that he was flying.

★   ★   ★

Bobby awoke in a chilly white room. There was a door, dim figures moving beyond the frosted glass. He was still floating, hardly conscious of his own body. The whiteness of the room hurt his eyes. He closed them, opened them again. Now it was night. Yellow light spilled through the glass. The figures moving beyond had globular heads, no necks, tapering bodies.

One of the figures paused. The door opened. The silence cracked like a broken seal. He could suddenly hear voices, the clatter of trolleys. He was conscious of the hard flatness of the bed against his back, coils of tubing descending into his arm from steel racks. His throat hurt. His mouth tasted faintly of liquorice. The air smelled the way the bathroom cabinet did at home. Of soap and aspirins.

"Your eyes are open. Bobby, can you see?"

The shape at the door blocked the light. It was hard to make it out. Then it stepped forward, and he saw the soft curve of May's cheek, the glimmer of her eye.

"Can you speak?"

"No," he said.

May turned on a light over the bed and sat down with a heavy sigh. He tried to track her by moving his eyes, but after the brief glimpse of her face, all he could see was the dimpled curve of her elbow.

"This is hospital?"

"Yes. You've grown up."

Hospital. Growing up. They must have taken him here from home. Which meant that it had been a difficult change.

May said, "You're lucky to be alive."

Alive. Yes. Alive. He waited for a rush of some feeling or other — relief, gratitude, achievement, pride. There was nothing, just this white room, the fact of his existence.

"What happens now?" he asked.

"Your parents will want to see you."

"Where are they?"

"At home. It's been *days*, Bobby."

"Then why . . ." The taste of liquorice went gritty in his mouth. He swallowed it back. "Why are you here, May?"

"I'm having tests, Bobby. I just thought I'd look in."

"Thanks."

"There's no need to thank me. I won't forget the times we had."

Times. We. Had. Bobby put the words together, then let them fall apart.

"Yes," he said.

"Well." May stood up.

Now he could see her. Her hair was cut short, sitting oddly

where her fat cheeks met her ears. Her breasts hung loose inside a tee-shirt. Along with everything else about her, they seemed to have grown, but the nipples had gone flat and she'd given up wearing a bra. She shrugged and spread her arms. He caught a waft of her scent: she needed a wash. It was sickly but somehow appealing, like the old cheese that you found at the back of the fridge and needed to eat right away.

"Sometimes it happens," she said.

"Yes," Bobby said. "The bitter milk."

"No one knows really, do they? Life's a mystery."

Is it? Bobby couldn't be bothered to argue.

"Will you change your name?" he asked. "Move to another town?"

"Maybe. It's a slow process. I'm really not an uncle yet, you know."

Still a child. Bobby gazed at her uncomfortably, trying to see it in her eyes, finding with relief that the child wasn't there.

"What's it like?" May asked.

"What?"

"Being a grownup."

"Does anyone ask a child what it's like to be a child?"

"I suppose not."

His head ached, his voice was fading. He blinked slowly. He didn't want to say more. What else was there to say? He remembered waiting stupidly as his brother Tony sat up in bed watching TV that first morning after he'd grown up. Waiting as though there was an answer. But growing up was just part of the process of living, which he realised now was mostly about dying.

May reached out to touch his face. The fingers lingered for a moment, bringing a strange warmth. Their odour was incredibly strong to Bobby. But it was sweet now, like the waft from the open door of a bakery. It hit the back of his palate and then ricocheted down his spine. He wondered vaguely if he was going to get an erection and killed the thought as best he could; he hated the idea of appearing vulnerable to May. After all, she was still half a child.

"You'd better be going," he said.

May backed away. "You're right." She reached for the handle of the door, clumsily, without looking.

"Good-bye, May," Bobby said.

She stood for a moment in the open doorway. For a moment, the light fell kindly on her face and she was beautiful. Then she stepped back, and all her youth was gone.

"Good-bye, Bobby," she said, and glanced down at her wrist-watch. "I've got things to do. I really must fly."